A brand new vampire. The lover who got her killed. And a desire neither can deny.

Crimson Oath

Tatyana Vorona used to be human... until she met the dark and mysterious Oleg Sokolov. He lives in a world of power, blood, and betrayal. And now so does she.

By helping him, Tatyana helped herself to an early grave. Then she rose again as a vampire with the ability to manipulate water. Tatyana is in hiding, trying to master her magic, blood lust, and the terrifying draw she still feels toward the man who set all this in motion.

He might control fire, but flames of desire have a will of their own.

Oleg's empire was shaken by his daughter's betrayal and the bloodshed that followed. Now someone else is trying to take advantage of the chaos to destabilize his rule further. He should be hunting them down, making an example of anyone who dares to challenge him.

Instead, he's searching for *her*. No matter how far Tatyana runs, he's determined to return her to his side. And when it turns out she's hiding right underneath his nose, he'll do whatever it takes to make Tatyana his. Permanently.

Fire and water collide in this steamy romantic fantasy about a new vampire that won't submit and her powerful lover who must learn to bend in order to keep her. CRIMSON OATH is the sequel to BLOOD MOSAIC, and takes place in the same expansive world as Hunter's popular Elemental Series.

Praise for The Firebird and the Wolf

If you like enemies-to-lovers, slow burn, blood bonds, elemental vampires, forced proximity, anti-hero, modern vampires... then you'll love *Blood Mosaic* by Elizabeth Hunter. What an absolutely enthralling start to The Firebird and the Wolf series!

— Jamie Williams, Amazon.com

Ms. Hunter weaves storylines expertly. She pulls on threads that in the end, make a tapestry of love, intrigue, and the violent world of vampires. Any fan of fantasy will love this book!

— Shelly K., Goodreads Reviewer

Cinematic scope and intriguing characters populate this modern day vampire saga filled to the brim with staggering drama, betrayals, fascinating world building/history, an intimate and complicated slow burn love, and a morally grey vampire in a suit (that can wield an axe like The Northman.)

— Lisa C., Goodreads Reviewer

Hunter is a master at world-building and creating complex characters. I can't wait for the next one to come out.

— Kate, Goodreads Reviewer

If you're a fan of *Discovery of Witches* or Diana Gabaldon's writing style you'll enjoy this book. If you're interested in Eastern Europe and history, you'll enjoy this book. If you're a fan of vampires navigating the modern world, you'll enjoy this book. If you're a fan of messed up family dynamics, you'll enjoy this book. If you're a fan of slow-burn romance, you'll enjoy this book.

— Lauren Bollen, Amazon.com

Welcome to a lushly seductive world where power is currency and everyone pays to play the game. 5 stars. Absolutely loved it. I devoured this book within a day.

— Shea.Reads.Always

I am infatuated by Elizabeth Hunter's intellect and writings because she challenges the limitations of my beliefs and mind. Ever creative, never rote, always fresh. Dynamically complex characters, evolved twisted plots and and fresh witty dialogue.

— Calista Cates, Amazon.com

CRIMSON OATH

BY

ELIZABETH HUNTER

Crimson Oath

The Firebird and the Wolf
Book 2

Elizabeth Hunter

Recurve Press, LLC

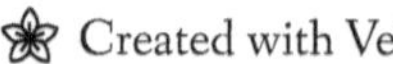 Created with Vellum

Chapter 1

Oleg

The vampire walked up the hill, bathing in the full moonlight and enjoying the crisp ocean breeze that whipped off the Black Sea.

It was spring in the small village on the Crimea, and while war had touched many of the larger towns and cities, in this isolated hamlet, fruit trees were in bloom and pushing flowers, bright yellow mustard dotted the roadside, and lavender fields filled the air with their unmistakable scent.

The vampire carried a gift for his quarry. He wasn't a barbarian, after all. She would give him the information he was after, and she likely wouldn't remember a thing afterward.

And if she did...

Well, he would deal with that eventuality when it occurred.

Oleg Sokolov hadn't become the vampire lord of the Kievan Rus by accident. He didn't take chances, but he didn't borrow trouble either. One middle-aged human was not a threat to him, which was why his chief boyar and the rest of his security were waiting at the paved road.

He walked past a wooden barn and up to an old farmhouse with a fresh coat of paint. The shutters were decorated with bright red flowers, and wood trim showed the evidence of fresh repair. The garden was planted, and green heads of lettuce were already springing up in the raised beds.

A newly built dovecote sat next to the house, sheltered by a high fence and protected from the foxes and martens by a dense screen.

Before Oleg could put his hand on the gate, a low, rumbling growl alerted him to the presence of a dog.

A massive shepherd dog of indeterminate heritage crawled out from under the porch and slowly walked toward him. He was three foot at the shoulder with a black face and smoke-grey fur.

"Hmm." Oleg lifted his chin. "No one ever accused the Vorona women of being careless." He met the dog's eyes. "Nice to meet you, sobaka."

The dog curled his black lip before a thunderous bark broke the shadowy stillness and quieted the burbling coos of the pigeons in the cote.

Oleg raised an eyebrow at the barking dog. "Good. You have alerted your mistress." He stepped back and lowered his hand from the gate. "Very well, I will wait here."

It only took moments for the door to open, and the familiar sound of a shotgun being cocked met his ears.

The dog walked to the porch steps and sat, quieting his growl when his mistress shushed him.

"I expected one of you weeks ago," a voice called from the dark house. "You're slow."

Oleg lifted his eyes to the shining barrel of the shotgun and nodded. "We wanted to give you time to settle in."

Anna Asanova stepped out from the shadow of the doorway and onto the porch, the shotgun pointed at Oleg's chest. "I'm settled. What do you want?"

"What do you think I want?"

"I don't know where she is."

"Are you telling me Tatyana hasn't made contact with her own mother?" Oleg shook his head. "I don't believe you." He'd also been tracking her mobile phone usage. Anna was getting calls from someone in Georgia, but he couldn't be sure it was his prey.

"I didn't say she hasn't been in touch. I said I don't know where she is."

Oleg shrugged. "You know that gun will not kill me."

"I've been told you can die by losing your head," Anna said. "I'm willing to fire a few times if that's what it takes."

She wouldn't be alive by the second shot, but Oleg didn't have any desire to kill her. Not if he could help it.

He stepped forward and lifted the package in his left hand. "I brought you a cake."

Silence.

The dog noticed the bright pink pastry box and let out a high whine. A second later, Oleg saw a drop of drool fall from his dark jowl.

"Dymka." Anna's disappointed tone made Oleg smile. "You glutton."

"It's chocolate smetannik," Oleg continued. "I think it might be your favorite. And maybe Dymka's too." He put his hand on the gate, and this time Dymka stepped forward but didn't growl. His eyes were fixed on the pink box.

"Stoyat!" Anna barked, and the dog started growling again.

"Anna," Oleg warned. "We both know I could have come here with a dozen vampires if I wanted to harm you. All I want is to talk. I'm worried about her."

"Why?"

Oleg put his hand on the latch for the gate, and Dymka started barking again. The dog's hackles went up, but Oleg kept his eyes fixed on Anna. "Your daughter became a vampire because of me. Because my people did not protect her. She may not technically be under my aegis, but that doesn't mean I am indifferent to her."

Far from it, but Anna didn't need to know that.

Tatyana Vorona haunted his thoughts. It had been over a year since she had fled from him, but her piercing blue eyes met Oleg every time he fell into day sleep. Her voice whispered in his mind. And her blood moved in his veins.

He couldn't rid his thoughts of her, and the last thing he wanted was to hurt her mother.

Oleg wanted the woman back, and he was a very patient predator.

He lifted the pink pastry box again, and Dymka quieted, but he didn't sit.

Anna sighed. "I am going to regret this." She lowered the shotgun. "Oleg, you may come in." She looked at the dog. "Dymka, priyatel."

Immediately, the dog relaxed and walked to the gate with a wagging tail, sitting down as Oleg eased open the latch and swung the gate inward, keeping his eyes on the shepherd.

"He won't bite you unless I tell him." Anna waited for Oleg to approach the porch.

Oleg held his hand out and petted the dog's black ears. He was a handsome animal with shoulders that reached Oleg's waist and a head that nearly came to his chest. That said, once Anna had called Oleg a friend, he appeared completely relaxed.

"He's well trained."

"Did you come here to ask about my dog?" Anna leaned on the doorframe as Oleg approached the house. "Or did you come about my daughter?"

OLEG SAT AT THE TABLE, THE SMETANNIK COOLING IN THE antiquated refrigerator and a homemade cake on the table. Anna boiled water for tea, and Dymka, ever watchful, sat in the doorway of the kitchen, staring longingly at his mistress.

There was a curled-up cat on the sofa, but the animal only opened one eye, blinked at him, then went back to sleep.

"When did you get the dog?" he asked. "You only arrived a few weeks ago, but he seems at home."

"A neighbor of mine keeps sheep." Anna glanced over her shoulder. "He'd already trained this one for the animals, but as he got bigger, he wasn't getting along with the other dogs so much. When I told my neighbor I was looking for a farm dog, he gave me Dymka." Anna shrugged. "He's good company. Keeps the foxes away from the birds."

Tatyana had once told him that her mother liked her birds more than most people, so protecting them was probably as much a priority as keeping vampires away.

"I have someone watching the farm," Oleg said. "He shouldn't bother you, but if there is danger, he'll be able to deal with it." He lifted the serving knife and cut a piece of cake for Anna and himself as she brought the teapot over to the cozy kitchen table.

She poured two cups, first for Oleg, then for herself.

"Spasibo," he murmured.

"You're welcome." She pulled the teapot back. "Well, I don't know if you're actually welcome, but you're welcome to tea."

Oleg shrugged. "Fair enough."

He'd been in the old farmhouse before, the first time when he had to explain the immortal world to Tatyana and her mother. Not much had changed, but the house was a little less worn. A little more secure. There were a few new windows, and he suspected she'd had insulation added, because the interior was warm even though the night was cold.

"She sends you money?"

"She sent me plenty." Anna glanced at him as she sat. "I don't need her money. The farm is good now, and I'm renting out our apartment in town."

Anna Asanova was so obviously Tatyana's mother that Oleg found it difficult not to stare at her. She wasn't old—in her late forties at most—but her eyes were tired, and her life had been harder than her daughter's. Still, the resemblance was enough that Oleg searched her face, looking for traces of the woman who had become his obsession.

"You left the country for a while."

"Yes." Anna blew on her tea.

"But you came back."

"Yes."

"Did Tatyana arrange it?"

"Did she?" Anna narrowed her eyes. "I'm not sure."

He'd been impressed by how thoroughly the woman had disappeared. Whoever Tatyana was working with—likely the same hacker or hackers who had helped her find all the money his thieving daughter had stolen—was very, very good.

If they were willing to work with vampires, he might hire them for himself.

"Do you really want to ask me about Tatyana moving me?" Anna looked up. "Or are you worried about her like you said?"

"I am worried about her." And he wanted to know how she'd done it, but that was secondary.

"Why are you worried?"

"The people she went to..." Oleg shrugged. "I don't trust them."

Tatyana had fled his territory and ended up in the court of Arosh, the ancient fire vampire who ruled quietly in the Caucasus Mountains. While Oleg's allies ruled the cities of the Eastern Black Sea, in the mountains they bowed to the Fire King, and no one traveled there save for those Arosh allowed.

"You may not trust them," Anna said, "but she does."

"So she is still there?"

Anna turned cool eyes on Oleg. "Are you asking me to snitch on my own daughter?"

"I am asking you to think about her safety."

Anna pursed her lips. "She seems safe to me."

"So you've seen her?"

She rolled her eyes. "What do you think, Mr. Vampire?"

"I don't want to presume. You could be communicating via carrier pigeon."

He would never underestimate these women again.

Anna smirked. "Did you like that? That was *my* plan, you know."

"I thought as much." Tatyana had managed to slip under his nose and send her mother into hiding with nothing more than a few birds.

"You think I've visited her when you haven't?" Anna asked. "I have a phone now, don't I? She has a computer. I may not know about computers like my daughter does, but I know how to video chat. My daughter is fine."

So she was somewhere with internet access. Unfortunately, these days that could be anywhere. Even the Fire King might have entered the twenty-first century by now.

Or Tatyana could be heading into the nearest city to call her mother. Oleg would tell his operatives in coastal Georgia to watch the internet cafés and libraries for any sign of her.

He was grasping at straws.

"Tell me" —she took a bite of cake— "why do you care about my daughter? She got you your money, didn't she?"

"Yes." He followed Anna's lead and cut into his cake. Vampires didn't need human food, but it had been a day or so since he'd eaten anything, and his stomach was empty. If he went too long without consuming human food, it would cause discomfort.

The cake was too sweet, like most modern food, but he could tell it was baked well. "You're a good baker," he said. "Did you plant the garden too?"

"What are your intentions toward my daughter, Mr. Vampire?"

Oleg froze. "My... intentions?"

"Yes." Anna stared at him. "You come to my farm—which she wasn't happy about, I'll have you know. When I told her I was moving back, it started a very big fight. And now you're asking about her when she doesn't work for you anymore. Are you in love with her?"

"Don't be ridiculous. Your daughter is my responsibility."

"Are you the one who made her like this?"

Thank God, no. "Of course not."

Anna shrugged again. "So you are not responsible for her. I am her mother. I am responsible for her. That Zara, the one who hurt my Tatyana, you are responsible for *her*, yes?"

"Zara is dead now. She won't be bothering you."

"Huh." Anna blinked. "I thought that, but Tatyana wouldn't tell me."

Tatyana probably didn't want to scare her mother, but Oleg thought all the Vorona women could use a little more fear in the back of their mind. They were remarkably fearless, and it could easily get them killed.

"Did you kill her?" Anna asked. "Or did Tatyana?"

So Anna thought her own daughter was capable of killing someone.

An interesting insight.

"She's dead," Oleg said. "That's all you need to know. But someone *was* helping her." He glanced over his shoulder. "So don't let Dymka get too friendly." He took the too-sweet cake that Anna had made and tossed a good chunk over toward the dog, who quickly gulped it down. "Except for me. He can be friends with me."

Anna muttered under her breath. "Maybe you two deserve each other for breaking my brain."

"Will you give her a message?"

"No." Anna snorted. "You want me to pass messages for you like you are schoolchildren?"

"What? No." Oleg blinked. "Not schoolchildren, but there are things—"

"I am not your messenger girl," Anna said. "If you want to kill me, you'll kill me, yes? I don't get involved in my daughter's love life. I'm not that kind of mother."

"It's not about her love life." Oleg felt his skin heat.

"Well, it seems to me that you are very interested in Tatyana, and since she's not working for you anymore, I don't know what other reason—"

"There are people who want to kill her." Oleg didn't raise his voice. He didn't believe in raising his voice. He believed in others quieting down so they would listen.

Anna went quiet.

After a long moment, she asked, "Who? Who wants to kill my daughter?"

"My enemies." It wasn't a lie. Necessarily.

If Oleg's enemies knew that Oleg had fixated on her, they would want to kill her, so the key to her future safety was for him to be as indifferent as possible.

"Why would they want to kill her?"

Because I care about her.

He wasn't going to tell Anna that.

"She's young," he said quietly. "Zara bragged to the immortal world about her clever human bookkeeper, and now that bookkeeper is a vampire and she's a vampire with connections so good that she was able to make her mother disappear."

"Why is that anyone's business but hers?"

"More than one of my kind is worried that if Tatyana could steal money from Zara and get away with it, she could steal money from them too."

Another exaggeration, but it worked, because Anna's eyes went wide.

"She wouldn't," Anna snapped. "Tatyana is an *honest* person."

"Do you think so? She stole from me."

"I don't believe you." Anna's cheeks were red with indignation. "My daughter is not a thief."

Oleg shrugged. "I didn't want to believe it about my own daughter either." But he had always known Zara was a thief. "Sometimes our children make unwise choices."

The wheels were turning in Anna's head. That was all he

needed. He just needed Anna Asanova to reach out to her daughter so he could track Tatyana down.

Oleg finished his tea and stood. "I am trying to help your daughter. I'm trying to keep her from making more mistakes. Drawing more attention to herself."

Anna stood, but she said nothing.

Oleg walked toward the door, patting Dymka's head as he walked out. "The next time you speak to her, tell her that I'm looking for her and so are others. Tell her that whatever mountain cave she's hiding in, she's going to have to leave eventually."

Anna lifted her chin. "And you'll be waiting?"

"Yes." Oleg nodded. "I'm immortal, Miss Asanova. I can wait a very long time."

Chapter 2

Tatyana

"No one is trying to kill me, Mama." Tatyana kept her eyes on the screen, which was hidden behind a heavy silicone case. "He's trying to get information from you. Do you remember everything?"

"He didn't touch me."

"Not once?"

"No." Her mother narrowed her eyes. "But he did touch Dymka. Can he use his special mind powers on dogs? Is that why Dymka liked him?"

Oleg's "special powers" were the same as Tatyana's, an electrical current called amnis that ran under her skin like an extra sense. It let her manipulate humans, like the ones working at this very quiet bar in Kutaisi where she was using the Wi-Fi.

With a handshake, Tatyana could alter the humans' cerebral cortexes to wipe their short-term memories. It was also the reason she had to use the homemade silicone case for her laptop.

Computers and vampire amnis? They didn't get along.

It was her third laptop this year. She'd shorted out the others.

"He's trying to scare you." She glanced at Samson, the silent wind vampire who had flown with her to the city at the base of the mountains. "This is why I didn't want you to go back to the farm."

Kutaisi was the unofficial borderland between the territory under Arosh's control, which stretched northeast into Central Asia, and that under Alina Machabeli, the vampire ruler of coastal Georgia and some of northern Turkey.

"And what was I going to do? Stay in Kherson with strangers?"

Her mother had been in a safe house in Kherson for over a year before she broke.

Tatyana had known it was going to happen. She could tell her mother was miserable. The fact that she was safe wasn't as important as who was watching her birds.

But by then Tatyana was fairly sure that if Oleg was going to kill her and her mother, he would have found a way. Even though her mother had been in Oleg's territory, he'd basically ignored her.

Tatyana rubbed her temple. "You were *safe* in Kherson. That's why I sent you there."

Talking to Anna couldn't provoke headaches anymore, but her mother could try. And she tried very hard.

"I'm safe here," Anna said. "Your vampire didn't do anything to me."

"He's not my vampire, Mama."

"In fact, he said he has someone watching the farm."

"Watching the farm?"

"Yes, for my safety."

Her mother actually sounded reassured.

By Oleg. The fire vampire.

Tatyana had considered sending her mother to Romania or Turkey, somewhere out of Oleg's territory, but her mother would have been even more miserable somewhere that no one spoke her language.

And Tatyana wasn't completely sure how far Oleg's territory stretched. Sometimes it seemed like it was endless.

From what she'd learned while hiding in Arosh's court, Oleg

Sokolov, vampire lord of the Kievan Rus, controlled the territory from the Caucasus Mountains and east of the Volga River, skirting the edge of the Caspian Sea north to Siberia and clear over to Mongolia.

But *control* could be a very loose term.

In the immortal world, powers were constantly shifting, and it was all Tatyana could do to keep track of who ruled what territory and how strict that control was.

The vampire world operated more like medieval city-states than modern governments, and the past year and a half had been one lesson after another in going with the flow.

"He said he was going back to Odesa," Anna said.

Tatyana frowned. "Arosh?"

"Who is Arosh?" Anna asked. "I'm talking about your vampire."

Of course her mother was still talking about Oleg. "Right."

"Who is Arosh? There is a different vampire now?"

"Arosh is the one I'm working for at the moment." It wasn't exactly true, but it was enough to satisfy her mother, who would be stressed if she didn't think Tatyana had a job.

"Good. That's good to keep busy, Tanya."

Work tires you, but it's better to be tired than stupid. She could hear her grandfather's words in her mind.

Tatyana *wasn't* working for Arosh; she didn't need money. Maybe ever again.

She'd calculated the value of the gold and jewelry she'd taken from Oleg, and it was enough to keep her comfortable for a very long time.

If she lived past a century, she might need to work some things out, but she was frugal by nature. She wasn't prone to lavish displays like Oleg, and she didn't have anyone to support except her mother.

Every now and then, a pang of guilt hit her about the theft of the gold bars and jewelry, but Oleg himself had told her the treasure she'd taken belonged to her sire Zara, who was dead.

So it didn't count as stealing.

Technically.

Calculating all of her sire's treasure along with the money Oleg had paid her after she found Zara's loot made Tatyana realize that she was well and truly rich.

As long as Oleg didn't try to get Zara's gold back.

"So Oleg is going back to Odesa." Tatyana nodded. "Good. That's good." Odesa was farther from her than Sevastopol.

"How does he move so easily everywhere? Is it all by boat?" Anna had left Sevastopol by boat, so she assumed anyone fleeing without government permission had to go by boat.

"No, he's just rich." And he had human authorities in his pocket and specially built planes. "Rich people can do anything whether they're human or... not human."

The first thing Tatyana had learned after becoming a vampire was that human borders meant little to vampires unless they became a hindrance to movement. And even then, with enough bribery or violence, those hindrances often disappeared.

Okay, the first thing she'd actually learned was how miserable and overwhelming bloodlust was, but that was quickly followed by the territorial thing.

She glanced at Samson, but he was sitting in a booth and drinking a beer, ignoring the women who were hitting on him while he read a book.

For some reason, Samson liked Tatyana enough that he was willing to fly her to Kutaisi once a month to call her mother. It wasn't strictly in Arosh's territory, where she officially had safe haven, but it wasn't exactly out of it either.

Tatyana asked, "You didn't tell him we had a regular call time, did you?"

"No, but he knows I've talked to you."

"Did you tell him that?"

"No, he knew already!" Anna twisted her mouth into a scowl. "You think I would snitch on you?"

"I know you wouldn't mean to." But she had.

Oleg probably *suspected* that Tatyana called her mother, and

Anna had confirmed it. Which meant she would need to stop coming to the same comfortable spot and look for something new, because now she knew Oleg was watching her mother.

Her mentor Kato had told her she would need to vary her movements, but Tatyana had become comfortable with the same quiet bar where no one seemed to pay her much attention.

Damn it.

"We'll need to change the time for next month," Tatyana said. "Just in case."

Anna sighed. "I was finally able to remember this time, and now you want to change it. And you don't want me to write anything down. I don't have your vampire brain, you know."

"I know, but tell me..." Tatyana racked her brain. "Who is someone famous who has a birthday in March?" Her mother loved old movie stars and had a trivia-like knowledge of their lives.

"Liza Minnelli has a birthday on March twelfth." Anna pursed her lips. "I can't remember the year."

"Okay, that's perfect. Three and twelve." It was near the beginning of the month. "I'll call you on March twelfth at twelve in the evening. Midnight. Can you remember that? I'll call you on Liza Minnelli's birthday."

Anna nodded. "I can remember that."

"Good." She waved at her mother. "I love you. Be careful."

Anna muttered, "Becoming a monster has made you very sentimental."

No, it had made her very conscious that everyone she knew was probably in danger of early death. "I should go."

"Wait!" Anna raised her hand like she was still in school. "Your boss said to give you a message."

"He's not my boss anymore."

"I mean..." Anna shrugged. "You're still afraid of him, so he's kind of still your boss."

"I'm not afraid of him." She was *so* afraid of him. But probably not for the reasons her mother thought. "What did he want me to know?"

"He said that he was waiting for you to come out of your cave," Anna said. "But that others were waiting too." Her mother's voice got soft. "He said that other vampires want to find you. I think you might not be safe where you are."

He's waiting for you to come out of your cave, but others are waiting too.

A GENUINE WARNING? AN ATTEMPT TO FLUSH HER FROM HER safe haven in the mountains? Or an empty threat?

With Oleg, any of those choices was a possibility.

The vampire could be mercurial to say the least. Tender and protective one moment, domineering and imperious in the next.

Tatyana closed her eyes against the wind that beat against her back as Samson carried her above the low-hanging clouds that bumped against the Caucasus Range in northern Georgia. She could see scattered lights in the distance and suspected there was a party in progress.

The Fire King loved a party.

Since Samson was one of her only friends, Tatyana had prioritized learning the sign language he used.

She took one hand out and braved the cold, whipping wind. *Party tonight?*

Samson nodded.

At the harem? she asked.

He shook his head.

Good. If it wasn't at the harem, she wouldn't have to attend.

Since Tatyana didn't fall under Arosh's aegis—his vampire

authority—she couldn't work or stay in his castle. She didn't fall under anyone else's aegis either.

And it was starting to become a problem.

She was rootless and at loose ends in this complicated political world.

Since she didn't belong to anyone or have any official role, once Tatyana had been able to control her bloodlust, she'd been moved to Arosh's harem, which mostly consisted of human women and girls looking for refuge. There were a few vampires there, but mostly humans.

She didn't have to have sex with Arosh just because she was staying in the harem—though many of the women highly recommended it—but she *was* expected to put in an appearance at any of his parties with vampire guests, of which there were many.

Arosh found Tatyana amusing, and he introduced her as his "clever little stray cat."

Which sounded more affectionate in Farsi.

Most of the first few months in the mountains, Tatyana had to remain isolated, which gave her plenty of time to put her new vampire brain to use. She'd focused on learning Farsi first since that's what most of the vampires around her spoke; then she'd started working on Greek, which was another widely spoken language in vampire circles.

While Tatyana had always had an easy time learning languages in school, the ability to pick them up even faster with an immortal brain was truly astonishing. She now had a thorough knowledge of Russian, Ukrainian, and English and a working knowledge of Farsi and Greek.

Georgian was still escaping her, but she knew enough to get around, and many local people spoke English or Russian, at least enough that Tatyana could get by.

Samson landed behind one of the brightly painted stone buildings that made up Arosh's harem. The mountaintop compound was an oasis of gardens and fountains nestled in the mountains. They were surrounded by dense forests and alpine lakes, and the area was well and truly hidden from humans.

Samson set her down and lifted his hands to sign. *Ambassadors from Alina's court are visiting tonight.*

Should I stay hidden? Tatyana signed.

Samson shook his head. *He told me to bring you when we came back.*

Samson was in Arosh's line. Though the ancient king was a fire vampire, his blood came from the wind. Tatyana knew that if Arosh gave Samson a command, he could not ignore it.

She still tried. "They're from Alina," she whispered. "They could tell him I'm here."

Samson frowned. *Oleg already knows you're here.*

"Still, he doesn't need any more information about me. He's already talking to my mother."

The silver-haired wind vampire cocked his head and quickly signed, *Is she in danger?*

It was tempting. Samson was a zealot when it came to protecting women.

If she told him Anna was in danger, he would probably fly to her family farm, pluck her screaming mother from her kitchen, and fly her back.

And then she'd have to deal with her mother's opinion on a nightly basis.

Tatyana didn't want to lie to her only friend. "She's not in danger. Oleg came to check on her. He says he posted guards at the farm even. If he wanted to hurt her, he already would have. I'm fairly sure she's safe."

Samson pursed his lips but signed nothing. He crossed his arms over his chest.

"Go ahead and say it," she said. "I know you want to."

Families are complicated, he signed. *But your blood is connected to his. That means something in our world.*

"My sire is dead," Tatyana said. "And I still don't even know how I feel about it, but I know Oleg is *not* my family."

Some nights Tatyana woke up weeping, clutching her chest where there was a hollow ache. She hated Zara for putting it there. Hated her and loved her; then she hated herself for helping Oleg kill her.

"The last thing I need is Oleg putting his stamp on my eternity." She stood on her tiptoes and kissed Samson's cheek. "You're lovely. But whatever path I find in this world, it needs to be on my own."

"Aha!" Arosh smiled and stood when she entered the circle where he was holding court. He spread his arms in welcome. "It's my clever little cat! Where have you been?"

"Flying with Samson, Lord Arosh." Spring had broken in the mountains and flowers were blooming, but the air was still cold. "We just returned." She pressed her hands together and gave him a nod, which was the most common greeting in the court. "Thank you for this invitation to join you." She turned to the guests seated immediately to Arosh's left in the place of honor and nodded at them. "Greetings to your guests."

The chilly air didn't bother Tatyana once she'd learned how to control her amnis, so she was wearing a long-sleeved floral dress she'd borrowed from Cora, who was one of Arosh's mistresses and ran the harem.

Cora had taught Tatyana most of what she knew about court protocol, and she was quick to point out that every vampire court was different.

So much fun.

Arosh stood at the head of a low table that curved like a horseshoe around the room. A fire burned in a brazier in the center of the circle, and fountains trickled in the background.

Tatyana felt the low hum of energy from her element, and that hum was the only thing that kept her amnis in check while surrounded by so many humans and strange vampires.

Piles of intricately embroidered cushions were piled behind each guest. The music was low, played by three women on stringed instruments in the corner of the garden. Other human women floated about the room, offering wine, light dishes, and goblets of blood-wine flavored with honey.

"This is the young vampire I was telling you about." Arosh sat and pointed at Tatyana. "She is brilliant with numbers and computers." He lifted a finger. "It is sensible to turn the young in this age, my friends. They have an understanding of this new science that threatens us. It is wise to understand your enemy if you want to defeat him."

The visiting male and female vampire next to Arosh turned cool brown eyes toward Tatyana, looking her up and down as if she were an interesting bug.

"This is Oleg's bookkeeper?" the man asked. "The one his daughter turned?"

The one who killed her own sire?

Tatyana heard the unspoken question, but she didn't react to it. Vampires were worse than old women when it came to gossip, and she'd learned that lying and exaggeration were expected.

"Her story is her own." Arosh waved a careless hand. "But she would be an asset to any organization. I am sure of it."

Wait, what was this? Was Arosh trying to get rid of her? Was this some kind of matchmaking situation? A job interview or something?

This was... not good.

Tatyana desperately wanted to leave the scrutiny of the court vampires, but Arosh had not dismissed her, so she stood there, free for all to examine with their cold, analytical stares.

Some were dressed in traditional local clothing, others were shrouded from head to toe. One man she didn't recognize appeared to be wearing military fatigues.

Arosh told Tatyana none of their names. She was being introduced to them, not the other way round. The invited guests murmured among themselves, but until Arosh excused her, Tatyana had to stay put.

She glanced at the Fire King and saw that he noticed exactly how uncomfortable she was at being put on display.

And yet he did not dismiss her.

Was it a test of patience? A trial of some kind?

She had been given sanctuary over a year ago, but now it appeared that Arosh wanted to pawn her off on someone else.

He's waiting for you to come out of your cave, but others are waiting too.

Was Oleg not bluffing?

Did Arosh know something she didn't?

Tatyana was on the edge of erupting in anger when Kato entered the garden with his young paramour Alexander on his arm.

"Brother?" Kato glanced at Tatyana, then turned back to Arosh. "Was my student waiting for me?" His kind blue eyes turned to Tatyana. "You are so understanding, my dear."

Alexander quickly added, "I'm so sorry we kept you waiting for us."

The tall human was nearly the same stature as Kato, but while the ancient water vampire was broadly built and as muscular as the statues of Greek gods he'd inspired, the human on his arm was a slim man with full lips set in a suntanned face and a long fall of wavy blond hair that went past his shoulders.

They made a stunning pair.

Kato crossed to Tatyana, leaving Alexander on the edge of the circle. He put his arm around Tatyana, and the tension drained from her shoulders.

She always felt safe with Kato.

The two vampires sitting on Arosh's left immediately rose and bowed their heads low.

"Great father," one said, "you honor us with your presence."

"Your Excellence," the woman said, her eyes fixed on the floor, "we are unworthy of your welcome."

So these two were water vampires. It made sense if they came from Alina's court, as she was also a water vampire. Their blood could probably be traced back to the ancient king with his arm around her.

Water vampires tended to be the most politically minded of the four elements, but maybe there was something wrong with Tatyana because she hadn't had any urge to politick or scheme since she'd been turned.

She was as introverted as ever and only wanted to be left alone to figure out her new eternity in peace.

"Arosh, why do you insist on flashing our brightest jewels when we have only just acquired them?" Kato kissed the top of Tatyana's head. "I have been training Tatyana myself," he said to the emissaries from Alina's court. "Her amnis delights me."

And just like that, the cold appraisal of the vampires around her turned to studied disinterest. If the ancient king of the Mediterranean had staked some kind of claim over the young one, she was not up for grabs.

The corner of Arosh's mouth turned up, and he and Kato exchanged a look that spoke volumes. Unfortunately, whatever language they were speaking wasn't for Tatyana to understand.

"Come," Kato said. "If my brother has finished introducing you, Alexander and I were hoping you could join us." Kato turned to Arosh. "Brother?"

"You may take her." Arosh waved a hand. "Tatyana, you are dismissed."

She pressed her hands together and bowed slightly. "Thank you, Lord Arosh." She glanced around the table. "A pleasant evening to all of you."

As soon as she reached the edge of the room, Alexander grabbed her hand and tugged her into the shadows. "What kind of trouble are you causing now?" He squeezed her hand. "You do keep things exciting around here."

"Come." Kato's voice was barely over a murmur. "Let's find a quiet corner so we can talk. There are ears everywhere at Arosh's parties."

Chapter 3

Oleg

Minsk, Belarus

Oleg strode through the darkened factory, his footsteps echoing in the hollow air. He glanced at the large four-wheeled tractors in the process of final assembly.

"The upgrades Polina did last year appear to have increased production," he muttered to Mika, who was walking beside him. "This facility has moved from ten thousand units per year to being on track to produce over fifteen annually."

"She was right to ask for the funds." Mika Arakis, Oleg's chief boyar, head spy, and personal enforcer, scanned the massive factory as they walked. "Humans will always need to eat. Can you believe these machines?" Mika pointed to one. "Imagine how quickly you could plow a field with these."

Oleg nodded. "Their ingenuity amazes me."

"Very clever humans," Mika said.

When Oleg and Mika had been human, it would have taken ten strong men over a week to do the work that one of these machines could do in a day.

Oleg shook his head. "Truly remarkable."

His commercial and political interests in Minsk were overseen by his daughter Polina, who had been running this area of his empire for nearly two hundred years.

A father wasn't supposed to have favorite children, but Polina might have been his. She was steady as a rock and had been at his side for over four hundred years. Her mind was a thing of beauty, and she enjoyed the logistics of empire.

If Oleg had an heir, it could very well be Polina.

She knew when an embrace was needed and when a slap was more appropriate.

The metallic aroma of vampire blood hit Oleg as soon as he reached the darkened corner where the factory's safety showers were located.

Instead of a worker washing off chemicals, the spare white stall was occupied by a battered vampire with dark hair, pale skin, and a sour expression. He was tied to a chair with twisted barbed wire, his feet were on concrete, and his eyes burned holes in Oleg as he approached.

"Polya." Oleg stopped at the edge of the area lit by searing white floodlights. "What did you find for me, my daughter?"

Polina rose from the chair opposite the bloody vampire and walked to Oleg, lifting her face to his and smiling. "Papa."

He kissed her forehead and both cheeks before he pinched her chin affectionately. "This is the driver of the truck that hijacked ours?"

"No, the driver is dead. He was human." She nodded toward the vampire in the chair. "This is the one who killed the driver before I could get my hands on him."

The vile criminals had beaten Polina's employee nearly to death, then hijacked a shipment of electronics that had been headed for Brest to be distributed to their Polish partners.

Polina's people had tracked the truck to a warehouse in Baranavichy and quickly dispatched the humans and vampires guarding it before bringing what appeared to be the ringleader back to Minsk.

"He's the last one," she said quietly. "There were no humans left by the time we got inside. Three dead ones though. I believe they killed them as soon as they realized we'd found them."

Humans had minds that could be bent with amnis. Humans could tell secrets even if they were trusted.

"And how many vampires?"

"Four."

Whoever was targeting Oleg's shipments was devoting resources to the job. This had gone beyond regional friction. "Did you lose anyone?"

"In this hijacking? One vampire. His people were skilled fighters, but the moment I grabbed this one, they all reacted. They were looking at him for cues."

"So he was in charge." Oleg glanced at the glaring vampire. "Language?"

"None that we heard. No names. No documents."

So not only good fighters but disciplined.

Oleg looked at the half dozen other vampires hanging around the periphery. Polina's staff. Let them witness an interrogation? Or would it be better for them to only hear the screams?

The vampire would be more likely to talk with a smaller audience.

"Tell your people they can wait outside," he muttered.

Polina barked at them and the waiting vampires scattered, leaving Oleg, Mika, and Polina alone with the vampire who had stolen their truck.

Polina nodded at Mika. "Mika, nice to see you."

"Polina." Mika was examining the beaten vampire with narrowed eyes. "This seems to keep happening."

"Yes, quite annoying." Polina tossed her long dark hair over her shoulder and stared at the man. "He gives me nothing. Perhaps he might speak to you, Mika. I hear you're very skilled with matters such as this."

Mika looked at the man and smiled, baring his fangs. "Ah, but do we have the time for my methods?"

The vampire didn't even flinch. Whoever he was, he was tough.

Or stupid. Perhaps both.

Oleg's factories in Minsk were the backbone of his legal manufacturing business, and usually the excellent roads that crisscrossed the country were perfectly safe.

But this had been the fifth hijacking in six months. Someone was targeting his businesses. No human companies had seen an increase in theft, so it wasn't a general crime wave.

This was an attack on Oleg.

He circled the man in the chair. "And no documents on him?"

"I looked for a wallet but he had nothing." She held up a phone. "Nocht compatible, and his case wasn't waterproof."

Water vampires always had waterproof cases on their phones, and the man wasn't floating away, which meant he was either an earth vampire like Polina or a young wind vampire who couldn't fly yet.

Oleg bent down, sniffing the blood that lingered on the man's collar. The cuts on his face had already healed. The man hissed but said nothing.

"I don't recognize his scent." He turned to Mika. "You?"

Mika walked over and sniffed the man's blood, then shook his head.

Oleg sat in the chair opposite the beaten vampire, where Polina had been sitting when they came in. "You know who I am?"

The silent vampire nodded.

"So you know you have a choice," Oleg said quietly. "You can tell us who hired you and she will kill you." He nodded toward Polina. "She's my daughter. I trained her on the sword myself. She will be quick. It would be painless."

The vampire might have glanced at Polina, but he still said nothing.

"Or you can stay silent, and I will burn you from the inside out," Oleg said quietly. "Do you know how that works?"

Nothing from the nameless one.

"First I'll cut off a hand." He shrugged. "Probably a hand. Then I force my fire into your veins."

The man's eyes ticked. It wasn't quite a flinch, but it was something.

Oleg continued quietly. "I don't know why my amnis loves blood so much, but it seems to follow the veins. Runs under the skin." He snapped his fingers and brought the soothing red-and-orange fire to his fingertips.

The liquid flames ran over Oleg's skin like mercury, slipping between his fingers, crawling up his arms, and moving from the palm of one hand to the other.

The vampire's eyes locked on Oleg's fire.

"Once my flames get inside, you won't die right away. It will take a long time for you to die. But you will feel *every* moment of it," Oleg said. "Or you can tell us who hired you to steal this truck." He shrugged. "Either way, you are dead, so being loyal to whoever paid your people is useless. They are dead. You will be dead. Your silence doesn't matter anymore."

"My silence keeps the others safe," the man blurted. "So kill me however you like." His eyes rose to Oleg's. "But I won't talk."

"Well." Oleg wiped his hands on a cool towel that Polina handed him back in the factory manager's office. "He was correct. He didn't talk."

"That was frustrating and satisfying at the same time," Polina muttered. "At least I can tell Mr. Goretski's family that the men who nearly killed him have been taken care of." She curled her lip. "Unless Ivan tells them first."

Oleg tossed the ash-stained towel on the counter before he leaned against it and crossed his arms over his chest. "What does that mean? Has my favorite brother in Moscow involved himself in this?"

"Didn't you hear?" Polina was clearly annoyed. "Our driver was receiving medical treatment here in Minsk, and the doctors said he was recovering very well. And then Ivan sent a private plane for the entire family so he could see a neurological specialist in Moscow."

What are you doing, Ivan?

"Did the man need a neurological specialist in Moscow?"

"According to the neurologist here in Minsk? No. He was receiving the same care as he would receive in any hospital. We pay for private doctors, Oleg. This has always been company policy. You know this."

Working for vampires could be dangerous, which was why Oleg was quick to offer benefits to his many employees, and one of them was excellent medical care if they were ever injured on the job. He had a reputation for being generous with his humans, but it was mostly out of self-interest.

Happy humans made for loyal workers who were less easily turned.

Now his brother was stepping on his daughter's toes.

Mika offered a thoughtful "hmmm" but nothing else.

Oleg sat on the edge of the metal desk in the factory office. "Who contacted the family initially?"

"The manager of the shipping company. He called as soon as we realized Goretski had been hurt. We quickly moved him to a private hospital; then I called the man's wife as soon as I woke that night and got the report."

"How many days later did Ivan send the plane?"

"Two nights later. Goretski was out of the coma, but Ivan's men showed up at the hospital from 'company headquarters' in Moscow."

Polina snarled when she used air quotes. "The boys from Moscow had the woman on the phone with Ivan himself, reassuring the family there was an apartment in Moscow near the rehab facility waiting for them. All expenses paid."

Polina knew as well as Oleg did that it wasn't necessarily who caused the problems but who showed up fix them.

Humans were easily swayed.

Mika asked, "So are we all thinking that Ivan could be involved in this?"

"He's not a stranger to provocation," Polina said. "But attacking humans under my aegis like this? He's never gone quite that far. If he did—"

"Easy." Oleg put a hand on her shoulder. "Throwing around accusations will get us nowhere. My brother is the governor of a major region in our empire."

"And the head of a criminal gang," Mika said.

Oleg shrugged. "And yet there are many in our clan loyal to him."

"He's been running his mouth to anyone who will listen about how you dealt with Zara," Polina spat out. "As if that crazy bitch didn't have it coming. You were too patient with her."

"Your sister is dead now; it doesn't matter."

"But it does." Polina lifted her chin. "Because Ivan is using it against you. And your druzhina may know what goes on behind the scenes, but the average area leader?" She pointed at the door. "Those men out there cleaning up the ashes? They think Ivan is great. They congratulated me for calling in a *favor*" —she nearly spat out the word— "a favor to help that poor man's family."

Mika muttered, "You didn't disagree with them, did you?"

"Of course not!" Polina hissed. "How could I without looking ungrateful? I nodded and smiled and acted like it was the least I could do for our people." She shook her head. "Ivan is a thug. They used to hate him."

"Yes, but that's when his men used to puff their chests and make problems along the border areas," Mika said. "Ivan has stopped all that."

"Because he's the one that started it."

Oleg had to smile. "My brother is the master of creating a problem and then showing up to solve it. He has always been this way. It's strategic thinking for small minds."

"That may be." Polina kept her voice low. "But right now he's telling a story that those vampires out there are hungry for. And all of them are listening."

They were back on the plane before Mika finally blurted out what he'd clearly been holding in for hours. "The vampire you just killed was Poshani."

"And this is why you have a job." Oleg settled into his seat in the custom plane they'd flown to Minsk. "His accent was definitely Poshani."

"Eastern Poshani to be precise." Mika closed the metallic cage that enclosed Oleg's personal compartment. "You need to call Radu. Or I could call Kezia if you'd rather."

"Not all Poshani vampires work for Radu," Oleg said quickly. "Or the clan. This could mean nothing. He could have been an outcast."

"An outcast with four partners who were probably also Poshani?" Mika sat next to him. "Their people are everywhere in our territory."

Cesar, Oleg's air steward, came to check on them and offer a bottle of blood-wine, but Oleg declined with a wave of his hand and Cesar retreated back to the galley.

Moments later, Oleg felt the plane moving toward the runway.

"The Poshani are our allies. Our relationship has never been compromised," Oleg said. "Other than some bitching from Ivan, their people have never caused us problems. They pay us handsomely for roaming access to our territory."

"As they should," Mika said.

As the plane's engines built up speed, Oleg felt that same clench in his belly. The same dip and fearful thrill he'd experienced the first time he left the earth.

Machine-powered flight. It was a truly marvelous thing. Airplanes were one of the few things that still got his heart beating.

Human ingenuity had always interested Oleg. Unlike many of his kind, he was curious about the modern world. He had no nostalgia for the past. The past was dirty and violent and cruel.

And yet so many of his kind clung to their history as if it were a precious jewel. The Poshani were the perfect example.

Had their lives fundamentally changed in the past millennium?

They were a vampire clan like none other in the world. Uniquely coordinated between their human and vampire elements, many did live in cities and operate in the modern world, but the majority maintained the itinerant lifestyle of their ancestors.

They were traders, builders, fighters, artists, and more than anything, they were fiercely loyal.

Perhaps if Oleg's history had been marked by that kind of loyalty, he might cling to it as well, but he was the son of Truvor the Red, a cruel warlord who'd seen himself as above humans and nearly all vampires.

"You should have a meeting with Radu." Mika glanced out the window, but he was already opening a book. The vampire read voraciously. This night it appeared to be a volume of Spanish poetry.

Obviously Mika had not been sired by Truvor the Red.

Oleg's sire detested learning about anything that wasn't related to violence or greed. He made a habit of pitting his children against each other, and Oleg's brother Ivan had picked up many of his habits even though he'd hated their sire as much as Oleg did. He'd also inherited Truvor's loathing for anything different or anything he couldn't understand.

Like the Poshani.

The clan was enigmatic by design and often spread lies purposefully to mislead the immortal world. Radu of Bucharest was one of their leaders—the public face of the Poshani clan—but Oleg knew that Radu had two coregents, a brother and a sister, who held equal power.

"I can tell the pilot to make a detour to Bucharest," Mika continued. "We could be there in a couple of hours and open the house. Cesar could call the butler before we land."

Oleg picked up a magazine. "No need just now." He opened it, but he couldn't concentrate. His eye caught on an ad for a perfume. The image was of a blond woman walking through a field of lavender.

Mika noticed the ad. "Is she one of your ex-girlfriends?"

"No."

What would Tatyana have looked like in the sun?

Oleg had the absurd thought that he could build a light-proof warehouse as large as the one they'd just left, plant it with lavender, and put enough lights in it that Tatyana could have her own lavender field to walk through like the ones near her family farm.

"Oleg?"

He looked up. "What?"

Mika narrowed his eyes. "You're thinking about the woman again."

"What did your people in Kutaisi find?"

Mika didn't roll his eyes, but Oleg could tell he wanted to. "She's been going to an internet café, bar-café kind of thing. The bartender remembered her coming in with a silver-haired man."

"The wind vampire." Oleg had to swallow the urge to snarl audibly. The vampire was a favorite of Arosh's; more importantly, he was the immortal who had flown away with Tatyana in his arms.

"The two of them come in fairly regularly," Mika continued.

"How regularly?" Had she taken this silver-haired immortal as a lover? Was she attached to him? Oleg felt his fangs aching in his jaw.

"They come in once a month. Same day of the month. Around the same time. She's been going there for over six months."

Six months meant that she'd mastered her bloodlust at a year or less. Good. That was good. She would have more freedom that way.

But the same place for six months? It wouldn't only be Mika who noticed a pattern like that. "When is her next meeting time?"

"Yesterday."

Oleg curled his lip at Mika. "And you didn't tell me?"

"It doesn't matter," he said. "She didn't show."

Damn.

But good. His visit to Tatyana's mother must have spooked her.

"She won't go back."

"Not if she's smart," Mika said.

"She's smart." He wouldn't be this fascinated with her unless she was intelligent. "I wonder if she knows we could track her down anywhere in Arosh's or Alina's territory and she'd still be perfectly safe."

"Physically safe? Probably." Mika turned back to his book. "I don't think she's *physically* afraid of you."

Then why did she run away?

Oleg had been rethinking their last night together like a detective, analyzing every word. Every expression. Every movement she made before she fled his house and his protection.

You are mine, he'd whispered to her. *I am patient. But you are mine. And when you are ready, you will give me your fangs.*

He'd all but asked for her fangs in his neck, the ultimate intimacy between vampires.

And she had run.

Perhaps she had a fear of commitment. Considering her family history, that was not unexpected.

"Oleg, you have to stop." Mika shook his head. "I feel a kind of... distant obligation to her too. Do you think I've forgotten what happened to her and Elene? But you have to leave her alone. Ivan is becoming a problem, and if you don't deal with him—"

"Call Bucharest." Oleg folded the magazine and snapped his fingers at Cesar in the galley. "I changed my mind about Radu. Get the house ready. It would be good to touch base with a terrin of the Eastern Poshani for a number of reasons, and we can ask him about this Poshani who hijacked our truck."

Mika glanced at Cesar, but the human was still well out of earshot. "The Poshani vampire who is now very dead?"

Oleg switched to an old dialect of Estonian that Mika spoke. "The Poshani practice blood price. I'll have to make some kind of financial settlement when we find the man's immediate clan, but Radu will be reasonable considering the circumstances."

"Fine." Mika nodded. "It's spring, you know. Radu and all the Poshani will be getting ready for the kamvasa."

"Then we'd better catch him before he disappears into the wilderness for six months." Oleg turned to Cesar. "Call the house in Bucharest. And tell the pilot to change our destination."

Chapter 4

Tatyana

Caucasus Mountains, Georgia

Kato leaned forward and made sure to keep his voice low. "It's time."

Tatyana looked around the party that had been raging for hours. It was only an hour until dawn, and not an immortal had departed.

Arosh's human women were nodding and blinking slowly, some from exhaustion and others probably from blood loss.

The musicians, being vampires, still played as strong as ever, though the tenor of the music had shifted to a slower pace.

"It's time for what?" Tatyana asked. Was something going to happen at the party? Her fangs immediately fell. "You must remove Alexander immediately."

"Nothing like that." Alexander moved his hand to Tatyana's forearm. "The party is safe. He's talking about Arosh's protection, dear one."

She was immediately soothed by his touch.

Alexander had to be the most steady human she had met in her entire life. He was probably in his late thirties, and he looked like a carved statue. Appropriate, perhaps, since his partner was a water vampire who was so old he didn't even remember being human.

Before the modern era, the oldest and most powerful immortals ruled empires that covered continents. The world was more diffuse then. Humans were scarcer and resources were limited to the most powerful vampires who could control the most territory.

Kato had been one of those emperors, ruling the ancient Mediterranean with strict control, fighting with Arosh in the East and allied to Saba, the oldest known vampire, who ruled across the African continent.

Massive powers clashed in the ancient vampire world, but as humans thrived and grew, resources became more plentiful. Territories could be broken into new pieces, ruled by younger vampires, and the time of the ancient empires passed.

Over centuries, Arosh and Kato had turned from bitter enemies to reluctant and then dear friends. As brash and intense as Arosh was, Kato was the sea—vast, generous, and deadly when he was roused.

Tatyana turned to the ancient vampire who had become her mentor. While Zara had been her sire in fact, Kato had become the vampire who taught her how to be immortal.

"Arosh means to withdraw his protection?" Tatyana blinked. "Why? What did I—"

"Not immediately," Kato said in a soothing bass. "And you have done nothing to anger him. He will grant you time. He will allow you to think about it. But that display back there was him telling you to start thinking of your future."

"Which... can't be here?" She felt as if she were barely out of vampire primary school and was being told to go make her way in the world. She'd expected to have to leave eventually, but she had so much more to learn.

"You know we would both love for you to stay here," Alexander said. "But this is not our home." He glanced at Kato with a raised eyebrow. "Though perhaps very soon, we may find a new place of our own where we—"

A pair of drunken humans burst into laughter behind them, clearly inebriated and being led away from the vampires by two of the older women in the harem.

Alexander smiled. "Where we might live a quieter life."

Tatyana turned to Kato. "Can an ancient, terribly powerful vampire emperor have a quiet life?" She glanced at Alexander. "I don't really see you two living in a seaside cottage."

"Don't worry about us," Kato said. "Right now you need to think of yourself. Where are you going to go, Tatyana? What are your plans?"

"I don't know." Her heart was in her throat, and she could not get her fangs to retract. "I cannot go back to Oleg's territory."

"Why not?" Kato's gaze was steady. "It has been over a year, and there has been no sign of retaliation for your actions. He's a strict ruler, but he is not an unreasonable man. There is no reason to think that being in his territory would be dangerous for you."

"It's just..." Tatyana pressed her lips together.

Not even Kato knew she'd stolen—taken her rightful inheritance —from Oleg. It wasn't something she had advertised, though some in Arosh's court clearly had their suspicions.

She kept her voice soft. "I have my reasons."

She wasn't afraid of Oleg. Exactly.

She was afraid of how he might sway her will once she returned to his orbit.

And there was no way she could return to his territory and not be in his orbit. It was as if Oleg had his own magnetic field.

"He is your sire's sire," Kato continued. "He has a blood responsibility to you."

And also the beginning of a blood bond because Oleg had taken her blood numerous times. Though she hadn't questioned it at the time, now that Tatyana knew more about blood bonds, she was second-guessing her every interaction with the lethally attractive fire vampire.

"I don't think Oleg has as much generosity as you give him credit for," she said. "I don't trust him."

Liar, a little voice whispered in her mind. *You don't trust* yourself *around him.*

Alexander's voice was soft. "She did kill Oleg's daughter. No matter what he says, he could be harboring a grudge."

Tatyana knew not everyone believed her story about killing Zara. In fact, most of them didn't. Rumors flew in the vampire world. Some said that Oleg had killed Zara long before Tatyana had been turned. Others said that Saba the earth vampire had killed Zara for her role in spreading a vampire poison. Still others claimed that Oleg had killed Zara in retaliation for Zara killing Oleg's dead mate.

None of those rumors were true, but Tatyana kept her mouth shut and tried to ignore the whispers and curious eyes.

Most of Arosh's court seemed to think that Tatyana fleeing from Oleg was all part of a lover's spat, which could frequently be lethal when it came to vampire relationships.

"You're frightening her," Alexander said. "It is too much, my love."

"She needs to be a bit frightened," Kato said. "I want her to survive."

Tatyana had woven a complicated web of lies during her time in Arosh's court, but the more she learned about how vampires lied about their origin, the more she thought the double-talk and gossip only helped her reputation.

Alexander put a calming hand on her shoulder. "If Oleg threatens you for killing Zara, he'll only be condemning himself. He can't blame you for her death without admitting he lied to Saba."

Kato added, "And threatening you would make him an outcast in civilized vampire society when he's been working for decades to bring his territory into better relationships with other leaders after Truvor's reign. Zara's death has already damaged his image—"

"Or elevated it," Alexander muttered, "at least in certain circles."

"But those are not the circles that Oleg wants to move in person-ally or financially," Kato said. "I knew Truvor. Oleg is not like him. He's stern and can be unforgiving, but he honors duty to his clan. He values loyalty above all else."

Loyalty like... not stealing millions in gold and sentimental jewelry purchases from a man who'd already paid you millions for your work?

Shut up, conscience.

"I don't want to return to Oleg's territory," Tatyana said firmly. "I understand that I have to think about my future, but Oleg is not going to be a part of it."

The following night, Tatyana walked across the harem compound with a garment bag, headed past the kitchen gardens, the rose garden, and the water garden toward the most luxurious part of the mountaintop retreat where Cora lived.

Cora was the woman in charge of the entire harem, having recently risen to the role of headwoman after the most senior of Arosh's women had retired to a luxury home on the Black Sea.

It was a profitable venture to be one of the Fire King's favorite lovers.

Cora kept a massive closet of clothes in her house that ranged from casual outdoor gear appropriate for hiking or swimming to evening wear, all available to borrow for short or long term. Arosh sent Cora and some of the older women on luxury shopping trips to replenish the clothes a few times a year.

Tatyana had never been dressed so well in her life. It was like living with a team of stylists as her next-door neighbors, and all of them were fine with you borrowing their clothes.

It was also practical for the women in the harem. Many of them came to Arosh's compound with little or nothing. Many were running from abusive homes or desperate situations.

Tatyana suspected that it stroked Arosh's ego to be their savior, but at least he was doing something productive with his ego.

And if some women repaid that favor with blood, sex, or both, Tatyana was not going to judge.

Except Arosh. She could judge Arosh.

Tatyana waved at two women who were sitting near a fountain, reading a book between the two of them. She recognized the book as a popular romantic fantasy. Both girls looked up at Tatyana, then back at the book, letting out a little bit of laughter.

Had she been that carefree when she was their age? She didn't think so. Tatyana felt like she'd been old for as long as she could remember.

The atmosphere in Arosh's harem was much like the atmosphere within the dormitories at her university. It was not unpleasant, but then, she was one of the few vampires and she was given a good amount of space. Most of the women knew everything about each other, and gossip was a way of life.

But Cora and the older women kept the younger ones in check. Cora was in her forties, a stunning brunette with olive skin and dark eyes. Tatyana had heard she was born in Damascus, but she had no idea if it was the truth. Most of the women spoke Georgian, but the ones who'd been there the longest spoke Farsi like Arosh.

Tatyana tapped on Cora's door.

"Come in."

She entered the house to see the dark-haired woman in front of a mirror, spraying some kind of fragrant oil over her freshly washed curls.

She glanced at Tatyana from the corner of her eye. "Hello, Miss Vorona. How can I help you?"

"I'm bringing back the dress I borrowed. Thank you."

"Of course you are welcome. That blue is an excellent color on you." Cora glanced at her, then back to the mirror. "There is a rack behind the door. You may hang it there."

Tatyana turned and saw at least a dozen dresses in identical garment bags. "Thank you for the loan."

"Of course, of course." Cora carefully pitched her voice to be breezy, but Tatyana immediately sensed a thread of tension in her tone. "Since you are here, I need to speak to you about Lidi, Aisha, and Natia."

Tatyana frowned and turned after she'd hung up the dress. "What about them?"

"You're paying all of them for their blood." Cora didn't look away from the mirror. "And only them?"

"Kato told me a human should only give blood once every three months." Tatyana was confused. "And that I need to feed from a living donor at least once a month." She could pay for blood-wine and donated blood, but Tatyana had to admit that she felt stronger after feeding from live donors.

"Yes, of course you should buy blood from those willing to give it," Cora said. "This is obvious."

"So have Natia, Aisha, or Lidi complained? If I've done something wrong, I apologize. I don't want to use the excuse that I am young, but some of the etiquette here—"

"No, it's not that." Cora waved a hand at her.

"I do not understand what you're trying to say." Tatyana thought she'd perfected the balance of lulling humans into a relaxed and pleasant state without awakening their lust.

That had been a surprising and revelatory lesson the first few times Kato had overseen her feeding from a live donor. Multiple lessons were learned.

Cora continued, "According to the girls, you're far more considerate than the men who visit the court."

Were all humans this frustrating? Or had she simply become more impatient with doublespeak? "I continue to not understand the problem."

Cora finally turned from the mirror, a slight frown resting between her eyes. "Are you doing it for economy? I know you are young. Is buying bagged blood less money than paying the girls?"

"No. It is more expensive."

Cora's eyes went wide. "So why are you feeding from only three of my girls?"

"Isn't it slightly..." How could she explain? Paying for blood felt a little like paying for sex. "Isn't it exploitive?"

"Why would you say that? We don't force them to give their blood." Cora appeared to be offended. "Most of these girls have no money. None. You are a *nice* vampire. You have money. They don't need a pleasant ear or a polite smile from you. They need money if they're going to make some kind of life other than this."

Tatyana was starting to see what Cora was getting at.

Arosh paid for everything his women might need, but he didn't give them a salary. Their life could be fully provided for, but it would only ever be what he gave them.

For some of the women, it was all they wanted. Safety. Pleasure. Companionship.

But any money or gifts they received from vampires they entertained was theirs alone. If they found a patron or a lover among his guests, the Fire King wished them well and sent them on their way. The majority of the younger women left when they'd saved enough money to have a different life and could start fresh in a new place.

Tatyana hadn't put together that by only feeding from the same three women, the rest of the harem might be offended.

"It would be one thing if you had a romantic relationship with one or all of the girls, but they say..." Cora shrugged. "You don't appreciate women that way."

"I *do* appreciate them," she said, "but not sexually. I wish I could like women more than men," she muttered. "It seems simpler."

"Eh." Cora shrugged. "Relationships are drama no matter who they are with. You're a young vampire; you'll branch out." Then she pointed at Tatyana directly. "But while you're here and have money, you pay my girls. You have everything, and they have nothing. You pay in gold, yes?"

Samson had helped her change some of her gold bars to gold coins.

"Yes, I have gold."

"Good. Then stop paying Arosh's men to fetch you bagged blood when there are women who need the money right here." She pointed toward the courtyard outside her house. "You're a vampire now. You're not going to be their friend. You're not going to be their sister. But you can be their patron. You can help them survive. Do you understand me now?"

Tatyana nodded. It was another lesson. Another revelation.

She wasn't in a dormitory of potential friends; she was a water vampire who needed blood. These women could provide it, but this was a transaction, not a friendship.

Cora turned back to the mirror. "If you need some ideas for girls who would suit you, let me know what you're looking for. That's what I do, Miss Vorona."

"Perhaps you should give me a list of girls who need some income," Tatyana said. "You know them better than I do."

"Excellent. I will have a list sent to you within the hour, but Karolina would be a good one tonight."

Tatyana could tell from Cora's tone of voice that it had been exactly the response she wanted from her.

Know your place, vampire.

You're useful to us, just as we are to you.

They were not here to be Tatyana's friends.

OLEG BRUSHED STRANDS OF HER HAIR BACK FROM HER forehead. "She has to be practical. It's not about you; it's about taking care of her people."

"Like you take care of your people?"

"Yes." He wrapped his arm around her waist and pulled her into his body. "I'll take care of you. Did I not satisfy you enough tonight?"

His skin was warm and heated when it touched her. She could feel his amnis brushing against hers. Familiar, wanting. Even though there was nothing between them, their energy still pulled them closer.

He bent his head to her neck and licked along her collarbone before he trailed his fangs along the sensitive skin of her neck.

Soft lips nibbled under her ear, and she smiled when his beard tickled her skin.

"You took care of me very well." She put her arms around his shoulders and tried to pull him closer. "Very, very well."

Closer.

He reached down and ran his fingers along her thigh, drawing it up and over his leg, opening her body to the length of him that lay hard between them.

"Tatyana," he whispered. "Why did you run?"

"You would be my whole world." She closed her eyes and reveled in the pleasure he pulled from her body. "We both know how it would be."

"Yes. Because you are mine." He kissed across her jaw until his lips hovered over hers. "You belong to me only. Not to anyone else. Only to me."

She met his eyes, dark storm grey like the clouds before it snowed. Burning cold into her very soul. He sucked the breath from her lungs when he looked at her that way. "Why do I dream about you?"

"Because you know that you're mine." His lips landed on hers, and she closed her eyes.

You know that you're mine.

You know that you belong to me.

TATYANA BLINKED AWAKE, HER BODY FLUSH WITH UNSATISFIED yearning for the vampire who consumed the few moments of dreaming that eternity granted her.

Was it him? Did he have some magical power to send these constant dreams to her? Why were the few moments in time when she could dream about her human life consumed by the very being who'd caused her to lose it?

Her emotions swung between fury and grief.

She'd never wanted this. She didn't want to be a vampire.

She'd wanted to be an accountant. She wanted to have a boring office job in a medium-sized city, meet some nice man she could tolerate and have a few children. Take summer holidays on the farm where she'd spent her childhood. Watch her babies grow up. Help them with their schoolwork. Take them to dance class or tennis practice.

Tatyana felt hot, blood-tinged tears track from the corners of her eyes.

But she couldn't even have that. After years of taking care of her mother and working for others, she was deprived of even a hint of normal life.

She would never see the sun again. She would never know what it meant to be a mother. She would never wade in the sunshine along the shallow water of the Black Sea or sit on a dock and fish while she watched the sunrise.

The most mundane human activities now felt like precious pearls that had been ripped from her neck and scattered on the ground while other, more powerful feet stomped on her simple dreams.

Stop. Tatyana heard her mother's voice in her mind. *Just stop it.*

No more of this morbid talk. You could have died, and you didn't. You should be grateful.

To be a vampire?

Yes, she should be grateful. Would she rather be dead?

She didn't want that. It might be coming for her, but she would fight it.

Because now she had fangs.

Some nights Tatyana felt like she was living on borrowed time, and in those moments—like those desperate, breath-catching moments when she'd been standing in the middle of Arosh's guests—she realized that she was nobody in this world.

Then again, she'd been a nobody as a human. At least now she had gold, fangs, and could only be killed by fire or a sword to the neck.

And that...

That was not nothing.

Chapter 5

Oleg

Radu le Basarab—wind vampire, Poshani terrin, and all-around pain in the ass—had a club in downtown Bucharest called Zarvă, which smelled of human sweat, pungent perfume, and spilled beer.

While the vampire lounge was soundproofed, less crowded, and less odorous than the human part of the club, it was still not Oleg's favorite place to meet.

"It costs Radu so much money to make a place so cheap," Mika muttered.

"Quiet," Oleg said. "Be respectful."

"We're not there yet."

"Fine." Oleg watched the streetlights as the car drove through empty city streets. "Get it out of your system now so you can play nice."

More curses in rough Estonian that left Oleg smiling.

He'd tried to lure Radu to his town house with the promise of showing the vampire a new piece of art Oleg had acquired in Cologne the year before. Radu was a lover of any art but especially anything by Marc Chagall, and Oleg had purchased a beautiful new Chagall piece that was currently hanging in his Bucharest library.

But Radu had insisted on Zarvă, so Oleg and Mika took a car to the back alley where the vampire entrance to the club was located and waited as Oleg's security staff and Radu's negotiated who and how many were allowed into the club.

Mika made a face when he heard the thumping music. "I will never understand this man."

Oleg wasn't sure he understood Radu—how much did any vampire understand another?—but he could appreciate the scope of the immortal's interests. He owned clubs and bars but also a thriving chain of fresh grocers and numerous farming operations.

"He could have asked to meet us at the cowboy bar," Oleg said. "This place isn't that bad."

Oleg's man gave them a nod; then Oleg, Mika, and two of their soldiers were allowed to enter the club and walk up a set of stairs to a second story that overlooked a churning human dance floor.

Inside the vampire section, the dance music had been muted to an acceptable level in consideration of immortal ears, and since the human club was packed, the vampire club was as well.

They left their security standing by a wall and walked through the dimly lit club, which was decorated with luxurious velvet wallpaper and leather-upholstered booths. As they threaded their way through the booths and tables, Oleg detected different traces of amnis in the air.

Two young vampires he recognized from Alina's court, probably in Romania on holiday.

A solitary, dark-haired woman who smelled of ashes and dust. She had the distinct air of Arosh surrounding her.

A jovial table of Greek vampires, newly freed by the recent turnover of their own court.

And in the corner, a former lover named Maria sat with two broad-shouldered, matching vampires who looked like square-headed Cossacks.

Maria glanced Oleg's way and lifted her glass in a silent toast.

He inclined his head, and it wasn't lost on him that Maria had been forced to substitute two men to replace him.

In the far corner, Oleg saw a small clutch of Poshani Hazar guards holding court with a group of human women who all wore small ruby pins at their neck. Radu's hired donors.

The Poshani vampires watched Oleg and Mika with smiles on their faces and suspicion in their eyes.

Their lord waited for his guests in a velvet-shrouded booth where servers slipped in and out with large bottles of blood-wine, trays of caviar, and other delicacies.

"Mika Arakis." One of the Hazars nodded at Mika, then at Oleg. "Lord Oleg, you are welcome."

"Duke, how are you?" Mika asked.

The man scanned them up and down, glanced at his men by the wall, and lifted his chin. "All is peaceful, thanks to the clan."

Oleg asked, "Ready for spring?"

The corner of Duke's mouth turned up. "Always."

They walked toward the curtained corner, and Mika pulled back the drapes.

"My friend!" Radu stood and held out his arms. "Welcome."

He was a barrel-chested man who was probably turned in his mid-thirties, with dark hair, dark eyes, and the sculpted cheekbones characteristic of the Poshani people.

When Radu lived in Bucharest, he was the life of the party, throwing lavish dinners featuring human chefs flown in from across the world. He collected art and wept openly when he went to the ballet, which was frequently.

Radu was also smart as hell, disappeared from public life for six months at a time, and had a mouth like a Moscow taxi driver. He loved hunting and fishing, knew nearly every vampire in Eastern Europe, and ran a moving safe house called the kamvasa.

"Radu." Oleg walked over, embraced his ally, and patted Radu heartily on the back. "Don't tell me you're forced to find women at the nightclubs now."

Radu guffawed and motioned Oleg to sit down. "Hardly, hardly." He craned his neck to look around the lounge. "But who doesn't enjoy being surrounded by beautiful women, am I right?"

Mika looked their server up and down as she set crystal goblets in front of them. "A beautiful woman is never a hardship," he said. "Thank you for meeting us on short notice."

"It was fortunate you called." Radu's smile fell, and he flicked his fingers at the human who was serving them, sending her away and leaving only Oleg, Mika, and Radu in the quiet, curtained booth. "I was already hearing rumors that made me uncomfortable, my friend."

Radu picked up an open bottle of blood-wine and filled their goblets before he filled his own, lifted it, and took a drink. After his initial sip, Mika and Oleg both joined him.

"We dispatched at least one vampire from your clan." Oleg believed in directness. "He and a group were operating in our territory with a team of human thieves. They beat our truck driver into a coma before they stole the freight and took it to a warehouse."

Radu wasn't wearing a smile anymore. "Was this the first incident?"

Oleg looked at Mika.

Mika said, "This was the fourth incident in six months. It was vexing enough that Polina called Oleg about it."

"Your daughter is a capable ruler." Radu lifted his goblet and drank. "If she called you, it is not without reason."

"Thank you, and I agree." Oleg's eyes never left Radu. "We don't know if any of the other vampires killed were Poshani. The one left refused to speak more than a few words. I understand a blood price must be offered to his clan, but given the circumstances..." Oleg spread his hands. "You must understand our concerns as well, my friend."

"Our people have lived in your territory for centuries," Radu said.

"The Poshani have no interest in interfering in our hosts' businesses. It goes against every law of hospitality we hold sacred."

Hospitality codes among the Poshani were inviolable. They had strict rules about interference with any people or organization that offered them roaming rights, and if a vampire bartered for shelter within their seasonal caravan—the kamvasa—they were protected by any and all means for the agreed-upon dates.

"Who was he?" Mika leaned across the table and kept his voice low. "Do we have a problem?"

Radu waved a hand. "He was one of Vano's men, but my brother had disciplined him for a minor infraction and the young one took it too much to heart. He struck out on his own. His sire was upset by his death, but Vano has made it clear that the blood price will be all the recompense he is given. Sami was working outside the organization."

"Do you know who they were working for?" Mika asked.

"Not yet, but I'll keep asking," Radu said. "His sire has questions too."

"The other vampires we killed along with him," Oleg asked, "none of them were yours?"

Radu shook his head. "Not that I know of. We felt Sami die, but he was the only loss."

When an immortal child died, a sire felt it in their own body. Their amnis was tied together, so the moment the Poshani vampire had been killed, everyone with a blood tie to the dead would have known it.

"How is your employee?" Radu asked.

"Recovering in Moscow." Oleg swirled his blood-wine before taking a sip. "Thank you for asking."

"Sami's sire will be making financial settlements with you for the damage to your human."

Oleg raised a hand in the expected objection. "That is not necessary."

"You must allow him." Radu pressed on. "This is our way."

"Your clan has suffered a death, and my driver is still alive."

"But he is injured, and we must make this right for his family," Radu continued. "And for you, our ally."

Oleg had bargained with the Poshani for many years. Three times offered was a sincere overture. If he rejected Radu's recompense, the Poshani terrin would be offended.

"If you insist," Oleg said after a long pause. "I will pass this settlement to his family. I'm sure his wife and children will be grateful."

"And of course, the greater harm is to the appearance of conflict between our people." Radu leaned his elbow on the table. "Any appearance of division between the Poshani and your empire will be seen as a weakness and an opportunity to exploit both of us."

Oleg sipped his blood-wine and lifted one shoulder in a reluctant shrug. "I cannot disagree with you. Much as I would like to."

"The Vashana is being held at the end of the season, of course. And this year is Vashana Zata, which only occurs once a century."

Vashana was the yearly festival and grand gathering of the Poshani clan, human and vampire, and it was held at the end of the kamvasa season, before the winter set in and the Poshani went to their settled homes or commenced traveling out of their territory if they couldn't stand remaining in one place for too long.

"The centuries pass swiftly, old friend. The Vashana Zata is this year?" Oleg sipped his blood-wine. "I had no idea."

Which was not a lie. The Poshani were so secretive he doubted many outside the clan knew that a major event of this magnitude was happening in the woods of Eastern Europe.

Oleg had attended Vashana before, but Vashana Zata was something different. That was the festival where new leaders of the Poshani would be chosen, and usually one or more of the current terrin would pass their ceremonial goblet to a successor to keep the power moving.

Previous terrin would retire and become trusted advisors, but it was considered unwise among the Poshani to have power given to one individual for too long.

"Is it time for your retirement?" Oleg smiled. "You're young. You've only been terrin for what? Two hundred seasons?"

"Admittedly, I do not know if I will continue as a leader." Radu shrugged. "The terrin are chosen by the people. Perhaps there is one who is more beloved or better qualified than me."

"You are being modest," Mika said quickly. "The Poshani have thrived under your leadership."

"Mika Arakis, you are too generous." Radu inclined his head. "I am only one of three."

"Nevertheless," Oleg said, "my boyar is not incorrect."

"And I am conscious of the compliment you have paid me by traveling to me so quickly after this unfortunate incident." Radu did appear pleased. "I think it would benefit both our people to be more public about our alliance. Would you do me the honor of being my witness and guest for the Vashana Zata at the end of the season?"

Oleg spread his hands. "My friend, I would be delighted."

Mika and Oleg woke the following night and immediately flew to Tbilisi, the vampire and human capital of the Republic of Georgia where Alina Machabeli, a water vampire of great political skill, had ruled for over one hundred years.

Unlike in Bucharest, Alina had agreed to meet Oleg for a private dinner at his town house in the old Vera neighborhood.

The Georgian regent arrived in a vintage Mercedes sedan, accompanied by two guards who waited in the foyer while Oleg and Alina visited.

"Oleg, it's good to see you." That night Alina wore a draped suit in mossy-green silk. She handed Oleg a box of candy and a bottle of locally produced blood-wine that he immediately handed to his house manager.

"Thank you." He stepped forward and offered his hand. "I've heard this vineyard is excellent."

"I should hope so—it's mine."

She smiled as he kissed her knuckles, and Oleg was reminded that she had a charming dimple in her right cheek.

"Will you join me?" He gestured to a door. "I thought we could meet just the two of us since this is not a formal visit."

"Thank you."

"No, I must thank you for seeing me on short notice." Oleg guided Alina to the conservatory. "You have indulged my hasty schedule."

She had been turned as a mature woman, and the appearance of age lent Alina an air of sophistication and wisdom. She had a smattering of silver at her temples, but the rest of her hair was deep brown, and her eyes were a rich hazel-green with fine lines in the corners that emphasized her expressions.

For her comfort and as a show of good faith, they were meeting in a room with a large fountain and no fireplace, though heat was pumped through the intricately tiled floors.

"Your orchids are thriving." Alina walked over to survey the glass wall where dozens of the flowers hung. "What a marvelous collection."

"My house manager dotes on them, and I am the fortunate recipient of her botany skills." Oleg stood next to Alina, following her eyes. "You take an interest in botany yourself, I remember."

She turned to him. "Don't pretend like you didn't choose this room because of it."

"I chose this room because it's as beautiful as my guest," Oleg said, "and has two very comfortable seats. Shall we?" He gestured to the large rattan chairs by the fountain.

"Of course." Alina settled into her chair and pulled a silver cigarette case from her inner suit pocket. "Do you mind if I smoke?"

"You're asking me?" Oleg snapped his fingers and brought a

flame to his hand, lighting Alina's fragrant cigarette before she sat back in her seat.

"I was disappointed to hear about Zara," she said. "So much potential."

Oleg put on a brave face and slid a crystal ashtray closer to Alina. "We haven't spoken since it happened. Thank you."

"I know how dear she was to you and Luana."

"Luana doted on her." *To an extremely unhealthy degree.*

"It was a regrettable situation, but with her smuggling activities..." Alina gestured with her cigarette. "Sometimes our children walk paths that lead them to destruction."

"Indeed." The perfect segue. "I'm fortunate to have Polina and Juliya so close."

Alina smiled. "I believe you are what humans refer to as a 'girl dad.'"

"Ha!" Oleg smiled in genuine amusement. "Technically Juliya is my brother's daughter, but I cannot disagree. My sons often accuse me of favoring my daughters, but that's probably because none of them are running a territory for me right now."

"Is that going to change?" Alina's eyes narrowed. "I wondered why you wanted to speak directly. Has Zara's death shifted things?"

"Lazlo was already ruling the territory I'd initially had Zara overseeing, so there have been no changes. And none on the horizon that I anticipate."

"Lazlo and I are friendly. Well" —Alina blew out a delicate stream of smoke— "as much as Lazlo is friends with anyone. I'm happy to continue working with him."

Oleg's empire was roughly divided into eight territories overseen by a combination of his children and his brothers. Some of them were crowded and dense, like the territories around Kyiv and Moscow. Others were wild and barren, barely territories at all, like the massive Siberian plateau ruled by a quiet and deadly boyar named Lidik.

"Stability is a virtue in our world," Alina said. "I am glad to hear that no changes are imminent. I wish the humans were as virtuous as the vampires these days."

"Ah, but they have short, fiery lives, do they not? They must make their mark in eighty years, not eight hundred."

"You speak truth."

"Speaking of humans," Oleg said. "I am curious how Zara's newly turned daughter is faring in Arosh's court. Have you heard anything of her?"

Alina tipped her ash into the crystal tray. "Arosh's court is not my own. When the Fire King reemerged, he made it very clear that I would respect his territorial integrity or be erased from history."

Oleg was sure the invasion still stung, so he was quick to add his own concessions to Arosh. "Yes, I had to be somewhat flexible with my territories east of the Volga." He shrugged. "But there was little economic interest there, so not a great loss."

"The same for me in the mountains. A fair exchange for a friendly alliance with such a powerful and ancient immortal. Arosh's court is secretive, but we are on good terms."

"Are you saying you know nothing of Zara's daughter?"

"I'm saying I do not interfere with those who remain in Arosh's territory."

Oleg smiled. "Am I to understand the Fire King has not allowed the woman to leave his compound in over a year?"

"She's not a woman—she's a vampire now." Alina lifted an eyebrow. "And I never said that."

Oleg was quite thankful Tatyana was both female and vampire. "So she *has* been in your territory?"

Alina's lips curved in a smile. "What do you want, Oleg?"

"Tatyana Vorona and I parted on complicated terms, considering what happened with her sire."

"Yes." Alina narrowed her eyes. "There are many rumors about how and when she was turned."

"What do vampires love more than gossip?" Oleg spread his hands. "I only want what is best for the woman. I consider her..."

Mine. "...part of my extended clan, and she was good friends with Elene."

"Speaking of terrible losses." Alina shook her head in genuine regret. "I am sorry, Oleg. A drowning? Such a tragedy."

Oleg could never let on that his own daughter had killed such an important human under his aegis. "Truly, Elene was irreplaceable. She was something of a mentor to Tatyana, so you understand my concern."

"Of course." Alina took another puff on her cigarette. "My sources tell me Miss Vorona has refused to return to your territory."

"I don't know why that would be."

"Was she your lover?"

Oleg felt his fangs ache. "Does that matter?"

"It seems to me that young vampires often have wild emotional swings," Alina said. "And it seems that she has recently lost her human mentor. Perhaps she only needs time to settle into her new life."

"You're probably right."

Alina reached into her jacket and withdrew another case, this one about the size of a deck of cards. "I do have security footage from a bar in Kaspi that you may find interesting." She held the case toward him. "If you like."

There was a twitch directly under Oleg's eye, and his amnis jumped beneath his skin. Irritating. He hated to show any sort of weakness around others, even an ally.

He reached out his hand and took the case. "Thank you, Alina. I'll give it to Mika if you think it might be of interest."

"Of course." Alina smiled and stubbed out her cigarette butt in the crystal ashtray. "Now you must tell me where your house manager obtained that red Masdevallia orchid. It's a stunning specimen, and I do love collecting rare beauties." She smiled. "I believe we might have that in common."

"It's unedited." Mika looked at the computer screen in the main security office in Odesa. "But after about six hours of the footage at triple speed, I caught it."

His chief boyar was standing beside one of the humans who operated the technology in the security office while Oleg was standing over the young man's shoulder, at a safe distance from the machine.

"What?" He leaned forward, and the computer began to waver.

"No." Mika held up a hand. "He'll show you, but don't break the equipment."

Fire vampires were even more reactive to electrical current than the average immortal with amnis. Oleg had always assumed there was something about the volatility of their energy that simply set anything electronic on edge.

"Fine." Oleg stood up straight. "So show me."

The camera was pointed at the bar and the register, so the majority of the footage was simply humans coming and going, servers grabbing trays, and bartender after bartender pulling pints of beer, mixing drinks and—

"There." Mika pointed. "Did you see?"

Oleg shook his head. "Back it up."

Mika tapped the shoulder of the young human who was operating on the computer. "Back up a few minutes and put it at regular speed."

There was no sound, so the room they were in was utterly silent save for the hum of the electronics when the young man pointed at something on the screen and tapped several controls.

Suddenly there was simply black-and-white footage of a bar, as if they were looking on from a balcony over the action.

There was clearly music in the club because a few people were dancing on the edges of the screen while two women sat at the bar, talking into each other's ears, and a young man wearing a cap sat at the corner, looking at a computer screen through heavy, black-rimmed glasses.

"I don't recognize anyone."

"The picture isn't great, but wait." Mika held up a hand. "Not there yet."

As they watched, a white head passed parallel to the bar, and the two women turned to look.

"The silver-haired one," Oleg said. "But does he—"

"Wait."

Oleg kept watching as the silver-haired vampire glanced over his shoulder at something, then walked to the corner where the young man was sitting.

He leaned down and said something, and then immediately the young man stood up and the two walked out of the screen.

"Did you catch it?" Mika asked. "Does he need to rewind?"

"No." Oleg didn't need him to rewind the footage. He knew exactly what Mika had seen.

Mika pointed to the frozen image on the screen where the silver-haired vampire had grabbed the hand of the person working on the computer. "The young man—"

"Was not a young man." Oleg recognized Tatyana's breasts even when they were covered by a bulky sweatshirt. Her delicate wrists. The curve of her neck and her jaw. "I saw. Is there more?"

Mika shook his head. "It was so quick, but then I went back and rewound it, watching her, but other than working on her computer, she doesn't do anything else. No meetings. No video calls. She orders a glass of wine she doesn't drink and sits there working."

Had she cut her hair? Dyed it? Or had the cap covered her glorious golden hair so thoroughly that Oleg had missed it? The quality of the camera didn't help, but he felt blind.

Blind and frustrated.

If she could sit in a corner for hours and he wouldn't recognize her, how was he supposed to find her?

"Obviously, once you are near to her, you'll be able to sense her," Mika continued, "so I'll keep collecting footage from area bars with Wi-Fi connections. I'm sure she's using a VPN, so IP addresses will be useless, but visually we can be on the lookout for a young woman, or anyone who might be in disguise as—"

"No." Oleg's eyes were drawn to a much clearer target. "She's a young, recently human woman who can probably blend into many or all environments. As beautiful as she is, she can make herself somewhat forgettable. It's useless to track her."

Mika raised both eyebrows. "You want us to stop tracking her? She has no reason to think we know she's going to Kaspi, and there are numerous bars and restaurants where she could access the internet."

"No, don't bother tracking her." He pointed to the screen and the carved profile of the man with the silver hair. "Track *him*. I've never seen him with his head covered. He doesn't speak, and I don't see him touching anyone. Everyone who sees him will remember a silent giant with silver hair." Oleg nodded. "He is how she's moving around. Track him."

Chapter 6

Tatyana

She went to Samson's quarters with her backpack ready, expecting the accommodating wind vampire to be ready to take her. It was her scheduled night to call her mother, and she only had two hours to find a connection.

But Samson started shaking his head the moment he opened his door.

Not tonight, he signed.

"What do you mean?" Tatyana whispered. "It's Omar Sharif's birthday, and I only have two hours."

Samson had come to his door wearing nothing but an open white shirt and a pair of loose black pants. *Arosh told me that you need to stop going into town,* he signed.

"But why? I'm not bothering anyone." Shit. If her mother didn't get a call, she was going to panic, and then Anna would probably call Oleg because apparently they were getting together for tea regularly and Oleg had sent her mother a new-to-her vehicle for the farm.

The fact that the vampire knew her mother would never take a new truck and had sent her one with just enough wear that it could be accepted as a present irked Tatyana to no end.

The man was too perceptive by half.

Samson continued, *Arosh says you need to be planning for where you are going next, not playing video games online.*

"Oh my god, does Arosh think I'm playing video games?"

Okay, she *was* playing video games sometimes, but very badly and only so she could use the direct-message features to talk to Grimace about options to disappear.

Samson shrugged and didn't look pleased about it, but he also didn't look like he was in the mood to defy Arosh.

No one in the compound was going to defy Arosh.

Stay here, Samson signed. *You don't need to go anywhere if you don't want to. You don't have to run.*

Tatyana nearly growled. "That's not what Kato and Arosh seem to think."

Samson's eyes burned into her, and he stepped forward. *Stay here,* he signed. *With me.*

Tatyana felt her heart stumble. She lifted her eyes from Samson's beautiful chest and to his ghostly, pale grey eyes. His features appeared carved out of the rocks that surrounded them, but his lips were full and gentle.

She knew he was prized as a lover in the harem, and women were quick to share his skills, but though Tatyana had felt a sexual pull, she had never acted on it. She was short on friends in the immortal world, and losing one for a sexual fling didn't seem like a great idea.

Stay with me, and he won't send you anywhere, Samson signed. *We could be happy, Tatyana. You could be content with me.*

He had given her a nickname in the language he used, a *T* sign that curved from his temple down his jaw, mimicking the way her long hair fell into her face sometimes.

"Do you..." Tatyana didn't know what to think. "Do you really care for me, Samson? Or are you just worried that I've got nowhere else to go?"

He signed nothing else, but she saw the truth in his eyes.

Not love. No, it was nothing that passionate, but caring. Concern.

And yes, desire. Who was to say what might happen in a year? In two? In a decade?

"You know, before I met him" —she felt tears threatening her eyes — "you were exactly the kind of man I was looking for. You're kind. Thoughtful. You take care of people. You are *very* handsome." She laughed a little bit. "And you make me feel peaceful."

He lifted one shoulder in a shrug. *Those are good things.*

"I know." She nodded and forced a smile. "I'm not saying I don't feel it." She stepped closer and kept her voice low. "I could probably fall in love with you if I let myself."

Samson pulled her into his room, closed the door, and bent down, cupping her cheeks with both hands and pressing his lips to hers in a velvet kiss.

His energy touched hers, then pulled back, glancing against her amnis in a delicate dance as his lips softly moved against her own.

It was gentle and tempting. Tatyana knew she was right. If she let herself, she could fall head over heels for this gently powerful man. She felt the elemental strength he wielded floating in the air around her, and the silken press of his lips against hers was mimicked by the brush of air against her skin.

It wasn't a roar of passion. It wasn't a roar at all. Samson's kiss was a seductive whisper, and part of her yearned to cling to the safety he offered even if it wasn't with her whole heart.

You are mine! Oleg's voice roared in Tatyana's mind. *You belong to me only. Not to anyone else. Only to me.*

Tatyana pressed her hand to Samson's chest, and he immediately withdrew. "I can't. I shouldn't."

The vampire heaved a deep sigh, cocked his head to the side, and signed, *The Varangian?*

Tatyana shook her head. "I don't know how I feel about him. Does that make any sense? I hate him, but he's in my blood. Until I get more distance from him, more time..." She crossed her arms over her chest. "You deserve someone who wants to stay here for *you*, not because she's on the run and only wants to be safe."

The corner of Samson's mouth turned up, and he stroked a hand over her shoulder. *That's not the only reason you'd be happy here. We could be very good together.*

"Maybe someday we will be," Tatyana whispered. "But if I stay right now, you'll always wonder if I stayed for you or because I had no place else to go. You know I'm right."

Samson dropped his hand from her shoulder and looked away, pursing his full lips. Then he bit his lip a little bit and shook his head. *What do you want me to do?*

"Can you tell Arosh I'm looking for a place to go?" Tatyana asked. "Can you tell him I need this time to find some options that don't involve going back to Oleg?"

I'll tell him —Samson stepped back and quickly buttoned his shirt— *when we get back from calling your mother.* He glanced at an old clock on the small table by the door. *After all, it's almost Omar Sharif's birthday.*

THE CREEPING FEELING THAT SOMEONE WAS WATCHING HER never went away even when Tatyana hunkered down in a corner of the quiet bar. Samson remained near the door as he always did, and there were no visible security cameras, though that was no guarantee they weren't there.

Cameras could masquerade as anything now, though most clubs and bars wanted the patrons to know they were being watched for security reasons.

She'd logged on, caught up with her mother, listened to her mother talk about the lavender border Oleg had planted on the narrow road leading to Anna's house, and then she'd quickly logged into her accounts, left a message for Grimace, and flown back to Arosh's compound with Samson.

She'd been looking over her shoulder all night, so returning to the tightly controlled compound felt like a relief. She still remembered the overwhelming feeling of safety the first time she'd flown in. The first night she felt secure.

Understanding more about vampire life now, Tatyana knew that it was an illusion. All of it was an illusion. There was no true safety in this world—there was only struggle, negotiation, and finding short seasons of reprieve before it all started over again.

This was not a restful life, but her mother was still alive. As long as Anna was alive, Tatyana would be too.

When her mother passed? She couldn't say. That was too long in the future. For now her only focus was finding a safe and relatively stable place to rest her head.

And drink some blood.

She tapped on the numbered door that belonged to the next woman on Cora's list.

Sibella Ardelian. Room 315.

Not a name she'd heard before. Armenian maybe?

Having a room in the 300s meant that Sibella was new to the compound, so Tatyana was hoping strongly that Sibella wasn't new to vampire feeding. She still felt like an awkward newcomer to the exchange.

A voice came from behind the door. "Who is it?"

She spoke thickly accented English, so Tatyana responded in English as well.

"I'm Tatyana Vorona. Cora said you would be expecting me?"

The woman opened her door, and Tatyana looked down. She was tiny and petite, rubbing dark brown eyes that were thickly lashed as she yawned.

"I thought you were coming at dusk." She glanced over her shoulder. "Sorry, I went to sleep because I guessed that you had fed from someone else." Her brown eyes turned from sleepy to suspicious. "You're Tatyana?"

"Yes."

"Do you have an ID?"

What an odd question. "No."

"Then how do I know that you're her?"

Tatyana was irritated now. "Do a lot of young female vampires live here that I don't know about? If you don't want to give me your blood, there are six other names on my list." She started to turn.

"Wait!" Sibella called out. "I suppose you are right. Come in."

If she was new, maybe she didn't realize how secure Arosh's compound was. Perhaps that was the reason for her overt suspicion.

"No human has ever been killed by a vampire in Arosh's home." Tatyana walked in, and Sibella pointed to a table where she set her backpack. "You must be new."

"So are you." Sibella walked over and turned on the lamp beside the bed. "Because I guarantee you some humans have been killed here."

"How do you know?" Tatyana took a seat on the short sofa near a low bookcase. It looked like the most comfortable place to take the woman's blood.

"Because you're vampires," Sibella said with a wave of her hand. "Accidents happen. You just want blood, right?" She'd walked over to the small kitchenette and was drinking a tall glass of water. "I don't do sex with women or old men, but if you get affectionate, I don't care so much."

"No problem. I just want blood. I don't like connecting the two either. Makes things..." She flashed to a memory of Oleg at her vein. "Makes things complicated."

"Giving blood is always complicated." Sibella rubbed her fingers together in the universal sign for money. "But lucrative for me."

"Is that why you came?" She noticed that Sibella didn't seem shy or insecure in the least. The longer she spent with the young woman, the more she set Tatyana at ease.

"Yes." Sibella spoke frankly. "I'm saving up for a big purchase. The girls where I come from, they know if they want to make real money, a year or two in Arosh's compound is very profitable." She sat next to Tatyana and shrugged. "Donate your blood. Get paid very well." She looked around. "And live in luxury in the mountains while you're here." She winked at Tatyana. "Maybe have your pick of the best-looking immortals in the court, starting with the king himself."

Tatyana smiled. "So Arosh isn't an old man?"

Sibella offered her a coy smile. "The Fire King is a god. Rules are a little different for gods, aren't they?"

Tatyana laughed a little bit. "You're funny."

"I'm Poshani. Our humor is our greatest defense."

"Poshani?" She'd never heard the name. "Is that where you're from?"

"You've never heard of Poshani?"

Tatyana shook her head.

"Ah, you are new." Sibella sat back and spread her arm over the back of the small couch, a tiny queen in her domain. "Poshani are a clan. We travel, like Roma people, but we're a little... different."

"Because you know about vampires?"

"Because we have a lot of them ourselves," Sibella said. "Our clan leaders are all vampires. We work with them, we elect them to their positions, and they take care of us."

Tatyana had never heard of such a thing. "So you've known about vampires..."

"My whole life." She shrugged. "My uncle is a wind vampire now. Well, my great-uncle. He's one of the Hazar of the kamvasa now."

Tatyana shook her head. "I do not know what any of that means."

"The kamvasa is..." Sibella pursed her lips. "Well, it's our caravan. It moves in the spring, all around Eastern Europe. Poland, Belarus, Russia, Romania, of course. While the weather is warm, we move."

"That sounds fun."

A giant road trip with your friends and family. If Tatyana had a family like that, she'd never want to leave it.

"It's our way of life." Sibella looked into the distance. "It's going to be hard remaining here for two years, but it's the quickest way to get my own caravan."

"Your *own* caravan? I thought you said—"

"My own rig, I mean." Sibella leaned forward. "A bus? A little trailer? Something like that. I don't want to live with my parents forever."

Okay, *that* made sense to Tatyana.

"I've been there." She reached out and offered Sibella her hand to shake. "And to support you, I am happy to be your paying customer. Thank you for your blood."

"Very nice to do business with you." Sibella cocked her neck to the side.

Tatyana held up a hand. "Amnis?"

"Please." Sibella nodded. "But no altering my memories."

"I can do that." Tatyana put her hand on Sibella's arm and let her amnis creep up her skin, soothing her and lulling her into a dreamy, relaxed state.

"You know..." Sibella's voice was already drowsy. "I have immortal family, but I don't think I'd ever want to have to drink blood."

Tatyana couldn't blame her.

The young woman continued, "But my uncle seems happy enough to be a Hazar."

Tatyana talked to her to gauge her mental state. "You told me about the kamvasa, but what's a Hazar?"

"They're... the guards." Sibella's shoulders relaxed, and her head dropped to the side. "On the kamvasa for... the paying guests."

Tatyana had been about to lower her mouth to Sibella's neck, but she pulled back when she heard what the woman had said. "What do you mean, paying guests?"

"Sometimes..." Sibella shrugged. "It's worth a lot of money to vampires to be able to disappear."

"Disappear?"

"The Poshani hide them," Sibella whispered. "I won't know

where they are. The vampires don't even know where they are because the darigan move the kamvasa in daylight." Sibella giggled a little bit. "No one can find you. What do they call it in the movies?" She smiled. "A safe house, yes? It's like a... moving safe house. But for *vampires.*"

A moving safe house.

For vampires?

Tatyana felt her heart pick up, and Sibella's blood wasn't the only thing exciting her now. She lowered her head to Sibella's throat and slid her fangs into the human's neck.

Her blood was sweet and hot, sliding down Tatyana's throat like nectar. She put her arm around Sibella's back and drew her close, supporting her body as the young woman went limp in her arms.

Tatyana was going to drink fully that night.

And then Sibella was going to tell her more.

Kato was waiting for Tatyana in Arosh's main hall when she finished feeding. The Fire King was seeing guests and holding court that night, settling disputes from vampires under his aegis, welcoming guests, and accepting gifts and tribute that poured in from Siberia to Central Asia.

"Good evening." She sat next to Kato and glanced to his right. "No Alexander tonight?"

"He's sleeping." Kato put his arm across the back of Tatyana's chair. "Arosh was looking for you earlier."

"Oh?"

"Samson told him that you'd gone into the city again," Kato murmured. "He wasn't pleased, but he didn't say anything to Samson."

Because she was one of Samson's favorites, and Tatyana was

beginning to feel like her being friends with Samson was more of a liability for the wind vampire than a gift.

Two vampires stood in front of Arosh in the middle of the room, both with their heads bowed respectfully, as Arosh heard their dispute about a small river valley they both claimed in Chagan Basin.

"I'm looking at options right now." Tatyana kept her voice as low as her mentor's. "I might have an idea."

"Keep in mind, I am your teacher," Kato said. "I am willing to extend my connections."

"In Greece?" Tatyana had always wanted to see the Greek Islands.

"Not Greece. I have extended clan in the Americas," Kato said. "But if you *are* interested in Greece, I have a ceremonial seat in the court of Alitea. That is an option."

Alitea was a hidden island in the Mediterranean and a very old seat of power for ancient immortals. "Alitea sounds—"

"Of course, if you want to go to Alitea, you'll be under Saba's aegis."

Tatyana remembered the ancient vampire who made even Oleg afraid.

No, thank you.

"I think there may be an option closer to home," she whispered. "Do you know about the kamvasa?"

Kato was silent for a long time. "I know about it. I have never been a guest."

She felt Arosh's eyes on her when two representatives who looked like businessmen walked forward and spoke quietly to him.

Disputes were heard publicly, but they looked more like representatives from another court. They turned their heads and glanced in her direction.

"They're from Alina's court in Tbilisi," Kato murmured. "Oleg recently visited Alina to discuss common interests. And possibly you."

"How do you know?"

"Because I spend time here instead of jetting off with wind vampires and playing on my computer."

"I am not playing—" Tatyana swallowed her words when a vampire in front of them whipped his head around and looked straight at her.

"There is reality, and there is perception of reality." Kato spoke in his teaching voice. "Tell me which is more important for you in this moment."

"Perception of reality," she murmured.

"Exactly." Kato glanced at her from the corner of his eye, all the while facing Arosh's seat of power with his arm stretched across the back of the settee, framing Tatyana with visible protection. "You know what you are doing. I know what you are doing. But Arosh does not see you spending time in court, making alliances, or learning about the immortal world."

The vampires from Alina's court slunk away. Was *slunk* a word? They seemed to ooze away from Arosh until they were standing straight again, bowing toward him before they turned, both of them looking at Tatyana with pointed glares.

"Kato's favorite," Arosh called, "come to speak with me."

"He's going to try to interview you in front of the court, but don't let him," Kato said. "Request a private audience. Call on his mercy. He'll give it to you if you say it's for a matter of the heart."

"A matter of the..." Tatyana stood and stepped quickly toward the center of the room.

The Fire King did not like to be kept waiting.

Before Arosh could speak, Kato's words were tumbling out of her mouth. "Merciful Lord Arosh, if I could speak with you privately about a matter of the heart."

For fuck's sake, that could *not* work. She sounded like a fawning, sentimental fool who had a crush on her schoolmaster.

But while a "matter of the heart" might have made her blush as a human, Arosh seemed to consider it thoughtfully.

"Of course, my dear." His voice instantly softened. "Please follow me." He motioned her to the private chamber behind his throne, and Tatyana followed him in a slight daze.

It had worked?

Well, shit. What was her matter of the heart?

She had to think up a sad story and quickly.

Arosh sat on a low couch near a brass brazier with glowing coals and patted the seat next to him. "Come and sit with me."

Tatyana sat in a slight panic.

"I can see that you are nervous to speak with me," Arosh said. "But you may speak freely and depend on my confidence."

"Thank you, Lord Arosh." She stumbled, biding for time. "I'm sure this matter is... Well, I know how busy you are. How important the company gathered tonight must be."

Arosh loved flattery. It was as good as food to him.

"You are a guest of my house." The fire vampire put a hand on her back, his touch warm and comforting. "You must depend on my graces as your host. I can see you are conflicted, but why?"

"Because my... feelings." Oh, she was terrible at this. He was going to know she was lying the minute she opened her mouth. "I know you want me to return to Oleg, but I'm afraid of him!"

Okay, that was the truth.

Arosh's hand on her back paused. "Is this because Oleg was your lover and now you have feelings for my son Samson?"

Tatyana blinked. "I do have feelings for Samson." Her voice was quiet. "But... my heart isn't free from Oleg's influence."

It was the truth. The absolute truth.

Damn.

"Your mind is still very human," Arosh said. "I have seen this before with newborn vampires. And though you are over a year immortal now, you are an infant in immortal life."

"Yes, Lord Arosh." He was right. She was still stumbling and bumbling most of the time.

"When it comes to matters of the heart, you still think like a human. Perhaps you believe you will have a singular, great love in this life." He smiled indulgently. "But that is rare for our kind. You will love many through the centuries, with many types of love. Leave room in your heart for many loves."

"Thank you." She turned to him, surprised by the understanding in his voice. "That is very wise."

Arosh smiled kindly. "Would you like to have sex with me now?"

And there it was. "No, but... thank you."

"I am only offering because it would give you great physical pleasure." He patted her shoulder. "I do not have an interest in your heart."

"And I appreciate your offer, but Samson is very dear to me."

And vampire morals were flexible, but maybe not *that* flexible.

Arosh smiled. "Samson has the purest heart of any vampire I have ever known."

"I agree," Tatyana said. "But *my* heart isn't pure. It's twisted with worry for my mother and fear of how I am going to find my place in this world. Fear that I won't be strong or smart enough to protect her. Fear that simply by being a vampire, I might be putting her in danger."

"I hear that fear in your voice, but you also impress me, Tatyana Vorona." Arosh leaned back. "I admire your loyalty to your family— even though they're human—and I believe you have the potential to be a force in our world. I thought you would enjoy spending time in my court, but you seem to want to spend time with humans more than vampires."

"I appreciate my time in the court, and I will be loyal to Kato for the rest of my life." It was the absolute truth. "But I am also conscious of finding my place in the wider immortal world as you suggested."

He raised one dark eyebrow and pierced her with his hawklike gaze. "By spending time in human bars and clubs?"

Tatyana felt surer now. This she could explain. "By sending messages through my computer to those I know. My own allies, if you will. I hide in bars and clubs to use their resources."

Arosh frowned. "I am listening and learning."

Surprisingly progressive of him. "I come from a generation that doesn't send letters or use phones. We use our computers the same way you would send a messenger to a court."

"I see more clearly now." Arosh nodded thoughtfully. "I will tell you, Alina is not pleased that you dart in and out of her territory. She worries that it sends the wrong message to an ally that she must work closely with."

"Oleg."

Arosh nodded.

"I don't want to attract his attention either, which is why I am looking at keeping a low profile, at least for another few months."

"Not here?"

"Everyone knows that Oleg's bookkeeper is in Arosh's court," Tatyana said. "How can I keep a low profile here?"

"And not in Alina's territory?"

Tatyana shook her head. "I don't want to put you or Alina in that position."

Arosh leaned back. "Then where would you keep a low profile?"

"I don't want to tell you exactly," Tatyana said, "but it might be right under Oleg's nose."

Chapter 7

Oleg

"Track the wind vampire," Oleg told Mika. "That is how she's moving around Arosh's and Alina's territory. If we find him, we find her."

"But don't kill him?" Mika asked.

Oleg wanted to say yes. He still remembered the image of Tatyana's delicate hand being held by the other man.

But that was an irrational and jealous reaction. It was beneath him.

"Do not kill him. It would create an international incident," Oleg said. "But he should understand that Tatyana is mine."

"He's Arosh's favorite," Mika said. "If we offend him, it *will* create an international incident."

"We don't need to offend him, we just need to find him." Oleg pointed at the computer on Mika's desk and snapped. "Make it happen."

"Make it happen," Mika muttered. "As if I snap my fingers and produce vampires out of thin air."

"He's a wind vampire, but he's keeping to Alina's territory," Oleg said. "Probably because he doesn't want to skirt too close to my territory north of the Caucasus."

"We have more spies there."

"Exactly." Oleg stared at the pictures someone had printed off of the profile of Arosh's son and Tatyana in the club.

Once he saw her, he went back and watched every moment of her time in that bar, watched every movement. Tried to read her lips.

She was very good at concealment. How irritating.

Oleg lifted his chin. "Get the plane ready. I want to visit the mother."

Mika walked out, muttering in Estonian, but Oleg didn't care.

If he couldn't have Tatyana under his control, he'd at least go reassure himself that her mother was firmly in his territory and under his aegis.

"And Mika!" he shouted at his boyar's retreating back. "Order her a cake."

ANNA ASANOVA NARROWED HER EYES AS SHE WATCHED HIM EAT a piece of the apple tart he'd brought from the baker at his mansion in Sevastopol. She was in a housecoat and wearing a sleeping cap on her head.

There was something still oddly menacing about her.

"What's wrong with my daughter?" She glared at him.

"Nothing." He set his fork down. "Why do you think something is wrong?"

"Because you show up out of nowhere at" —she glanced at the clock on the wall— "three in the morning. And now you're eating an apple tart in my kitchen."

Oleg heard Anna's carrier pigeons softly shuffling in their cote outside. "How are your birds?"

"You know they're fine. Answer the question."

"I can't find her," Oleg admitted. "I am worried."

"You told me you knew where she was."

"I do. Roughly."

He'd never personally been to Arosh's compound in the Caucasus Mountains, but he knew approximately where it was. Unfortunately it seemed that access to the compound was only via wind vampire, and the Fire King was unlikely to allow him to fly up for a friendly chat with Tatyana.

Anna shook her head. "You don't like when you're not in control of things, do you?"

"Of course not." He jabbed a fork at the apple tart. "No one likes being out of control."

"Most humans live long enough to learn that control is an illusion."

"I'm far older than you," Oleg said. "Far, *far* older."

"Yes, but you became an immortal young, like my Tanya." Anna waved a hand at him as if brushing off an annoying insect. "So you don't know everything, Vampire Man. You were young and powerful, and then you became a vampire and became even more powerful. So when I say that all control is an illusion, you don't really believe me even though you know I'm right."

Oleg set down his fork. "What is your point, Anna Asanova?"

"You think you control your world?" Anna leaned forward. "You control nothing. Governments turn on their people. Relationships fail. People *die*. And you don't always get a warning that it's going to happen." She snapped her fingers. "All your plans can be gone in the time it takes for a bus to drive around a corner."

Oleg frowned. "Not having a plan is unacceptable when others depend on you."

"You were turned before you understood what it means to be weak." Anna shrugged. "So in this, I'm wiser than you."

"I have people who depend on me," Oleg said. "I have to maintain control to keep them safe. And your daughter needs my protection."

"She was still alive two nights ago," Anna said. "So that's been... over a year and a half now?" Anna pursed her lips. "It seems like she's staying alive on her own."

"Alive and hiding."

"So?"

Oleg leaned forward, frustrated and wanting to smash something, but it wouldn't be Anna. Not if he wanted Tatyana back. "She shouldn't have to hide."

"So who is scaring her into hiding?" Anna raised an eyebrow. "It's you, isn't it?"

"She has no reason to fear me."

"That I do not believe." Anna lifted a finger. "No matter how kind and considerate you have been to me. Tatyana is a smart girl. A practical girl. If she is afraid of you, she has her reasons."

Oleg said nothing, but he sipped the tea she'd brewed for him in the middle of the night. Perhaps the woman had some wisdom. She knew nothing about the vampire world, of course, but she might have some insight into her daughter.

"If my daughter is afraid of you," Anna said, "then you need to ask yourself why."

One month later

WHY ARE YOU AFRAID OF ME, LITTLE WOLF?

Oleg had found her.

It had been nearly a month of carefully listening to whispers and watching patterns—as well as paying off a few of Alina's people—but he had found her.

He peered over the wall of the quiet pub in Gori, a small city in a river valley. The bar was attached to a pub with excellent Wi-Fi and a thriving community of young people who sat in groups around firepits, talking and laughing as they enjoyed their beers and cocktails.

The moment he'd reached the perimeter of the city, he'd felt the blood he'd taken from her burst to vibrant, violent life. It took every degree of Oleg's self-control not to storm into the bar, throw her over his shoulder, and march out like a Viking raiding a village.

The simmering desire to possess this woman who tormented his mind gnawed at his gut.

The pub was on the edge of town, and the outdoor beer garden where Tatyana was sitting glowed under the gentle light of a half-moon and soft yellow string lights that hung overhead. The sky was a deep, vibrant azure, and the breeze was warm and fragrant with the scent of a nearby orange grove.

She sat in the corner. Alone, always alone, while the silver-haired vampire watched the door.

Mine.

Oleg waited in the darkness, drinking in the sight of her after so many months. The elemental torment he felt was one-sided. She had never taken his blood, and if she felt anything from him, she wasn't showing it.

> *"You think I'm a bully?"*
>
> *"No. I said you pretend to be a bully."*
>
> *"You're not afraid of me."*
>
> *"Sometimes I am, a little bit."*

But why did she fear him? Did she fear his fire? Did she fear for her control when he tempted her to give him everything?

> *"You think I'm lying?"*
>
> *"Maybe you're telling the truth. But remember Ivan and the fire-*

bird. Even when you start with the best of intentions, things will go wrong."

He saw Mika strolling toward the side gate where the entrance to the beer garden was located and the wind vampire's head go up.

Spotted.

The vampire whipped his head around and hit something on the table that made a clanging noise.

Tatyana's head darted up.

Mika walked into the bar.

Tatyana was already on the move.

She slipped her backpack over her shoulders and ducked into a hallway where Oleg could no longer see her. A snarl ripped from his throat, and he walked out of the shadows toward the beer garden, but the silver-haired vampire was already gone.

He'd either taken to the air or he'd walked so fast that Oleg's eyes hadn't caught him because he was distracted by watching Tatyana.

Mika was already headed back to the shadows of the trees across the street where Oleg was waiting.

As Oleg stepped across the gravel-strewn road, a wall of air slammed into him from the front, knocking him off his feet and knocking him into a stand of cedar trees.

He fell to the ground, bracing his hands on the needle-strewn ground, and smoke simmered from under his heated palms.

The fucking wind vampire had broken his line of sight, and he'd lost Tatyana.

"Look for her!" he shouted at Mika.

Another wall of air, but this time Oleg caught a glimpse of his attacker, who was perched in the top of a nearby tree like a white-headed raptor. His body was cloaked in black, so the only visible part of him was his pale hair and face.

Oleg kept his eyes on him, stalking toward him with flames licking at his collar. "You."

The pale one sneered and flicked his fingers, which sent another stream of air whipping around Oleg, wrapping around his legs and nearly knocking him over as the press of wind constricted his feet.

He snapped his fingers, lobbing a ball of fire up and into the tree.

Despite the damp spring night, Oleg's fire was so intense that it caught in the branches of the cedar tree and burst to hungry life, eating away toward the peak of the evergreen and making the pale vampire fly into the night.

"What are you doing?" Mika ran back and nearly shouted at him. "You can't start a forest fire in Alina's territory." He lifted a hand and threw a cooling mist over the tree, dousing the fire just as the humans in the bar noticed the flames. "I know you can feel the woman, so *you* follow her. Ignore the other one."

Oleg turned and slipped back into the shadows, stalking toward the front of the restaurant and the double doors that opened inward.

He ignored the hubbub of the patrons as they ran to the windows to see the smoldering cedar tree and reached for the thread of connection that linked his blood to Tatyana's.

There was a pulse in his blood and an elemental nudge that sent him toward the back of the restaurant where an archway led to a dark hallway.

He could scent her as soon as he stepped inside.

There was the sound of a crashing door and a quick flash of moonlight before the hallway was dark again, then another slam of wind.

This time Oleg was expecting it. He felt the pale vampire's amnis before it hit him, and he braced himself as he shoved forward, snapping his fingers and bringing a handful of fire to his palm.

The dark figure pulled the hallway door open again and the silver-haired vampire reached for her, wrapping his arm around her waist, prepared to take to the air as soon as the door opened.

Before they could move, Oleg struck, sending his fire down the center of the hallway.

It collared the silver-haired vampire in a living torque of blue flame.

Arosh's son froze. If he moved an inch, the flames would engulf his face.

The door outside closed softly, and the dark figure stepped forward, pulling down the hood of her sweatshirt as she walked toward him. "Oleg, stop."

The sound of her voice stirred something in his chest.

Rage and delight.

She was calm. So calm. Like a doe skirting the attention of a hungry bear.

Oleg didn't want her to be a doe. He wanted her to be a wolf. Her wary voice made him irrationally angry. He bared his fangs at the wind vampire, who watched Oleg's flames encircling his face.

"Oleg." She repeated his name. "Take it away. Please."

The silver-haired vampire was frozen, his eyes glaring at Oleg, but he could do nothing without burning his face.

"You found me. I'm here." Tatyana raised her hands and took another step toward him. "Let him go. You want me, not Samson."

Oleg reveled in his power, making the flames dance and hop around the vampire with gleeful abandon. He smelled a hint of singed hair.

Tatyana saw what he was doing and snapped at him. "Oleg, stop this now!"

There you are.

Oleg kept his hand up, continuing to collar the silver-haired vampire with his flames, but he turned his attention to the woman who had plagued his mind since the moment she'd flown away from him.

"Hello, little wolf."

She was even more beautiful than his memory had created. Her hair was a smidge longer, and the sun-touched blond had given way to a richer honey gold.

Her skin was paler than he remembered, which made her sky-blue eyes even more vibrant.

Her blood leaped in his veins, urging him closer.

Tatyana closed her eyes. "What are you doing to me?"

"I told you," Oleg said carefully. "You are mine." He turned his eyes back to the wind vampire. "Now take a breath, calm your friend, and let's sit and talk in a civilized manner. If he doesn't attack me, I won't attack him. Does he understand?"

"Yes, he understands you," Tatyana said scornfully. "What do you want? You want to have a nice, friendly drink?"

"Dinner," Oleg said. "Not here. Sit down for dinner with me. Mika and your friend can wait here to give us some privacy." He pulled his fire back to his palm, and the silent vampire's shoulders relaxed. "I also think it's important to note that your friend attacked me first."

The pale one shrugged one shoulder.

"I'm not arguing about this with either of you," Tatyana said through clenched teeth. "Samson, please wait here with Mika." She put a soft hand on the vampire's shoulder, and they exchanged an incomprehensible look and some signs to communicate.

Then Tatyana turned to Oleg with narrowed eyes. "You." She marched out of the hallway, brushing past Oleg and sending his amnis into a frenzy. "Follow me."

Chapter 8

Tatyana

She was so angry.

Because not only had he tracked her down, threatened her friend, and maneuvered her into an intimate dinner in a beautiful restaurant that overlooked the river, the minute he appeared and she felt his amnis, something in Tatyana settled and sighed in relief.

She hated him. She hated what he did to her. She hated what he made her feel.

Oleg sat across from her, a white cloth napkin draped over his lap, sitting like an emperor in a charming, upscale restaurant serving traditional Georgian fare. From what she'd seen at the other tables, it appeared to be a fish restaurant, and all the dishes smelled delicious. A bit overpowering to her sensitive nose, but delicious.

Unlike the smaller hostels and bars that catered to backpackers and Western tourists, this menu was entirely written in Georgian, and as Tatyana didn't read the language and spoke only a little, Oleg had ordered for both of them.

What a surprise.

"I'm not hungry," Tatyana said. "I fed last night."

"You should still keep something in your stomach to be comfortable," he said. "You're a creature of the body, despite your power. I ordered caviar and some local smoked salmon."

"I don't like smoked salmon." She loved smoked salmon and remembered preparing it with her grandfather after he went fishing in the summer months.

Oleg snapped his fingers, and in seconds, the server was at his side. He said something else in Georgian that was so quick Tatyana didn't catch it, but the man nodded and ducked away with a small bow.

"Since you don't like smoked salmon" —Oleg stared at her— "I ordered some fried chicken strips from the children's menu. Perhaps those will suit your current mood."

God damn him. She wanted to laugh, but she couldn't.

"Arosh is going to be angry with you," Tatyana said. "Samson is his favorite son."

"Is that why you are so cozy with him?" Oleg sipped the glass of white wine the server had poured for them. "Currying favor with the Fire King through his favorite child?"

"Samson is a friend," Tatyana said. "He has protected me."

"From what?" Oleg stared at her with cool grey eyes.

From you.

From too much attention.

From the whims of his father.

"Arosh won't be happy with you," she repeated.

Oleg set his glass down and folded his hands gracefully on the table. "Maybe, but he can say nothing. We're not in his territory, and his son attacked me with no provocation."

Tatyana couldn't help but stare at Oleg's hands. They were hands that had brought her pleasure so intense that she'd wept. They were hands that had wiped tears from her face and washed blood from her body.

"Tatyana."

She blinked and looked up, striking the tender memories of this vampire from her mind.

"I'm here," she said quietly. "As you mentioned, we're in Alina's territory. I have permission to be here. I'm assuming you do as well. What do you want?"

"I want you to come back with me," he said softly. "I don't care about the gold, if that is worrying you. And I was going to give you the jewelry anyway."

"You were going to give me your dead mate's jewelry?"

"*My* jewelry," Oleg emphasized. "Jewels I had collected that I wanted you to wear. The jewelry is not important."

"Does anyone else know I stole from you?" She was guessing not. "Does Mika even know?"

"So you admit you stole from me?"

Dammit. She'd slipped up. "I admit nothing. Zara was my sire. The gold I took was hers. You yourself told me that a sire would send her children into the world with a settlement of gold. I took a very small percentage of what I was owed." She dropped her voice to barely a whisper. "Especially considering she murdered me and turned me into a vampire without my consent."

Oleg smiled at her. "I have missed you."

"I cannot say the same about you."

He cocked his head. "So you intend to remain in the Fire King's harem?"

"Don't make it sound like something it's not. He's not keeping a harem of women to use for his sexual whims. It's a refuge."

"I can tell you haven't had sex with him. I'd smell him on you."

"Trust me, it has been suggested."

"So why not indulge?" He leaned forward. "Do you miss me?"

Now she wished she *had* slept with Arosh just to keep the smug expression from his face.

Ugh. No. She didn't want to sleep with anyone.

Except Oleg.

That irritating voice in her mind could shut the hell up.

"Taking a lover isn't high on my list of priorities right now," Tatyana said. "I've learned much in Arosh's court."

"Maybe, but it's not where you belong."

"And where *do* I belong?"

"With me," he said. "In my organization."

Tatyana blinked but said nothing.

"Let us be practical." Oleg leaned back and ran his fingers along the edge of the table. "Elene told me before she died that she wanted to hire you. She said you are brilliant, and I do not disagree. Amnis will have only improved your mind; you would be a tremendous asset to the Sokolov organization."

Whatever strong-arming she'd expected from Oleg, she hadn't expected him to offer her a job.

"Come back to Odesa," Oleg said softly. "Whatever is between us, we have time to explore it. I have no desire to rush... whatever this might be." He reached across the table, and the tips of his fingers stroked along the back of her hand.

There was an instant rush of desire, a feeling of comfort and peace.

Tatyana pulled her hand away. "Don't use your amnis on me."

"I'm not using amnis on you. I can't do that now that you're a vampire, remember?"

"You do something to me," she whispered. "Don't pretend you don't."

Oleg pulled his hand back, but he leaned forward and dropped his voice. "Whatever effect you might feel, it is coming from you as much as me."

"No." She refused to admit how much she wanted him.

She wanted to crawl into his lap, curl up with his arms around her, and sniff his neck.

He smelled of incense and cedar.

He smelled like her grandfather's smokehouse.

He smelled like home.

"Tatyana." Oleg's voice was soft and tempting. "Come back with me. Tonight. We can be in my home in Tbilisi by dawn. We can be back in Odesa tomorrow night. Or at your mother's farm. You know she misses you."

"Don't." She raised a hand. "Don't use my mother in this."

"I've been taking care of her and—"

"She doesn't need you to take care of her." Tatyana felt her temper rise. "*I* am taking care of her. She needs you to leave her alone."

"So she can grow old without her daughter?" Oleg's voice grew harder. "So she can putter around her farm with her birds and her cat and her dog, with no family to comfort her? No company save for the trees and the ocean? What kind of life—"

"Don't talk to me about *life*," she hissed. "Because no matter what gifts you give my mother or what promises you make to me, you and I both know that *you* are the reason that I no longer have mine. You are the reason she will never have grandchildren. That every hope she had for my future has turned to ash."

Oleg sat back, and the blank expression that fell over his face like a mask told Tatyana he hadn't forgotten. He hadn't forgotten at all.

He would never admit fault because admitting anything meant admitting that he had failed. He'd failed to protect her from Zara. Failed to keep Elene alive.

"You say you want me to come back with you, but how can I trust you?" She dropped her voice to a whisper. "How can I trust you when you told me yourself that you wanted me to give you the fangs out of my own mouth?"

Oleg sat back and blinked. The blank expression fled, and his eyes returned to their typical calculating expression. "Did I say that?"

"I remember it very clearly." Tatyana's voice grew harder. "You may want me defenseless against you, but no matter what I make of this life that is forced on me, I will *never* give up the little power I have."

A smile tugged at the corner of his mouth. "I see." He crossed his arms over his chest, and then his mouth twitched again. "This is... very interesting."

"Is something funny to you?"

"Not at all." His voice slid into his typical, seductive register. "I acknowledge what you are saying, Tatyana Vorona." He nodded slowly. "And I respect it."

She blinked. In a hundred years, she would not have expected Oleg Sokolov to tell her he respected her. "So you understand why I must develop my independence," she said. "And you will leave my mother out of this."

He lifted his wineglass and sipped the fragrant, golden wine. "Don't be ridiculous—I'm still going to take care of your mother. She's in my territory."

"Oleg—"

"And while I respect your quest for... independence, volchitsa, you are still mine." He set his wineglass down. "Oh look." He turned to her and smiled. "Your fried chicken pieces have arrived."

THEY WALKED ALONG A BEND OF THE RIVER THAT RAN THROUGH the heart of Gori, through small parks, past apartment buildings with lit-up windows, and across a bright red bridge.

Part of her wanted to walk back to Samson and fly away.

The bigger part of her understood that coming to some kind of peace with Oleg was a good step, one that might bring her more peace in the future. And meeting with him in Alina's neutral territory was about as safe as she was going to get.

"Think about my offer," he said. "You know how vital Elene was. I readily admit that her loss has left a huge void in my organization, and it's one that you could help fill."

"I will agree to think about it."

"You can call me." He pulled a plastic-cased mobile phone from his pocket. "Do you want my phone number?"

"Oleg Sokolov doesn't carry a phone." She cocked her head. "Who are you? A body double?"

He smiled a little bit. "Mika was getting annoyed with me. He says he wastes time tracking me down or chasing my guards to find me when he wants to tell me something." He shrugged. "So I relented and acquired a mobile phone."

She narrowed her eyes. "But you love annoying Mika."

"I know. I got the phone; I didn't give him the number."

She couldn't stop the laugh. "You're such an asshole."

"He would be bored if I became too cooperative." Oleg's voice softened. "It is good to hear laughter. We do not laugh as much since Elene died."

Tatyana's smile fell. "How is her family?"

"Devastated." His voice was rough. "I speak to her daughter regularly. She is my goddaughter; it's my responsibility to take care of her. Elene's son and her husband want nothing to do with me."

It was good to speak about someone that Tatyana had considered a friend. Someone she'd hoped would be a mentor.

"I envied her life," she admitted. "I wanted to be her. Successful professionally. Respected like that. To have a family and a husband." Tatyana shook her head. "She had everything."

Oleg stopped walking, and Tatyana turned to look at him. "What?"

"You can still have those things." He frowned a little bit. "You've seen very little of vampire life so far, and you're not in a... typical vampire court."

She huffed out a breath. "So the vampires in your organization live quiet lives, do they? Get married. Settle down. Only pick up the battle-ax Monday through Friday?"

"No." He smiled. "The men and women of my druzhina live warriors' lives. Some of them are mated, but they usually do not have families."

"So what Elene had is not—"

"But one of my daughters in Minsk adopted two children last year with her human partner." Oleg sighed and started walking again. "I would prefer that they married in the church, but Polina said it is not necessary, and I am trying to be understanding of her modern ways."

"What?" Tatyana could only blink. Oleg sounded so... conventional. So paternal. "She has human children?"

Oleg turned and kept his voice low. "I trust you to keep that information to yourself. Please recognize that their lives are precious to all in my clan, but their mortal nature puts them at increased risk from my enemies."

"I would never" —she shook her head— "I would never tell anyone."

"Thank you." He continued walking, cocking out his elbow and waiting for her.

Tentatively, Tatyana put her arm in his. "She's your daughter?"

"For four hundred years now, yes. A brilliant businesswoman and a very fair-minded governor. She overseas my territory in what is called Belarus now. The borders are different than when I conquered it, because of humans. But it's in that region."

"I didn't know."

She'd known Oleg's vampire brother was in charge of the area around Sochi and Crimea where her mother lived. She supposed it made sense that one man couldn't rule a vast empire without over-seers of some kind.

"All I am saying," Oleg continued, "is that most immortal organizations are much like human governments. Yes, there are martial wings of every court—every king must have an army—but much of the day-to-day business of what I do is mundane. We make money. We invest. We build factories and create jobs."

Tatyana was swiftly shifting pieces of knowledge in her mind. "I remember seeing some payroll accounts when I worked for Zara, but I thought it was all..."

"A front?" Oleg smiled. "For our nefarious operations?" He chuckled a little bit. "No, it is all real. One of my companies is a leading manufacturer of agricultural equipment in Europe and Central Asia."

What Oleg was describing sounded much more like a modern multinational corporation than a criminal organization. "People will always need to eat."

Oleg grunted. "Yes, and wise immortals understand that the health of humanity directly affects our well-being."

Vampires, of course, also needed to eat.

"Over the centuries, I have made many things," Oleg said. "I like being productive. My sire enjoyed making war, and I have waged war when it was necessary, but war is wasteful. I avoid it when I can."

"I wish human governments understood that better."

"Hmm." Oleg shrugged. "Whether at war or peace, farming is a good industry. Plows and harvesters feed soldiers and civilians alike."

"One of Zara's companies was a greenhouse manufacturer." Tatyana remembered some of the accounts. "At the time I thought that was normal, but after I knew what she was, it seemed strange."

"She had greenhouses for many reasons," Oleg said. "Some of them legitimate." He pressed her hand into his side. "So you see, even my juvenile and unstable daughter employed many people. Including you when you were human."

"Until she stopped paying me."

"Imagine if she hadn't." The corner of his mouth turned up. "We would never have met if she'd just paid her bills."

"Oleg—"

"I can't regret it," he said quietly. Oleg stopped at the apex of a bright red pedestrian bridge that looked over the water and stared down at her, her arm still locked with his. "Can you blame me?"

His eyes were soft, and with her enhanced vision, the night took on a luminescent grey quality that looked more like twilight than darkness.

For a moment he looked like just a man. A warm man who smelled of cedar cologne, holding her arm safe in his.

Tatyana's eyes fell to his lips, full and curved in pleasure.

She reached up and touched his beard, scratching her fingernails along the edge of his jaw as a low hum came from his chest.

He leaned down, angling his head toward hers, but a moment before their lips touched, he paused. "May I kiss you?"

She should say no. "Yes."

His mouth was a revelation. Soft and searching, he coaxed her lips open, and when his tongue touched hers, she felt human again, and every inch of her body heated.

They were in the middle of a park, but it was nearly three in the morning. She inhaled the scent of his skin, and for a moment she forgot everything else.

He was a man; she was a woman.

It was a kiss, and it felt like the first time she had ever been kissed. The gentleness was nearly painful. Her eyes were closed when Oleg pulled his mouth away.

"How could I regret anything?" he said softly. "You are becoming an *extraordinary* vampire."

Vampire.

The spell broken, Tatyana opened her eyes and saw Oleg's fangs extended, long and sharp in the bright moonlight. She felt, more than saw, his power whirling around him.

Her blood pulled her back to him. She felt a burst of swirling anger, need, lust, and desperate longing that burned in her throat. She wanted to sink her fangs into his neck and pull the life from him until he was on his knees and begging.

Tatyana cringed at the image and took a step back.

"Tatyana?"

Bitterness stained her tongue. "You may not regret that I was kidnapped, beaten, and basically killed, but I never wanted to be a vampire."

His chin lifted and he stepped back. "But you *are*. You might as well make the best of it."

He held out his hand, but she ignored it and kept walking down the arch of the bridge and back to the pedestrian path.

Make the best of it?

Tatyana swallowed her anger and tried not to fume.

Too bad. So sad.

Sorry that you lost your ability to walk in sunlight, have a family, and live a normal life where you don't have to drink blood every other night to keep from being a ravenous monster, but can't you just make the best of it?

It could be worse!

It could *always* be worse. Her mother never passed up an opportunity to remind her of that.

Oleg took long strides and caught up with her, following her up the path, across a street, and toward another set of apartment buildings that hugged the riverbank.

They were walking in silence, away from the tourist areas and toward the tree-lined riverwalk. Streetlights were getting farther apart, and the sound of traffic dimmed in the distance.

The moon was high, and lights in the apartments were scattered as human families slept.

"Tatyana, I think we should—"

"I want to go back to the bar and find Samson."

She was ready to leave.

She and Oleg weren't at each other's throats. Maybe now that he knew she wasn't obsessed with him—though the kiss was regrettable—and she knew that he wasn't going to track her down for taking Zara's gold, they could simply go their separate ways.

He could live his blood-soaked vampire existence being an undead emperor to thousands, and she could try to carve out a corner of eternity that didn't suck out her soul.

That was all she wanted. A little bit of peace. A space that felt like home. Safety for her mother.

"They're going to try to rob us."

Tatyana stopped and turned when Oleg spoke. "What?"

He stood still, hands in his coat pockets, and nodded at a clutch of dark-clad men who had broken away from the shadows under a tree and were lurching in their direction. "They think we're lost tourists."

She hadn't even noticed them, lost in her thoughts and fuming at the silent vampire beside her. "Oh good. Another excuse for you to rip some heads off."

He shrugged. "If they irritate me or threaten you—"

"As you very recently reminded me, I'm not human anymore." She glared at him from the side. "Just wait here and let me talk to them."

"You?" He had the gall to look amused. "You're going to talk to them. Excellent. I hope they don't have knives. Let me know when you would like my company, little wolf."

Tatyana stalked over to the boys, most of whom looked like teenagers, and snarled, "Where the fuck are your mothers?"

The young man in the front of the pack froze.

"Well?" Tatyana continued. "Where are they?"

The young man in the front of the pack looked confused. "We... what?"

He answered her in Georgian, but Tatyana responded in Russian, in the best attempt at grandmotherly shame she could manage. "Do they know you're out so late?" She pointed at the apartment buildings behind them. "Is that where you live?" She looked at one of the boys, who looked barely old enough to pee standing up. "You! What is your mother's name?"

"Uh..." He stammered. "M-Marie. Her name is—"

"Shut up, Georgi."

"Oh!" Tatyana kept going. "So I should walk back and start pounding on doors and asking Marie why Georgi is harassing people out for a walk at night, yes?"

"Fuck you, bitch." The words might have come from the tallest boy in the group, but his voice was wavering. Just a little bit. Nevertheless, he reached into his pocket and pulled out a knife. "You're crazy. So shut up and give me your—"

Faster than the knife could rise, she darted over to him, yanked the blade from his hand, twisted his wrist, and gripped the boy's throat in her hand, slamming him to the ground before she turned to the biggest one, who had barely had time to react.

She grabbed his ear, pulled him down to her face, and hissed in his ear. "Go. Home." She flooded his skin with amnis as she spoke and watched his pupils go wide. "Go home and apologize to your mother for being a bad son."

The boys were scuffling in the long grass around their friend on the ground, stunned by Tatyana's sudden attack and the limp way their ringleader drooped in her arms.

She let him drop to the ground before she turned to them and spoke quietly. "All of you go home and apologize to your mothers for being shameful, irresponsible little fucks who don't have jobs and aren't in school."

They said nothing, but they picked up their friends and shuffled back into the shadows of the trees along the riverbank. Moments later, Tatyana heard them start to run.

Oleg wandered over, his hands still in his pockets and an amused expression on his face. "I've never thought about using maternal guilt to deal with humans. Unexpectedly effective. Should I call for a car?"

"They were dumb little boys." She turned to him. "I knew plenty of them at home. You would have ripped their heads off and killed them."

Tatyana felt a pang in her chest when she realized that half those boys she'd grown up with were probably dead already. Bombing. War. Crime. All of them could kill as easily as a vampire.

The world was filled with monsters, and now she was one of them.

"I probably would have only needed to kill the ringleader." Oleg stared into the darkness. "But I did not need to." He looked at her.

"See? I told you that you're going to make an extraordinary vampire."

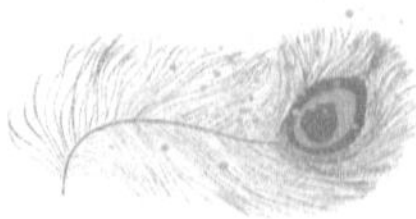

THE FOLLOWING NIGHT, TATYANA WOKE ON AROSH'S MOUNTAIN with Oleg's scent still clinging to her skin. She washed her face, put on clothes that would be acceptable for court, then walked through her door, heading toward a room in the furthest corner of the compound.

Two sharp raps later, the Poshani human named Sibella opened the door, narrowing her eyes when she saw Tatyana.

"It's only been a few days. You can't feed from me again, and I told you I'm not interested in anything else with you."

"I don't want sex or blood from you." Nevertheless, Tatyana pushed her way into the room and pulled out a thick roll of US dollars she kept stashed in her room. "But I do have a proposition."

Chapter 9

Oleg

The night following his pleasant dinner with Tatyana, Oleg was mulling over their conversation in his mind. Revelations had been made. This was progress.

It was an interesting and unexpected thing to have such a moment misunderstood so thoroughly. What Oleg had actually said was that he wanted Tatyana to give him her fangs. What he'd meant as a passionate declaration had been understood as a threat.

Interesting.

"What has you smiling?" Mika scowled at him. "You instigated a minor international incident between you and one of the Fire King's favorites in Alina Machabeli's territory, and humans witnessed people flying and setting trees on fire. I'm surprised you're not already trending on social media."

Oleg chuckled a little bit.

"You think this is funny?" Mika held up a phone. "I've already had her security chief making snide remarks in my ear this evening, and I haven't even heard from Daria or Morella or Angel or one of the other Amazons Arosh has working for him."

"Does he employ any males at all?" Oleg mused.

"Only a few," Mika muttered. "I've heard that he trusts women in security positions more than men."

Oleg pursed his lips. "An argument could be made for it."

Mika flipped him off. "I'm not retiring, so don't get any ideas." The water vampire sat back in his seat. "Or maybe I should, considering I'm sick of all of this. We should be dealing with Ivan's links to rogue Poshani soldiers and random vampires showing up in Polina's territory. Instead, I'm chasing after a woman who has made it clear she doesn't want you."

He raised a finger. "She very much wants me."

Mika rolled his eyes. "Yes, of course she does. That's why she flew back to Arosh."

Oleg smirked. "A little bit of pursuit is good for the soul, Mika. Things that come to you easily are not as treasured as those you must fight for."

"So philosophical for someone chasing after sex."

Oleg reached over and slammed his palm against Mika's chest, driving the wind from the vampire's body before he gripped his lieutenant's throat.

Oleg bared his fangs, and Mika froze. "Enough." The growl came from his chest. "You think I'm chasing a woman like a horny schoolboy? You think I only want her sex?"

Mika narrowed his eyes and pushed Oleg's arm away. "Clearly I underestimated the hold Tatyana Vorona has on you. Should I be concerned?"

"She will be in our organization," Oleg said. "Elene saw her potential, and so do I. And that was before she became a vampire mentored by an ancient."

Mika wasn't convinced. "She doesn't want anything to do with us because we're the ones who got her killed."

"Don't talk to me about life, because no matter what gifts you give my mother or what promises you make to me, you and I both know that you are the reason that I no longer have mine."

It was very irritating when Mika had a point.

"You are not entirely wrong." Oleg stretched his neck to one side, then the other. He didn't like disciplining Mika, but sometimes his chief boyar became a little too confident in his position. "I will convince her. It may take some time, but she is mine."

Mika said nothing for an hour, but Oleg could hear all but hear the silent Estonian curses battering his mind as he read a report that his human assistant had already sent from Polina.

"Mika."

Mika looked up from his book. "Yes, Knyaz?"

So someone was feeling a little irritated. That was fine.

"Set up a conference call with Polina when we arrive in Odesa," Oleg said. "I want to fill her in on what Radu and I spoke about."

"Of course." He reached for the small notebook he kept in his jacket pocket and made a note. "Did you have notes for me about your meeting with Alina?"

"It was mostly a catching-up meeting. I wanted to reassure her that Lazlo would remain in charge of our neighboring territory."

"And ask about Tatyana."

Oleg looked up, stared into Mika's eyes, and the vampire lost his snappish tone.

"She gave you the video footage of Tatyana," Mika said. "That footage that led us to a minor international incident in Gori. Alina won't be pleased if she thinks Arosh will point the finger at her."

"Did *she* give us the footage?" He paged through Polina's report. "Or did someone else? We have so many sources, it's impossible to say. It might have been anonymous."

"Very well." Mika nodded slowly. "Arosh's people will want to know why we were tracking his son."

"If they ask, tell them I had an important computer security question for Tatyana and I know she's an expert."

Mika frowned. "That might work as long as Tatyana doesn't say why you actually wanted to meet with her."

Tatyana admit that she took Zara's gold, Oleg's jewelry, and was running from her own feelings for him?

"She won't say anything." Oleg glanced at Mika. "Trust me."

"And I'm assuming you want me to continue keeping tabs on her and Arosh's son?"

"No."

Mika put his notebook down. "No?"

"No." Oleg glanced up. "I slipped a phone into her pocket. We'll be able to find her anywhere now."

"When she finds it, she'll destroy it."

Oleg shrugged. "Check the signal when we get back to Odesa. She'll keep the phone."

His daughter's face filled the screen that hung over his mantel in his personal office in Odesa. She was holding one of the twins, the ornery little mite named Natalya who loved to stay up at all hours with her mama.

It was convenient for Polina, but it annoyed her partner Alexi and the nanny.

"Look at her." Oleg's heart warmed when he saw the little one sitting in Polina's lap. "She's growing very fast."

"Yes, she's trying to climb up and down the stairs by herself now." Polina smiled. "She drives Alexi mad."

"He loves it." Oleg had been suspicious of the man, but ten years into his relationship with Polina, the pair seemed settled despite Polina's unwillingness to marry.

"He does." Polina tapped Natalya's cheek. "Tati, don't you want to say hello to dedushka?"

"Absolutely not." His children having children was not a common occurrence, so though Oleg was overjoyed by the delightful little humans in his clan, he was nobody's grandfather. "Tati, can you wave at Papa Oleg?"

The little girl lifted her hand and curled her fingers in a wave.

"See? She'll call me Oleg. That is enough."

Natalya's blinks were getting longer and longer, and she was starting to curl into Polina's chest, so his daughter picked up a manila folder on her desk as she rocked the baby to sleep. "So after Radu told you the vampire's name was Sami, my people were able to dig a little more."

"And?" Oleg glanced at the little one, but the toddler was falling asleep.

"Sami Novak was his government name," Polina said, "but once we tracked his credit card, we found rental records online that listed him with a few others."

"He had rental records?"

"Short term only," Polina said. "He used an online placement service that caters to businesspeople who do remote work. And more than once he listed two other men with him—Manfred Novak and Danior Kosinski. Sometimes Danior had a different last name, but it was almost always Sami with Manfred and Danior."

"Do we think they were two of the others at the scene?" Radu had told him that Sami was the only Poshani vampire killed, but Manfred could easily be a Westernized version of Manfri, and Danior was a common men's name among the Poshani. "Radu said that only one of theirs had been involved."

Polina lifted a shoulder in a slight shrug. "It's possible Radu was misinformed. Or maybe someone didn't want to admit that a few Poshani vampires went rogue. No one wants to look like they're not in control of their people."

Possible. Likely even. Poshani justice was swift within the clan.

They were free spirits in the vampire world, but adherence to cultural norms within the clan was a necessity. A rebellious Poshani put the entire community at risk.

"If these other two were also Poshani and involved with the truck robberies," Oleg said, "this problem could be bigger than we anticipated."

"There is no way of confirming it at this point. We've put alerts on their known credit cards, but so far none of them have been used." Polina set the folder down. "What are you going to tell Radu?"

"Nothing right now. We don't know anything definite, and if I ask him, I'm casting doubt on what he's already shared with me."

"He won't want to lose face," Polina said. "He'll shut you down."

And no one could keep a secret like the Poshani.

"He invited me to the Vashana at the end of the season," Oleg said.

"That's months away." Someone had come into Polina's office, because she held up a finger when Oleg started to speak. "One moment, Papa."

A human nanny walked over and took the sleeping girl from Polina's arms, not sparing a glance at the video screen in the room.

Polina trained her people well.

After the nanny left and closed the door, Polina spoke again. "The Vashana is at the end of the season, but there have been four truck robberies in six months, and this last one nearly killed our driver. We need to shut this down and make a statement."

"I agree." Oleg mulled over his options. "I'm going to fly to Moscow to see the driver. I need to give him some cash from Radu's people anyway. I told Radu I'd deliver it personally."

Polina made a face. "Say hello to Ivan."

"I'm not going tonight. I'll give it a few days." He closed the file on Sami Novak because there was nothing else to do at the moment. "Sami Novak is dead. All his conspirators are dead. Maybe this was an isolated string of robberies, but only time will tell."

She sighed. "You're right."

"And you're impatient." Oleg smiled. "I want you on a video call tomorrow night."

"Why?"

"I'm calling a meeting of the governors. We need to put a permanent replacement for Elene in place."

Polina's jaw tightened. "Elene is not replaceable."

"I realize that on an emotional level, and I know how close the two of you were," Oleg said. "But SMO is suffering from lack of clear leadership. The overseas shipping arm of the company is central to our corporate plan over the next century, and the current political situation with the humans needs a steady hand. We must hire a replacement who can fill the gap."

"Fine." Polina was clearly unpleased, but she was a businesswoman too. "Send me any files you have on possible replacements and a secure link. Unless you want to send a plane for me and Alexi."

"A screen meeting is fine for now," he said. "And there are no candidates yet. I'm asking everyone to put forward their best, so think about who could step into the role from your region."

"Human?"

"Yes. Day meetings are a necessity, so yes. I want to promote from within the organization, but I'm open to ideas. When the final vote happens, it will be in person."

"Understood." She reached toward a button on her desk. "I think Natalya's crying again. I'll see you tomorrow night."

"Polina?"

"What?" Her eyes darted toward the door.

"I love you, and I'm proud of you," Oleg said softly. "Give my granddaughter a kiss."

OLEG SAT AT THE HEAD OF A TABLE IN ODESA, SURROUNDED BY five vampires, a trusted human scribe, and three screens bearing the faces of three of his governors.

"My most trusted governors," he said to start the meeting. "It is good to see you all."

While his druzhina—his inner circle—was heavily represented in his governors, there were two vampires, his brothers Ivan and Pavel, who had also been granted governor seats despite the fact that they were *not* in Oleg's personal circle.

Both oversaw key areas of his empire. Pavel was one of his oldest living brothers and had overseen his northern ports for centuries. Oleg's most troublesome brother, Ivan, oversaw Moscow and much of the Russian heartland with the criminal gang he'd created.

"Lidik is in Odesa." Pavel was on a screen and his voice sounded accusatory, but that was nothing new. "I did not know that exterior governors were flying in."

Pavel was distant, cold, and extremely efficient. He could also be as irritable as a wet cat.

"Lidik happened to be in the region for something unrelated." Oleg glanced at the Siberian woman who sat stiffly in the corporate conference room.

"I'm meeting one of my children tomorrow night," Lidik said quietly. "She recently relocated from Kashgar to Capadoccia."

"It's lovely to see you." Polina was also on a screen. "Will you be in the area more often now that she's moved?"

"Doubtful." Lidik glanced at Oleg. "I'll be here when the knyaz requires it, as always."

Lidik rarely left Siberia, and Oleg was fine with that. She was dressed in traditional Siberian clothing, mostly fur, despite the balmy spring weather in Odesa. Her long hair was braided elaborately, and she stared at the table in front of her, tracing the pattern of burl on the polished wood.

The wind vampire wasn't blood related to any of his clan, but four centuries before, Oleg had saved her life. As a result, Lidik was more loyal to him than most of his blood relations.

She was also a favorite of Polina and his brother's child Juliya, who was sitting next to Oleg in the conference room.

"If we could take roll for the scribe," Juliya said, "we can get started with the meeting. This is procedural but important."

"I don't know why any of that nonsense is necessary." Ivan's resonant baritone voice rolled over the room, filling the space. "When did we start keeping records like humans? We don't have shareholders, brother."

"It's necessary because I want it," Oleg said. "That is all you need to know."

Ivan stared at him for a moment; then his face broke into a wide smile. "How modern! Very forward thinking, brother."

Ivan usually addressed Oleg as *brother* even though they'd never been close. It was as if he received pleasure by reminding Oleg that— despite their mutual dislike—they shared Truvor's blood.

Oleg hadn't realized that Ivan was in Odesa, and he was slightly annoyed that his brother had slipped into the city under his nose.

He glanced at Mika, but the Estonian only lifted one dark eyebrow.

Oleg had a purpose for the minutes of the meeting. He had every intention of looking over the candidates for chief financial officer alone with Mika and possibly with Tatyana. As recently human, she would have valuable perspective on the matter.

"Pavel." The vampire's clipped voice started the roll. "Present via screen."

"Mika, present in Odesa."

"Polina," his daughter called. "Present via screen."

"Lazlo," Oleg's oldest brother grumbled from a screen in the corner. "And I'm staring at Oleg's face on a television again. For the record, he's still an ugly bastard."

Oleg smiled, and all the vampires around him chuckled.

He did notice the scribe carefully jotting down Lazlo's words. Lovely. That would amuse Tatyana.

"Rudov." Oleg's last brother spoke. "And I am present in Odesa."

Normally both Rudov and Ivan would have attended via screen, but Ivan had shown up unannounced for some reason, and Rudov happened to be in Odesa to confer with Juliya about the current situation with the Crimean ports.

"It's rare for us to have so many governors in one place," Oleg said. "Which is why I wanted to call this meeting. We need a new CFO, and I'd like it to be a human from one of your organizations."

"An excellent idea," Ivan said. "I have several very talented people who could step into the role. I'm not eager to part with any of them, but for my dear brother?" Ivan nodded. With consequence. "I would make the sacrifice for our clan."

Moscow was an economic powerhouse, and Oleg had no doubt that Ivan had a half dozen superb humans who could fill the role.

Unfortunately, all of them would be loyal to Ivan. Not Oleg.

"That's enormously generous," Oleg said. "Tonight we're simply offering names. And take some time to think about it." He looked at Pavel, sensing the objection even before the fastidious vampire spoke. "Think carefully about the role and who this person will be succeeding. Elene Beridze will be impossible to replace, but we must do our best."

"I don't think the small commercial interests in my sector have produced any humans who could replace Elene," Lidik said. "But I'll think about it."

"I have two people in mind," Rudov said. "I imagine Juliya can guess at least one of them."

Juliya was the governor of the region west of the Dnieper River and going southwest toward Romania, which meant her region held both Kyiv and Odesa, while Rudov governed the region south of Ivan's and stretching to the Black Sea. The two often worked closely, particularly on shipping and logistics.

Rudov was also Juliya's sire. While technically she was under

Rudov's aegis, she had sought permission from her sire to pledge loyalty to Oleg's authority and Rudov had granted it. The two made for a powerful and stable duo in a region where human politics could be turbulent and bloody.

"I want to hear all your ideas," Oleg said. "I'm going to outline what I'm looking for; then you can ask any questions you may have. Think it over, then send me individual files on your two best candidates and I'll consider them. We will meet again in a month to vote."

He looked around the room. "I will have the final say, of course, but I do want your opinions."

Eight voices spoke. "Yes, Knyaz."

Eight faces. Eight nods.

Eight very strong personalities.

Oleg knew that without their cooperation, he could never govern a region as vast as the Kievan Rus. In fact, he often thought about breaking up the empire he'd taken from his sire.

Glancing at Ivan, he knew it was impossible. The idea of dividing Truvor's empire was akin to shattering a stained-glass window.

Each part of it supported and held the next. Without the whole of it, there were countless sharp edges.

And sharp edges led to bleeding.

The Immortal Empire of the Kievan Rus was tied together by history, war, and blood.

It was Oleg's responsibility to keep it whole.

Chapter 10

Tatyana

She was sitting at a bar in Kutaisi and the music was pounding around her. It hurt her ears, but it was the best way to mask the sounds of the video game she was playing since she couldn't wear headphones.

—I have a plan.

The left side of her screen was exploding as her character was devoured by aliens yet again. Other players in the game were shouting insults, but Tatyana ignored them. She was focused on her conversation with Grimace.

Who was still shooting at the aliens even as they messaged each other.

—whats the plan?

—I have a place I can hide, but I might not have internet there

—blasphemy pidge

—I know the plan won't work unless I can put something together

—what do you need?

—hardware

Excited emojis filled the screen.

—yesssss tell me more

Sibella had explained a little bit of what she might expect by hiding in the kamvasa, and since secrecy was key, all electronic devices were confiscated. Apparently the Poshani would give you a mobile phone or tablet to call the outside world every now and then, but that wasn't enough for Tatyana.

She needed to be able to check on her mother. She needed to be able to check her investments and trade the cryptocurrency where she'd hidden some of her fortune.

—I need a computer that doesn't look like a computer. But it has to be insulated. RFID blocked. All that.

Tatyana had created her own shortcuts for using human computers. Gloves helped and so did plastic, but this was another level of construction.

Tatyana's character erupted back into life like a tiny digital vampire, and she started fighting her way through what looked like a South American jungle populated by tentacled aliens as she continued to chat with Grimace.

—who are we hiding from? Grimace asked. —civilian or professional?

Maybe she was making assumptions, but Tatyana was guessing that the Poshani vampire clan didn't have the kind of cybersecurity professionals that Grimace was used to working with.

—civilian. smart, but civilian.

—easy-peasy, pidge, timeline?

—two weeks.

—now you're trying to kill me.

—if you hide it in a well-constructed suitcase, that will probably be enough

Her character took the first blow from a hairy tentacle.

She locked her eyes on the left screen and aimed a futuristic rail gun at the head of an enemy alien as she saw Grimace filling up the right side of the screen with furious typing. When the alien was finally dead, she turned back to see what he'd typed.

—i have an idea. thank you for an amusing project. i wont need my friend to do this, but i will need a delivery location. the finished product will probably take about a week since i can do it myself.

—perfect. Use this address for delivery— she typed in the address of a hotel in Kutaisi where Samson knew the owner —message me when you ship it.

—done.

—thank you and you know you'll get paid.

—ur adorable, pidge. one of these days...

—one of these days what?

She smiled at his words. Grimace was always threatening her about meeting in person, but she had a feeling that he'd be an old man before they ever met.

Tatyana, of course, would still be young.

Unlike her character, who had once again been killed by an alien. This time dual tentacles ripped her head off from two directions, spraying blood everywhere before her character crumpled to the ground.

—ur so bad at this game

—thx I know. Can we just play cat café next week?

—lol no

"You're leaving me again." He brushed a piece of her hair away from her face. "Come back."

"You can't keep showing up in my dreams without my permission." Her words tried to push him away, but she clung to him, wrapping her arms around his waist, heating her body against the burning pillar of his muscular frame.

He was like a fireplace, warming her skin in the cold chamber in the mountains. She let her fingers take liberties in the dream, running her hands along the ridges of muscle at the small of his back. His skin was smooth, the fine hair that should have softened his skin burned away by the fire that ran through his veins.

She leaned into the rough texture of his beard on her neck.

His soft lips brushed against her skin when he spoke. "Stay with me."

"Why did you look for me?" Cold tears gathered in the corners of her eyes. Tatyana felt cold. All the time, she felt cold. "Why do you make me remember missing you?"

"Because you're mine."

It sounded so simple in her dreams, and she knew she was dreaming. He was too gentle. Too comforting.

Dream Oleg was the lover she craved, his gentle strength wrapping around her like a heavy blanket. When she was in her dreams, he drove the cold away.

"Closer."

Her skin was bare and pressed to his. His arms encircled her. His hands soothed her skin, stroking up and down her back, his fingers dancing over the rise of her hips and teasing the delicate skin of her inner thigh.

Delicious desire danced in her blood, and when he lifted her leg, spread her thighs, and slid into her body, she let out a soft sigh.

Yes.

This was what she needed. He filled her, and his steady, thrusting hips drove the cold from her body. Delicious pleasure started at her toes, filling her as he whispered unintelligible sweetness in her ear.

When the pleasure crested, she cried out, and he swallowed her sighs with his mouth. Their kiss went on and on and on until it was everything and all she felt was his body in hers, his blood in her mouth, his amnis twisting and melding with her own.

When Tatyana opened her eyes, the room around her was black and empty.

Cold tears lingered on her cheeks.

"Are you sure about this?"

"I'm not sure about anything." She was meeting with Kato in the watery fortress on Arosh's mountain where her mentor had hidden for centuries when his mind went blank.

The Kato she knew was not the powerful emperor of the ancient world because that immortal's mind had been wiped and rewritten by a poison centuries before. Even with an antidote, it had taken years to recover a fraction of his memories.

"The Poshani *can* be trusted," Kato said. "The human did not lie to you. But you'll be cut off from the world for six months at least. Are you sure you want that?"

"That's the best part." Tatyana waded into the water, wearing a simple black bathing suit she'd found in the clothing supplies for the harem. "It will get me out of Arosh's long and lustrous hair."

Kato smiled. "He's very proud of his hair, you know. It's hard for fire vampires to keep their hair when they light themselves on fire so regularly."

She smiled. "Barbarians."

He winked at her. "The worst of them."

Kato's quarters contained a vast, Roman-style bath built with marble and gold. Warm, rose-scented steam suffused the air, and marble benches lined the walls. She could see Alexander lounging in one alcove, holding an open book and talking with someone she couldn't see.

This was Kato's domain, and Arosh didn't trespass unless his old friend allowed it, which meant it was Tatyana's favorite place on the mountain.

"Let's practice a water thread first," Kato said.

"It's a useless party trick." Tatyana wished they could practice manipulating water in the air or even pulling a wave, but though Kato had given her the basics of those elemental powers, he tended to focus on fine motor skills, not great shows of power.

"It's good for control." He snapped his fingers. "Draw a thread."

"Fine." She put her hands together under the water and focused her amnis as she drew one hand up, pulling the water between her fingertips and raising it until a thin, shining line of water quivered in the misty air.

"If you're not sure about the Poshani, why don't you stay here?" Kato watched her hold the thread of water between her palms. "Keep it stable."

"You and I both know I need to leave, and six months of hiding gives me more time to plan." She held the water thread steady between her hands, feeling the immaterial power of her amnis quivering like an excited puppy.

"Going from one hiding place to another is not a plan."

"Maybe not, but right now it's all I have unless I want to return to Oleg's territory or live under Saba's aegis in Alitea."

"There's the United States. Territories are not as old there, and I have connections I'm offering."

"I don't know anything about that world." At least the Poshani existed in Eastern Europe. That felt slightly familiar.

"Your control gets better every night," Kato murmured. "Very good. Hold it a little longer."

She felt her mind ache from the strain of maintaining the delicate line of water between her hands. "Hiding in the kamvasa gives me six months of safety. Who knows what will happen in six months? Maybe Oleg will decide to retire and I can go back to Sevastopol. Maybe the Poshani will love me so much they decide to adopt me."

"Oh yes. Both of those things are very likely."

"I can hope."

"Your control is impressive," Kato said. "Now don't let it break, but release it into one palm."

Tatyana didn't breathe as the shimmering line of water wavered and flowed, gathering like a silken thread in the center of her left palm.

She let out a breath when the small pool of water rested in her hand.

"Excellent." Kato smiled. "Never forget, your power is absolutely average for a new vampire."

"Please." She poured the water out of her hand and into the warmed pool. "Stop your flattery or it will all go to my head."

"Teaching such an average pupil is an enjoyable exercise for me." Kato ignored her sarcasm. "Brute strength isn't an option for you, so precision will be your best tactic. Control will be everything, and your power will grow from there."

"I remember when I was still human." Tatyana shook her head. "Zara seemed so powerful to me."

"She was average," Kato said. "Like you. But compared to humans, you are very powerful now."

"And very vulnerable," she added. "No light. Forced to drink a single food source or I'll shrivel up. Forced to sleep during daylight. I only have half the time I did as a mortal."

"True." Kato lifted his chin. "That is the bargain of immortality and elemental power."

"And I am forced to abide by that bargain."

For as long as her mother was still living.

Tatyana put both her hands on the surface of the pool and felt the water swirl around her fingers, comforting her with its energy.

At least the water loved her. It filled the air around her and caressed her skin. While her amnis might feel like a barely restrained puppy at times, the element it controlled was a sinuous and delighted cat.

"It is worth it?" She looked up at Kato. "Waiting out the centuries for my power to grow before I feel safe?"

Kato smiled. "You could always find a shortcut. Mate and exchange blood with an old and powerful vampire."

She felt the memory of Oleg's fangs at her neck and the corresponding surge of arousal she quickly tried to tamp down. "That will not be happening."

"Your body reacted just now," Kato said. "Were you remembering Oleg?"

"Do you have to ask?" She'd confided in Kato months ago when she'd been feeling particularly vulnerable and desperate.

The craving for Oleg was a stubborn glitch in her mind, and her emotions ping-ponged between anger and longing. She was convinced that he was doing something to her, even across the miles that separated them.

"How many times did he take your blood?"

She shook her head. "I don't remember." She still craved his fangs in her neck. She wanted them. She yearned for his bite.

The bastard.

"When you were a vampire, yes?"

"Yes." Why was he asking about this? It was like talking about sex with her father.

If she had a father.

Kato frowned. "And you never took his?"

"What?" Her eyes went wide. "No."

"Didn't you want to?" Kato leaned along the edge of the pool, and the water danced around him. He glanced at Alexander across the room. "I don't think Alexander would mind you knowing that I take his blood."

She had to smile. "I assumed that you did."

"If he were immortal..." Were Kato's cheeks a little red? Could vampires blush, or was it her imagination? "I would want him to bite me in return. That is all I'm saying."

Tatyana sat in the corner near to Kato, but not too close. This conversation was awkward enough. "Oleg and I were lovers, but we were not like you and Alexander. The two of you love each other. You have mutual respect. It's very obvious."

"When my lovers have been human," Kato said, "taking their

blood was an enjoyable part of sex. But a blood exchange between vampires is a much more intimate thing. I have told you about this."

"It creates a tie." Tatyana understood that now even though she hadn't when Oleg had bitten her.

"I know your feelings about Oleg are complicated now," Kato said, "and I will do nothing to defend his actions. You were too young and vulnerable to understand what was happening with that exchange."

"It wasn't an exchange," Tatyana said. "That's the point. He took my blood to control me. I never took his."

The corner of Kato's mouth inched up. "Ironically, he's probably feeling the loss quite keenly. Your amnis will take years to leave his blood, but his amnis never touched your system. If it had, it would have been much harder for you to leave."

Tatyana blinked. "What?"

"That's why I would never take the blood of a vampire now without asking for their own bite in return," Kato said. "It was wise of you to keep your distance, Tatyana. If you'd given him your fangs, it would have been much harder for you to leave."

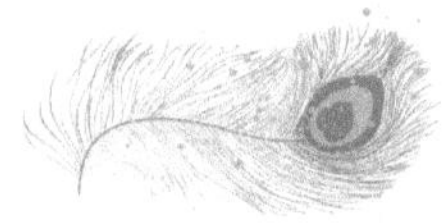

If you'd given him your fangs, it would have been much harder for you to leave.

THE WORDS KEPT BOUNCING AROUND HER MIND AS SHE WALKED back to her rooms in the compound after leaving Kato.

If you'd given him your fangs...

Tatyana unlocked the door to her windowless room and locked it behind her. The scent of Oleg filled her senses.

Damn that vampire. He was everywhere. Absolutely everywhere.

She walked to the coat hanging in the closet, the one she'd worn two nights before in Gori, the night that she'd seen him again, and somehow he'd embedded his scent in her clothes, on her skin, and even done something to her mind that made her dreams about him even more vivid.

She couldn't join the Poshani kamvasa fast enough. Now that she'd told Kato, she was itching to leave.

Tatyana had put the call in to the number Sibella had given her, requested passage, and had been quoted a price, but she hadn't heard anything that confirmed her place with the Poshani safe house. Would Saba's court end up being her only option?

Either way, she knew her days in Arosh's court were numbered.

She opened her closet and hung up the thick robe she'd donned when she left Kato's quarters. She glared at her coat she'd worn in Gori the night Oleg found her. It smelled like warm cedar and frankincense and a little bit of leather. She hadn't touched it since she returned, but every time she opened her closet, it was like Oleg burst out and kissed her.

Fuck.

Maybe she should put that damn coat out of its misery and burn it, but her mother had given her the warm wool garment when she'd moved away for university, and she loved it even though it was a little too big.

It was just her luck that she'd been turned at a point in her life when she was underweight from stress. She would now be bony for eternity.

Tatyana dressed in a court-appropriate pair of pants and a warm wool tunic that Kato had given her in his signature blue color. She would fill the rest of her night sitting in Arosh's court and listening to him as Kato's pupil.

Maybe that would feed the Fire King's ego enough to leave her alone until the Poshani decided to return her call.

At the back of her mind, she worried that they would not return her call at all. Sibella had warned her that not all who applied for passage in the kamvasa were granted a place, and Kato had warned her that the Poshani were aligned with Oleg, though they remained an independent clan.

Would Oleg sabotage her place in the vampire safe house? The longer she went without a message from the strange vampire clan, the more worried she became.

Someone rapped on her door. "Tatyana Vorona," a voice called. "The Fire King requests your presence in the throne room."

Damn.

This could not be good.

"Your actions put our entire race at risk," Arosh said. "There was video taken and posted on your computers and on the human television channels."

It had taken a few nights, but apparently the news of Oleg and Samson's fight had made it to Arosh's ears.

Fantastic.

Samson stood with a blank face on Arosh's right side, staring at the ground.

Tatyana stood in the middle of the audience chamber with Kato standing beside her. She said nothing. Correcting Arosh's understanding of the internet and social media seemed like a poor use of words when he was this angry.

She kept her voice soft and placating. "My lord Arosh—"

"Don't you think your anger would be better directed at the Varangian?" Kato interrupted her, glancing to his right where the oily representatives from the Georgian vampire queen were standing. "Granted, Samson might have overreacted to Oleg's intrusion, but he's not the one who started a forest fire. Wouldn't it be more appropriate for Alina to speak to Oleg about this?"

The two Georgian vampires whispered to each other, and Arosh glared at Kato.

"Brother, your student has caused her last problem in my court. She will leave, or she will be confined to your quarters."

"I understand," Kato said. "She is already in the process of moving, but if you desire that she live with me until she's ready to leave, I have no objection."

"The Varangian's interest in her is causing problems."

Tatyana couldn't take it anymore. She blurted, "This is bullshit!"

"Tatyana." Kato put a hand on her shoulder. "Not right now."

Arosh looked amused. "Oh no. Let her continue, brother."

"It is complete *bullshit*." She enunciated carefully in Farsi so there would be no mistaking her meaning. "It's not my fault that Oleg keeps tracking me. And it's definitely not Samson's fault. He was protecting me from two vampires who were not even supposed to be in Alina's territory." She looked at the two reps from Alina's court. "I don't understand why you are here. Go talk to Oleg if you want to know why he started a fire in Gori."

"You are his bookkeeper," one of them said quietly. "Everyone knows this. You should return to him."

"I'm not his anything." Kato's hand tightened on her shoulder, but she ignored it. "My sire is dead. I am under no aegis. I am Kato's student, and that is all I am."

That was all.

Because Kato had no empire. He had no territory. He had no aegis to offer her.

Tatyana felt the hollow in her chest. Even though her teacher stood behind her, a pillar of strength, she was still alone. Utterly and completely alone. She had no people. No sire.

She had no one.

Tears threatened her eyes, but she refused to cry.

She met Arosh's eyes. "I will be gone in one week."

One week fit the timeline Grimace had given her for getting a hidden computer to her. She still hadn't heard from the Poshani, so maybe that wasn't going to happen after all.

But one week gave her enough time to get her equipment, get her things together, and find a new place to hide. She wasn't a newborn anymore. She could be around humans.

Her year in Arosh's court hadn't been wasted. She would learn how to hide.

"I will take you at your word, Tatyana Vorona." Arosh looked at the Georgian vampires from Alina's court. "Kato's student is correct. If Alina has more complaints, let her take it up with the Varangian who attacked my son. As far as I am concerned, this matter is settled."

Kato whispered, "Tatyana, return to your room now."

She spun around and marched out of Arosh's audience chamber, feeling every vampire eye on her as she walked.

Alone, alone, alone. She was utterly alone.

She had a mother to protect, and she was utterly alone.

She felt a shivery sensation crawling over her skin, and she had the urge to run.

Run, run, run.

I'm still going to take care of your mother. She's in my territory.

For once, Oleg's promise didn't make her angry; Tatyana was relieved. She was pissing off vampires left and right, but at least Anna and the farm would be safe.

She trusted Oleg would keep his word because he was old-fashioned and, for some reason, her mother amused him.

At least there was that.

She made it back to her room without running into anyone who tried to talk with her, and nearly as soon as she locked the chamber door behind her, the phone on her desk started to buzz.

She looked at the screen, but the number wasn't familiar. Nevertheless, she touched the green icon to answer it. "Hello?"

"Tatyana Vorona?" a strange voice said in Russian. The accent wasn't familiar.

"Who is this?"

There was a low murmur in the background of the call.

"The Poshani approve of your caution. You have requested passage in the kamvasa."

Tatyana's heart leaped in her chest. Relief!

But her head was still in charge, and she no longer trusted anyone. "You have not answered my question. Who is this?"

More murmuring in the background. "You are speaking to a Hazar of the kamvasa. You are speaking to Sibella's uncle."

Tatyana let out a breath. "Okay." This wasn't a trick. "Yes, I have requested passage in the kamvasa."

"And you agree to our price?"

"Yes." The price quoted over the phone was a small fortune, but Sibella had warned her about that. "I agree to your price for a full season of shelter."

"Pack your things. Two suitcases only. No electronics or tracking devices. We will text you a bank account number tonight. On receipt of payment, a location will be sent to you. In two nights, you will be there."

Two nights? No! Her computer from Grimace wouldn't be ready. She shook her head. "I need more time."

"You do not have more time. If you no longer want passage—"

"Wait."

She'd have to manage. It was six months.

Six months. She'd be able to call her mother, but she'd be cut off from everything else.

For six months.

Tatyana felt like she was stumbling around in the dark, but she was out of options unless she wanted to return to Oleg's territory.

And they were promising her six months of safety.

"I'll be there," she said. "Text me the location and I'll be there."

"Very well," the voice said. "Welcome to the protection of the Poshani, Tatyana Vorona. We will meet you in two nights."

Chapter 11

Oleg

"You're fidgeting." Mika paged through another book of poetry on the plane. "You cannot be nervous about meeting this driver."

Oleg was flying to Moscow to meet the injured human driver from Polina's territory who had moved from the hospital to rehab. "I'm not nervous." He enjoyed meeting his humans. "I have simply been away from the citadel too long."

"Your castle isn't going anywhere."

It wasn't the castle that called him, it was solitude. It was space. It was physical activity. He'd been surrounded by vampires and humans and corporate constraints for too long. If he didn't get some time to himself in the mountains, he would end up murdering Mika.

He might do that anyway if the man continued sipping his blood-wine like that.

Slurp.

Had Mika always drunk wine so loudly?

Slurp.

Oleg curled his lip, growled low in his chest, and Mika looked up. The vampire blinked, then frowned when he saw Oleg's fangs.

"You don't need your castle—you need to fuck someone." Mika shook his head. "Forget about the Vorona woman and find a willing woman in Moscow." He pulled out a small black book from his pocket. "Do you want me to call one of your ex-girlfriends? There are two living in Moscow right now that—"

"Enough," Oleg snarled. "Fuck you."

"No, seriously, fuck *you*." Mika sighed. "You're going to end up murdering Ivan if you don't work out some of this tension."

Murdering Ivan sounded delightful. Oleg closed his eyes and imagined how he would kill his most despised brother.

Beheading with an axe was classic but somehow not enough.

He could rip Ivan's head from his body. He could dig his fingers into Ivan's neck and send his fire into his brother's puny brain.

He could tell Mika to leach the water from Ivan's system, then use Ivan's desiccated body as the center of a bonfire.

"You're actually imagining how you're going to kill Ivan right now, aren't you?"

"Why the fuck are we going into his territory?" Oleg muttered. "We could fly this driver to Sochi for a holiday."

"We're going" —Mika leaned forward— "because it is not Ivan's territory, it is *yours*."

Right. Moscow was his even though he disliked the city.

"You've allowed Ivan too much independence. When people hear the Sokolov name now, what do they think of?" Mika asked. "Weapons dealing? Drugs and alcohol?"

"And your point is?" Oleg didn't care what his reputation was as long as it kept his people safe. In fact, the worse his reputation was, the more enemies would keep away.

"When they hear Sokholov, they think of Ivan." Mika rolled his eyes. "Of all the Ivans."

Oleg's older brother had the irritating habit of siring children and naming them Ivan too. There had to be at least a dozen immortal Ivan Sokholovs living and working around the world, and the original Ivan thought it was hilarious.

"You will rein him in," Mika said, "or the druzhina will be forced to do something whether you like it or not."

Oleg cut his eyes to his chief boyar, but Mika didn't look away.

Outsiders often misunderstood the structure of his empire. Oleg was the head of the clan and the knyaz, but that didn't mean he ruled without consequences.

The druzhina would remove him and put another in his place if they had to.

"You wouldn't," Oleg said. "Because no one wants this fucking job but me."

And these days, he wasn't feeling very sure about that. When being head of the clan meant killing Truvor and bringing rogue vampires under control, conquering territory, and bringing order out of chaos, he had reveled in it.

These days being the knyaz of the Kievan Rus meant office buildings, computer files, board meetings, and paperwork.

And flying to Moscow to shake hands with humans under his aegis.

"I was not built for meetings," Oleg said slowly. "I was not made for looking through paperwork and files. What is this bullshit you have me doing, Mika? I'm sitting in Odesa when I could be—"

"Cruising down Central Europe in a longboat, pillaging at night and burning enemy soldiers?"

Oleg bared his fangs. "Maybe."

Mika stared at him and took another drink of blood-wine. "In this era, you pillage far more when you hire a good tax accountant."

Oleg let out a growl that rumbled in his chest and slammed the goblet of blood-wine from Mika's hand. "You drink too loudly."

Mika looked at the spilled blood leaching into the carpets in their compartment. "You're giving Cesar a raise."

"Fine," Oleg snarled. "He's probably overdue for one anyway."

"Find the Vorona woman and fuck her," Mika said. "Or find *someone*. You're becoming unbearable to live with."

A ding sounded over the communication system.

"We are starting our descent into Moscow," the pilot said. "Please ready the plane for landing."

Oleg clasped the man's rough hand in his own, making sure to warm his skin before the contact. "It's good to see you doing so well. I know you're recovering faster with your family here."

The driver named Goretski had tears in his eyes. "I could never have afforded this care without you, Mr. Sokolov."

They were meeting in the spacious living room of an apartment near the rehabilitation center where Goretski was learning how to walk again. According to the doctors Oleg had met at nightfall, the man would regain most of his physical abilities, but his peripheral vision had been permanently damaged. That night he sat in an easy chair near the fire, but Oleg could see the walker nearby.

Polina was already arranging alternate employment for the man in their organization since he'd no longer be able to be a commercial driver.

"It's not even a question." He glanced at Goretski's pleasantly round wife. "I am honored you made the time to see me and introduce me to your family."

"Of course, Mr. Sokolov." Goretski and his family only knew Oleg as the CEO of the company, not as a vampire. Luckily, Oleg had perfected the art of blending in centuries before.

The Goretski family consisted of this middle-aged driver, his wife, and two teenagers who stared at Oleg with wide eyes. The boy was scrawny and still growing. The girl still had round cheeks, but she would be a beauty when she grew into her dramatic features.

Oleg turned to Mrs. Goretski. "I understand that the children have had school tutors while your husband is recovering."

"They have," the woman said. "And my office gave me a leave of absence to be here."

"I'm glad. If you have any problems with them, please let us know."

Goretski's wife was a civil servant in Minsk, and Polina's people had more than a few connections in the government.

"I hope the tutors have been adequate. I know the children are probably missing their friends." He glanced at the two teens. "Education is most important, and we don't want yours to suffer because of this horrible accident."

"They've had a wonderful time here in the city," Mrs. Goretski said. "And Anna is taking drawing lessons while she's here."

"Anna." Oleg smiled. "My dear friend's mother is named Anna. What a beautiful name for a young artist. I hope I am able to see your drawings someday."

Her voice was barely over a whisper. "Thank you, Mr. Sokolov."

"I'm taking martial arts," the boy said. He puffed up his chest when he spoke.

Oleg lifted his chin in respect for the young man's boldness. "An excellent idea. I hope you'll be able to continue that discipline when you return home."

The boy's cheeks were a little red, but he nodded. "My teacher said there's a studio in Minsk where I can keep practicing."

"Excellent."

"Oleg!"

He heard his name called and carefully plastered on a smile before he turned to face his brother. "Ivan."

"I see you've met this wonderful family." Ivan blustered into the room, wearing a navy-blue suit and a blood-red tie. "Families like this, they are the backbone of our company, are they not?"

"They are."

"With two fine children, yes? A beauty for a daughter and a son who already has that tough mindset, eh?"

Ivan ruffled the boy's hair, and the teen beamed from the attention.

His brother had always been a flatterer, and Oleg could see that Ivan's compliments had the intended effect on both Mr. and Mrs. Goretski. They held hands, both beaming with pride.

"I'm relieved that we were able to keep the family together while Mr. Goretski recovered," Oleg said. "It was a generous move to bring them here."

"Ah, but I know the rehabilitation center here is world-class," Ivan said. "One of my own sons was treated here."

Was it after you beat him to a pulp yourself or did you set one of your vampire children on him?

Oleg didn't say it, but their own sire had made a habit of beating them ferociously or pitting his sons against each other for amusement, and Ivan had picked up that trait.

Even as knyaz, Oleg was reluctant to intervene in Ivan's internal affairs. After all, most of his sons came to him as lower-level human soldiers who'd worked their way up Ivan's criminal organization. If they wanted to sign up for Ivan's form of torture, that was their own business.

"We don't want to keep you longer." Oleg inclined his head toward Mr. Goretski. "I know it's very late, and your doctors said you needed rest. I'm glad we were able to meet tonight."

"Oleg, did you have time to discuss the matter we spoke about earlier?"

He had no idea what Ivan was talking about, but he didn't let on. "Of course."

"Peter and Gabriela, be well." Ivan pointed at the couple. "I'll see you tomorrow night, eh? You promised a cake for me."

"Of course, Mr. Sokolov." Mrs. Goretski smiled broadly. "I haven't forgotten."

"I hope not." Ivan patted the man on the shoulder before he walked toward Oleg, joining him as they strode from the room.

They were out the door and walking down the marble-clad stairwell before Ivan spoke again. "You've been spending a lot of time in Georgia."

"Have I?" His actions outside the territory were none of Ivan's business.

"These hijackings, they're mostly in Polina's and my territory. But if there are issues on the eastern border, you know that I can take the lead on these matters."

I'm sure that's what you want.

"It seems to me that Polina has the matter well in hand." Oleg kept his voice easy. "She's dealt with the group. The criminals who were attacking the trucks were eliminated." Oleg paused on the stairs and turned to Ivan. "Do you have reason to think there is a larger organization behind them?"

Ivan's eyes glittered. "If your daughter has killed them all, I would not worry. She is as brutal as her sire."

Oleg took the compliment even though it came from Ivan. "Thank you."

"I just know that sometimes it's easy to miss a snake in the grass."

Ivan and Oleg were nearly the same height, which meant that when Ivan threatened Oleg with a smile, he met his brother with merry eyes.

Oleg smiled back, showing a hint of his fangs. "I would never underestimate the ability of a clever snake to hide."

He started down the stairs again, and the hair on the back of his neck stood at attention as his amnis reacted to Ivan's badly veiled threats.

"Then again" —Oleg paused at the base of the stairs— "there are fewer and fewer clever snakes still lurking around Moscow, aren't there?" He glanced over his shoulder and just barely caught the look of disdain on Ivan's face. "You've killed anyone smarter than you."

Ivan was not particularly intelligent, but he carried a brutal, scheming ability to manipulate people, and he was adept at seeing weaknesses.

"I heard a rumor that Zara's clever bookkeeper is in the Fire King's court." Ivan swerved to a topic Oleg had not expected. "Odd that she would be there. Arosh has no modern business presence that would necessitate someone with her skills."

Oleg frowned, pretending to be confused. "Are you talking about Zara's youngest? The young woman who was working with Elene?"

Ivan's eyes narrowed, and his lips curved in a satisfied smile. "You know exactly who I'm talking about. Perhaps she is Alina's now. How did you let a little bit of a girl slip from your control?"

"Zara's daughter is always welcome in our territory, Ivan, but she is very young. I am not a captor for young vampires who want to roam."

Oleg could say more, but he knew when Ivan was trying to bait him. The worst thing he could do was reveal how much he was paying attention to Tatyana Vorona.

She would immediately become Ivan's target.

Ivan took another step toward Oleg. "So you're not trying to get her back?"

Oleg shrugged. "What is she to me? When she has finished her time in the Fire King's court, she will likely return home. Our kind tend to return to their roots, do they not?"

Ivan was certainly in touch with his roots.

Oleg was more and more convinced that leaving his brother alive after Truvor's death had been a mistake. If Truvor had an heir in brutality, it was Ivan.

"A pretty little thing and a computer genius too, from what I hear," Ivan said. "Perhaps she's the person you're looking for to take Elene's position."

"I'm sure she's very bright, but we need a human for the role." Oleg leaned into Ivan's turn of conversation. "So who are your candidates?"

Ivan frowned. "What?"

"The CFO role, of course."

Ivan was trying to bait him and provoke a reaction. The best way to counter his brother was to not react. Pretend to be focused on mundane business matters and treat Ivan like an afterthought.

It would drive the vampire crazy.

Oleg patted his older brother's shoulder. "Rudov and Juliya have already sent me names, but I haven't heard anything from you, and I know you have people who deserve consideration. I hope you're thinking carefully about it."

They stepped out of the building and into the spring streets of Moscow. The building they left was painted a bright yellow color, and it bordered a park where blossom-covered branches created an arch over the sidewalk.

"Oh, I am." Ivan sneered. "Filling corporate desks is my top priority."

"Good, good." Oleg smiled. "Leave policing the territories to Polina, brother. You're better suited to the city."

It was the absolute worst insult one could give to one of Truvor's sons.

Oleg spread his arms. "Such a beautiful spring we're having, yes?" He stepped toward the street where a black-windowed car had just pulled up to the curb. "I'll see you soon. Send me your candidates! I can't wait to see your top talent."

Oleg slipped into the black sedan, and the car pulled back into slow evening traffic as Ivan grew smaller in the rearview.

Mika held out a manila folder. "You were right. They were here."

Oleg nodded. "In Moscow?"

"They stayed on the outskirts, but there are records of Sami and Danior Novak staying in a hotel in Krasnogorsk two weeks before the first truck hijacking."

"Any evidence that they met with Ivan's people?"

"No, but that's not the worst part."

Oleg paged through the files, but his eyes only skimmed them. "What's worse than my own brother trying to undermine my shipping operation and beating my human employees nearly to death?"

"It's possible that Ivan didn't poach those soldiers from the Poshani. I called my little bird in Ivan's office. Vano le Krizenov had a meeting with Ivan at the same time that Sami Novak was staying here in Moscow."

Oleg's head shot up. "No."

Mika nodded.

"We need to get to the airport tonight," Oleg said. "How long is the flight to Bucharest?"

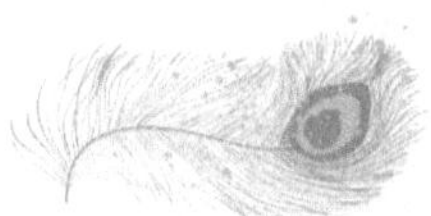

THEY LANDED IN BUCHAREST TWO HOURS PAST MIDNIGHT, AND Mika made another call to his connection in Radu's office as soon as they landed, but again there was no answer.

"Still nothing?" Oleg asked.

Mika shook his head. "It's just going to her voicemail."

"What are our options?"

"You really think this is some kind of emergency?"

"Vano is a Poshani terrin," Oleg said. "There are three supreme leaders of that clan, and he is one of them."

"And it's time for the kamvasa to start."

The roaming safe house meant the Poshani clan was about to start its big seasonal caravan, and most of their leadership would be out of communication with the outside world.

"Still," Mika said. "It's possible that his meetings with Ivan were for completely legitimate reasons—"

"It's possible." Oleg nodded, gripping the door in his hand. He heard the plastic crack, and he released it.

"Vano does handle most of the human-facing businesses," Mika said. "Radu and Kezia deal with internal matters, and Vano is the moneyman."

"Yes, but if it was a business matter, why didn't we know about it? Vano should be dealing with Polina or Juliya in Kyiv, not making calls to Ivan's personal secretary."

"Tank." Mika spoke to the driver. "You remember Radu's club?"

"Yes, boss."

"Take us there."

Oleg looked at Mika in the back of the black sedan.

Mika shrugged. "You wanted options, those are our options. If we can't get him on the phone, he's probably at that atrocious club."

Oleg turned to watch the darkened windows. "Radu told us that Sami Novak was Vano's man, but he implied that Vano and Sami had a falling-out. I don't think Radu was lying to me."

Mika nodded. "But Vano could have been lying to Radu."

"I don't trust Vano," Oleg said. "I never have, but he's only one of the terrin, and his power is checked by Radu and Kezia." Oleg felt a snarl working its way up his throat as the sedan stopped in traffic and his frustration peaked. "The Vashana Zata is being held at the end of the season, Mika. I'm supposed to go and witness it."

Mika kept his voice even. "If Vano is plotting with Ivan without telling his brother or his sister, the Poshani have a major problem."

"And if Vano is scheming with Ivan—and Radu and Kezia *do* know about it—then *we* have a problem." And hundreds and hundreds of secretive, skilled Poshani humans and vampires roaming freely through their territory.

The Poshani's traditional territory was not like other vampires. They had no single homeland, though their presence in Romania was significant. They crossed boundaries and maintained host relationships with numerous vampire rulers, who gladly worked with a clan of loyal and discreet humans and vampires who were skilled artisans and tradespeople.

In the previous century, Oleg had used Poshani contractors to build factories and compounds, trusted them with the plans to his personal offices and homes, and spent millions to hire their people.

They came to do a job, were paid generously, and then moved on.

Oleg had never worried that those secrets could be compromised because the Poshani valued trust and secrecy above all.

"What do you want to do?" Mika asked softly.

"I want to speak to Radu before I jump to conclusions."

"Understood."

Oleg wasn't willing to break an old alliance because of suspicion. More than likely, there was a perfectly legitimate explanation.

Traffic picked up again, heading toward downtown Bucharest and the flashing lights of the clubs and bars where humans wandered, hailing taxis or staring like zombies at their mobile devices.

They pulled up to the back entrance of Zarvă and immediately exited the vehicle. Oleg brushed away the polite greetings of the security guards as Mika introduced them.

Moments later, they were walking up the stairs to the sound-proofed vampire lounge that overlooked the dance floor.

Mika walked into the club before Oleg, scanning back and forth before he waved Oleg inside. "I don't see him."

Oleg's eyes narrowed on a familiar head of dark, curly hair. "I don't see Radu, but I do see his sister."

Kezia le Almásy, terrin of the Poshani and sister of Radu and Vano sat in the corner booth where Radu had met them weeks before, sipping on a glass of blood-wine and luring Oleg in with her eyes.

She was one of the singularly most seductive women Oleg had ever met, though they'd never been lovers. She bounced between human men and immortal women as powerful as she was, though Oleg had always suspected that her truest companions were entirely hidden from sight.

He walked across the club and couldn't stop the smile that tugged at the corner of his lips. He waited patiently as Kezia's sandy-haired bodyguard patted him down.

Mika wisely kept his distance.

"Kezia." Oleg greeted her with a nod. "You're even more stunning than I remember."

It was true. The Poshani leader's skin was pale, and her full lips were red. A crown of nearly black curls surrounded her face, high-lighting the delicate features that lured her prey.

"Oleg Sokolov." She smiled and motioned him closer. "So much power coming to visit me. Sit. You seem tense. Can I help you with that?"

"You don't want sex with me." He stretched his arm across the back of the booth and let a ripple of blue flame dance over the back of his hand. "I would burn you."

"Perhaps I would enjoy it." Kezia's kohl-lined eyes watched his hand. "You're looking for Radu."

"I am."

"He's already gone." She turned back to look at him and let her fingers dance in the air. "Off to the kamvasa, darling. There are guests to be greeted, and he's the most congenial."

"You're running late?"

She smiled coyly. "I like to make an entrance."

"So where is your roaming summer camp starting this year?"

"Wouldn't you like to know?" Kezia pulled out a slim cigar. "Do you mind?"

"It would be my pleasure." Oleg snapped his fingers and pulled a flame from the dry air, holding it out to Kezia so she could light her cigarette. "I need to get a message to your brother."

"I can carry a message for you, or you could buy passage in the kamvasa." The corner of her mouth turned up. "I think it's going to be a very interesting year."

"The Vashana Zata is this year, yes?"

"Radu said he invited you to the party."

"So if he trusts me enough to invite me—"

"Ah, ah." She wagged a finger at Oleg. "That location will be sent much later. Until then, you'll have to remain in the dark like everyone else."

"It's important." Oleg leaned forward. "I would not press the issue if it was not very, very important, Kezia."

She narrowed her eyes and blew a thin stream of smoke across the table. "Tell me what this is about," she said softly. "And I'll decide if it's important enough to bother Radu."

Chapter 12

Tatyana

Samson flew Tatyana to a squat parking garage in the Georgian city of Zugdidi two nights later. She carried only one large backpack with two changes of clothing, the coat her mother had given her, and nothing else.

Kato was sending her computer and the rest of her belongings to her mother at the farm. She had no idea when she would see any of it again. She'd messaged Grimace about the job she had to cancel, but she hadn't heard back.

She was heading into the wilderness with no computer. No mobile phone. Nothing.

Tatyana felt naked.

They landed in pitch-darkness, the cloudy sky overhead giving them cover in the middle of the night, and Samson's face was grim as he took the backpack from her and started walking down to the second level where the instructions had told her to meet her Poshani transport.

"Can you please be kind?" Tatyana said softly. "I had very limited options at this point."

Samson spun and pounded his chest before he signed angrily. *Me. You had me.*

"We both agreed that me staying with you because I was desperate for shelter was a bad idea."

Samson shook his head and started walking again.

"And when you're not pissed off at me for leaving, you're going to realize that I'm right." She ran to catch up with him. "Samson."

He flipped up his hand. *Shut up.*

"Fine," she muttered. "What an excellent parting this is. You act as if I'm dying when I'm basically going on vacation for six months."

He didn't sign a word.

Tatyana followed him down to the next level where he abruptly stopped and stared ahead.

There was a black transport van waiting at the end of the garage with three people standing by its side.

Tatyana felt her stomach drop. This was it.

Samson reached out and took her hand, folding her cold fingers between his own.

"Thank you," she whispered. "Kato and Alexander say the kamvasa has never lost a guest. In a thousand years, not once."

Samson nodded.

"So I'm safe with them."

He let go of her hand. *Did you pay them?*

"Of course."

Then you are safe, he signed. *Poshani hospitality laws are considered sacred.*

"Okay." She let out a shaky breath and took his hand again. "I won't know where I am, right?"

He shook his head.

"They said I'll have a tablet though. So I can video-call you. Check your messaging app. I'll try to call as soon as I can."

He nodded.

"I'm scared," she whispered. "My entire vampire life has felt like

I'm hopping from one knifepoint to another. I just want to find someplace to rest."

Samson stopped, turned, and set her backpack down so he could wrap her in a firm embrace. He pressed her head to his chest, and though his heart was silent against her ear, it was comforting anyway.

After a few moments, he pulled away and signed, *Let this be your rest. For six months, you will have nothing but time. No worries about your safety. No worries that Oleg will find you. No worries about my father being impatient. You will be safe in the kamvasa.*

Tatyana nodded.

Use these months to look in your heart. Powerful people join the kamvasa. You might even find a vampire you would like to work for. Use this time to make connections and breathe.

"I will."

And at the end of six months, if you want me to come and find you, I will. Samson rolled his eyes. *I can piss off my father and get away with it.*

"You are wise and kind," she whispered. "And I'm probably a fool for passing up the chance to be with you."

The corner of his mouth turned up. *You're in love with Oleg.*

"I'm really not. He's just in my head."

Samson shrugged. *Think about it.*

"I'll take your advice, but right now I better go to these people. They're going to think I'm stalling."

They work for you now. They can wait.

She took a deep breath.

Tatyana didn't need to breathe. She could sink herself to the bottom of a lake and stay there for days if she wanted to. But the act centered her.

She stood on her tiptoes and pressed a kiss to Samson's cheek. "I'm ready."

Then we go. He picked up her backpack again, took her hand, and tugged her arm to get her walking.

As they approached, Tatyana saw that the three figures were two women and one man. One of the women was human, but the others were vampires.

"Miss Vorona?" The vampire woman stepped forward. "It's very nice to meet you. I'm Carlotta, and this is David and Alissa."

"Hello." She glanced at Samson. "I only have one backpack. I don't have many clothes or... anything."

"That's fine," Carlotta said. "If you find that you need additional garments, there are seamstresses in the kamvasa." She held out her hand. "May I?"

Samson passed her the backpack, and Carlotta handed it over to Alissa.

"Forgive me, but Alissa must check the bag for electronic signals or trackers," Carlotta said. "This is for your safety and ours."

"Of course."

Much to Tatyana's surprise, the sensor that Alissa waved over her backpack started to alert.

"What?" She looked at Carlotta with wide eyes. "I didn't bring anything. I promise you."

"It's possible that someone placed a tracker in your luggage without your knowledge." The woman glanced at Samson.

"Samson wouldn't." Tatyana took his hand. "He's my friend."

Alissa smiled. "If you could open your bag please?"

Tatyana moved to the open back of the van and noticed a tan-colored box that looked much like a large coffin in the cargo area.

"That is your transport box," Alissa said. "To keep you secure until we reach the kamvasa. It locks from the inside, and we cannot access it once you lock it."

"Okay." It still looked like a coffin.

She looked over her shoulder at Samson and hated that a tiny part of her suspected Arosh had convinced him to plant something in her bag.

Alissa waved the sensor over her carefully rolled-up clothing, and the only thing that alerted was her old coat.

"What the…" Tatyana unrolled it and immediately searched the pockets, her hands finding the problem immediately.

She pulled out what looked like a burner phone in a hard plastic case.

"The last time I wore this was that night in Gori." She pursed her lips and turned to Samson. "This is Oleg. He must have put it in my coat and I didn't notice." She turned to Carlotta. "I used to work for Oleg Sokolov. You should know he's been trying to get me back. This…" She held up the phone. "This was probably his attempt to track me without me knowing it."

Carlotta held out her hand, and Tatyana put the phone in her palm. The vampire smiled as she closed her hand around the small phone. "Not even the knyaz of the Kievan Rus can find you once you enter the kamvasa," Carlotta said. "I'll take care of this."

She handed the phone to Alissa, who put it in a grey bag with a metallic coating, and then she turned back to Tatyana. "Are you ready?"

Tatyana looked at Samson, who nodded. *Go,* he signed. *Call me when you're settled.*

"Yes." Tatyana smiled. "I'm ready."

Tatyana woke in darkness and silence with a burn at the back of her throat.

The air smelled of moss and pine, but she saw nothing. She reached out and patted the side of her transport box, eventually finding the small keypad that was embedded in the side.

She quickly punched in the code she'd entered the night before, sighing with relief when the lock beeped and the lid of the box popped up and slid to the side.

Tatyana sat up and saw a faint light glowing somewhere like

dawn peeking through curtains. The soft yellow light grew in strength, and within a minute, her surroundings became visible.

There were no windows, only a small, glowing lamp that simulated the dawn.

The transport box had been placed on a bed in a luxurious travel trailer that was bigger than her first student apartment in Kyiv.

The wide bed was on an elevated platform, and two sliding doors had been opened while she slept.

Down a short set of stairs there was a sitting area with a table, a leather couch, and a wall of books that was secured behind clear cabinets.

There was a chess set positioned on a built-in desk, and a silver carafe sat on the table with a crystal goblet next to it. There was also a beautiful arrangement of fresh wildflowers spilling over a ceramic bowl.

Past the small library, there was a large rack along one wall, filled with what Tatyana was guessing were bottles of blood-wine.

Beyond the living area, there was a small kitchenette, but it took up hardly any space in the trailer. Past that, another set of French doors that had been cracked open. She could see a tub and shower beyond.

There were no windows and only one door, though she could see a skylight over the kitchen with a sliding cover that could probably be used by wind vampires.

The floor was wooden, adorned with thick Persian rugs, and the caravan smelled like leather, wood oil, and lemon.

The scent reminded her of home.

Tatyana let out a small burst of laughter. If the Poshani had been trying to make her feel at home, there was nothing like that combination of scents, which reminded her of her grandparents' farmhouse in Crimea.

She climbed out of the fiberglass box, which took up a good portion of the bed. "Where am I supposed to put it?" she muttered.

Perhaps her hosts would come and take the transport box away now that she was... wherever she was.

It was an odd sensation, not having any idea at all where she was in the world. Had she traveled out of Russia? Was she in Romania? Poland? Austria? Tatyana could be traveling in a place she'd never been before, and she would have no idea at all.

She was wearing the same clothes she'd been in the night before, which was reassuring. There were no unfamiliar scents on her skin. She walked down the stairs and toward the table with the carafe. She suspected there was fresh blood inside, and when she cracked the lid, she smelled it.

Her fangs grew long in her mouth, and she quickly poured the blood into the goblet, drinking it down to quench the burning sensation at the back of her throat.

Once her hunger was sated, she noticed an envelope tucked under the bowl of wildflowers.

She opened the envelope and slid out the letter inside.

Dear Miss Vorona,

Welcome to the kamvasa and the hospitality of the Poshani people. The darigan are our human staff who guard and take care of your caravan during daylight hours. The Hazar guards will protect the caravan during the night.

Your guards will protect both you and your home with their own lives, so be assured that you are entirely safe during your respite here.

Welcome to your home for the next six months. Your privacy and comfort are our top priorities. When you are ready for more introductions, simply step out of your door.

May the blessings of the Kali be on you,
Clan Poshani

IT WAS A LOT TO TAKE IN, BUT TATYANA WAS IN NO MOOD TO throttle her curiosity. She was dying to go outside. She walked to the door and turned the key.

The door swung open, and Tatyana saw two steps leading down to an open meadow where long grass waved in the distance. Rolling hills covered by dense pine forests surrounded the meadow, and bright yellow flower heads nodded in the soft breeze.

At the sound of the opening door, a dark figure turned from looking over the meadow. The man wore a dark ruby jacket that tied at the waist and a pair of loose trousers. He smiled and spread his arms when he saw her.

"Welcome to the kamvasa, Tatyana Vorona. I am your host, Radu."

TATYANA AND RADU STROLLED THROUGH WHAT COULD ONLY BE described as a mobile town, complete with houses in the form of caravans both modern and traditional, mobile restaurants and taverns, and every kind of shop imaginable.

There were clothing shops like Carlotta had mentioned the night before. Leatherworkers selling purses, belts, and bridles. Wagons selling instruments and musical paraphernalia, along with pharmacies, medical wagons, and even what looked like a rolling library.

"The kamvasa will move at regular intervals throughout the season," Radu said. "Sometimes we'll be in a place for a week, sometimes only a few nights. It will all depend on the conditions on the ground, determined by the darigan."

"So the darigan run everything while we sleep?" Tatyana glanced at the humans passing them, noticing that none of them gave her a second look. They were clearly accustomed to vampires walking in their midst.

"Correct." Radu continued, "For everyone's safety, it is important that you do not attempt to ascertain your current location. This is for your protection and our own."

"Of course."

"And in the top drawer of the desk in your caravan, you will find a vampire-compatible tablet connected to our virtual private network."

"So I can call my mother?"

Radu nodded. "Of course. You are not cut off from the world; you are simply protected from its dangers. You can make audio and video calls from a select number of secure messaging applications. The network cannot be traced."

"Thank you." It would have to suffice. Radu didn't mention the mobile phone that Oleg had planted in her coat, so she didn't bring it up.

"Do you have any questions about feeding?" Radu said. "Fresh blood will be delivered to your caravan every night, placed in the locked delivery box by the door, but there are human donors also available if you prefer a live donor. It is included in the cost of your stay."

"Thank you. I'll let you know if I need one." She'd need at least one live donor a week in addition to her nightly donated blood, but it seemed rude to bring it up while surrounded by so many humans.

Two shrieking children ran across the grassy lane, giggling as they passed her and Radu before they disappeared into the trees.

"What a wonderful way to grow up," Tatyana said. "So free."

"They are out late tonight because it is a Friday and there is no school tomorrow." He smiled. "Otherwise, the little ones are usually in bed at this hour."

In addition to the shops and taverns, there were mobile schools that were closed up tight, obviously intended for the many children she saw everywhere through the camp.

Tatyana smiled. "It's nice to be around children again."

"Our young ones are our treasures, Miss Vorona. The future of our clan."

"Please call me Tatyana. I'm still young myself. I've missed being around... normal people."

She'd grown up in a neighborhood where many generations lived together. Living in Oleg's hotel, his compound in Sochi, and then residing in Arosh's court meant she hadn't lived among the friendly chaos of humanity in years.

Radu smiled. "We do extensive security checks on all of our guests, so I am sure this is an unnecessary warning, but I must tell you that any crime or offense against our human family will lead to your immediate death."

"Right." Tatyana nodded, trying to hide her reaction. That was... direct.

Of course, any vampire hiding from the world could be the hunter as easily as the hunted.

"No offense intended, of course."

"None taken." Tatyana was quick to assure him. "I understand your caution, especially with so many families around."

"Every Poshani family wants to join the kamvasa," he said. "It is the center of our clan life. Of course, not every family can make it every year. Work, school. The outside world often intrudes."

"That makes sense." It still seemed like a lot of people surrounding her, and most of them were human. Far more humans than vampires.

And all of them greeted Radu. He could easily be mistaken for being a gregarious favorite uncle save for the lethal air of power he carried.

"Do you have any questions? I should tell you, if you feel uncertain about the protection of the darigan during the day—which is unnecessary but understandable if you are new to our clan—there is a secure day chamber built into the bottom of your caravan."

"I didn't see it."

"That is intentional, of course." He smiled. "But I can show you how to access it. Like your transport box, it can only be opened from the inside."

"Is someone taking the transport box from my trailer?" She pointed over her shoulder. "It's quite large."

"No one will enter your trailer without your permission, not during the day or the night," Radu said. "But simply push the bell in your kitchen area and the darigan will come to remove it. You can also call for housekeeping if you would like cleaning."

"Thank you."

As they walked, Tatyana saw there were vampires and humans gathered in open-air taverns and restaurants around the meadow. Soft music filtered through the air from a group of musicians playing traditional music on guitars and violins.

"Is that Poshani music?" she asked.

"It is." Radu smiled. "Do you know anything about our history?"

"I tried to do some research online, but there's almost nothing."

"We prefer privacy," Radu said. "Our culture is very ancient with roots in Asia, but we have traveled across the centuries into Eastern Europe. The father of our clan was turned into a wind vampire many centuries ago, and he put in place our current way of life."

"Humans and vampires living together?"

"There is no immortal hierarchy here," Radu said. "If anything, our immortal family members exist to serve our human sisters and brothers. We protect them, and they protect us."

"But you're one of the... rulers, correct?"

"Elected by the people," Radu was quick to add. "I serve with two others, my brother and my sister. All decisions are for the good of the people." He spread his arms. "And we live in peace and prosperity."

Tatyana heard in Radu's statements a generous spirit but also the privilege of the powerful. She hoped the human members of the Poshani felt as important as Radu seemed to make them, but when she looked around, it seemed to her that all the people playing instruments, serving drinks, or running shops were human.

Vampires, on the other hand, were sitting and being served or speaking in hushed tones with other vampires and humans.

Interesting.

"If I wanted to learn the Poshani language," Tatyana asked, "is there a class?"

Radu's eyes lit up. "You honor our people with your interest."

"I'm here for six months," Tatyana said. "I don't have a job. How else could I keep busy except by learning something new?" She was already eying the intricately embroidered caps and knitted shawls she saw on some of the women.

"I will think on this," Radu said. "I might know of a tutor who could help you."

When Tatyana was young, her grandmother had tried to teach her things like knitting and embroidery, but with schoolwork and taking care of her mother, she'd never had time. Now, with months stretching before her and no computer to distract her, perhaps it was time to learn such things.

She was away from vampire politics and intrigue. She was in a place where her every need was seen to, and she could rest. Perhaps it was time to see what kind of life she could build when she wasn't embroiled in immortal intrigue or in fear for her life.

She was going to take Samson's advice. She was going to rest her mind and breathe.

"Ah!" Radu saw something in the distance. "I see my sister at the tavern. Come and I will introduce you to Kezia. She has only just arrived from Bucharest."

Chapter 13

Oleg

Oleg sat in front of the pale computer programmer, keeping his gaze steady on the man even as the human perspired.

The thin man was shockingly pale for someone who was physically able to access sunlight. From the smell of his body, he ate too many fried foods.

They were sitting in a conference room, and Mika had sent this man to him to explain why Tatyana's phone was no longer working.

Apparently his yelling at Mika wasn't getting results, so his chief boyar threw a human computer programmer at him, probably guessing that Oleg would be more polite to loyal human staff than he would be to his old friend.

Mika was correct, but this sweaty man *was* testing Oleg's patience.

Oleg frowned. "Are we working you too many hours?"

The man blinked, clearly surprised by the turn of conversation. "Wh-what? No, Mr. Sokolov. Not at all."

"What did Elene put in place two years ago? Something to do with health?"

The man frowned. "The employee wellness program?"

"Yes, that." Oleg flicked his fingers. "Do you have need of it? Do you have need of a doctor?"

The young man shook his head. "I don't think so?" His face grew even paler. "Do I have cancer?"

"Why would I know this?" Oleg asked. "I am not a physician."

"Did you... did you smell something? Vampires can smell cancer, can't they?"

"Do I look like a beagle?"

His eyes went wide. "No, sir."

Did beagles smell cancer? No, they were the dogs that sniffed for food at the airport.

Humans were so strange and limited.

"I did smell something," Oleg said.

The man's eyes grew glassy. "I knew it. What will I tell my mother?"

"I smelled your sweat. You smell like fried potatoes and plastic."

The young man's face froze. There was a flash of relief and then an abashed expression as his cheeks grew red. "Oh."

"Of course, you might have cancer, but I'm only smelling the fried potatoes." Oleg picked up a cup of black coffee that his secretary brought for him. "You should go to the doctor," he said. "Maybe go for more walks. Get a dog. Leave the house."

"Yes, Mr. Sokolov," the man whispered. "I will take better care of my health. I promise."

"You are capable of being in the sun," Oleg said. "This is a privilege that only humans have. Do not waste it. What is your name?"

"Grisha... Grigori, Mr. Sokolov."

"A good, strong name," Oleg said. "So you should take care of your health, Grigori. Enjoy the outdoors more."

"Yes, sir." He pointed at his computer. "Mr. Arakis said you wanted me to explain something to you?"

"Yes, but I want you to remember that I was concerned about your health," Oleg said. "Because the Sokolov group believes in... human-employee wellness."

Grisha nodded. "I've been thinking about going to the gym."

"Is the gymnasium indoors?"

"Yes."

"Then don't go there." Oleg waved a hand over his face and frowned. "You're as pale as a vampire. That is not good."

"This conversation is not going the way that I thought it would," Grisha muttered.

"No, because I was distracted by your smell of plastic and fried potatoes." Oleg folded his hands on the table. "I gave someone a phone to track where she was, and my personal secretary who oversees these things says she can no longer see the location."

It had been in Arosh's fortress for several nights, then it was in a parking garage, then it had simply disappeared.

"Oh." Grisha opened his laptop and began typing. "Have you tried calling it?"

"No."

"Okay." The human frowned before his eyes went wide. "Does this person *know* she has the phone?"

"I expect yes. By now she would."

"But she hasn't called you."

"No."

"Does she have your phone number?" He frowned. "Do you *have* a phone number?"

"I do." Oleg pulled the slim electronic device from his pocket. It was the first phone he'd ever had, and there was only one number programmed in. The device was in a thick plastic case, and he handed it to his secretary every morning to take care of it while he slept. "I programmed that number into the phone."

"But you haven't called her?"

"No." It was up to Tatyana to call him. He wasn't going to chase her anymore.

Well, he was, but he wanted to give her the feeling that she was reaching out to him, not being tracked. "Is there a way to discover where the phone is right now?"

Grisha folded his hands and leaned forward. "So if the phone's battery has died, we cannot find it."

"Why not?"

"You gave her a phone," Grisha said. "Not a chip or a tracker of some kind? Like... a tag?"

Oleg scowled. "She is also not a beagle."

The human lifted both hands. "Of course not, but the most likely thing that happened is that she didn't know she had the phone, so the battery died. And once the battery dies, a phone is essentially dead."

"I see." Oleg hadn't thought about batteries. He turned over the black plastic thing in his hand. His phone was always charged. He'd assumed they were self-powering. "Interesting."

"But if she turns the phone on, I can track it," Grisha said. "If you give me the number, I can put an alert on it so if the phone is turned on and pings a tower, I can triangulate it and find a location. If that happens, I can let you know. Or your secretary."

Very little of that made sense to Oleg, but he nodded anyway. Mika said the young man was one of their most competent computer employees.

"Yes," Oleg snapped at him. "Do that."

"Of course." Grisha started typing again. "Tell me the number please?"

Oleg rattled it off, then pushed back from the table. "Good. You must send a message to Mika or my secretary when you find it."

"*If.*" The man sounded a little panicked. "If I find it. If she doesn't charge the phone—"

"Yes, yes." Oleg waved a hand as he stood. "She will charge it."

His little wolf would be too curious where the phone came from. Or she would know where the phone came from and she would want to berate him for being pushy or overbearing or something like that.

Mika walked into the room just as Oleg was standing up. "Are you finished?"

"Yes, my young friend is going to track Tatyana's phone and tell me when it turns on again."

"If she hasn't thrown it away or shorted it out," Mika said.

"She won't do that." Oleg lifted his chin. "What do you want?"

"We encountered someone who may have information about the matter in Minsk."

"Excellent." Oleg turned to look at Grisha. "Keep me updated. And please go outside."

"Y-yes, Mr. Sokolov."

Mika kept his voice low. "I have news from Polina."

They walked through the offices of SMO International where humans tapped on computers and spoke into headsets in a myriad of languages, ushering the flow of goods around world shipping lanes.

"And what has my daughter found?"

He'd told Polina that Ivan might be working with Vano and his clan. The head of the Eastern Poshani had his headquarters near the border of Polina's territory, so it made the most sense for her to follow up the lead.

"Polina has found a ghost," Mika said quietly.

Oleg stopped in the middle of the hallway, nearly knocking over a short secretary who was carrying two cups of coffee.

"Who?" he growled.

The wide-eyed secretary scuttled off.

Mika waited for the hallway to clear. "Danior Kosinski is not dead."

"That's one of Sami Novak's frequent roommates, correct?"

"Yes."

So this was another vampire who had attacked his people.

"It would be more correct to say that Danior is not dead *yet*." Oleg thought about Mr. Goretski using a walker at the age of forty-two.

"Her people stopped a truck at the Polish border trying to cross into Belarus with a load of stolen liquor," Mika said. "One of her men recognized the name and the face from a briefing a few weeks ago. She's holding the humans the vampire had with him, but she sent Danior to the citadel."

"Excellent." An excellent excuse to go to his favorite home. "Call Cesar and get the plane ready."

Oleg was going home.

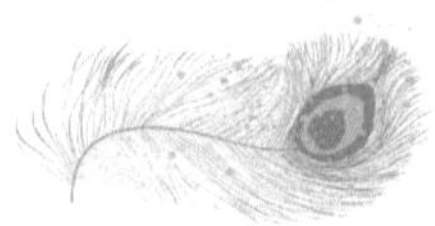

THE WIND VAMPIRE WAS BURIED IN ONE OF OLEG'S DUNGEONS, his neck broken and his body encased in the earth. Oleg sat in a chair on the other side of the dungeon and watched him.

"You risk the ire of the Poshani." Danior sneered. "When my people find out you have taken me—"

"Your people already think that you are dead." Oleg sipped a cup of black Ceylon tea flavored with orange peel. It was excellent. "I've already paid the blood price to Vano's people through Radu. You do work for Vano, correct?"

The man shut his mouth and stared at the wall.

Oleg set the cup on the round table his servants had brought into the dungeon and brushed a flaming hand over his chest.

He was shirtless, not because of the warm spring night but because occasionally letting his fire creep out and cover his body seemed to terrify the wind vampire currently buried up to his neck.

Mika was sitting backward on a chair and looking down at Danior. "You're in Vano's family, aren't you?"

Danior said nothing.

"We can keep you here for quite long like this," Mika said. "I've heard that the worst thing you can do to a Poshani vampire is contain them. It poisons your blood."

Danior was admirably silent, but his eyes flicked to Oleg as the fire vampire stood and walked over to the buried vampire.

Oleg crouched down and allowed the flames to ripple over his chest, covering his body like living armor. "You stole from me, hurt my people." He shrugged. "Sometimes business is business. But I have no patience for betrayal."

"How can I betray you?" Danior said. "You are nothing to me."

"Do the Poshani not roam through my territory?" Oleg said. "Do the laws of hospitality mean nothing to you? I am your *host*, Danior. Your kamvasa exists in my lands because of the safe passage I provide."

The vampire curled his lip. "The Poshani do not need your safety."

"Because Vano has made a deal with Ivan?"

There wasn't much. Just a flicker in the corner of Danior's eye. Nothing certain.

Oleg smiled. "Is that his little scheme? Ivan thinks he's the lord of his own territory to make agreements with Poshani terrin?"

Danior pursed his lips. "I know nothing of Truvor's clan."

Oleg's arm darted forward and his hand closed around Danior's neck, collaring the vampire with an iron grip.

As the vampire watched with wide eyes, the flames crept down from Oleg's shoulder, inching closer and closer.

"Stop," he whispered. "Stop."

"*My* clan." Oleg kept his voice mild even as his hand tightened. "Did you have something to say about my clan?"

"I misspoke," Danior choked out. "I only meant that you and Ivan—"

"You mean my governor?" Oleg said. "My inferior?"

"Yes." Bloody tears leaked from Danior's eyes. "Forgive my mistake, Lord Oleg."

Oleg pulled back his fire and released Danior's neck. Then he took a long breath and let it out slowly. "I feel as if you're still holding something back from me, Danior. This is disappointing."

"Perhaps he needs to stay in the citadel for a bit longer." Mika stared at the man like a snake watching a mouse.

"I think you are correct," Oleg said. "I'm sure he'll be able to dig himself out tomorrow night. There's no rush."

Danior's fangs jutted from his mouth, cutting the edge of his lip, but he remained silent.

"After all," Mika said, "Vano and the rest of the clan already think Danior is dead." He stood up from the chair. "You've paid the blood price to his clan."

"Which means that technically" —Oleg waited until Danior met his eyes— "your blood belongs to me."

OLEG STAYED IN HIS CHAMBERS THE FOLLOWING NIGHT, enjoying the solitude and the quiet. He was working on a new piece, a round table with a blue-eyed wolf in the middle of a dark forest. He set sapphires for the eyes and used milky-white glass pieces in grey and white for the fur.

Along the edge of the table, surrounding the forest, was a border of dancing fire.

"A bit obvious, don't you think?"

He turned and saw her rolling her eyes from where she lounged in an upholstered chair in the corner of his room. Her smart mouth was pursed in wry amusement, so he set down the tesserae in his palm and walked toward her.

"Do you like interrupting my work?" He spread her legs and knelt between them, running his hands up the soft flesh of her outer thighs.

She was wearing a floating blue dress that reminded him of a ballet costume. It glittered in the low light of his day chamber, the soft lamplight picking up the silver threads woven through the fabric.

The softness of her dress contrasted with the sharpness of her tongue. "Is it even possible to distract the great artist when he is at work?"

"Yes." He leaned closer, nipping at her chin before he captured her mouth. "You distract me. You won't leave me alone."

She lifted her chin. "Says the man who would have me under his thumb."

"I don't want you under my thumb." He pulled her hips closer, pressing his erection into the soft juncture of her thighs. "But I do want you under me."

"If you had me every night, Oleg Sokolov" —she lifted a hand and threaded her fingers through his hair— "you'd quickly tire of me."

He heated his lips and trailed them along her jaw. "I could never be tired of you."

"Liar."

"Can you read my mind now?"

"Maybe."

He pulled back and stared at her. "I wanted to see you in sunlight with the light in your hair."

Her blue eyes met his. "That can never happen now."

"If it was possible, I would build you a world where the day belonged to you."

"Not even you are that powerful."

"I would lay waste to an army for you. Conquer an empire."

"Do you think that would impress me?"

"I don't know what would impress you." He frowned. "I really do not."

She pressed her hand over his chest, where his heart used to beat. "I don't want the things you care to give me."

"So what do you want?"

"What do I want?" She slid her hand up and stroked the back of his neck. "What do I want?"

"I want to know."

"I cannot tell you." She pulled him closer and pressed her lips against his in a kiss that tasted of a spring morning and smelled of night-blooming jasmine.

Oleg slid his arms around her waist, intoxicated by the delicate kiss.

It was a taste of tenderness when he wanted to gorge himself on her. He wanted to sink his teeth into her flesh. Wanted her fangs to bruise him.

But instead, she teased him with tenderness.

"Oleg," she whispered.

"Yes."

"Oleg."

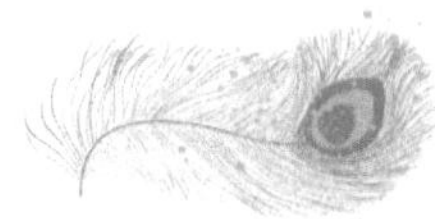

"OLEG!"

His eyes flew open at the sound of the banging on his door.

He had been dreaming. Oleg couldn't remember the last time he'd dreamed. He could still feel the infuriating delicacy of her kiss.

Throwing his legs over the side of his bed, he walked to the thick oak door that blocked his day chamber from the rest of the castle, pulling on a pair of pants and trying to ignore the raging erection his dream had provoked.

"What do you want?" He threw open the door to see Mika on the other side.

His boyar frowned. "Were you still sleeping?"

"No."

Mika opened his mouth, then closed it. "Grisha has a hit on the phone."

"She turned it on?"

"Apparently." Mika cocked his head. "But the location appears to be in Sweden."

"Sweden?"

Mika shrugged. "Grisha thinks it's a false trail. She must have figured out a way to hide the location."

"Of course she would." His little wolf was a genius with her electronic toys. "Where is my phone?"

Mika held out the black device in the rubber case. "Don't break this one too."

"Go." Oleg took the phone and slammed the door shut. Then he threw a blanket over his shoulders and sat in the chair where he'd been dreaming about Tatyana.

Using the stylus attached to the case, he touched the button with Tatyana's name, then tapped the icon to make the speaker work.

He waited to hear her sweet, sarcastic voice.

"This has gone on long enough," he muttered. "Tatyana, you need to come home." He mentally rehearsed what he would say.

Her mother missed her.

She was needed at the company.

He needed her.

No. That sounded desperate.

"Hello?"

Oleg jumped to his feet when a man's voice answered the phone. "Who is this?"

"Who is *this*?"

"Look at the phone and you know who this is," he snarled. "Where is Tatyana?"

There was a pause, then a hesitation. Then a low, familiar laugh.

"She's safe, old friend. Very, very safe."

The line went dead, and Oleg threw the phone against the stone wall of his day chamber before he let out an angry roar.

He knew that voice.

And he knew exactly where Tatyana had fled.

Chapter 14

Tatyana

A month into her protected tenure with the Poshani, Tatyana was starting to feel at home. In fact, she was so at home she was starting to feel bored.

She'd learned a decent amount of the Poshani language, met and mingled with the other vampire guests, and was starting to learn the guitar. Yet every night, she battled the urge to run a marathon, swing an axe, or punch something very hard. Embroidery and knitting were not a satisfying outlet for her energy.

Perhaps she was not meant for a peaceful life.

In the back of her mind, she could hear Oleg laughing at her.

The caravan was camped in another scenic meadow, this one overlooking the rolling hills of a valley where twinkling lights glittered on the far side of the river in the distance.

That night there was a play happening in the middle of the meadow with human and vampire players acting out a production of *The Government Inspector*, a ridiculous comedy about mistaken identity and human corruption.

Apparently it was a favorite of the older vampires and humans in the kamvasa. There was a Poshani theater company that did a new play every week, and while they often performed original stories, there were many human-penned favorites thrown in.

Tatyana walked away from the center circle of paying vampires, with their brightly decorated caravans and constant entertainment, and wandered to the outer circles of the kamvasa where the humans who ran the operation actually lived.

There was something in the air that drew her away from her own kind and toward the nostalgic hum of human life.

Fridays were the most active nights for the Poshani. Children ran through the camp with their friends and cousins, shops and restaurants stayed open longer, and taverns were full.

"Tatyana?"

She turned when she heard a familiar voice.

"It is you." Rumi smiled. She was one of the human women who spoke fluent Russian and had agreed to tutor her. "What are you doing out here?"

Rumi was a mother of two and one of Sibella's cousins, but she was also one of the head cooks for the kamvasa. She was in charge of the main dinner at dusk each night when Poshani vampires could join the human darigan for a meal.

That night she was wearing a stained apron and stirring a large pot hanging over a large wood-fed firepit. Tatyana breathed in what smelled like a spicy paprikash or goulash.

"I was just walking." Tatyana looked around. "I hope that's okay."

"You are welcome anywhere in the kamvasa." Rumi wiped her hands on her apron. "Do you want some food? I know there is a dinner served before the night's entertainment, but if you'd like something different—"

"No." Why had she come? Why had her feet led her away from her fellow immortals and toward the humans, many of whom regarded any non-Poshani vampire with guarded distance.

Bread. She'd been smelling the baking bread.

"I was wondering..." Tatyana felt awkward. "This may seem like a strange request."

Rumi smiled a little bit. "I have a hard time imagining that you would ask for something strange." She picked up a long wooden paddle and started to stir the stew again. "Trust me, some of the requests we hear from our paying guests would make your ears bleed."

"Somehow that doesn't surprise me." Tatyana had found the other paying guests to be more than a little weird.

There were three other vampires staying with the kamvasa who had signed on for the entire season like Tatyana, though she was informed that it wouldn't be unexpected for some guests to come later or leave early. It all depended on their arrangements with Radu.

Rumi smiled. "Not much surprises me anymore."

Tatyana watched the fire under the giant pot and thought about Oleg holding fire in his hands like it was a purring cat. "Some of the others are so old I can't imagine what they would want."

There was a vampire named Darius who was in the caravan parked next to hers, and the first word that popped into her head when Tatyana met him was *old.*

That ancient Persian looked like a statue half the time. He barely stirred, and when he did, he moved so quickly she didn't know how he blended into the modern world.

Then again, it was very possible he didn't blend in at all, and that's why he was a frequent guest of the kamvasa.

Rumi smiled and switched to Poshani. "Do you want to practice your language?"

It would be good to work on her skills with a subject so domestic and friendly.

Tatyana continued in the same language. "Do you have any bread?"

"To eat?"

"No." She switched back to Russian. "Sorry, I haven't learned the word in Poshani." She held out her hands. "Bread to knead. To bake. Anything that you need to bake."

Rumi's eyebrows went up. "You want to knead bread?"

"I used to bake when I was a child," she said. "With my grandmother. I'm pretty good at kneading."

"Ha!" Rumi was delighted. "If it were colder, I would take you up on your offer in a second, but we only let vampires knead bread in the winter."

"What?" Tatyana frowned. "Why?"

"Your energy." Rumi pointed to Tatyana's hands, then returned to the stew. "The yeast loves vampire energy. When it's warm like this, it will rise too fast and throw off the texture."

Tatyana's mouth fell open. "You're joking."

"I wish I was because vampires make excellent bakers." Rumi winked at her. "Do you know any fire vampires we could borrow?"

"I... No." She stammered. "I mean... No."

Rumi looked like she wanted to ask more about that, but instead, she pointed at the stew. "You can stir this if you like" —she glanced at Tatyana's hands— "so I can chop onions for the next batch. If it gets too hot, you know how to cool fire down, yes?"

Pulling water from the air and directing it to put out a fire was one of Tatyana's earliest lessons with Kato. "Yes, I can do that."

"Good. If you let it stick, the darigan will never let you forget it." Rumi left Tatyana stirring the goulash and walked over to a wooden table that had been folded down from the side of a kitchen wagon. "So you made it a month before you got bored."

She smiled. "I have never been a person who did not have a job. Even when I was a child, I had chores with my mother or my grandparents."

"Like baking bread?"

"That was a pleasure," Tatyana said. "Mostly I shoveled a lot of shit."

Rumi barked a laugh. "I've never heard a vampire who'd admit to something like that."

This was so much better. Talking with Rumi while she chopped onions and Tatyana kept the stew moving over the fire felt like being back in her grandmother's kitchen.

"My mother keeps birds," Tatyana said. "Pigeons? She loves them, but they shit a lot, you know."

"Bird shit is good for the garden."

"That's what she always said too. Our neighbor would take buckets of it and give us vegetables in return, so it was a good trade. We had the roof apartment, so no garden for my mother unless we went to the farm where she grew up."

"You're young, aren't you?" Rumi asked. "For a vampire."

"Yes." Tatyana nodded. "I'm new at this life."

"But you're not with your sire?" Rumi frowned. "That's hard to be away. You should be with your sire."

Tatyana felt a burning pain in her chest where Zara's blood had tied them together. "We had a complicated relationship."

"Family is always complicated." Rumi said nothing else. "Still, you must be doing well for yourself if you can afford to be here."

Tatyana smiled. Poshani humans were not deferential around vampires. Polite, yes. But also blunt. It was wonderful. "Unlike most of the older vampires, I'm actually quite good at computer technology."

Over the years, she'd discovered that vague references to computers often let people assume she was whatever they wanted to imagine. In her experience, most people thought that those who worked in technology could make a lot of money, and they usually didn't ask how.

"My brother would love to meet you." Rumi scraped a chopped onion into a bowl and started on another. "He works in Vano's office with... information systems or something like that?"

Tatyana filed that information away for future use if necessary. "Vano is the terrin who will join the kamvasa later, correct? The one who takes care of most of the human business matters?"

Rumi nodded. "He used to keep the main Poshani offices in Kyiv, but he has relocated to Warsaw these days."

"Of course. The current political situation..." She trailed off with a meaningful shrug.

"You know how it goes."

"I do." If there was one thing that felt normal to Tatyana about immortal life, it was the constant shifting of power and politics.

"Other people, they get attached to land," Rumi said. "Attached to buildings and statues and schools." She curled her lip. "And then when they lose something, they go to war."

"Not the Poshani."

Unlike other vampire clans, the Poshani had territory that seemed to be constantly shifting.

Rumi kept chopping onions. "We understand things differently than settled people. Nothing is permanent in this life, is it? Family keeps us together. Traditions keep us together. The kamvasa keeps us together. Money, buildings, houses... They can all disappear." She snapped her fingers. "Like that."

The snap took her back to Oleg.

"I don't like the snapping thing any more now than I did when I was alive."

"You're still alive, volchitsa. Your teeth are just sharper now."

She was still alive, and every night she existed, her teeth got a little sharper, her outlook a little more cynical. It felt good to talk with Rumi about baking bread. About childhood chores and the complicated universality of family.

"So what is the camp gossip?" Tatyana kept stirring the goulash, careful not to let the bottom of the pot burn. "Are there any dramas I should know about?"

Rumi smiled. "You are a strange vampire, Tatyana."

"Considering the vampires I have known in my short life, I'm going to consider that a compliment."

A WEEK LATER, TATYANA SAT ON A CUSHIONED SOFA SET UNDER the stars. Her trailer was once again in the inner circle of the Poshani camp, lush carpets had been laid across the grass, and a light meal of smoked fish and caviar was set out on an open-air buffet as the children of the kamvasa put on a delightful play of their own composition that they called *Baba Yaga and the Three Sisters*.

"But you left my doll in the woods," a little girl shouted from the stage in the center of the meadow. "And now I must go find it and... and Baba Yaga will eat me alive!"

One of the sisters was played by a red-cheeked boy who clearly was reveling in the extra attention of being the only boy in the cast. "Little sister, don't worry about the witch in the forest. You're too skinny to be a good meal."

The human and vampire audience laughed at the boy's high-pitched voice and silly expressions.

"Come, little sister." The oldest girl held out her hand. "Let's go to Papa's barn. We will take the rope from the cow and tie it around your ankle. If you get lost, all you must do is follow the rope and it will lead you back home."

"And don't forget to wear the cow's bell around your neck to scare off the witch." The boy twirled a blond curl of the wig he was wearing.

"Don't be silly!" The smallest sister was indignant. "If she thinks I'm a cow, she will definitely eat me for supper."

The audience of humans and vampires laughed and clapped as the children ducked behind the green velvet curtain to prepare for the next scene.

Tatyana couldn't remember the last play she'd enjoyed so much.

The children were silly and stumbling and exactly as enthusiastic as children should be in a play they had written themselves. The audience cheered and clapped with abandon. The musicians performed a score for the little players as if they were a professional troupe, and the costumes were lavish and carefully fitted.

A moment after the musicians took the stage for the scene change, she felt vampire energy approaching.

Tatyana sat up, and her amnis went on alert. The damp night air drew to her skin, only to relax a fraction when she realized it was Radu.

The clever wind vampire raised his hands and approached carefully in the darkness. "May I join you?"

She motioned to the space on the sofa beside her. "Please. I'm sorry if I seemed alarmed. I wasn't expecting anyone to join me."

Most of the paying guests kept to themselves, though she'd shared a drink with Madina, another vampire who had joined the kamvasa for the season.

Madina seemed overly curious about her origins, so Tatyana had spent most of the evening smiling, nodding, and talking about the skill of the Poshani musicians and the comfort of her travel trailer.

Unlike talking to Rumi, vampire small talk was not enjoyable. At all.

Madina seemed very important and very brusque. She probably thought Tatyana was a vapid idiot, but Tatyana didn't care. She didn't know the woman, and something about her felt hungry and scheming.

"How are you enjoying the play?" Radu said. "Can you follow what they are saying? My sister Kezia says you are becoming quite conversational in Poshani."

"Yes, I understand most of it." Tatyana's eyes turned back to the stage as a little girl in a red dress walked out from behind a curtain with a bright white rope around her ankle. "Perhaps I need to speak with children before I try adults."

Radu smiled. "We are all children when we are learning something new. I think it's wonderful that you're curious about our language and traditions," he said. "Most of our paying guests are not."

She glanced at him from the side. "Then that is their loss, to be so incurious."

"Perhaps the worst insult for an immortal."

"Perhaps their doom," she whispered. "I'm young, and I'm still learning about the world. Imagine being as old as Darius and uninterested in how the world has changed around you." Tatyana shrugged. "I think a vampire wouldn't live for very long if they were unwilling to learn new things."

"You remind me of Oleg Sokolov," Radu said.

Her head whipped to the side and she stared at him, the children's play forgotten. "Is that so?"

"I believe you worked for him," Radu said, "for a time."

"I did."

Though no one had called her "Oleg's bookkeeper" since she'd been there, it didn't surprise her that rumors had spread of their connection. She knew the Poshani did checks on vampires before they let them in the kamvasa, and it was highly likely they were traveling through Oleg's territory that season.

If Radu noticed her reaction, he didn't comment on it. "It's an admirable thing to be as old as the Varangian and still be curious. One of the things that has kept him in power, I think. His willingness to change with the times. And, of course, his willingness to be ruthless for his people and to protect their interests above all else. As a leader, I admire that."

"Yes, he's very protective." She looked back at the stage, though some of her enjoyment for the play had waned. "At least, protective of people and things that belong to him."

Radu leaned closer and dropped his voice. "I hope you understand that though we are allied with the Varangian, your safety and privacy are our first priority," he whispered. "If anyone is looking for you—even someone who is our ally—the kamvasa will not betray you. That is our responsibility as your host. When you are a guest of the Poshani, we will protect you with our lives."

She turned to Radu. "The children on the stage," she whispered. "Do they belong to you?"

He narrowed his eyes. "All Poshani children are my responsibility. I am their terrin."

"So if anyone threatened them," she said, "you would protect them."

His dark eyes glinted in the lamplight. "As if they were my own blood."

"I would do the same," Tatyana said quietly. "In fact, I would kill for them. I have known they existed for only a few weeks, but I would commit violence to keep them safe. Ask me why."

"Why?"

"Because there is innocence in the world, and it deserves to be protected," Tatyana said. "For no other reason than that it exists."

Radu stared at her a long time before he inclined his head. "I respect you, Tatyana Vorona."

"I used to work for Oleg," she continued. "And yes, I am sure there are ways that we are similar. But we are not the same."

Radu reached into his pocket and took out a folded piece of paper. "This is for you."

"A message?"

"A phone number." He held it out. "He said you would want it."

So Oleg had tried to call. Which meant he knew that she was with the kamvasa even if he didn't know where they were. "He presumes much."

"The number is yours to do with as you like." Radu held his hand toward the fire. "I can burn it if you like."

"Give it to me." She grabbed the paper and stuffed it into her pocket.

"Very well." He turned back to watch the children on the meadow stage. "A reminder that calls from the tablet in your trailer cannot be traced. All your communication either by text or voice is encrypted."

"Thank you." She shifted in her seat. "I probably won't call it; I'll probably burn it."

"That is your prerogative, my friend." Radu smiled a little bit.

"But you can tell him you gave me the number."

"Only if you want me to."

"Oh no." She pursed her lips. "I want you to tell him."

Tatyana glanced at Radu, but he was watching the stage with amusement in his eyes.

The little girl on the stage spotted her doll leaning against a wooden tree. She crept forward on her hands and knees, crawling toward her doll.

Only to let out a high-pitched shriek as she was yanked back by the rope around her ankle.

"Baba Yaga!"

Chapter 15

Oleg

"It's not because of the woman." Oleg was on a video call with Polina, who was in Minsk, while Mika sat across from him at the table. "It is possible that Ivan is working against us using Vano's people."

Polina's eyebrows went up. "So you want me to violate a long-standing agreement and find the route of the Poshani kamvasa?"

"Radu needs to know that his clan might have been compromised."

"We *know* that Ivan is working with Vano's people," Mika said. "We don't know if Vano is part of it." He shrugged. "I never liked that asshole."

"Ivan or Vano?" Polina asked.

"Ivan." Mika curled his lips. "Maybe both."

"The question remains" —Oleg broke into their bickering— "we don't know if Ivan lured Vano's people away from the Poshani clan or if Vano is going behind Radu and Kezia's back to work with Ivan. Are these independent troublemakers, or is there a bigger problem?"

"That's what Vano has claimed," Polina said. "When we discovered that these were Poshani vampires who had hijacked our truck, he implied they were rogue troublemakers estranged from the clan."

"Is it possible the greater Poshani clan have allied themselves with Ivan?" Oleg asked. "I have a good relationship with Radu, but he's only one of the terrin. My relationship with Kezia is very superficial."

Mika said, "Power inside the clan might be shifting."

"Exactly," Oleg said. "These are questions that we need answers to. That's why we must find the kamvasa."

It wasn't because Tatyana was with them.

It wasn't *only* because of that.

"The caravan has been roaming for nearly two months now," Polina said. "I suspect they're in the eastern part of my territory, but I don't know for sure because I do not ask! They pay us well for those roaming rights and for privacy."

Mika was writing something in a small notebook he kept his pocket. "It's been the arrangement for centuries, Oleg. If you want to change our treaty with the Poshani—"

"I don't want to change it over the long term, but this year is different."

"Because of the woman," Mika said.

"Because they're choosing new leaders this year."

"You know" —Mika seemed to ignore him— "she'll only be there for a few more months, and then you can lure her back to Odesa."

Polina nodded. "She probably wants more money. Not many of our kind are technologically talented, so if she's as skilled as you say—"

"It's not a question of money." Oleg was trying to be cool, but his fangs had been on edge since he'd heard Radu's voice on the other side of Tatyana's phone.

The moment he'd acquired another phone after he'd broken the second one, he called Radu back, asked him to pass his number along to Tatyana, and then he'd waited.

For three weeks.

Oleg wasn't willing to call Tatyana's phone more than once. That would make him look desperate and attract too much attention toward Tatyana.

"Your father is very grumpy right now, Polina." Mika glanced at Oleg. "Personally, I think he needs to go hunting."

"The deer are plentiful at the country house," Polina said. "Alexi was just up there last weekend with some friends and—"

"I don't need to go hunting." He didn't want to hunt down a deer; he wanted to hunt down Tatyana Vorona. He just didn't want to create a problem with an old ally while he was doing it. "I need to find the Poshani kamvasa."

"It's not that we *can't* find it," Polina said. "Of course we could. But even asking around will create problems, Papa. They guard their route carefully, and even a hint that we're looking for them will cause offense."

"You've been invited to the Vashana Zata," Mika said. "Surely we can wait for a few more months. So far, no more trucks have been attacked, and Ivan seems to be quieting down."

"I know," Oleg said. "That's what puts me on edge."

"I spoke to Vano in Warsaw a few nights ago and casually brought up Sami Novak again." Polina lifted a finger. "I did not mention Danior. I believe he still thinks that all Sami's friends are dead."

"Good." Oleg and Mika spoke at the same time.

"And Vano didn't mention Ivan at all. Was very friendly, very eager to work on the housing project I proposed in Grodno."

Oleg asked, "So Vano is playing like he's still on good terms with you?"

"He *is* on good terms with me," Polina said. "We have no proof that Vano is working with Ivan. Some of his people obviously are, but Vano can be an asshole. An independent-minded immortal might not want to stay under his thumb."

Mika looked up. "I have to agree with her. We can't assume that

Vano is going behind our backs with Ivan. If we can be double-crossed, so can he."

"I don't like any of this," Oleg said. "And in a matter of weeks, Vano is probably going to disappear into that stupid roaming safe house."

With Tatyana.

His Tatyana.

"We need to find the kamvasa," Oleg said. "Do it, Polina."

His daughter groaned. "This is going to screw up the Grodno project."

"The future stability of Sokolov Industries is more important than one project." Oleg's voice was clipped. "I don't need an exact location. Get me a rough estimate and I'll do the rest. If Vano's people have a problem with it, they can speak to me directly."

"Yes, Papa." Polina's voice was subdued. "Of course."

Moments later, Polina disconnected the call and Mika stared at Oleg.

"What?" Oleg was suddenly in a foul mood.

Three weeks. What was she doing in that damned caravan? Taking up knitting? Tatyana would only be interested in knitting needles if she could stab him with them.

"Tell me this isn't because of the woman," Mika said.

"We suspect a centuries-old ally might be double-crossing us and working with my most dangerous sibling, and you think I'm over-reacting?"

"No." Mika shook his head. "I agree with you that we need to find out what's going on, and probably we need to kill Ivan. But I question the urgency. What's the rush? Why not wait until the fall?"

Because by the fall she could have formed a connection to someone else. Someone equally as powerful. Someone who didn't have the history that he did.

"Because the Poshani people are choosing new leaders at the end of this season." Oleg stood up. "The Vashana Zata only happens once every hundred years. Radu might be thinking to retire. If Vano is going behind the backs of his brother and sister—putting the safety of their entire clan at risk—then I owe it to my old friends to let them know."

OLEG RETURNED TO HIS PRIVATE APARTMENT IN ODESA BEFORE dawn after hours of dealing with tedious business matters that Elene should have been handling.

His fucking daughter.

He wanted to kill Zara all over again. For many things, but mostly for killing one of his dearest friends, and then he would kill her again for giving him more paperwork.

Oleg couldn't find it in his heart to regret Tatyana becoming a vampire even though he regretted how it was done. But Elene?

He missed her dearly. Perhaps he would see if Elene's daughter and grandchildren would like a holiday. He missed the sound of children.

There was a strange buzzing somewhere in his room, and he went on alert.

What could it be? Could someone have secreted an explosive device in his apartment? That wasn't possible. Mika's security team regularly swept for any electronic devices and...

Oh.

He had an electronic device of his own now.

Oleg walked to his desk and opened the drawer. The phone—the one with a number that only one person had—was ringing.

He picked it up and touched the green button, putting it flat on his desk and glaring at it. "Hello?"

"You really got a mobile phone."

He sank into his upholstered leather chair and spread his hands on his desk, trying not to grab the device as he listened to her voice. "I did."

This wasn't a dream.

She kept talking. "Have you given the number to Mika yet?"

"No. If I did, he'd just want to talk to me."

He heard a low laugh from her, but the speaker wasn't good enough. The mobile phone didn't capture the richness of her voice. It was tinny and irritating.

"Your voice doesn't sound right."

"The connection should be good." Her voice dropped into that absent, thoughtful tone that she often had when she was mulling over a problem. "But I'm using a VPN, so it's possible—"

"You're not here." Oleg sat back in his chair and looked at the phone. "I can't hear your actual voice, just the electronic version of it."

"Ah. Yes, that's the way phones work."

"So I've heard."

"Which shouldn't be a surprise since you *planted a phone on me.*"

"I gave you a brand-new phone with my number programmed into it," he said. "In case you wanted to call me."

"You wanted to track me, Oleg."

"If I wanted to track you, I would have planted a tracker, not given you a phone."

"Oleg—"

"I like the way you say my name." He closed his eyes. Ridiculous. He sounded like a schoolboy. "There's always a slight hint of scorn. I was talking with my daughter earlier. She was being very deferential. It was annoying."

"How terrible for you."

The corner of his mouth turned up. "The sarcasm transmits surprisingly well."

"Why was she being deferential? Were you being terrifying?"

"I am never terrifying." He sat back in his chair and stretched his legs out. He couldn't smell her scent, but it was always amusing to parry with his favorite bookkeeper. "I'm a very modern immortal leader. I don't hang any of them by their toes anymore. I haven't disemboweled anyone in years."

Or had he? He'd have to ask Mika.

"Oh yes, not terrifying at all. Tell that to one of the vampires or humans you've killed."

"Obviously that's not possible because they're dead."

"Fine, tell it to Marta then. I'm assuming she's still alive."

"Who is Marta?" Did he know a vampire named Marta? Did one work for him?

"Elene's secretary. She's still working for you, isn't she?" Tatyana sounded alarmed.

"Oh, that one. Yes, she's quite well."

"Good."

Oleg shrugged, then questioned why he was shrugging when Tatyana could only hear his voice. "In fact, she probably deserves a raise because she's taking on much more than she was doing when Elene was alive."

"I'm sure she is. Also, she's terrified of you."

"No, that's not possible," Oleg said. "She's attracted to me. I can smell it."

Tatyana sighed. "Please don't ever tell that poor woman you can smell that she's attracted to you. It may surprise you, but being terrified of someone doesn't necessarily mean you're also not attracted to them."

Oleg frowned. "That seems very unhealthy."

"I was both terrified and attracted to you when I was human," Tatyana said. "Was I unhealthy?"

"But you're not terrified of me now," he said. "And that is the important thing."

Tatyana didn't say anything.

"Volchitsa." He softened his voice. "Tell me you do not fear me."

"Not..."

He leaned closer to the phone, wishing he could smell her blood.

The scent of her hair. Wishing he could touch the vibrant energy that ran through her veins. "I do not want you to fear me, Tatyana. Not ever."

She let out a soft sigh. "Why was your daughter being deferential earlier?"

Fine, change the subject.

The hair on the back of his neck prickled, and there was an aching twist in his chest that he tried to ignore. "I was asking her to do something she didn't want to do."

"Ah."

"She will do it."

"I'm sure she will."

"And not because she is terrified of me," Oleg added. "Because she knows that what I am asking is important for our organization."

"I'm not going to ask."

"You should." He propped his chin on his fist and stared at the small black rectangle where his lover was speaking.

"I don't work for you anymore," she said. "It's none of my business."

"But it could be. I would actually like to have your opinion on this, but considering I know where you're hiding—"

"I'm not hiding," she said. "I'm taking a very luxurious vacation with interesting people."

"Camping for six months is not a luxurious vacation, volchitsa. Not when you could be spending your summer on a yacht in the Mediterranean with me."

She was silent.

"Would you like to change your plans?" He smiled. "I have a lovely, light-safe vessel docked in Portofino. Give me the word and—"

"I love it here actually."

He barely suppressed his sigh. He was both relieved and irritated. "Well... good. Radu isn't a bad sort, and he will keep you safe."

Because if he does not, I will hunt him down, pull his heart from his chest, and feed his innards to my wolfhounds while he watches.

Oleg didn't say that aloud.

And he wouldn't have to feed Radu to his wolfhounds. Despite his irritation with Tatyana's second disappearance, the creeping fear he'd been enduring for over a year while she resided in the Fire King's court had eased. Living with the Poshani was the safest she could be outside his own aegis.

"There is something very precious here." She spoke softly. "Something... sort of wonderful." Her voice was even more addictive when it was soft.

"What is it?"

"I don't know yet."

"Tatyana—"

"Have you visited the farm lately? My mother said workers came and fixed the roof of the barn. She hadn't even told anyone it was leaking."

"I told you I'd take care of your mother." He crossed his arms over his chest and leaned back, closing his eyes as he pictured Tatyana curled up somewhere. She would have her feet up in her chair because she was small and didn't like her legs dangling. "I've been busy in the city," he continued. "But I'll try to visit her soon."

"You don't have to visit her."

"I know you call, but she misses you. You should—"

"Don't ask me to come back again." Her voice was nearly a whisper. "Please don't, Oleg."

He felt his fangs aching in his jaw, but he kept his eyes closed and pictured Tatyana as if she were sitting in front of him. Sitting on his lap, her head resting on his chest. He could wrap his arms around her and listen to her slow heartbeat. Her long hair might tangle in his beard.

Such an odd, domestic image. The ache was twisting in his chest again, and he curled his hand into a fist. "I want you back."

"Please, Oleg. Don't—"

"I miss you." He reached out, slammed his hand on the phone, and the plastic device sizzled and melted under his flaming hand.

Mika raised an eyebrow. "You broke another phone?"

"Yes."

"What happened?"

"It melted." Oleg leaned against the wall of his boyar's office, staring at the stacks of files on Mika's desk. "You're busy."

"Yes, but I can send someone to get you another Nocht-compatible device. Anton!"

"Don't bother Anton," Oleg muttered.

A short human popped his head into the office. "Yes, boss?"

"Oleg needs a new phone."

To his credit, Anton didn't ask. "Right away. Same number?"

She might want to call him again. He couldn't call her, of course, because the number was blocked.

"Yes," Oleg growled. "Same number."

"Yes, sir." Anton scurried away.

Mika crossed his arms over his chest. "You're giving me the number this time."

"It's not necessary." Oleg looked at the state of Mika's desk. "Do you have someone who can take over your duties here in the office for a few weeks?"

"Yes." Mika narrowed his eyes. "Why?"

"I think I may need you out of the office for some time."

"Because you want to... go to Las Vegas for a poker tournament?"

Oleg smirked. "That does sound amusing, but no."

Now that Oleg had decided what he was going to do, that annoying twisting sensation in his chest was no longer bothering him.

Polina would tell him the rough location for the kamvasa within days.

Once he had that, he didn't need anyone else. He'd taken

Tatyana's blood. Her amnis would lead him to her once he got close enough.

He'd be able to find her within a few days, if not sooner.

Mika was clearly suspicious. "Perhaps you're wanting a holiday in Italy? It's been too long since you've enjoyed the boat."

"No."

"Business trip to Argentina?" Mika spread his hands out. "Buenos Aires is beautiful in the fall, and it's been too long since we visited the ranch. What an excellent idea."

Oleg smiled a little. "I had something much closer in mind."

His boyar's smile looked a little more like he was baring his teeth. "Then why do you need me to leave the office?"

"Because you, me, and Lazlo—and maybe Ludmila and Oksana—are going on a hunting trip."

"What an excellent suggestion. Polina was right. Her country home is very welcoming. Please say you're craving venison and not—"

"We're going to find the kamvasa ourselves." Oleg clapped his hands together. "What fun. Once Polina gives us a region, it should only take a few days."

Mika stood, walked to the door, and closed it carefully before he spoke again. "This is a terrible idea, and you're going to anger Radu and the rest of the Poshani."

"We can camp in the wilderness like old times."

"You mean the times your druzhina was bloody, hungry, and trying to root out the last of your sire's old allies while other vampires tried to kill us every night? Those times?" Mika curled his lip and walked back behind his desk. "This is a ridiculous idea."

"Lazlo can dig us comfortable caves. You can make that wonderful hunter's stew you learned from that old man in Slovenia. Ludmila will be ecstatic."

"Because Ludmila's ideal retreat is a cold stone cave and anything more than a plank to sleep on, she considers a frivolous luxury." Mika leaned toward him. "Why are you doing this? And don't say it's because of internal Poshani politics or for the benefit of an ally."

"What can I say?" Oleg walked over and slapped Mika on the shoulder. "I feel the need to get out of the city," he said. "Reconnect with my element."

"You're a fire vampire," Mika said. "Why don't we fly to Hawaii and you can play in the volcanos while I enjoy some beautiful women?"

"I'm glad you're so excited about it." Oleg patted the back of his friend's head. "We are getting back to our roots."

"I hate you, and I'm giving myself a raise."

"That's fine." Oleg strolled toward the door. "Summon the others. This is going to be fun."

Chapter 16

Tatyana

"Tatyana Vorona."

She turned when she heard her name coming from the red-painted tavern.

Kezia, terrin of the Poshani, was waving her over.

"Hello." As months with the Poshani passed and Tatyana became accustomed to the rhythm of life in the kamvasa, she had also started noticing ripples. "How are you tonight?"

Not cracks. Not yet. But while the surface of life flowed smoothly—humans and vampires going about their daily duties in a steady rhythm—Tatyana was starting to feel other currents beneath the surface.

And in the heart of those, Kezia was a very large stone.

"Come and join me for a drink." Kezia pointed to the chair across from her.

"Thank you." Tatyana walked over and took a seat, facing the dark-haired woman.

Tatyana had met Radu's sister, not at one of the lavish parties that were thrown for the paying guests but near the cooking tent when she'd been joking with Rumi and some of the other human women.

They had been teasing Tatyana about how she pronounced some Poshani words but complimenting her on how quickly she was picking up the language.

Kezia had quickly joined them, blending into their conversation like a visiting sister and keeping her eyes on Tatyana the entire time.

After Kezia's arrival, Tatyana had been slow to speak, but she listened to everything the women and Kezia spoke about, filing it all away in her quickly growing mental file about the Poshani.

"How has your week been?" Kezia asked. "I hear there will be a new play tomorrow."

"But will it compare to *Baba Yaga and the Three Sisters?*"

"I heard!" Kezia put a hand on her chest. "I cannot believe I missed it."

"It was so charming."

"The children, no?" Kezia sipped her wine. "They are a delight."

"Yes, they make the camp very lively." And alive. It was past midnight, so all the children were asleep in their tents and trailers, but she could hear a baby crying in the distance, and the sound comforted her. "It's been a quiet week, but I tried that restaurant you told me about. It was excellent."

"The lamb ribs, yes?" Kezia kissed the tips of her fingers. "From the Floreas' wagon? They are so tender."

"And not too strong." Tatyana had always enjoyed the taste of mutton, but it was a very pungent flavor for vampire tastes. Kezia had suggested a small wagon that sold ribs, and Tatyana was surprised at how much she enjoyed them.

"Yes, they only use the spring lambs for vampire guests." Kezia waved a server over, and the young man poured a goblet of blood-wine and set it in front of Tatyana. "The ones who have only taken their mother's milk. That's why it is so delicious."

Tatyana felt her stomach drop. Well, she would not be eating *that* meat again.

She'd grown up on a farm, so she had no illusions about where meat came from, but her grandfather had never taken spring lambs or young calves.

We give them a good life, and they give us meat. But we must give them a good life first.

She could hear her grandfather's voice in her mind, but she didn't want to be rude to one of the Poshani leaders. Not only was it undiplomatic, she was not in her own culture, and she was keenly aware of that.

While Radu seemed to be the favorite uncle, joking with everyone from the old men to the youngest children, Kezia focused on the women of the kamvasa, checking in with them, asking about the night-to-night needs, picking their brains about what the gossip was around the camp.

Tatyana also saw the Hazars—the immortal guards who patrolled the air around the caravan—reporting to Kezia and Radu regularly.

"Has your brother Vano joined the kamvasa yet?" Tatyana asked. "I feel like I've met everyone else."

"Even Fynn?"

"Yes, even Fynn. Briefly, but I did meet him." The nearly silent vampire sounded German, but he kept to himself. The only thing he seemed to be interested in were the dancing nights where he enjoyed the attention of young Poshani men and women who performed for him.

And Tatyana had no opinion about that.

"Vano is coming next week," Kezia said. "He's helping to transport a new guest from France who will be staying with us through the end of the season like you. So a few months."

The prospect of new company was welcome. Even though she'd been spending more time with the humans of the kamvasa than the vampires, it would be pleasant to have new possibilities for conversation. "It will be nice to see a new face in the evenings."

"Oh yes." Kezia's lips curled into a smile. "I think you will enjoy the French vampire's face, and maybe more than his face if you're looking for some light fun."

Tatyana's smile froze. "I see."

Kezia laughed. "Don't need a lover yet? Or are you still enjoying the afterglow from Arosh's skills?"

"I'm not looking for a lover." The immediate image of Oleg jumped into her mind.

No. He was not her lover despite the tender words and teasing they'd shared the other night.

She had no idea why she'd called him.

Liar.

She knew. Obviously she knew.

I miss you.

The damned man had said that in the tender voice she heard in her dreams, and then the line had gone dead. She'd even tried calling back, and it went straight to a voicemail that had not been set up.

What was Oleg about?

Tatyana's irritation must have shown on her face because Kezia laughed.

"Whoever you are angry with, sleeping with René would be a brilliant way to get revenge. He's very good, and the two of you would be gorgeous together. But I recommend him only if you aren't looking for anything serious."

"I appreciate the advice." And she'd file that away with any new restaurant recommendations Kezia gave her. She sipped the sweet blend of blood and port in the blood-wine the server refilled. "I'm not looking for anything like that right now."

Of course not, because you're mine.

She mentally told Oleg to shut the hell up, then turned her attention to the women who were delivering trays of food to the tavern wagons. "You know, the chefs for our vampire dinners cook like they come from the finest restaurants in the world."

Kezia nodded. "They do. The current chef de cuisine we stole from a Wallace hotel in Australia. I lured her here myself."

"She is exceptional," Tatyana said. "But I think I appreciate the family cooking more. It reminds me of home."

"You are very kind." Kezia's gaze softened to something that was slightly less scheming. "Most immortals see the kamvasa as a kind of relic. Almost like a moving museum."

"Oh no. It's far more than that." Tatyana shook her head. "It is a journey that keeps your culture alive. A road from the past to the future." She looked at her wine. "I'm sorry. You know this, of course."

"No need to apologize." Kezia narrowed her eyes. "Thank you. I'm glad you feel that way about our family. For that is what we are. A family." Her face slipped back into a diplomatic mask. "You must tell me about where you'd like to travel now that you're an immortal. Have you visited Asia yet? I have some wonderful recommendations if you're looking for ideas."

"Thank you."

Despite Kezia's pretty words about her people, in the back of Tatyana's mind, she wondered if the vampire's attitude toward the humans in the kamvasa was as detached as her attitude to livestock.

Because if there was one thing Tatyana had learned about vampires, it was that some of them definitely saw humans the same way they did livestock.

Pamper them, take care of them, but they are there for your convenience.

We give them a good life, and they give us blood.
But we must give them a good life first.

Chapter 17

Oleg

Ludmila, Oleg's most silent sniper, was as close to cheery as he had seen her since the Second World War when Oleg had set her loose on the Nazis invading Russia. She was whistling as she threw two large duffel bags into the back of one of the old Land Cruisers parked outside Oleg's castle in the Eastern Carpathian Mountains.

Her mate, Oksana, on the other hand, was less than pleased. "Why are we doing this?"

"To find his girlfriend," Ludmila said. "You know, the pretty little blond one." She smirked at Lazlo. "Your brother, he has a type, doesn't he?"

"Yes." Lazlo sounded as cheery as Ludmila. "He likes them pretty, blond, unhinged, and hostile."

Oksana said, "I thought Tatyana was in the Fire King's court."

"Not anymore," Lazlo said. "She booked passage in the kamvasa for the season."

The three knew Oleg was there, but they didn't care, which was part of the reason he had chosen them for his druzhina. He didn't need people who would kiss his ass—he needed smart warriors who could think for themselves.

Even if that made them annoying as shit sometimes.

"This should be fun." Ludmila smiled. "The Poshani are very good at covering their tracks, and they will become violent if they discover us."

Lazlo narrowed his eyes. "There is something wrong with you."

"I don't like boredom, old man."

"Shut up," Oleg barked. "All of you. Keep packing."

Oksana glanced at Oleg. "You know, I want to clarify that pretty, blond, and hostile is not a bad type. That's basically my mate if she were blond."

"True." Lazlo nodded. "And brother, you've had sex with far worse."

"The supermodels," Ludmila muttered.

"The heiresses were worse," Lazlo said. "At least the models had jobs."

Oleg walked over and lifted an ice chest into the back of one truck. "Enough."

"I heard she did not kill any humans her first year." Ludmila patted Oleg's shoulder. "So that's good."

"I heard that Kato the Ancient became her teacher," Lazlo said. "A lucky turn. She has Dzbog's favor."

"Okay, yes." Oksana angled a rifle case into the back of the second Land Cruiser. "She may be favored by a Slavic rain god, but remember, *I* was her first teacher."

Ludmila insisted on packing enough weapons to take out a small army. Oleg didn't think filling half the vehicle with weapons was strictly necessary, but when he'd suggested leaving them behind, Ludmila had looked at him like he'd suggested running through the streets of Moscow stark naked in the winter.

"And such a good teacher you were." Ludmila patted her mate's shoulder. "Lazlo is right. Mary herself favors that young one. She's very lucky."

Mika walked over and leaned on the Land Cruiser next to Oleg. "You know, the religious mix among your soldiers would be rich fodder for an academic."

Oleg's chief boyar had been busy making one telephone call after another, trying to arrange his responsibilities so he could be out of mobile phone range for at least two weeks.

"Pagan." Oleg pointed to Lazlo. "Orthodox." He pointed toward Ludmila. "Along with a few followers of Mohammed, and don't you burn rowan branches at midsummer to some thunder god or something?"

"That's just tradition," Mika muttered. "Are we almost ready?"

"Yes." Oleg looked at Mika's phone. "Are you bringing that thing?"

"There is still work to be done." Mika scrolled through the device as he spoke. "Not all of us can drop everything to track down a woman and—"

"Be very careful right now," Oleg said quietly. "I've been listening to the three of them for the past half hour."

Mika looked up. "Track down the Poshani to warn them about a possible security breach in their inner hierarchy."

"Yes, exactly."

"Which is none of our business," Mika said, "but something we are doing only from the charity that lives in our hearts."

"So glad we're clear on that." Oleg glanced at Mika's phone. "Anything else from Polina?"

"Vano is gone, and another truck was hijacked."

Oleg stood up straight. "What?" If there were more missing employees, he would have to delay his plans to find Tatyana no matter how persistently she was plaguing his mind.

Mika raised a hand. "It appears to be human-on-human crime this time," he quickly added. "Polina's people reported it to the police. No harm to our employees. They were held with weapons at the Russian border and the truck was stolen, but no violence. No one was hurt."

"What was the cargo?"

"Electronics," Mika said. "Mobile phones mostly. There were trackers in the container, but they were disabled."

It was hardly an unusual crime, but it still irritated Oleg anytime something was stolen from him. "Perhaps we need to start putting armed guards with our drivers."

"That's a possibility that Ivan has suggested."

"Let me guess, he would like to employ his own men?"

Mika smiled. "What do you think?"

Oleg could easily believe Ivan would target Oleg's trucks, creating a problem just so Oleg would have to hire Ivan's people to solve it.

It was something Oleg had done to rivals in the past.

"Where was the truck stopped?" Oleg asked.

"Smolensk."

"Hmm." The city was a border area in Oleg's empire, roughly where Polina's governance ended and Ivan's started.

"Yes, I thought it was interesting too." Mika was looking at his phone again. "Ivan has been sending daily updates about the police progress."

"How helpful. Does he think we don't know he has the Russian police in his pocket?" Oleg asked.

"We're playing along for now," Mika said. "Unless you'd like me to do something more... proactive."

"This will be his people again. Ones he can keep on a tighter leash."

"Yes, Polina and I have both considered the possibility."

Oleg was going to have to do something about Ivan.

He was going to have to kill another brother.

But one problem at a time.

Right now he needed to find Tatyana and also figure out if Vano could be trusted. He wanted to keep the Poshani as allies if he could. He didn't relish driving people from his territory, and frankly, he made a generous income from nothing more than giving them the right to roam freely.

"You realize that if Radu finds out that we've tracked down the kamvasa in violation of our agreement, he could attack us and no one would blame him."

"Yes." Oleg pushed away from the vehicle when he felt the reverberation of the door slamming behind him. "That's why they're never going to realize we're there."

Chapter 18

Tatyana

"I saw him," Rumi said. "And for that one, I might not care about the fangs."

The women around the cooking wagon hooted with delight.

"I saw him too." A woman named Desiree elbowed Tatyana while she was stirring a pot of beef and barley soup. "Tanya, did you see him? He's your kind. You have to have met at the welcome dinner."

"I met him." She shrugged. "He's nothing special."

"Oh no." Rumi pointed at her. "I don't believe you for a moment. If you had a heartbeat, you'd be blushing."

"She has a heartbeat, it's just slooooooow."

The three women around the cooking fire laughed out loud, and Tatyana felt like her cheeks would crack from smiling. She hadn't felt like this... maybe ever.

Rumi was there, and Desiree, who was a little older than Tatyana. There was also an older woman in her forties named Katrina, whose quick wit and stories kept everyone in stitches.

"Okay, I would never ask a Poshani vampire this," Katrina said.

"But blood flow is what makes the good times *good* if you know what I mean." She motioned below her waist while Rumi and Desiree smirked. "So does it take forever to have an orgasm when you're a vampire?"

"Katrina, what a question!" Rumi waved a hand at her. "Tanya, ignore her. So rude."

"Okay, but I really am curious now." Desiree cocked her head. "I've never thought about that before."

Tatyana pushed through her embarrassment and forced herself to answer. "I think it's the amnis." She lifted a hand and pulled a wave of fog toward them, cooling down the cooking fire. "You know, our energy."

"Yes, that makes sense." Katrina wiggled her hips. "Now to try that out with the very fine Frenchman."

Tatyana joined Rumi and Desiree as they laughed.

René DuPont, French vampire and guest of the kamvasa for the rest of the season, had arrived the night before, and rumors of his looks and charm were already spreading like wildfire through the ranks of the Poshani women.

"Seriously," Rumi said. "I swore off vampire lovers years before I married Hanzi, but if I were single? I might consider letting that one bite me."

"Do all Poshani girls have vampire boyfriends?" Tatyana asked. "Is it common?"

"We all go through a phase," Katrina said. "I had immortal boyfriends and girlfriends when I was young, but I only ever loved one."

Tatyana blurted out the question before she could stop herself. "What happened?"

Katrina smiled sadly. "I got grey hair."

"Oh, what an asshole," Rumi said. "You never told me that's why you broke things off with Iza."

"He didn't say anything," Katrina said. "But I could see it. He was drifting away and looking at younger women." She shrugged.

"What can you do? I broke things off a year after I turned thirty-six. He'll stay beautiful forever, like that Frenchman. I needed to move on."

"Never try to have a real relationship with a vampire," Desiree said. "Our mothers all tell us the same." She looked at Tatyana. "Romantic relationships, I mean. Friendships are different."

"Of course!" Rumi quickly added. "You know we're only talking about the men."

Tatyana said nothing, but her heart warmed at the idea that these women, mortal or immortal, actually considered her a friend. Or at least a possible one.

Tatyana shook her head. "I'm telling you, forget about René DuPont. I've met his kind before. He's probably just another man, only looking out for himself. And you can't see a pretty face in the dark."

Rumi hooted. "Unless you're a vampire."

"Okay, you might have a point." Tatyana smiled and started stirring the soup again.

"Have you met more handsome than him?" Desiree's eyebrows went up. "Come on, Tanya. You don't tell us anything about your past."

"I have." She'd been open with the Poshani women. Not about how she was turned, but where she grew up. "What didn't I tell you?"

"She means your past boyfriends." Katrina winked. "From the way you talk about men, I'm betting you were burned."

Tatyana froze. "What?"

Radu knew about Oleg. Had he told others in the camp about her past with the fire vampire?

"Oh, come on," Rumi said. "Who hasn't been burned by a man?"

Oh.

Ohhh. She let out a silent breath. "Exactly. Who hasn't been burned by a man?"

"Come on." Katrina nudged Desiree. "She said she was in the Fire King's court. I bet she got burned by the best there."

Rumi laughed. "We've all heard the stories about Arosh."

"Every Poshani girl knows about Arosh," Desiree said. "I spent a few years in the Fire Court myself." She rubbed the tips of her fingers together. "How do you think I bought my van?"

"It's a good thing as long as you're smart about it." Rumi nodded. "Not all of us go to university like Katrina and get office jobs."

Tatyana hadn't asked, but it sounded like Katrina had a remote job of some kind in technology, working in the business offices in Warsaw when she wasn't on the road. She'd only joined the kamvasa in the past few weeks.

"Jobs are boring," Katrina said. "I need to know more about Tanya's past with sexy vampires."

"I don't..." She smiled. "I'm not going to tell you that."

"Oh, it was serious then." Desiree sidled closer to her. "Now we definitely need to know."

"He wasn't..." Was she actually going to talk about this? "He was very possessive. Very overwhelming."

"In a bad way?" Rumi asked, not looking up from the carrots she was chopping. "Hanzi is possessive, but he's a pussycat if I growl at him."

"Ah, that was the problem then," Tatyana said. "I didn't try growling; I'll remember that for next time."

All of them laughed at her, and Tatyana was hoping they'd change the subject.

No such luck.

"A lover should be possessive," Katrina said. "But they should also know they're not the center of your world. We have lives, yes?"

"Exactly," Tatyana said. "A person should have their own identity."

"If you're young, that's harder," Rumi said. "Give it time." She looked at Tatyana. "You have a lot of that now."

Chapter 19

Oleg

It was three weeks after they started that Oleg finally felt a stir in his amnis.

"South."

Lazlo was driving. "What?"

"We need to head south."

He'd taken Tatyana's blood multiple times before she left him, both for greed and for her own good. He could use that blood bond to find her. He could also use it to protect her.

He'd used it to pull the pain of her sire's death from her and keep her alive. He'd gathered the pain of Zara's death into his own body as he felt her amnis die in his own blood.

The combined pain of his and Tatyana's loss had sent him to his knees.

Tatyana's blood had tormented Oleg when she left and comforted him when she was near.

Now he could feel it stretch and reach out, the amnis he carried with him searching for her elemental power and drawing Oleg closer to her physical location.

He was so sure of her whereabouts, Oleg felt that if he looked over his left shoulder, he'd catch a glimpse of her from the corner of his eye. "We need to drive southwest."

"We just came from there, but if you say so." Lazlo pointed to the map in the dashboard. "Look at that and find me a route."

The first week of searching, they'd left the paved roads and driven through the wilderness, traversing gravel and dirt paths, exploring remote farming regions, forests, and isolated river valleys.

The second week, he started to feel hints of her blood in the air as Tatyana's amnis stirred to waking in his veins.

But now...

"I can feel her." He grabbed the map and looked for a route that would take them closer. They weren't traveling off road yet, but they would. Eventually they would be on foot.

"When we get close enough, we'll have to park the vehicles," Lazlo said. "The Hazar will be patrolling."

The Hazar—Poshani wind vampires famed for their keen sight and martial skills—were Oleg's greatest threat through this endeavor. They would attack first and ask questions later if they deemed an immortal a threat.

The Poshani planned their routes carefully, threading their way through isolated villages and getting near enough to urban centers to restock their supplies without drawing an excess of attention to their people.

It was an intricate puzzle as complicated as one of their traditional dances, and Oleg had always respected them for it.

Unfortunately, that caution and stealth was standing between him and his prey.

Mika, Ludmila, and Oksana were in the rear vehicle, leaving Lazlo and Oleg in companionable silence.

Lazlo kept his eyes on the dark road as they bumped through a forest. "Is she worth this, brother?"

"What does that mean?"

"You know what I mean," Lazlo grumbled. "We're risking the anger of an old ally so you can find this woman."

"Despite what you all think, I am actually concerned that Vano could attempt a coup within the Poshani clan."

Lazlo grunted. "He's always been too friendly with Ivan."

"Exactly." They had acquired a government map that estimated the roads, but it was only slightly accurate. "There is a fire road about half a kilometer ahead. Turn left on it."

"Yes, boss."

"And yes."

"Yes, what?" Lazlo said.

"She's worth it." Oleg kept his eyes on the map, refusing to look at his brother. "I think she has the potential to be a very extraordinary vampire."

"You wouldn't be you if you didn't want to collect pretty, bright things and fix them on the walls of your castle."

Oleg frowned. "What are you talking about?"

"You've always been drawn to the unusual," Lazlo said. "You collect women like that. That's why you were drawn to Luana." He looked to the side. "I'm not implying that this one is mentally unbalanced like Luana was, but..." Lazlo nodded. "She's interesting."

"I don't *collect* women."

"Of course you do." Lazlo slowed down and steered the Land Cruiser onto the narrow dirt road. "You like rescuing the birds with broken wings and fixing them. We all do it. That's how we make amends."

"For what?"

"You know for what, you idiot," Lazlo grumbled. "We destroyed entire cultures under his command. We leveled towns and turned rivers red with blood."

The haunting sound of human screams whispered in the back of Oleg's mind. "We had no choice."

"We did!" Lazlo barked. "We could have chosen death. We could have all chosen death, and some of us did."

Oleg stared ahead. "What would our deaths have accomplished? Death would have been *easy*," he spat out. "We could all become sad martyrs weeping before our gods and begging forgiveness from our ancestors while the world we left behind burned to ashes."

Lazlo nodded slowly. "You're not wrong."

"If you and I, Pavel and Rudov, and the rest of the decent ones had chosen death, all of the Kievan Rus would be ruled by Ivan and his kind."

"Did I say we were wrong?" Lazlo shrugged. "I'm only saying we all choose our own way of making amends. Some of us try to keep the wretched mortals from destroying the earth, and you took the shattered remains of a monster's empire and made it slightly less violent and brutal."

There was nothing Oleg could say to that, so he kept quiet.

"So if you want to collect interesting and beautiful women to make your eternity slightly less horrible, I cannot blame you for it."

"I am not *collecting* Tatyana Vorona," Oleg muttered. "She's infuriating. Headstrong. Dismissive. And so stubbornly independent I'm probably going to have to lock her up to keep her safe. I am beginning to believe she has a death wish."

"And if she does?"

"That's *unacceptable*." Oleg felt his fire itching to break over his skin at the thought.

Lazlo was silent for a long moment, then burst into laughter.

The sound was so startling that Oleg could only stare.

"You fucking idiot." Lazlo wiped bloody tears from his eyes. "She's nothing you want and everything you need." He burst into another peal of laughter, then slapped Oleg's shoulder. "I love it."

"You're an idiot and you know nothing," Oleg muttered.

"You're going to fall in love with her. You're half in love already."

"Please shut up or I will kill you."

Chapter 20

Tatyana

In the quiet hours before dawn, long after Rumi, Desiree, and Katrina had turned in for the night, Tatyana walked away from the kamvasa, nodding at the Hazar on the perimeter who caught her eye.

"I'm just going down to the lake," she told the guard.

"We'll be watching," the man said with a slight nod.

The Hazar were ever-present at night, the guardians of both the humans and the vampires in the kamvasa. They were a silent army that only surfaced when necessary. Sometimes to report something to Radu or Kezia and sometimes to return an adventurous child who had wandered too far.

She felt the vampire's watchful eyes as she walked down to the edge of the glassy lake, the moon and stars reflected in the mirrorlike surface.

She sat on the edge, perching on a fallen log, and watched the water react to her amnis, crawling up the shore to touch her bare feet where she stretched them toward the water.

The night was balmy—the heat of the day had lasted well until midnight when a slight breeze picked up and swept over the lake, bringing relief to the humans with air cooled by the water.

They had arrived in the small valley two nights before, and in the distance, she could see a tall mountain range. She still had no idea where she was geographically, but for the first time since she'd become a vampire, she was starting to feel at home.

It had nothing to do with the comfortable trailer where she'd collected a small wardrobe, stacks of books, and an interesting collection of rocks from the rivers and lakes they'd passed.

It wasn't the journals she'd started to keep again for the first time since she was a child.

It wasn't the ever more familiar rhythm of Poshani, but that was part of it.

Within the isolated bubble of the Poshani kamvasa, Tatyana had remembered that she loved music and she missed dancing.

She remembered what it felt like to joke with friends.

She remembered what it was like to close her eyes at dawn and not fear what might be coming the following night, because she knew who she would see, and she knew what they expected from her.

The kamvasa was starting to feel like home, and she felt an ache in her heart that they had already passed midsummer.

Two more months and this refuge would be gone. After that? What was she supposed to do?

The water kissed her feet, soothing the electric energy that had started to churn in her blood.

Safe.

You are safe.

The water reassured her, and Tatyana took a steadying breath. Whatever happened after the kamvasa came to a close, she realized that she could find her way in the world. She felt more confident moving among vampires, and she'd even considered talking to Radu about a job.

She could live for a long time on the money she had, but Tatyana knew she needed employment to be happy. Perhaps there was some part of the Poshani business she could help with.

After a peaceful hour, Tatyana stood and made her way back to the heart of the kamvasa, nodding at the Hazar who'd been watching.

She found her trailer with ease even though it was identical to the others in the center of the camp.

But the moment she put her hand on the door, she froze.

It couldn't be.

His scent was unmistakable. She could feel his amnis in the air.

Her blood came to furious life, and she yanked her trailer door open, prepared to start yelling for the Hazar, but the moment she walked into her trailer, his hand came over her mouth.

Oleg bent down, locked his eyes with hers, and pressed his forehead to hers, his lips against the fingers that were pressed to her mouth. "Shhhh. It's me. It's me."

She tore his hand away and hissed, "I know it's you!"

He didn't move. They were frozen, inches apart, and her amnis was raging.

Not in anger.

In the safety of her silent trailer, there was nothing but him and her. His skin smelled of earth and ashes. His breath was warm on her lips.

She wasn't afraid. She was furious.

And so hungry for him she wanted to weep.

Tatyana put her hand on his neck and closed the inches left between them, meeting Oleg's mouth in a furious kiss.

Chapter 21

Oleg

The kiss lasted only for a few seconds, but it was enough to leave Oleg smoking.

Tatyana pulled away and grabbed moisture from the air, dousing the ripple of fire that rose on Oleg's neck.

"Get yourself under control." She looked around the dark trailer. "Do you want to kill us both?"

He could feel her cool breath on his lips, and her angry whisper touched his skin like a caress. "I would never let that happen, but well done, volchitsa. Your control is excellent."

"I don't need your compliments." Her voice was scornful, but even as she spoke, her head was angling toward his again, drawn to him as he was to her.

"You have them, nonetheless." Oleg had washed his body in a nearby river before he slipped into the camp, washing off weeks of mud and ashes.

"How did you get in here?"

"It wasn't easy." His palm was warm on the side of her neck, and he could feel her amnis reaching out and flowing across his skin.

The Poshani Hazar searched for elemental energy first, and

for a vampire as old and powerful as Oleg was, keeping his amnis under tight control was a herculean feat. The effort it took for him to conceal his elemental power felt like a noose around his throat.

"You cannot be here." Tatyana's voice wavered between irritation and concern. "If the Hazar find you—"

"They'll only find me if you call for them." Oleg angled his head to the side and breathed in the scent of her. Fresh water and roses. He battled the bizarre temptation to fall to his knees. "Are you going to call for them?"

Their lips weren't joined, but they were only inches apart. "And start a fight when I know you probably have an entire army hidden somewhere in the woods?"

"Not an army." His hand slid from the side of her neck to her shoulder, and he stroked his thumb over her collarbone. "Only a few people and all ones you know."

It didn't matter if she called for them. Now that Oleg had found her, he wasn't going anywhere.

She's nothing you want and everything you need.

He banished Lazlo's laughing words from his mind. Tatyana was definitely what he wanted.

She looked up and met his eyes. "Oleg, what..." She shook her head. "What are you doing here?"

"You ask as if you don't know." While his left hand drifted over her collarbone, his right hand slid around her waist and pulled her body closer. "I told you; I missed you."

Her jaw clenched for a moment. "You said that; then you hung up on me."

She let him pull her closer and pressed her body into his. Her words might have been angry, but her body and blood knew exactly what they wanted, and it wasn't a fight.

Oleg felt as if he'd been starving and now a banquet was laid out before him. He could smell her arousal, and his cock was already hard.

It took every ounce of self-control not to grab her, throw her on the wide bed, and tear her clothes off. He wanted to drape his body with hers. He wanted to taste every inch of her skin. He wanted to sink his cock into her body and his fangs into her neck.

The memory of her taste was sweet on his tongue.

"I missed you." Now that he'd admitted it, he couldn't stop saying it. "You have infected my mind."

The moment Oleg had come within a mile of her, the amnis he carried in his blood woke like a roaring lion. He'd nearly torn off Mika's head when the vampire had told him to be careful and take his time.

"I *infected* you?" She pushed him back. "What is that supposed to mean?"

He narrowed his eyes. "Perhaps *infection* was the wrong word."

"You *cannot* be here." Her whisper was stronger this time. "You have violated your own agreement with the Poshani, and if Radu finds you—"

"So call him." Oleg moved back to her, crowding her against a wall and lowering his face to hers again. "Call him." He bent and whispered, dragging his lips across her skin, "I will not stop you."

She put her hands on his shoulders and pushed him away. "I should call them. I should scream for them right now." Despite her words, her eyes dropped to his lips.

Tatyana was as hungry for him as he was for her.

Oleg reached down, tore off the ragged T-shirt he was wearing, and threw it on the floor. Then he braced his arms around her, leaning into the wall and caging her body with his while he bent his head down and breathed in her scent.

"Do you remember what it feels like to need a breath?" He watched the expressions flicker across her endlessly fascinating face. "I don't. It's been too long."

"It burns." She fisted her hand and pressed it against her chest. "Right here."

Oleg's eyes dropped to her chest. "Yes, it does."

Her energy tangled with his, and the moisture in the air drew to her body while Oleg continued to carefully leash his power.

"You can't be here." She repeated herself, but this time it was barely a whisper.

Her hands lifted, and her fingertips were damp when she touched his skin. Her element sizzled against his chest, and steam rose around them, redolent with the scent of woods, water, and roses.

"Tell me to leave," Oleg murmured. "I know I have trespassed. Tell me to leave, and I will go."

Her bright blue eyes lifted to meet his gaze. "Maybe you have infected me too."

"Enough." He wrapped his arms around her and lifted her up as their lips met.

Tatyana wrapped her legs around his waist, and he braced his hands under her rounded bottom, kneading her delicate curves as he started walking to the bed.

Finally. *Finally.*

Her mouth tasted like wine. He was drunk from her kiss, and he was barely keeping his body under control. His throat was on fire, and all he wanted was to taste her blood and drink in her pleasure until she wept.

"No." Tatyana yanked the back of his hair, and Oleg barely kept from snarling. "Shower. Water."

"Smart." He changed direction and headed toward the scent of water.

Sliding the door open, he realized that he'd underestimated the luxury this caravan offered.

This was no rudimentary camper. The bathing area was nearly as large as the bedroom, and as he braced Tatyana against the wall and started unbuttoning the shirt that covered her skin, she reached out and flipped on the water.

Oleg arched his back when ice-cold water hit his neck.

"Sorry." She fumbled with the levers. "Let me just—"

"Not important." Nothing was as important as being *in* her. The water would keep his amnis at bay, which felt like an actual problem for the first time in several hundred years.

He was honestly not sure if he was going to lose control.

What was she doing to him? He gripped her shirt with one hand, tore his mouth from hers, and used his fangs to rip away the material blocking her body from his.

"Oleg!" She hissed. "Put me down."

He curled his lip and growled in the back of his throat but placed her on the floor where she stepped out of her now-soaked clothing and lifted her chin.

There was a drop of blood on her lower lip where his fangs had cut her lip. He lifted his hand, and his fingers hovered over the small wound. His hand was trembling. "What have you done to me?"

Chapter 22

Tatyana

What had she done to *him*? What was he doing to *her*?

Tatyana felt everything at once.

She was angry and she was relieved.

He had violated her sanctuary and she was happy about it.

He was the bane of her existence and the only man she wanted in her bed.

Oleg touched her lip, wiping a drop of blood from her mouth before he lifted his thumb and licked at the dark red drop of blood that was smeared on his skin.

His lip curled up, his fangs fell, and she saw the moment that his control utterly snapped.

Her water met his fire, and the room around them filled with steam. Oleg fell to his knees, spread her legs, and fixed his mouth at the apex of her thighs.

Tatyana's knees buckled as a spear of pleasure shot from the tip of his tongue, up the heated center of her body, and straight up her spine.

Oleg took her ankle and lifted her leg over his shoulder a moment before she would have fallen to the ground. His hand held the small of her back, and her shoulders rested on the wall of the shower as water poured around them both, sizzling against his skin as fire erupted on his shoulders, only to be doused and erupt again.

She wanted his fangs.

Tatyana reached down, one hand grasping for anything while she teetered on the edge of screaming.

He let go of one hip and gripped her hand in his, weaving their fingers together as his other arm wrapped around her thigh and reached up, tweaking her nipple as he feasted on her sex.

"Please," she sobbed, biting her lip so hard she tasted blood.

She felt her body begin to erupt and Oleg released her, shoving down his pants and driving into her with one hard thrust as her amnis burst across her skin in waves. She threw her arms around his shoulders as his hips drove her into the wall.

Her climax cascaded around her like a waterfall, rippling up her back until she was shaking with pleasure.

She didn't breathe. She'd forgotten how.

Oleg was silent, but his hands gripped her, and the hard length of his erection pierced her in the most pleasurable way. She wrapped her arms around his shoulders and clung to him. Her nails dug into his neck, and she smelled his blood in the air.

Yes, this.

Yes, him.

This one. This man. This monster.

Mine.

The feral whisper in her mind made her gasp, and Oleg took the advantage, capturing her lips with his own as his thrusts slowed and deepened, turning the corner from a frantic invasion to a slow and steady ride.

She wanted to suck his blood and taste the thick sweetness on her tongue. She wanted to lap at his cock and run her fangs over the turgid skin.

Oleg took his time, bending down to change the angle of his

thrusts as he hit her clitoris from his new position and sent her tumbling into pleasure again.

"Too much." She dug her fingers into the muscle at his neck, and Oleg snarled, throwing his head to the side as he snapped at her thumb with his dull front teeth.

"Mine." He pulled back when he heard her small gasp, locking eyes with her as he pinned her to the wall. "You are mine."

Was she?

Or was she the one who possessed?

Her mind was utterly clear, completely focused. Her amnis felt sharper than it ever had.

There was a ripple of blue fire riding his shoulders. Keeping their eyes locked together, she pulled the water to her palms and smoothed her hands over his burning skin.

"Shhh." She leaned forward and pressed a kiss to the side of his neck. She closed her eyes and imagined sinking her teeth into his skin, swallowing hot gulps of his blood that would slide sweet down her throat.

Yes. She could picture it in her mind, and her mouth watered.

"What have you done to me?" Oleg's voice was halfway between anger and wonder. "Tatyana—"

She captured his mouth with her own, cutting off words that might have made her think too much.

She didn't want him to speak. She wanted his body, his fangs, and his fire.

Oleg wrapped his arms around her waist and pressed Tatyana so close to his chest that there was nothing between them save for their rioting amnis that reached out, caressing fire against water before it exploded in pleasure when Oleg came.

She felt his climax through her entire body, minute bursts of energy over every inch of her skin as he pulled his amnis back so hard she thought his body might burn to ash from the inside.

He leaned against her, holding her tight as his body remained linked with hers.

Mine. She heard the whisper in her mind again.

This powerful monster. This burning fire.

Tatyana felt a surge of feral pride and a possessive instinct that reached up and wrapped around her throat.

Mine.

The water poured over them, and when she looked up, Oleg's eyes were closed.

It was as close to peaceful as she had ever seen him, and she was ready to sink her teeth into his shoulder to mark her territory.

This was not good.

She needed some distance. She needed to *think*. And she couldn't do that with Oleg anywhere near her. "Oleg."

"Hmm." He stroked a hand over her head, running his palm down the wet length of her hair.

"It's nearly dawn."

He opened his eyes and looked to the side. "Yes, I feel it."

"What are you going to do?"

He slowly set Tatyana down and eased away from her body.

Empty. She felt empty when he left her.

What are you doing to me?

What were they doing to each other?

"You need to go," she whispered. "You can't be here."

"You keep saying that." He trailed a finger over her ear and down the side of her neck. "Are you sending me away?"

"We never shared a day chamber, and I don't imagine you want to start now." Tatyana, flush with pleasure and hungry for blood, felt her head swimming. "You need to go before dawn because I'm going to wake up hungry, and I don't want you here."

It was a lie, and from the sly smile flirting at the corner of Oleg's mouth, he knew it as well as she did.

She wanted him. She wanted him in her bed. She wanted to wake at dusk, sink her fangs into his neck, and ride him until her head exploded.

She wanted his blood in her veins, and the sheer ferocity of that desire had her stepping away from him.

"As you wish, little wolf." Oleg reached down and grabbed the sopping-wet black canvas pants that were pooled on the floor of the shower. "But I'll be back."

"You're risking a huge problem with Radu and Kezia if you even try to—"

"I'll be back." He hooked his forearm around her neck, pulled her into his chest, and pressed his lips to hers in a long, mind-spinning kiss that had her stumbling back when he released her. "Not tonight. But tomorrow night I will be back. And we will..."

Do this all over again?

"We will talk." Oleg lifted his chin and pinched her chin between his fingers, angling her face up to his. "Yes, I believe we have things to discuss."

"Talking is overrated." She crossed her arms over her chest, suddenly feeling exposed. She reached over and turned off the shower, leaving both of them soaking wet and dripping.

"Hmm." Oleg rolled his shoulders back, and in a ripple of elemental power, the water that had dotted his shoulders turned to steam. "We shall see."

He leaned down and breathed warm air over her neck, licking out and giving her shoulder one last kiss before he turned and walked out of the shower, leaving her alone.

Tatyana reached over and grabbed for a large bath sheet, but by the time she walked out of the washroom, Oleg was gone.

Chapter 23

Oleg

He dropped to the ground and rolled under her travel trailer a moment before a Hazar landed on the grass in front of the door.

There was a quiet knock. "Miss Vorona?"

Oleg froze, curious what she would do.

The door opened. "Yes?"

"Are you safe?"

"Quite safe, thank you." Her voice held just a bit of arrogance. "A friend of mine just left. Is there a problem?"

No doubt the Hazar had noticed the explosion of elemental energy coming from Tatyana's trailer—a blind human probably could have felt the power of their combined climax—but the wind vampires had no idea who or what was causing the explosion in Tatyana's trailer, and they knew it wasn't any of their business.

The feet stepped back. "Of course not, Miss Vorona."

"Thank you for checking on me." Her voice warmed a little bit. "I appreciate your concern."

"Of course, surati."

"Good night." She shut the door, and moments later the Hazar flew away.

Surati.

Interesting. The Poshani Hazar had used the word for elder sister, and Oleg wondered if Tatyana understood the significance.

Surati meant sister, but it was also a term of respect for any woman who exhibited wisdom or good sense. The Poshani had taken to his little bookkeeper.

This both relieved and irritated him.

"A friend of mine just left. Is there a problem?"

"Of course not, Miss Vorona."

For some reason, Oleg felt his jaw ache when she referred to her "friend."

You idiot, she's talking about you.

No doubt the Hazar would assume Tatyana was entertaining another immortal in the kamvasa, and Oleg's eye twitched at the thought.

Who else was in the kamvasa? Was there a rival to interfere in his pursuit of Tatyana? Had that damned silver-haired vampire followed her?

In his rush to find Tatyana, Oleg hadn't spent any time investigating or watching who else might be taking shelter with the kamvasa this season.

She'd mentioned Radu and Kezia—was Vano still absent?

Oleg saw the sky starting to lighten, and he quickly darted out from the trailer, slipping from one shadow to another as he made his way from the center of the kamvasa to the edge of the meadow.

His amnis was jumping out of his skin, but his body was sated, which made keeping his power concealed slightly easier. The moment he hit the edge of the forest, he let some of his power loose and ran.

There had been no scent of another on her. That was good.

The cold night air fed his lungs and filled his chest. He could still smell her scent on his skin, and a primitive part of him reveled in the small marks she'd left in his neck. If he could turn them into scars, he would, but vampires didn't scar after they became immortal. Even the most severe burns healed eventually.

He didn't even breathe until he was a mile away from the kamvasa perimeter and nearing the cave that Lazlo had dug for them into the side of a small hill covered by stone pine.

Mika was sitting on a log just at the mouth of the cave, and he stood when Oleg came near. "Good. You're not dead."

"Did you think that was actually a possibility?" Oleg leaned against a tree. "Do you think they'd kill me? Or try to?"

"It's the Poshani, Oleg. Anything is possible when you've violated the sanctity of the kamvasa." Mika brushed his hands on his pants and turned to walk into the cave. "You'll be happy to know Lazlo is still brilliant at cave construction. He was finished with your day chamber before dusk."

"It's nice, isn't it?" Oleg looked up at the moon and the quickly lightening sky. "We haven't done this in three centuries, Mika."

"You mean you were missing cave life? Missing the lack of plumbing and burning food over the fire?"

"I missed spending quality time with my druzhina and watching their faces twist in annoyance when I take them away from their electronic toys and video entertainment." Oleg smiled. "Oh wait, that was just you."

Mika shook his head. "At least you fucked the woman. Feeling less stressed?"

Oleg spoke quietly and clearly so Mika didn't miss his words. "Speak respectfully unless you want me to kill you."

"I thought you'd be in a slightly more reasonable state of mind." Mika stood and rolled his eyes. "Apparently not."

That wasn't likely. If anything, that very quick taste of Tatyana Vorona had only fed his hunger for the woman.

"We'll be tracking the kamvasa for a time," Oleg said. "Tell the others. I'm going to my chamber to rest."

Whatever was happening between him and Tatyana, it was past time to sort it out.

Chapter 24

Tatyana

"Tatyana Vorona!"

She turned when she heard Kezia's voice in the meadow. They'd moved during the day, and Tatyana wondered if the Hazar suspected someone had intruded in the camp.

She saw Kezia walking toward her with a vampire behind her who had the bearing of a Hazar with his fitted black T-shirt and dark wrap sunglasses. He had sandy-brown hair cut military short and a square jaw.

From Tatyana's observation, wind vampires wore sunglasses when they flew, which made sense to guard against irritation of the eyes. And some vampires wore glasses when they looked at screens or bright lights.

But to walk through the camp wearing them looked ridiculous.

"Tatyana." Kezia called her name again and waved. "I'm so glad I found you."

Tatyana rose and walked to Kezia, greeting the woman with a light press of her cheek to Kezia's on one side, then the other, as the Poshani women had started greeting her.

"I am happy to be found," Tatyana said. "What a beautiful new spot the darigan have found for us tonight."

"Isn't it?" Kezia turned to the water. "This location is one of my favorites."

They were parked on the edge of a very large pond fed by a gently flowing stream, and instead of the kamvasa spreading in concentric circles, in this location it wrapped around the shore.

Many of the human wagons and trailers were opposite the central campsite, and the smell of cooking fires drifted across the water along with the sound of happy conversation and quiet music.

"Vano, you must meet our new surati, Tatyana Vorona." Kezia held Tatyana's hand and motioned to the man behind her whom Tatyana had thought was a guard.

Despite Kezia's warm introduction, Tatyana got nothing from Vano. Not warmth and not distance. The man's energy felt like a void.

Vano greeted her in Russian. "Welcome to the Dawn Caravan, Miss Vorona."

"The Dawn what?" She looked at Kezia.

"That's what many foreigners call the kamvasa." Kezia smiled. "Vano is our businessman. He's in charge of the money, so he talks with more foreigners than Poshani most nights. She speaks Poshani, brother. She picked it up surprisingly quickly."

Vano nodded a little bit. "You honor us."

"It's a beautiful and fascinating language."

"Some find it difficult to learn."

"I enjoyed the challenge. It's very nice to meet you."

"You are most welcome to our wandering home." Vano smirked a little bit. "Kezia and Radu say you have been a delightful addition to our traveling season this year. They sing your praises."

"They're very kind."

"It's good to get new blood into the caravan."

"The season is coming to an end too quickly," Tatyana said. "I love being here."

"Perhaps you will visit us again when you have the time." Vano's tone of voice didn't match his words. "I wish I could pull myself away from the office for a full season."

"You could," Kezia said. "But you love your accounts, brother."

Tatyana smiled. "You know, my background is in accounting."

"So I've heard." A smile touched his lips. "Oleg's clever bookkeeper."

"I did work for Oleg for a time." Tatyana kept her smile on like a mask. "I enjoy numbers, and he had an interesting job for me. I'm independent now."

If Tatyana wanted to keep in touch with her new friends in the Poshani, she might be looking to Vano for a job.

He cocked his head. "So you're independent of Oleg?"

Maybe not as much as I was before we fucked last night.

"We parted on good terms" —*and we were naked at the time*— "but yes, I'm independent of his aegis. I consult on a variety of book-keeping and technology projects."

Vano seemed to understand what she was getting at. "So if I needed an outside expert to wrangle our finances into the modern world, you'd be the person to hire?"

"Possibly." She cocked her head. "I have a background in technology, and I'm a vampire. It can be a complicated transition for our kind."

Our kind. She was talking like she'd been working with vampires for decades. "I think it's helpful to have someone with experience in both modern human business and immortal corporate structures to bridge that gap."

Dear God, was she talking herself into a deal with a vampire again?

At least this time she wasn't immediately drawn to the monster on the other side of the figurative bargaining table. Vano was about as charismatic as a roll of aluminum foil.

"An interesting thought." Kezia exchanged a look with Vano. "Something we might bring up with Radu before the Vashana."

Vano shrugged. "It's only three weeks away."

"But that is enough about work." Tatyana quickly caught on that Kezia wanted to change the subject. "Did I see them setting up the stage earlier?"

"Yes, the players have adapted *The Captain's Daughter* for the stage," Kezia said. "I am quite looking forward to it. They are performing tomorrow night, but they're doing a public rehearsal later if you want to watch."

"I look forward to it." Tatyana turned to Vano. "Do you enjoy theater?"

Just then, a gust of wind batted the back of her legs and tossed her hair into her face before swinging around and blowing toward Vano and Kezia.

Vano—who had been staring across the meadow—whipped his head back to Tatyana with a sudden and intense interest. His eyes narrowed. "I'm sorry, what did you ask me?"

"Theater." She held her breath in her lungs, freezing in place. "Do you enjoy the theater?"

She'd taken two showers that evening in addition to the dousing she'd shared with Oleg last night. The man couldn't possibly be embedded in her skin.

What was Vano smelling?

Vano blinked. "Theater? I enjoy it as much as anyone, I suppose." He nodded at Kezia. "I have a meeting with the darigan tonight. It was nice to meet you, Miss Vorona; I hope you enjoy the play."

Vano nodded slightly, turned, and walked away.

Tatyana still felt a knot of nerves in her belly, but Kezia didn't seem to be aware of any tension between her and Vano. "I can tell your brother is the life of the party, isn't he?"

Kezia burst out laughing. "Too true! He's the worst, but we love him." She shrugged. "We can't complain because he makes us too much money, and none of us like looking at contracts, do we?" She hooked her arm in Tatyana's. "Come. I heard through the rumor mill that you've taken a lover."

"This kamvasa is worse than an old people's home for gossip," Tatyana muttered.

"That means you must tell me all about it, or I'll make up my own stories."

"Absolutely not."

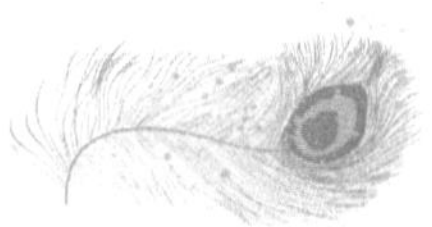

It was after midnight, and Tatyana hadn't seen Rumi, Katrina, or Desiree at the play rehearsal that night, which was far better than she'd anticipated. It had a straightforward plot, a courageous hero, and a sympathetic heroine. Along with a happy ending, it was exactly the kind of entertainment that Rumi would love.

Tatyana walked to the cooking wagons on the other side of the pond, wondering if there had been extra work she didn't know about.

"Rumi?" She called for her friends. "Desiree?"

If she'd been sitting in front of a play while her friends worked extra hard on some kind of project, she was going to feel guilty.

She slowed when she heard harsh voices in the distance.

"...this kind of waste." The voice was full of derision. "Do you think the clan has endless coffers?"

"So we need to stop giving the children snacks?"

Tatyana froze when she heard Rumi's voice.

"Are the small humans starving? No. They get enough food. They don't need cakes and treats all day. They should be working with their parents anyway, not playing in the forest like wild animals."

She crept forward, keeping to the shadows as she slipped around the corner silently.

In the distance, hidden between two old-fashioned vardos, Rumi and Katrina were standing across from Vano and a Hazar Tatyana didn't recognize.

"So is this how it is now?" Rumi asked. "You've seeded informers within the caravan to report back to you about every piece of coin?"

"Do you have any idea how much this operation costs?"

"I know how much some of the vampires are paying to be here." Rumi didn't back down. "And I know how hard my brothers are working in Minsk and Budapest building houses and stacking bricks so their families are provided for."

"It is not your role to question your terrin about how our labor is divided." Vano's voice rose. "Who do you think you are?"

Rumi lifted her chin. "It's not the role of the kitchen or even the terrin to tell Poshani parents how to raise their children. If they're hungry, we feed them." She slapped one hand in the other. "That is our *only* role."

"You waste our hard-earned money." Vano spat out his words. "Ungrateful—"

"Who is earning the money?" Katrina cut into his tirade. "Because I don't see you packing up trailer lines or hauling wagons, Vano." She sneered at him and said something low in Poshani that Tatyana didn't catch. "Don't you lecture us about work when you—"

Vano lifted his hand to strike the woman, and Rumi lifted her hands and shouted, "No!"

Tatyana nearly lunged forward, the air around her vibrating with evening mist, but Vano froze, and the Hazar with him leaned over and whispered something in his ear.

Vano's open hand turned into a pointing finger that he placed under Katrina's chin. Tilting her head up, he hissed, "Know your place, whore."

"Vano, this is unacceptable." Rumi straightened her shoulders and stepped between Vano and Katrina. "Not even a terrin may address the cooks of the kamvasa in this way. I will be speaking to Radu about this."

"You do that." Vano stepped back and straightened his shirt. "And stop feeding the children cakes."

Tatyana felt frozen. The idea of any of the vampires committing violence on the humans of the kamvasa felt like a slap across her own cheek.

Was this the dark side of the Poshani clan? She knew it had to be too good to be true. There was no community of humans or immortals where mutual respect was truly honored. That was a pipe dream, an ideal that she'd built up in her own mind because she liked it here and it felt safe.

She should have learned by now.

You're not a starry-eyed child, Tanya. Grow up.

She turned and started walking back to her trailer. It was only two in the morning, but maybe her mother would be awake. Maybe Anna wouldn't mind her call even in the middle of the night.

Her mind kept turning back to Rumi and Katrina standing in the darkness, chins lifted in defiance of the powerful vampire who was lecturing them.

Not even a terrin may address the cooks of the kamvasa in this way.

Tatyana stopped in her tracks and looked back over her shoulder toward the kitchen wagons. She should have known by Rumi's shock and Katrina's anger.

I will be speaking to Radu about this.

This was *not* normal behavior. Rumi was going to report Vano because it was abnormal.

She started walking back to her trailer again, but for the first time in months, she felt like there were eyes on her back.

Something was going on with Kezia's brother, and Tatyana knew she needed to watch her step.

For the first time in months, she did not feel safe.

Tatyana was watching the premiere performance of *The Captain's Daughter* the following night and wondering if Oleg was actually going to find her again. The kamvasa had moved after their brief and explosive meeting; she had no sense of where she was.

She'd briefly entertained the idea that she should wait in her trailer in case Oleg managed to find them, but then she banished that thought from her mind.

She was not going to wait for him. She was going to join her friends to watch the play, eat delicious food, drink some wine, and watch the stars. Then maybe if Oleg was in her trailer before dawn, she would talk to him.

But she would not wait for him.

The darigan had set out tufted sofas and luxurious pillows on the slope of the hill where the audience sat to watch the play. There was a natural amphitheater carved into the hill—or perhaps years ago an earth vampire had carved one out—and the ground was layered in rich wool rugs.

Vampires and humans tiptoed through the gathered audience to find a seat, waving at friends as children ran barefoot across the waving grass. The scent of paprika from the kitchen wagons wafted in the breeze.

Poshani, both human and vampire, greeted her by name as she sat on one side of a bright green sofa about halfway up the slope. A striped grey cat she'd seen near the kitchen wagons jumped up on the sofa, winked at her, then sat at attention on the far arm of the sofa, watching the grass.

Woodsmoke and dust. Fresh pine with a hint of wild violet. The summer night called to her, a symphony of scent and sound that filled her mind and piqued her amnis.

"Tatyana."

She turned when she heard her name. "Darius, how are you tonight?"

"I am well." The ancient Persian sat next to Madina. He touched the woman's shoulder, and both of them turned to nod at her.

"Tatyana."

"Madina."

On the edge of the gathering, she saw Fynn, who always seemed to be alone.

That night Vano sat with Fynn, and the two had their heads together. Both were wearing frowns. She couldn't look at Vano without seeing his hand raised to strike Katrina and his scorching insults.

She felt her lip curl instinctively.

"May I be so bold, mademoiselle?"

She turned and saw a blond vampire standing a little ways away. "Hello."

The man had blond hair, beautiful eyes, and full lips that were made for kissing. There was a dimple in his cheek and a playful expression on his face.

"You must be Tatyana." He took another step closer, addressing her in accented English. "Chérie, you are as stunning as Kezia reported. I am René DuPont des Trous of Tornai. It is an honor to make your acquaintance."

Tatyana disliked him immediately.

He was too charming. Too friendly.

And she was being rude. She responded in English even though she hated her accent. It was better than her French. "Good evening, Mr. DuPont. It's nice to meet you too. Welcome to the kamvasa."

He looked at the nearly empty sofa she was sitting on. "May I join you?"

"Ah, I am afraid that I am saving this seat for a friend." She plastered on a smile. "Perhaps for the encore performance tomorrow night?"

He raised an eyebrow and pointed at her. "I will hold you to your promise."

Had she promised anything? Lovely. Oh well. He would be her traveling companion for a number of weeks, so she should at least try to be friendly.

Her instinctive aversion to the man likely had more to do with being Anna Vorona's daughter than it did with anything he had done. She'd simply inherited her mother's suspicion of charming men.

The lights that were scattered around the hill were one by one turned off, and the lights on the stage shone bright.

"Welcome." The master of ceremonies swept onto the stage with a dramatic bow. "Guests of the kamvasa, brothers and sisters of the Poshani, welcome to the debut performance of *The Captain's Daughter*, an enchanting and romantic tale of love and struggle. War and loyalty."

The audience clapped, and Tatyana looked around to see where her fellow vampires were sitting.

There were Hazar hovering in the air, and the kamvasa guests were scattered around the slope. Darius and Madina were surrounded by servers, Kezia and René drank wine in an eclectic group of glittering vampires and humans, while Fynn was at his table on the edge of the crowd. Radu was sitting with him, drinking from a pewter goblet with his eyes on the stage.

Vano wasn't in her line of sight.

Tatyana tried to relax. What could the vampire do? She was surrounded by Poshani vampires and humans. There were lights on the stage. Nearly everyone in the camp had gathered for the play's premier.

The master of ceremonies continued. "Friends, Romans" —a scatter of laughter— "*Poshani.*" The audience clapped wildly and a few hooted. "We present... *The Captain's Daughter!*"

The lights dimmed again, and when they rose, there was snow blowing across the stage and a young man in thick clothes trudging slowly through what appeared to be a birch forest.

"Hello!" the actor called out. "Is anyone there to help me?"

In the dim shadows beside the stage, Tatyana saw a water vampire gathering fat snowflakes in her hand and blowing them across the stage with her cold breath.

Vampire-created stage snow. Tatyana couldn't help but smile. She was going to try making snow later.

"I heard you say you were saving this seat."

Her head whipped around when she heard him speak. Vano was standing in the darkness, his eyes fixed on Tatyana, pointing at the empty seat beside her.

How inconvenient.

"They must still be working." She gestured to the far side of the sofa. "Please, join me."

"I would be delighted." Vano wasn't wearing sunglasses that night, but he still reminded her of a Hazar with his black pants and black shirt. While most of the audience was dressed in festive clothing—Tatyana had donned a sky-blue sundress—Vano still appeared to be mimicking the guards.

"Your friends" —Vano kept his voice whisper-low— "if they are able to join you, I will move, of course."

"No, it's fine." She didn't think Rumi, Desiree, or Katrina would have time to watch the play even though they would love it. Vano's lecture the night before might have chilled their desire to be around vampires.

Especially the one sitting next to her.

She kept her eyes fixed on the play as the forest disappeared and the birch trees transformed into an old-fashioned military fort with men marching in dull brown coats as a red-coated captain shouted orders.

Drums pounded as the men marched and sang, and Vano scooted closer to Tatyana on the sofa.

"Kezia told me you've been spending time with the cooks." He smiled a little. "Are they the ones teaching you Poshani?"

She kept her voice low, knowing his keen immortal ears would hear her over the drums on stage. "They were kind enough to teach me, yes."

Though Kezia spoke to Tatyana in Poshani, Vano addressed her in very formal Russian.

"If you would prefer a language tutor with a higher level of proficiency, it can be arranged."

Tatyana turned to him. "Are you saying that the women who grew up speaking Poshani don't know the language well enough to teach me?"

"I'm saying that they are uneducated cooks and they speak like it."

"Hmm." Tatyana lifted her chin. "I grew up on a farm, running around like a wild animal, so I think the Poshani that I've learned suits me. Thank you."

His eyes glittered, and Tatyana realized she'd given too much away.

They don't need cakes and treats all day. They should be working with their parents anyway, not playing in the forest like wild animals.

Vano hadn't known she'd heard that exchange, but she'd just told him.

Stupid, Tanya. So stupid.

"Your friends must have told you about our discussion the other night."

There was no way she could refute that without admitting that she'd been eavesdropping. "I believe they will be sharing that conversation with Radu and Kezia. It is not something we need to discuss."

"Exactly." Vano's fangs fell behind his lips, but he allowed the edge of one to peek out at her.

A warning. Subtle but aggressive.

"Poshani business is for Poshani," Vano said. "You would do well to enjoy our hospitality, Miss Vorona. And do not forget that you are a guest in this place."

"I will never forget the hospitality of the Poshani," Tatyana said. "You can be assured of that."

Without another word, she stood and walked away. She wasn't retreating, but her hands had a slight tremor and her amnis was roused by his threat. If she stayed sitting next to Vano any longer, she was going to rip his head off. Or at least try.

Not exactly the proper etiquette for a theater performance.

She nodded at a Hazar guard as she passed him on the edge of the crowd.

The vampire cocked his head with a slight frown. "Is everything all right, surati?"

No, your terrin just threatened me and told me to keep my mouth shut about it.

She was angry and afraid. The bastard thought he could threaten her? He thought he could threaten Rumi and Katrina?

He could.

Vano was a terrin of the Poshani people, the power behind the kamvasa.

Tatyana tried to even her expression and stop her hands from trembling. "The lights were bothering my eyes a little bit." She touched her temple. "I'll catch the second performance tomorrow and remember to bring glasses."

"Of course, Miss Vorona." He bowed and watched her walk back to her caravan. "Enjoy your solitude and rest your eyes."

"Thank you."

She sensed him as soon as she got close. Tatyana walked up the steps and punched in her combination with the dangling stylus before she pulled the door open and walked into her trailer.

Her hands were still shaking, and her amnis was running high.

Oleg was lounging on the sofa in front of the small table, freshly showered and wearing a navy-blue shirt open at the collar. "The play sounded delightful. Pushkin, yes?" He looked up from the book he was reading. "Why did you leave?"

She stood, staring at him as the sense of rightness swept over her.

There you are. You arrogant, infuriating, know-it-all vampire.

There you are.

Dammit.

"Tatyana?" Oleg frowned and rose to his feet. "What happened?" He lifted his nose and sniffed the air before he growled and bared his teeth. "Who frightened you?"

Chapter 25

Oleg

His fangs were down, but Tatyana walked to him, stood on her tiptoes, and brushed a kiss over his jaw.

Her voice was breezy and unconcerned, a sure tell that she was upset. "I was enjoying the play but not the company. How did you find us so quickly?"

"Tatyana, I can smell your fear," he growled. "Who shall I kill?"

"No one." She sighed and sat on the sofa. "So domestic. The vampire lord of the Kievan Rus waiting for me after a night out with my friends."

She probably thought that would offend him, but Oleg frankly liked the image she put into his mind. He wanted to take her to plays and ballets and watch her enjoy them with her vampire vision, hear the music with new ears.

He liked the idea of waiting for her to return to a place they shared, knowing she would tell him about her evening and make him laugh with her sardonic humor.

"I smell adrenaline and cortisol," he said. "The same scent I have smelled on you when someone has frightened you. Tell me who it was unless you want me to walk to that gathering and start lighting vampires on fire."

"Will you calm down?" She stood and walked in front of him. "You are ridiculous," she hissed. "You cannot follow me through the world, killing anyone who makes me angry or afraid."

"Why not?" he snarled.

"Because you..." She let out a huff of breath. "Because it's ridiculous."

"You do not overreact to threats—I should correct myself—you do not overreact to threats from vampires other than myself."

"Overreact? You think I overreact to you?"

He looked down. "What do you call running from my house a few hours before dawn when you were only a few months immortal?"

"Survival?"

He growled. "And who was threatening you?"

"You!" Her mouth dropped open. "Not..." She let out a breath, stepped away from him, and walked to the far side of the trailer. "Not the way you are thinking."

He felt the loss, but he was frozen in confusion, which was not an emotion he experienced often. She was picking a fight with him, and he couldn't remember the last time someone had done that.

Centuries?

Maybe longer. Not even Mika was willing to go toe-to-toe with him, but this little girl thought she was a match for him?

Fine. They'd been dancing around this fight for months, and he had reached the limit of his patience.

Oleg walked over slowly, keeping his voice deliberately soft. "And how was I threatening you, Tatyana? How? By protecting you? By killing Zara?"

She said nothing, staring at his feet with her arms crossed over her chest.

"Perhaps I threatened you by pulling the pain of Zara's death into my own body so you wouldn't die from the loss of your sire when you were only a few months immortal?"

That got a reaction. She dropped her arms and took a step toward him. "You did not."

"Of course I did. I'm stronger than you. I knew you could survive her death as long as I had enough of your blood, and I was right."

Her eyes went wide. "That's why you took my blood? That's why you bit me?"

"No." Oleg walked over, leaned down, and growled in the back of his throat. "I took your blood because *I wanted it.*"

And he wanted more of it. The scent of fear was gone—the scent of her arousal had taken over. He wanted her blood, her kiss, her sex, her laughter. He wanted to see her dance, and he wanted her to be safe.

Fuck him, Lazlo was right.

"Who was threatening you?" he whispered.

She was frozen in place. "You felt your pain *and* mine when she died."

"Yes, and I'd do it again. Who was threatening you tonight?"

"I didn't want *you* to kill her." Tatyana pushed past him, but he grabbed her hand, keeping them connected even as she walked away.

"Tatyana—"

"I was going to kill her." She spun around. "I *wanted* to kill her. Or Mika could have done it. I knew it would hurt you and you'd already killed Luana—"

"You don't protect me!" Even the thought of it made him furious. "I've already told you this. That's not how my world works. *You* don't protect *me.*"

"Then what do you want from me?" She pulled her hand away from his grip. "You want me to need you" —her hand curled into a fist over her heart— "but you want *nothing* from me."

He shook his head. "You know that is not true."

"Oh, that's right. You want to *own* me." She walked to him and bared her fangs. "You want me like a trophy sitting in your dead mate's house, fucking you when you happen to remember that I exist." She lifted her chin. "What a lucky girl! To wait in the wings for the great Oleg Sokolov to grant me his attention."

Everything in his cold, hard chest softened, and he felt his heart beat once. "Is that what you think of me, volchitsa?"

"You want my world to be nothing but you." Her mouth twisted in a grimace. "You want to own me, but you want to know what is worse?" Tatyana blinked, and pink tears rolled down her cheeks.

Oleg said nothing.

"If I had stayed with you in Sochi, I would have let you do it." Her smile was bitter. "If I had stayed with you, I would have become nothing. And then..." Her voice dropped to a whisper. "*Then* you would have hated me."

He slowly straightened. "If you think that is what I want for your eternity, I have failed."

She said nothing, but she shook her head and wiped her eyes with the back of her right hand.

Oleg grabbed her hand and kissed the tears of salt and blood, tasting the flavor of his failure. "I will think of what you said tonight, and we will talk more tomorrow." He folded her small hand between both of his. "But tonight you must tell me who frightened you."

"Oleg—"

"Not because I do not think you are capable or intelligent, but because I am older than you and I know the immortal world better than you do. If there is danger, I want you to know what to do."

She said nothing.

"Will you acknowledge this? That I may understand the opaque politics of the Poshani better than you do?"

"Yes." She sighed. "Fine."

He waited for her to speak.

"Vano," she said quietly. "Vano threatened me."

Oleg growled. "I will kill him."

"No, you will not." She pulled her hand away from his.

Yes, he would. He'd been wanting to kill Vano anyway, and this was as good an excuse as any. He already suspected that the man was working with Ivan behind his back, and now he'd frightened the woman Oleg cared for.

"This is why I didn't want to tell you." She crossed her arms over her chest. "You shouldn't even be here, and if you march out and set Vano on fire—"

"I will not do that if you explain why he threatened you." Oleg put his hand on her shoulder and led her to the sofa across from the wall of books. "Unless you are in immediate danger, I will wait to kill him."

"You cannot kill him." Tatyana sat down. "Not for this."

Oleg sat next to her and waited for her to speak.

After a time, she started. "I've made friends with some of the human women who are cooks for the kamvasa. They're the ones who helped me learn Poshani. Vano arrived a few nights ago, and last night I heard him yelling at those women for wasting money by giving the children snacks and treats."

"That is ridiculous; the Poshani are not suffering financially." Unless there was something Vano was hiding, the Poshani businesses that Oleg interacted with were thriving. "Our organization works with them regularly, and their finances have no appearance of being in distress."

"I think it was a control and power thing." Tatyana frowned. "The financial argument is only a cover. I know how much I paid for my season here, and I have a feeling I got the family rate judging by how Radu and Kezia talk."

"To be fair, Radu would make you feel like you got the family rate even if he had gouged you." He reached over and took her hand, sliding her fingers between his own.

"That doesn't surprise me." Tatyana rubbed her thumb over his knuckles absently. "But I still think they charge others even more."

Her thumb stroking over his knuckles was intensely satisfying. "Did Vano know you saw him threatening those women?"

"He thinks they told me about it, and I didn't correct him. But Rumi already said she was going to talk to Radu about Vano's threats and disrespect, so I don't understand why he threatened me."

"He probably sees it as an internal matter. The Poshani try to always present a united front to outsiders, but like any clan, they have internal power struggles."

"That makes sense." She stared at the books, but she wasn't really looking. "There is more tension than I sensed at first."

"Be cautious around Vano." Oleg wanted to steal her away, but her words kept reverberating in his mind.

You want to own me. You want me like a trophy sitting in your dead mate's house, fucking you when you happen to remember that I exist.

He could not take her away from the kamvasa when she already thought the worst of him.

"I will be careful." She looked at him and raised an eyebrow. "And you?"

"I will not kill Vano for threatening you. Tonight."

She sighed. "I suppose I can live with that."

"Good." He nodded. "This has been a productive encounter."

She smirked. "No seducing me tonight?"

"No, I have decided that I am going to court you."

"What?" She blinked. "What are you talking about?"

"I am planning to court you, Tatyana Vorona." He tucked a strand of hair behind her ear. "Because apparently you think I only want you for a trophy, and that is not the case."

"Listen, I am sure in your own mind—"

"No." He leaned down and pressed a fast kiss to her mouth. "There will be no more arguing— Well, not about this. You asked me what I wanted from you? I will court you, and you will see what I want."

"Courting me." She leaned away and looked at him. "Who talks like that?"

"Someone who is significantly older than you," he muttered. "But this will be good. While you are still in the kamvasa, I will court you."

She shook her head. "What does that even mean?"

"We will spend time together, talk about many things, and share experiences that are not sex. So you will understand my character and I will understand yours."

She grimaced. "So... no sex? Just talking for another six weeks?"

"Don't be ridiculous," he said. "We can have sex and talk at the same time."

Oleg left her shortly after their discussion but took his time returning to the encampment with his druzhina. He waited on the edge of the kamvasa for nearly an hour, tracking the movements of the Hazar and second-guessing his decision to leave Tatyana in a place where other vampires might see her as vulnerable.

It wasn't that he didn't trust the Hazar, but if Oleg could sneak into the camp, it was possible that others could too. He wasn't the only one who could mask his amnis.

After an hour, he started back to the cave Lazlo had dug, enjoying the fresh night air as he walked.

"You're as stealthy as a bear in rut."

Oleg looked up. Ludmila was sitting in the low branches of a tree a few meters away and aiming a rifle at his head.

"Stop with the flattery. I'll buy you the new rifle you want."

"I already bought it." She clicked the safety on her firearm and set it in the notch of the pine. "Did you kill anyone while you were courting your little bookkeeper?"

Oleg narrowed his eyes. "Did Mika tell you where I was?"

"You smell like her." Ludmila sniffed the air. "She doesn't wear heavy perfume, but it's distinctive."

"It would irritate me that you know her scent, except you're a mated vampire." Oleg leaned against the trunk of the tree and looked at the faint light in the distance where the Poshani had circled their wagons. "Vano is in the camp."

"And?"

"He threatened Tatyana. And some of the humans who have befriended her."

"We should kill him."

This was why Ludmila was a favorite.

"I agree, but Tatyana doesn't think it's wise."

"Ugh." Ludmila grunted. "She sounds like Mika. 'Don't provoke known allies, Ludmila.'" She imitated the Estonian's accent. "'Stop maiming our business rivals' stupid employees.' If I maim them, they will learn not to be so stupid. How are they supposed to learn not to be stupid if they don't suffer physically?"

He narrowed his eyes. "You and Oksana don't have any plans to adopt children, do you?"

Ludmila shook her head. "She knows I would be too soft with them."

"It's amazing how your mate's thoughts mirror my own." Oleg felt the butt of Ludmila's rifle on his shoulder. He reached up and took the weapons so she could jump out of the tree.

"Vano is a weak little man who thinks he's smarter than he actually is." Ludmila looked into the distance at the same lights Oleg had been contemplating as she slung her rifle over her shoulder. "The Hazar nearly caught you earlier. I had to distract them. They may move the kamvasa again today."

"They won't. Kezia likes that little pond too much. They'll stay there for a week at least. The theater company just premiered a new play, and the stage is complicated to set up."

"They sacrifice security for entertainment."

"We all do sometimes."

"Are you talking about risking our organizational security so you can pursue the bookkeeper?"

Oleg ignored her. "Did you learn anything useful while you were spotting me?"

"There is a new guest," she added. "René DuPont."

"The French thief?"

"Is he French?" She narrowed her eyes. "I thought he was Belgian."

"Does it matter?"

Ludmila shrugged. "Probably to the French and Belgians."

"What do we know about him?"

"He moves like a cat." Ludmila glanced at Oleg, then back at the distant lights. "He moves like a good thief. Very quiet. He spotted you earlier, but he wasn't close enough to identify you."

"Do you think he's planning to rob the kamvasa?"

"That would be stupid." She shrugged. "But criminals are often stupid."

"*We're* criminals."

Ludmila grimaced. "Not anymore, boss. You're very law-abiding these days. It's lucrative—don't misunderstand me—but it can be a little boring."

"Perhaps I can convince some pirates to target our shipping fleet."

"That might be fun. I'm sure Ivan is already planning on it." She looked up at him. "You're going to have to kill him."

"René DuPont?"

"Ivan."

He'd known she was talking about Ivan, he just didn't want to deal with it right now. "I think I might be in love with Tatyana Vorona."

"That's not bad. She's not crazy like Luana if that's what you're concerned about."

"No, I'm more concerned with being in love with someone." He lifted one shoulder. "I did not plan on this."

"Life is unexpected. You think I planned on falling in love with a water vampire who collects painted ducks and enjoys watching English baking shows?"

Ludmila's mate Oksana looked like a rugby player, wielded an axe like a Varangian, and Oleg had witnessed her take the heads of three vampires with one broadsword strike.

"Oksana collects painted ducks?"

Ludmila sighed. "She found this pottery-painting café in Odesa that is open until midnight. There are five of them in the apartment now."

"All the same ducks?"

"No, different ducks." Ludmila frowned. "I believe there is a collection of complementary ducks that go together."

"Little ones too?"

"Yes, the little ones are the cutest, but they're harder to paint."

"Huh." Perhaps Tatyana was missing her mother's cat. "Maybe I should get Tatyana a kitten. She likes cats."

"If you are in love with this woman, do not give her gifts that require time, money, or maintenance."

"That's probably good advice." He frowned. "She thinks I want to own her."

"Of course you do. You want to own everyone and everything you care about, because then you can fit all the things you love into carefully controlled borders that you can protect."

"There's nothing wrong with protecting the things you care about."

"No, but you have never been known for your moderation, Knyaz." Ludmila looked up. "She's not your soldier, and she's not looking for a leader to follow."

"Then what is she looking for?"

"How am I supposed to know that?" Ludmila turned and started walking back toward Lazlo's cave. "That's what you have to figure out when you're courting her."

She's not your soldier, and she's not looking for a leader to follow.

LUDMILA'S WORDS WERE CIRCLING HIS HEAD THE FOLLOWING night as he watched Tatyana's trailer from the forest.

Tatyana had woken at dusk and gone to the play she'd skipped the night before. That night the performance was a repeat, the players were more relaxed, and more of the Poshani humans had joined the audience, including Tatyana's friends. When she returned to her caravan, Oleg was waiting for her.

And now they were playing a game of chess on the coffee table while he listened to her relate details about the play.

"I keep trying to figure out how that water vampire blows the snow across the stage." Her face was glowing as she moved a pawn to take his knight. "I want to try it, but no matter how much I concentrate, I can't get my breath cold enough to freeze water. Even when it's a very fine mist." She looked up with a slight frown. "Can you freeze water?"

"Freeze?" He smiled as he shook his head. "Definitely not. Heat is easier than cold, I think."

"Obviously for you." She sat back and waited for him to move. "Your turn."

"Is it?" Oleg didn't care about the chess game, but he very much cared about watching her delight as she took advantage of his distraction. He leaned forward, considering her queen's position on the board before he moved a bishop.

She rolled her eyes. "Are you trying to lose?" She moved her rook. "Check."

"Don't speak too soon." Oleg swiftly moved the previously positioned bishop to take her rook.

He wanted the game over, but not too quickly.

"Heat is easy because our amnis lives for vibration and vibration produces heat," he said. "It's a little more accessible for me because of my element, but any vampire can produce heat. That's how we keep our skin from being ice-cold around the humans."

"That makes sense." She cocked her head to the side. "But I cannot figure out the snow."

She was darling when she pursed her lips like that.

Oleg asked, "Was Vano at the play?"

Tatyana shook her head. "I didn't see him, and Rumi didn't mention him."

"Good. Did she report the altercation with Vano to Radu?"

"If she did, she didn't tell me, but she wouldn't because she doesn't know that I saw their fight."

He raised an eyebrow. "You didn't tell her?"

Tatyana shrugged. "I didn't want it to change anything."

"Why would anything change?"

"Because then I would be a vampire when she is in conflict with another vampire." She reached forward and repositioned her knight.

She was stringently independent, and he didn't approve of that streak in her. Self-sufficiency was a good trait for anyone, but vampires who isolated themselves and refused help usually didn't live long in his world.

"Your human friends know you are a vampire, Tatyana. If they are your friends, that will not matter." He reached for the glass of blood-wine she had poured for him.

"It does though. The Poshani say that vampires and humans are equal within the clan, but that's not true." She sat back and crossed her hands over her waist. "Surely you've noticed this."

"I have noticed that... I do not see Poshani vampires cooking goulash or building houses in Minsk." He smiled. "So yes. I see what you mean."

"Exactly."

"It is better than most organizations though."

She pursed her lips as she stared at the chessboard. "I will have to take your word for it, but it doesn't seem very equal to me."

"You still think like a human."

"I know, and I don't want that to change." She stood, walked to the sofa, and nudged his arms to the side so she could straddle his lap.

Oleg sat back and tried to ignore his cock, which had very definite opinions about Tatyana moving onto his lap. "You in this position tells me that you know you're losing this chess match."

"I acknowledge nothing of the sort." She leaned forward and put her face in the crook of his neck, inhaling deeply.

Oleg smiled and angled his head to the side. "You sniffed me."

"I like the way you smell."

"Vampire." He put his hands on her hips and rubbed gentle circles with the tips of his fingers. "You look beautiful in this dress."

"Thank you."

She was wearing some floaty, light green thing with slits at the sides that rode up her legs when she sat on him. He wanted to tear it off, but this might be the first time Tatyana had initiated intimacy with him in such a direct way.

Oleg was going to sit back and enjoy it.

She didn't move her head from his shoulder, and he could feel her breath on his neck.

"Tatyana."

"Hmm?"

Oleg put his hand on the back of her head, stroking her silken hair. "You asked me the other night what I wanted from you."

She laughed a little bit. "I have a feeling I know what you want." She spread her legs further, riding the heat of her sex along the thick ridge of his cock, which was heavy and hard between them.

"I told you what I wanted from you before you ever left me," Oleg murmured. "You just misunderstood what I meant." He angled his head farther to the side and urged her mouth toward his neck. "I told you, little wolf: *I want your fangs.*"

Chapter 26

Tatyana

There it was.

The same words he'd uttered over a year ago, but in the light of months apart and everything she'd learned about him, the meaning was far more clear.

He lay under her, not unlike her dreams, and her fangs were at his throat. She knew what this meant. What he was offering.

Her mouth watered, and a little voice whispered in the back of her mind: *You will not be able to leave him.*

Nevertheless, she opened her mouth, scraped her fangs over his skin, and watched his blood rush to the surface.

Oleg let out a guttural groan and dug his fingers into her hips. "Playing with your food, little wolf?"

Her food? She felt her mouth water, as if she could already taste the hot, sweet flood of him in her mouth.

His amnis crawled over her skin, teasing her nipples to sensitive points, raising goose bumps on her flesh.

Oleg sat preternaturally still, offering his blood to the predator she had become.

She licked at his neck, arching against him and riding the hard line of his erection between her thighs. The moment he fucked her, he would be master again, commanding her body and overwhelming her senses.

But this?

She breathed heated air against his neck and enjoyed the subtle reaction as his fingers curled into the flesh at her hips. He arched up, rubbing his erection against her aroused flesh, but he didn't move his head, baring his neck to her fangs.

He wasn't even breathing. The only sound in the room was her ragged breath against his skin.

Her choice.

Her bite.

His blood.

She drew her lips back and sank her teeth into Oleg's neck.

He let out a low, guttural groan of pleasure, and his hand moved to the back of her head. "Harder."

She bit down, all the while ravenous for him to fill her. She fumbled with the buttons on his trousers as she pulled blood from his neck.

Oleg finally reached down, tore his pants down the center, lifted her up, and seated himself to the hilt in her body.

She moaned at the pleasurable invasion, but her fangs never left his neck.

He said nothing, holding her tight as he thrust up over and over.

Tatyana rode him as she swallowed his rich, sweet blood. It was like nothing else she'd ever tasted. Wine after sips of water. She could feel his amnis flowing into her body, spreading through her veins, and the power of his fire twisted within her, joining them even closer than their bodies were linked.

She could take no more, and she released him with a gasp.

Oleg gripped the back of her hair in his fist and brought her bloody mouth to his lips, fusing them together in a kiss so savage that her head spun even as his elemental power surged through her.

Oleg put his hands under her bottom, as if he was going to lift her, then froze, eased back, and put his hands on her hips, lifting her up and down to ride his cock as she angled herself against him and focused on the swirling torrent of pleasure that was starting to pull her under like a whirlpool.

His amnis surging through her blood, his cock spearing her body, his voice whispering in a language she couldn't understand.

Oleg leaned forward, and Tatyana knew he wanted to take control, lift her up, flip her over, and make her scream.

Instead, he commanded her with tender hands and achingly slow thrusts as he felt her body start to tighten around him.

"That's it." He finally whispered something she could understand. "Come. Let me feel your pleasure joining mine."

Her body was a riot of sensation, but her elemental energy was a flood. His amnis. Her amnis. Flowing like twin currents in a raging river. She followed the crest of pleasure as it stole her breath, and Oleg cupped her cheeks in the palms of his hands, placing a gentle kiss against her gasping, open mouth.

She couldn't speak. She couldn't breathe.

When he came, he pressed his face into her neck and uttered her name with a ragged breath that sounded like it was torn from his chest.

His mouth was at her throat, and she was expecting his fangs.

She wanted his fangs.

Instead, he fluttered kisses over her skin and stroked his hands over her shoulders, along her exposed legs, and everywhere he touched, the tiny hairs on her body rose and followed him, caressing his fingers as he caressed her.

Tatyana was shaking.

She had destroyed herself against him, and all she wanted to do was hide.

She was too exposed. She'd been naked in front of Oleg, but now she felt like her very soul was laid bare.

"Tatyana—"

"Stop," she whispered, pressing her fingers against his lips. "Too much. I can't…" Her heart was an exposed nerve. "You need to leave."

Oleg leaned back, tilting his arrogant chin up and waiting until her eyes met his.

"I need to be alone," she whispered.

He didn't argue. The corner of his mouth turned up, but he said nothing.

Oleg was still in her body when he snapped his fingers and brought twin flames to his fingertips. He reached up and pressed his flaming fingers to the still-weeping fang marks she'd left in his neck.

Tatyana gasped when she heard the sizzle and took in the smell of burning flesh. "Oleg—"

"I don't mind your marks on my body, volchitsa." He smiled a little more. "I'd like to keep these for a while."

The flames left two red scars on his flesh, and Tatyana knew it would take months or even years for them to heal.

She was shaking and wrecked from an overload of sensation along with the rush of Oleg's powerful amnis flooding her body. She felt lightheaded.

She felt drunk.

Slowly she climbed off him, pulling her ruined sundress over her head and tossing it on the ground before she walked to the bathroom and threw on a robe, then cleaned herself up.

When she walked back, she saw that Oleg had pulled out the tail of his navy-blue collared shirt to cover the wreckage of his torn trousers.

She felt her skin heating up. "I'm sorry—"

"It's nothing." He cast a sly glance at her. "You're hard on my wardrobe, you know."

The flippant response jumped to her lips. "If you'd like to borrow a dress, you can have your pick."

He chuckled and walked over to her, grabbing her by the back of her neck and bringing her mouth to his in a hard kiss. "There she is."

She felt like she should say something, but she didn't know what. "Are you—"

"I'll bring some extra clothes the next time I visit." He pinched her chin, pressed one swift kiss to her forehead. "Sleep well."

Seconds later, he was gone.

Tatyana locked the door, double-locked it, and then crawled into her bed to hide.

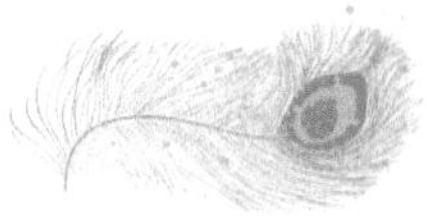

THE FOLLOWING NIGHT, OLEG DIDN'T COME, BUT HE LEFT A note in her trailer before dawn with a few words of apology, his next move on the chessboard, and a clutch of lavender he'd stuck in a glass.

Tatyana didn't mind. She was still working through the utter confusion of taking his blood and how it was making her feel.

Powerful, no doubt. She'd slept hard through the day, and that night when she woke, the usual burning in her throat was gone. She was barely hungry, and a single goblet of blood-wine was enough to sate her.

Two new trailers had appeared during the day, but she kept to her own caravan until the sound of strange voices had passed. When she snuck out, it was only to go see Rumi and Desiree, who were cooking for the evening meal.

"The man is a wind vampire, and his name is Benjamin Vecchio," Rumi said. "He's the son of Giovanni Vecchio, who used to go by the name Giovanni di Spada."

Desiree murmured something and crossed herself.

"Who is that?" Tatyana felt like they were talking about the boogeyman.

"Giovanni di Spada was a very vicious assassin." Desiree added a cup of spicy red paprika to the pot she was stirring, then swung the iron arm over the fire and spread the coals to lower the heat. "The old men use his name to frighten the children when they misbehave." She lowered her voice. "Don't wander at night or Giovanni di Spada will find you and cut your throat."

Tatyana's jaw dropped. "That's terrible!"

Rumi wrinkled her nose. "Yes, it's not good."

"And this new vampire is his *son*?"

"Apparently he was adopted as a child and raised with vampires." Rumi kept her voice low. "But he was sired not by his adoptive father but by Zhang Guo."

Tatyana had heard that name before, many times, in Arosh's court. "One of the Eight Immortals?" They were the vampire lords of most of East Asia, and rumors of their power and authority were impossible to avoid.

Arosh pretended to be civil with all of them, but he was highly resentful.

"So this vampire staying in the kamvasa is like... royalty or something?" Tatyana said.

She resented him immediately, which was probably unfair, but it seemed like everything in his life had been handed to him, and Tatyana couldn't help but resent people like that.

"The other vampire's name is Tenzin." Rumi was in full gossip mode. She put her knife down and spoke with her hands. "And she was Giovanni di Spada's old partner, but now she's mated to his son."

How... odd.

Rumi shrugged. "I know that probably seems strange, but they're vampires."

"Yes, vampire relationships can be very... complicated."

Oleg and Luana.

Luana and Zara.

Oleg and Tatyana.

She was exchanging blood with a man who was well over a thousand years her senior. Who was she to judge?

"If they're mated vampires, why do they have different trailers?"

Desiree frowned as she chopped another pile of onions. "That is unusual, isn't it?"

"I don't know. You can be mated to someone and still not trust them, I suppose." Rumi looked at Tatyana. "What do you think?"

"You're asking me?" Tatyana shrugged. "You've known about vampires longer than I have. I'm a baby in this world."

"You have a certain... glow about you though." Rumi winked at her. "So I think that you're learning more every night."

"I am not talking about this with you." The last thing she wanted was for her human friends to know or even suspect that she had a lover, especially one who was sneaking into the kamvasa under the Hazars' nose.

"Only three weeks more until the Vashana Zata," Desiree said. "Do you think that's why these new vampires have arrived?"

"I doubt it," Rumi said. "It's not like a former assassin or a vampire prince would be chosen by our people to take over as terrin."

"You never know," Desiree said. "There have been stranger vampires chosen to lead the clan."

"But not outsiders!"

Tatyana walked over to Rumi's table to help chop the onions. "What's the Vashana Zata?"

Rumi frowned. "You mean Radu and Kezia didn't tell you?"

Desiree waved at Tatyana to take over stirring the pot of paprikash and picked up the knife Tatyana had been using.

"They did not." Tatyana started stirring the cooking pot as the pungent smell of chopped onions filled the air.

"Vashana happens every year," Rumi said. "It's like... the general meeting. You'll see more Poshani come in—usually every family sends a representative—and disputes are settled, business is discussed, that sort of thing."

"So what's a Vashana *Zata*?" Tatyana asked.

Desiree shoved a pile of onions into a bowl and started chopping more. "That's where the terrin are chosen. It only happens every hundred years, so it's a very big deal. Sometimes a vampire will retire

—I've heard some people say Radu is ready to do something else—so if there's a vacancy, someone new will be chosen. It's a big honor but a big responsibility too."

"So there might be a new leader this year?" For some reason, that disoriented Tatyana.

"It's possible." Rumi muttered, "If there is, I pray to Sara-la-Kâli they take the ruby goblet."

Tatyana looked at Desiree.

The older woman smiled. "The terrin carry three goblets that were gifts of the Persian emperor at the beginning of our people's journey. One made of ruby, one of citrine, and one of emerald. Kezia carries the citrine, Radu the emerald, and the ruby one is Vano's."

Desiree whispered, "We're not big fans of Vano."

"I see." She wanted to ask if anyone was a fan of Vano, but that would probably be rude. It wasn't her place to say such things. She wasn't Poshani.

Tatyana's mind was whirling. She'd been halfway hoping until she met Vano that she might find some kind of job with the Poshani business even though she was an outsider.

And after she'd met Vano—and realized he was a bully—she considered asking Kezia or Radu if they needed someone with her skills.

She didn't need the money right away, but she wanted a job. She hated being bored, and she was hoping to stay in touch with her new friends.

"I've been wondering if the guests this year think they might be chosen." Desiree smiled. "Wouldn't that be a surprise?"

"Would anyone outside the Poshani clan actually be chosen as a leader?" Tatyana asked. "That seems like it would disqualify you."

"It's never happened before," Rumi said. "But it's not a rule. Who knows? It could be a good thing to have an outside perspective on things."

Desiree nodded. "I agree. A breath of fresh air."

"Kind of like having someone outside your industry on a corporate board." Tatyana nodded. "That makes a lot of sense."

Desiree smirked. "I heard Radu say he'd invited your old boss for the Vashana Zata this season."

Her stomach dropped. "Oleg?"

Rumi nodded. "Now Oleg Sokolov is an outsider that I can see the Poshani choosing. He's very well-known. People like him, and he's richer than a czar." She dropped her voice. "It seems like the clan might need an infusion of money."

"You're right," Desiree said. "Oleg is the kind Poshani might vote for if they needed someone new. Very popular."

Tatyana was frozen.

What was this?

What was he doing?

Was Oleg hunting her down in the kamvasa and making this proposal to "court" her simply a ploy to get closer and spy—

No.

That was ridiculous. If Oleg wanted to spy on the Poshani to maneuver himself into a position of power, he would have sent Mika, not come himself. He wouldn't have given Tatyana his blood.

Unless he wanted to make it harder for you to leave him.

"The Vashana sounds like an interesting party." She tried to cover the turbulent boil of emotions in her gut. "And even more cooking for the rest of us."

"You don't have to help us." Rumi smiled.

"I know you don't trust me to chop onions, but at least I can stir a pot." Tatyana smiled a little. "What else would I do? Drink wine and watch the dancers every night with the old people?"

Desiree said, "Our plan worked, Rumi. We finally recruited a minion for the kitchen, and we don't even have to pay her."

"Bwahahahaha!" Rumi pretended to let out an evil laugh, but she winked at Tatyana. "Who says vampires are the only ones who can scheme?"

. . .

"Hello!" A tall vampire with curly black hair waved at her as he walked over and started speaking in English. "I'm Ben. I heard you're from Russia."

What an absolutely American thing to say. She examined the new vampire with careful eyes. His energy was hot and bright. If she didn't know better, she'd think he was a fire vampire.

Tatyana narrowed her eyes. "Did Oleg send you?"

The man frowned. "All I said was 'hello, I'm Ben. I heard you're from Russia.'"

She hadn't realized she'd said that out loud. "You didn't answer the question."

She was stirring a large pot of goulash over the fire. She'd added the spices, but they needed low heat for some time before Rumi added the fish, which would cook quickly.

The caravan had moved during the day, and there had been no word from Oleg in three nights. She had that stupid vampire stuck in her mind and his blood in her veins.

Irritable didn't begin to describe how she was feeling.

"Okay." Ben Vecchio raised his hands as if in surrender. "Oleg did not send me."

"Good." With that answered, she turned back to the stew. Maybe if she ignored him, he'd go away.

She didn't really want to get to know him. Most of the vampires in the kamvasa kept to themselves, and that was fine with Tatyana. This American seemed overly friendly and was trying to speak with her in English, which was not her best language.

"Tatyana!" Rumi called in Poshani. "Is that stew ready for the fish?"

She answered her friend in the same language. "No, I just added the ground pepper. It needs to cook more."

"The fish is cleaned when you're ready for it." Rumi pointed to the table. "Just let me know."

"Another half hour maybe?" She turned her attention back to the fire.

The American vampire spoke again. "You're very good at languages. I've been trying to figure it out."

"Poshani?"

"Yes."

Tatyana looked up and sighed a little bit. He was not going away. "You're probably trying to fit it into a Roman or Slavic paradigm."

She might as well talk with him if he was going to insist. Maybe he wasn't an aloof asshole like the others if he was truly interested in the Poshani. She repeated what Rumi had told her about the language's history. "The Poshani language is primarily North Indian with borrowing from Hungarian, Turkish, and Farsi."

Benjamin Vecchio smiled. Was he baring his fangs at her? His teeth reminded her of a crocodile.

He looked overly excited. "You're a language nerd! How did you get to be a vampire?"

Her eyes went wide. What kind of immortal was he?

"None of your business." Maybe he didn't know he was being rude. He was from a different region of the world. "Do all Americans smile so much?"

"Probably." He held his hand out as if he wanted the spoon. "Can I help?"

Absolutely not. "You're a wind vampire?" If he was sired by Zhang Guo, he would have to be a wind vampire.

"I am."

"Then cool the stew. It's getting a little hot."

When he summoned his element, that was when she saw it. The vampire was as young as she was and could barely control all the power that was packed into his body.

It was like watching a baby try to handle a shotgun.

The wind he called was so strong the base of the goulash bubbled up and blew out of the side of the pot, nearly burning a Poshani girl who had just walked by.

The girl yelped and darted away.

Tatyana waved her hands at him. "Stop. Just stop."

He stopped, thank God, or she would have had to remake everything.

The man had the grace to look apologetic. "So if you don't want to talk about yourself—"

"I don't." Tatyana poked at the coals to rearrange the heat under the pot. "I know who you are. You didn't need to introduce yourself. Everyone knows who you are."

It was true. The entire camp was buzzing with excitement, partly because of the nearness of the Vashana Zata, partly because more and more people were showing up, and partly because new vampires seemed to be appearing overnight.

Her peaceful sanctuary was disappearing.

The American didn't look thrilled that he was the subject of curiosity. "That's so annoying."

"Your profile isn't exactly low." The corner of her mouth twitched. "Benjamin Vecchio, son of Giovanni Vecchio, immortal son of Zhang Guo, mate of Tenzin—"

"Wait, what?"

Tatyana looked up. "She is not your mate?"

Everyone in the camp said they were mated but simply lived separately.

"It's complicated." The American looked flustered.

That felt familiar.

Could Oleg be considered her mate now? They had exchanged blood. Not at the same time, but he'd taken hers. Then she'd taken his.

He was entirely possessive, and his attention was unwavering.

The American leaned in and lowered his voice. "Oleg?"

She curled her lip. How did he know?

Vecchio kept his voice low. "Okay, level with me. Does everyone assume Tenzin is my mate?"

He was clearly more concerned with his own love life than with hers. Good.

"Yes," Tatyana answered. "Is she not?"

"Tell me about Oleg."

His name coming out of this stranger's mouth made her want to snarl. Why was he so curious about Oleg?

She changed the subject. "It's difficult to remain hidden in this world, isn't it?"

"Which is so weird because the humans aren't supposed to know about us."

She rolled her eyes. "Be serious. Don't you think most of them know?" Tatyana was starting to feel like the entire world had to be aware of something so obvious. Maybe she'd just been walking through the world, oblivious, before she crashed into Zara.

"I think there are a lot of people who don't know a thing."

They trailed off into small talk about how he'd grown up and what they were both doing when they found out about vampires.

Did she lie? A little bit, but the American was far too nosy. He didn't deserve to know her entire backstory.

Then the man brought up Oleg.

Again.

"So Oleg isn't your sire?"

"What the hell business is it of yours? How rude do you have to be to ask questions like this?" It was like talking to a child. She only realized she'd spoken in Poshani when Rumi and Desiree laughed and the American looked confused.

"No." Tatyana tried to speak calmly. "Praise God, he is not my sire."

That would make all the sex extremely awkward. The sex she was dreaming about again.

"Asshole," she muttered.

"Clearly you're a big fan."

And she was falling for him, which made her a new breed of idiot.

"He's a... manipulative son of a bitch." There. Maybe the man would stop asking about Oleg now. She could feel Rumi's and Desiree's eyes on her.

Vecchio's voice was soft and sad. "Aren't they all?"

Huh. She hadn't expected that from someone who was raised in the court of a vampire assassin. "You tell me. You've known them longer than I have."

He was staring at the pot when he spoke in a quiet voice. "You'll find your people. Eventually you'll find them."

Now Tatyana felt like she'd stepped on a kitten who was following her around. The man didn't look arrogant anymore—he looked sad.

She wanted to warn him about wearing his expressions on his face so everyone could see them, but she wasn't his mother. "Yes, I hope so."

"So what brings you to the Dawn Caravan?"

"What brings anyone? I heard about it. I needed to get away."

They chatted back and forth a little longer, and Tatyana had to admit: he was an unusual vampire, and not only because of his abnormally strong amnis.

She wanted to ask Oleg about him. She wanted to know about Oleg's involvement with the Vashana Zata.

And she wanted to know why the energy in the camp had changed so abruptly the moment these two new vampires showed up.

The place that had been her peaceful sanctuary was off-balance.

Something was very, very wrong.

Chapter 27

Oleg

Oleg waited four nights to visit Tatyana. He figured that would give her enough time to rebuild the walls that had come crashing down when she'd taken his blood.

It was an experience he'd relived in his mind approximately a dozen times since it had happened.

Tatyana splayed over him, her elemental power misting over his skin like a kiss of fog as she rode him. The power on her face as she eyed his neck. The tentative touch of her fangs giving way to rampant, bloody desire.

Caution giving way to power giving way to desire. Then the near-instant rise of wariness again as the walls between them dissolved in a wave of joined pleasure. Utterly unexpected and completely novel.

Tatyana taking his blood was the singularly most erotic experience Oleg had ever had.

His amnis was alive in her body now, so even when she was distant from him, he felt a sense of her. She'd been vulnerable that night, bordering on afraid.

"You're not afraid of me."

"Sometimes I am, a little bit."

Now he understood her fear because a level of it had entered his own blood.

He didn't know what they were building or what path this bond would lead them toward, but Oleg was more sure than ever that Tatyana belonged to him.

After over a thousand years of life, discovering the unexpected was intoxicating.

"Boss." Mika's voice broke into his mental distraction.

"Hmm."

His chief boyar held up a phone. "Confirmation from Polina."

"About?"

"Vano and Ivan." Mika sat across from him on a fallen log. "Her people finally found someone at the gold exchange to confirm the transfers from Ivan to Vano. The first payment was two nights before the first hijacking, and the following payments matched the timeline of the other robberies."

"So Ivan was paying Vano's men to rob our trucks." Oleg frowned. "Even the ones headed into Ivan's territory?"

"Yes, which means that Ivan killed some of his own people in the robberies."

Oleg's fangs grew long, and he smiled. "That's excellent."

"That's horrible." Mika curled his lip. "I have no love for Ivan's people, but to be betrayed by your own sire and brothers—"

"Yes, it's terrible, and it's exactly something that Ivan would do." Oleg leaned forward. "The Poshani will hate it."

Mika nodded. "They will."

"We're still holding that Danior at the citadel, yes?"

"Yes, but according to Yuliya, he hasn't spoken again. Without your fire to frighten him, no other means of persuasion has worked."

Oleg mulled over an idea. "Ivan's betrayal of his own men could be useful."

Mika nodded slowly. "The Poshani—even a criminal like Danior—value loyalty above all. The vampire would find it despicable."

"We will wait and see if we need to use him."

"Good."

The Vashana Zata, the high festival of the Poshani, was only weeks away.

Within two weeks, Radu would send him a location, and Oleg could join the kamvasa without subterfuge. No more hiding. No more sneaking into Tatyana's trailer and risking the Hazar finding him. He could enter the kamvasa as an honored guest.

Now Oleg had other reasons to be at the Vashana this year. A snake was hiding in his territory, and he had a plan.

If he was successful, Vano would lose his status and his reputation, would be ousted from power, and none of the Poshani would ever work with Ivan again.

Business would suffer. Roaming fees would not be paid. And Ivan's lieutenants would bear the brunt of the loss.

Exactly as Oleg wanted.

Tatyana swung the door of her trailer open a moment before he reached it.

Oleg smiled as he slipped inside and shut the door. "You felt me approaching."

"Do you know an American vampire named Benjamin Vecchio?"

Oleg froze. "I know the name Vecchio."

"He's the nephew of some horrible assassin, and he's arrived at the kamvasa in the past few days." She looked distracted, and her amnis was surging erratically. "Something is wrong."

She was very intuitive. Yes, she would make an excellent mate.

Wait, what?

"That." She pointed at him. "What was that?"

"Nothing," he growled. "What are you talking about? You're acting crazy."

Mate? That was a ridiculous thought.

"No, I'm not. I felt something from you." She rolled her shoulders as if there was something crawling on her skin. "I do not like this."

"You're simply feeling the combination of our blood." Oleg waved a hand and walked farther into the trailer. "You'll get used to it."

"I don't like it."

"Then don't take my blood again!" Oleg snapped. He felt his fangs getting long in his mouth.

He *wanted* her to take his blood again. He wanted to bind Tatyana to him so tightly that it would be like ripping herself in half to leave him.

"I'm not going to apologize for being uncomfortable." Her voice was quiet. "Your amnis is much more powerful than mine, and..."

Oleg froze. "And what?"

"It's hard to think clearly when you're in front of me. My mind is completely focused on you. I want you close, and by close I mean that I would like to be sitting in your lap right now because my body does not feel like it is entirely my own."

Some of his anger retreated. He hadn't fully considered how much influence his amnis could have on a vampire so young.

"I understand," he said. "It is never desirable to feel out of control."

"The moment I felt you get nearby," she continued, "my mind became overwhelmed with..." Her forehead wrinkled in confusion. "What is this?"

"We are linked now. Both of us." Oleg walked to her and put his hands on her shoulders. He felt her amnis calm when it touched his own.

"My blood is not as strong as yours," Tatyana said. "It's not the same."

"I know what I felt after I took your blood, volchitsa. You will become accustomed to it."

Tatyana looked up with wide eyes. "Is this why you kept looking for me after I left?"

No.

"Yes." He nodded. "That is why it was difficult for me to leave you alone. Your blood was in my body, and I felt very restless."

Well, *that* wasn't a lie.

Tatyana sighed. "I'm still angry that you chased me, but I suppose I understand it a bit better now."

I chased you because you're mine.

And you should be my mate.

Fuck.

He'd had a mate, and she was highly unstable. The pain of having to kill her had devastated him, and Oleg was honest enough to admit it. He still felt the hollow pain of Luana's loss in his blood.

The fact that he wanted another one might be proof that Luana's instability had infected him after all.

Distract her.

Oleg saw she had replaced the chessboard with another game. "You ended our game?"

"Yes, I played ahead and saw that you would inevitably lose, so I had mercy on you." She was staring at the door. "You're welcome."

Oleg smiled, pleased to hear the vinegar return to her voice. "Such a kind opponent." He walked over to the coffee table. "What is this?"

She waved a hand, but she was still pacing. "Just a puzzle."

It looked like a kind of mosaic. "Hmm."

"Haven't you seen a puzzle before?" She walked over. "My mother loves them."

"Is this a competitive game?" He sat on the couch and immediately saw at least a dozen pieces he could put into place.

"Are you serious right now?" She sat next to him. "Have you never seen this before?"

"I have solved many puzzles, but this looks like a painting that has been carved into pieces." He shook his head. "Why would you do this?"

"Because it's fun to put it back together." She picked up a piece and pointed. "See? That's the picture it's supposed to make."

There was a box standing up on the table with a picture of boats in a harbor. It was a watercolor painting.

"It's not a competition." She tried the piece she held in one location, then another. "You do it with friends or you can put it together by yourself."

Oleg looked at a void where a small mast was isolated against a blue-green sea. He quickly scanned the pieces scattered on the table, found the piece, and put it in place.

"See?" She leaned against his side and placed another piece into the broken picture. "It's a good way to pass the time."

"Hmm." Oleg sat on the couch, enjoying the sensation of Tatyana's body pressed into his own. She was like a cat, leaning on him, and the weight was intensely pleasurable. "This is a children's game."

"There are children's puzzles, but this one has a thousand pieces, so it should take me a while to…"

Oleg quickly put a dozen pieces into place, working from the bottom of the puzzle up.

Tatyana nodded. "It seems that mosaic artists may have an advantage when putting puzzles together." She leaned her head on his shoulder. "You catch on quickly."

Oleg put his left arm around her and used the other to put pieces into place. She took a deep breath, and he felt her blood settle.

He turned his head and kissed her forehead. "I should not have stayed away from you."

"That is such a twenty-year-old asshole thing to do," she muttered. "I didn't expect game-playing from you."

"I wasn't playing games; you told me to leave."

"I didn't tell you not to come back."

Oleg paused in his relentless puzzle construction and turned to look at her. "I am sorry that I stayed away too long."

Tatyana looked up, meeting his stern gaze. "What are we now?"

He had no idea.

"Us." He kissed her forehead again. "Just... us."

More pieces of the boats. Starting on the long pier that jutted out into the water. Tatyana leaning into his side with her right hand resting on his thigh. Oleg leaning his cheek on her head.

Peace.

"I called you an asshole to the new vampire who joined the kamvasa," Tatyana murmured. "Once out loud and several times in my head."

"Is this a confession?" He smiled. "I'm sure it's not the first time you've called me an asshole. You might need to come up with some new insults, or you will get bored."

Piece by piece, Oleg built the dock until he was not going in order but building the picture from one element to the next.

"Who is the new vampire?"

"The one I mentioned." Tatyana reached out and started putting pieces of the sky into place. "Benjamin Vecchio."

A muscle near Oleg's eye twitched.

"You know him?"

"I know *of* him. He's very young and very powerful."

"I could tell. I was thinking he felt like a baby holding a shotgun."

Oleg chuckled. "You are not wrong. I do know his uncle."

"The horrible assassin uncle?" She sighed. "Are you friends with an assassin? Why am I not surprised you are friends with an assassin?"

"Not friends. But not enemies either. And he's a book dealer now."

"Now *that's* a change of career."

"His life and my life were not so different. Our sires both wanted a weapon, so that is what we became." Oleg finished the wooden pier and started on the shoreline, ignoring any sense of symmetry and letting the picture form organically. "That is usually the fate of fire vampires, milaya. You become a weapon or you become a king."

"You became a king."

He raised an eyebrow. "I became a knyaz. It's different. I'm a king who is a weapon." He continued putting the puzzle together, enjoying her delicate weight on his side. "If the weapon loses his edge, my druzhina will choose a new leader. No one is invincible."

"Do you ever think of leaving it? Like the book dealer?"

He paused and looked at her. "No. It is my responsibility to protect them."

She nodded.

"You must understand this," he said quietly. "I am not the book dealer. I will never leave my people."

She stared at the puzzle, her fingers curling around one piece. "I understand."

"Good." If she was going to be his mate, she needed to understand his role. "Why were you asking about Benjamin Vecchio?"

"He was asking about you."

Oleg's mind went on alert. "Why?"

"He thinks I am on the run from you."

"Why does he care? That is none of his business."

"I thought the same thing."

"Ignore him." He kissed her forehead again. "Ignore every man except for me."

She laughed a little bit. "Asshole."

"Tell me a new one." Oleg decided Tatyana's laughter was his favorite sound in the entire world.

No, it was the breathy moan of pleasure she let out when she orgasmed. That was his favorite. But her laughter came second.

"I hope you have another puzzle." The picture was over halfway complete. "I'm going to finish this one soon."

OLEG WAS STANDING ON THE EDGE OF THE FOREST THAT overlooked the kamvasa after he and Tatyana had finished two more puzzles and dawn was threatening the horizon.

He was watching the twinkling lights of the Poshani fires when he saw a fall of white flower petals drifting from a pine tree, dancing in the air until they settled on his shoulder.

He looked up and met the eyes of an assassin he'd known for centuries.

The wind vampire was dangling from a tree branch, peering down at him with her fangs out and a slight smile on her lips. "Hail, Varangian."

"Greetings, Khazar." He leaned against the trunk of a pine tree and crossed his arms as he greeted one of the oldest vampires he knew. "What you doing in these woods, Tenzin?"

He shouldn't have been surprised. If there was a Vecchio nearby, Tenzin was likely in the vicinity.

Like so many of his kind, she was an enigma. Tenzin of Penglai could have been an ancient or a teenage girl. Her black hair fell over her shoulders, and she wore black clothes. The only thing that made her stand out in the shadows was her pale skin and her fangs.

"Do I need an excuse to summer in Eastern Europe?" she asked. "The weather is perfect."

"You need an excuse to be in my territory."

She was likely over three thousand years old, and Oleg knew her well. Tenzin tended to frequent various hideouts in Central Asia, some of which overlapped his territory. They'd traded favors over the centuries, but mostly they kept out of each other's way.

Seeing Tenzin perched in a tree near the kamvasa was an unexpected wrinkle in his plans.

"Why are you spying on the Poshani?"

"I could ask you the same thing."

"*Spying* is an inaccurate word when they are crossing my territory. Are you here to kill someone?"

"No." Her answer was swift enough that he believed her. "At least not today. But there's always tomorrow."

Would Arosh have sent her? Saba? Tenzin would never work for Ivan because Oleg's brother disgusted her.

Who would have enough money to draw Tenzin to eliminate a mark?

"So why are you here?" Oleg asked. "Don't lie."

"But I enjoy it so much." She swung down from one branch to another. "I'm a guest of the Poshani." She dangled upside down and let her hair fall over her head. "So technically you're kind of in *my* territory right now."

That was a surprise.

Why would Tenzin be hiding from anyone? Most people in the immortal world considered her an urban legend, and the few who knew she truly existed would be wary to cross her.

"You're a guest? Of the Dawn Caravan?" He used the name that outsiders had given it.

"I was invited to the Vashana." Her eyes were wide and deceptively innocent. "You too?"

In addition to being an excellent and discreet assassin, Tenzin was also a very good thief, which made her invitation to the kamvasa an interesting choice. "Who invited you?"

She smiled. "That's a highly personal question that I am not going to answer."

First René DuPont, whom Ludmila had said was definitely a thief.

Now Tenzin?

Two well-known thieves were attending the Poshani's most important festival. It could not be a coincidence.

"What about you?" Tenzin asked. "Who invited you?"

"Me?" Oleg played innocent. "I am not here."

She stared at him. "That is an inaccurate statement. You are here."

"What I mean is, unless you want to create problems—"

"Which I do enjoy doing." She swung out, flipped over, and floated to the ground.

Tenzin had a habit of infiltrating immortal courts and blowing them up from the inside. He would call it a hobby in the same way that pyromaniacs enjoyed a pleasant campfire.

"Unless you want to create problems, I am not here," Oleg said. "At least not yet." He shrugged. "But I was also invited to the Vashana."

"Hmm." She smoothed a hand over her black tunic, and Oleg saw a neat curved sword sewn into the seam. "My partner and I were both invited."

"I hear that you're working with Vecchio again."

"Yes," Tenzin said. "But not the one you're thinking of. My partner is the nephew."

Benjamin Vecchio.

The powerful newborn who had been talking to Tatyana.

The newborn who had been asking about him.

Oleg pursed his lips. "Is he the one your sire turned for you?"

"That's..." Tenzin scowled. "How do rumors like this spread?"

"Because we're old and many of us are very bored." He smirked and crossed his arms over his chest. "So it's the nephew for you, is it? I thought you preferred women." He was fairly certain Ludmila harbored a long-standing fascination with Tenzin even though they had never met. "My best sniper will be crushed."

"I prefer to be alone," Tenzin said. "But Benjamin is my partner."

"I see."

"I very much doubt that." She floated toward him and inhaled deeply. "You smell of crushed roses and blood-wine."

He could feel her amnis surrounding him, probing his space. It was... intrusive. "Are you propositioning me?" That was a frightening thought.

Tenzin lifted her lips to bare the corner of her fangs. "My attention is elsewhere these days, Varangian."

"On your partner?"

She narrowed her eyes. "Oleg of Gardariki is known to be discreet, yet you lurk in the forest as if waiting for a lover."

She had used his old name on purpose to remind him he was younger than her. "What a fertile imagination you have."

"Is it Kezia?"

"Is this your business?"

She lifted her chin, and her smile grew wider. "You pique my curiosity."

"Go about your business, Tenzin. And stay out of mine."

"I do enjoy sparring with you." She spotted the small fang burns on his neck. "Nice fang marks."

He snapped his fingers and gathered fire in his hands, then let it crawl up his shoulders and circle his neck. "Please feel free to take a closer look."

Tenzin laughed and backed away. "You should be careful. There is conflict among the Poshani."

She was finally cutting through the bullshit. Good.

"Your partner, is he a mediator? Is that why he was invited?"

Tenzin partnering with a peacemaker was ironic to the extreme, but it would explain why she hadn't fomented any vampire coups in a few years.

"He's a thief."

Of course he was.

"Yes, that makes much more sense."

Which made three thieves in the kamvasa by Oleg's count.

Oleg sighed. "What are you there to steal, Tenzin?"

The first thing that jumped into Oleg's mind were the dishana, the greatest treasures of the Poshani people.

Carved from three massive jewels by an ancient king, the dishana were symbols of the terrin's power, and there was a mystical element to them as well. She who held the dishana held the power of the clan.

And since the Vashana Zata was happening this year, Radu, Kezia, and Vano would all have their goblets with them for the ceremony.

"Why would I steal anything?" Tenzin's eyes went wide. "You're so suspicious."

"Of you? Always."

She floated into the air. "They are expecting me, so I should go. Should I tell them you are watching?"

"Not necessary."

"And what will you give me to keep your secrets?"

He took a deep breath and pursed his lips. "A favor of my own choosing. At least a year from now."

She smiled, baring her fangs. "You amuse me, so I agree. I'll keep your secrets for now."

"Enjoy your night, Khazar."

Without another word, the lethal wind vampire disappeared into the night, and Oleg watched the black spot in the sky where she had been.

Three goblets, three thieves.

When a terrin resigned, their goblet would pass from the old to the new. But if one or even all those goblets was stolen, the ancient tradition would be broken.

This was the wrongness that Tatyana had sensed.

If the dishana were taken, the Poshani were ripe for a takeover.

Chapter 28

Tatyana

When Tatyana woke that night, her trailer was parked in an entirely new location.

She opened the door and saw a field of poppies that sloped down a gentle hill where the tall grass had been trimmed by workers holding curved sickles.

The darigan were building a bonfire in the center of a field as humans set up blankets and seats in a meadow where a gentle stream trickled through.

"Tatyana!"

She turned to see Radu walking toward her.

"Radu." The jovial head of the kamvasa had continued to impress her with his thoughtfulness and humor. "It's good to see you."

He stopped in front of her trailer and put his fists on his hips. "How are you tonight?"

"I'm well. Another beautiful landscape that looks like it came out of a picture book."

Radu winked at her. "The darigan take good care of us, do they not?"

Tatyana felt a genuine smile spread over her face. "I truly believe the Poshani have no equal in hospitality."

He put a hand to his chest. "If there is one compliment that will warm our still hearts, it is that one. Thank you."

She nodded toward the mowers. "What is going on?"

"Ah, the clan is starting to gather for the Vashana Zata. Kezia told you about it, I'm sure."

Odd that Radu assumed that, but perhaps he'd seen them together. The vampire appeared distracted, and his energy was... strange.

Tatyana sensed his amnis in an entirely new way. Oleg's blood? It was the only explanation.

"I did hear about the Vashana Zata. Lucky for me that I happened to choose this year to join your caravan. It sounds like a very special festival."

"And we are pleased that you will join us in our celebrations. The festivities will start to increase soon, but tonight a brother of ours has brought fireworks to enjoy."

Tatyana looked around at all the wildflowers and long grass. They were still green but drying as the summer waned and the autumn season started to turn.

"I see from your eyes that you anticipate the same thing I did," Radu said. "The grass is getting dryer this late in the summer."

"Would you like me to keep an eye on the fireworks tonight?" she asked. "I know you don't have many water vampires in the clan."

"You are correct, but of course, you are our guest first, so feel free to refuse."

"I don't mind." She waved a hand and gathered a bit of mist from the air. "It's an easy thing."

"Your heart is a generous one." Radu's eyes were warm. "It is no wonder that you have won the affection of so many of the people here."

"I consider a number of them friends," Tatyana said. "Being here has truly been a wonderful respite."

A jolt of fear stabbed her heart. Her time with them was coming to an end. After the Vashana, there were only six weeks left before the kamvasa stopped roaming for the season.

Radu must have seen the worry in her eyes. "Do you have plans for the winter?"

"My mother has a farm," she said. "I might return to visit her."

She didn't even want to think about Oleg yet, what a return to his territory might mean.

"Ah." Radu's face brightened. "So your mother is aware of your..."

"Yes." Tatyana smiled. "She knows what I am."

"And the rest of your family?"

"It's just my mother." Tatyana was quick to add, "She is a favorite of Oleg's, so they're friendly. Despite living alone, she always seems to have one vampire or another coming by."

Hopefully that would let Radu know that her mother was well-protected. She didn't *want* to distrust him, but when it came to Anna, Tatyana trusted no one.

Except—by some twist of fate—Oleg. Who seemed to hold Tatyana's mother in some strange and inexplicable regard.

"I see." Radu's eyes were laughing at her. "I have known your old boss for many years. Oleg is able to charm women of every age."

"But my mother has no use for charm," she said. "I think that's why he likes her. She insults him to his face."

Radu threw his head back and laughed. "Yes, I think he would enjoy that." He cleared his throat and hooked his thumbs in his pockets. "He is coming to the kamvasa soon. For the Vashana Zata. I invited him months ago, long before we knew..."

"The Poshani people have been more than welcoming to me." Tatyana was quick to reassure him. "I feel very secure here. Please don't be concerned about my comfort."

"The knyaz of the Kievan Rus has visited us many times."

Oh, you have no idea.

"Of course he would. He must be a very close ally."

"He is." Radu nodded. "But I didn't want you to be surprised by an unexpected face."

"I appreciate that." She motioned toward the stream. "When the fireworks start, I can go down by the stream. That way if any sparks are lit, I can put them out quickly."

Radu pressed both his hands together and bowed a little bit. "You are a credit to your clan and your sire, Tatyana Vorona."

She had no clan.

She had no sire.

Her heart twisted in her chest a little bit, but all she could do was smile.

TATYANA WAS NEARLY AT THE POSITION SHE'D CHOSEN NEAR THE stream when she felt a hand grab her arm and yank.

She sucked in a breath, and the amnis in her veins jumped to life at the threat.

Quicker than a blink, she whirled around, only to be met with nothing.

Darkness.

Then a whistle from above.

She looked up and saw Vano sitting on the roof of a nearby vardo.

Wind vampire.

"You walk very comfortably through our camp, Miss Vorona." One dark eyebrow arched up. "You should be more careful."

It was another warning, another attempt to push her under his thumb.

"Radu and Kezia led me to believe that my security is absolute within the kamvasa." She looked up and caught the silhouette of a Hazar hovering in the distance. "The Hazar are always watching."

"They are, and I am the one who trained them. In fact, many of them share my blood." Vano looked down at her as if she were a curious insect.

Tatyana had the distinct impression he was testing her.

"So they report to you?" She lifted her chin. "Should I go to your brother and sister and let them know that I do not feel safe?" Her amnis reached for the water nearby, and the mist in the air clung to her hands. "Perhaps I should ask Madina or Darius—René DuPont maybe—if they've also felt unsafe."

He didn't try to hide his fangs. "That would be unwise. After all, if you feel unsafe, it's likely because you are welcoming an outsider into your trailer when all are forbidden."

Oh, he was good.

Tell on me, and I'll tell on you.

Too bad Tatyana was a professional at hiding her true feelings. "I don't know what you're talking about."

Vano left the roof of the trailer where he was perched and hovered over her, making Tatyana crane her head to keep him in sight.

"So you deny that a vampire is sneaking into your trailer before dawn?"

Interesting. He had some of the information, but not all. He apparently thought Oleg was staying with her.

"I share my day chamber with no one." She stepped backward, away from the narrow alley between the trailers and toward the creek. She could feel her amnis become stronger every step that she took toward her element. "I don't trust easily. Especially vampires."

"Perhaps I've been misinformed."

"Maybe we should both meet with Radu and Kezia," she blurted. "I'm sure they want to know that you have safety concerns just as I have concerns about vampires treating humans as lesser Poshani and telling them not to feed hungry children."

Vano smiled. "You think you have something there, don't you?"

"I think you told me to mind my own business." Tatyana finally reached the end of the trailers and backed her way into the meadow, keeping Vano in sight. "You should take your own advice and mind yours."

She was going to have to tell Oleg that at least some of the Hazar had spotted him and those Hazar had reported him to Vano.

Maybe that meant that Oleg wouldn't be able to "court" her any longer, but the last thing she needed was a bloody and fiery vampire battle on her conscience.

Vano flew toward her, and before she could blink, he was in her face. So close that Tatyana felt his breath on her cheek.

"You should be careful, Tatyana Vorona."

She froze, and her hand curled into a fist. "So should you. You should know that I have friends, and some of them have very..." She turned and met his black gaze. "...*hot* tempers."

It was only her reluctance to provoke violence that had saved Vano from Oleg's wrath before. She didn't want to provoke a conflict, but if he continued threatening her like this, she wouldn't have a choice.

The corner of Vano's mouth turned up. "I see. Thank you, Miss Vorona. You've been very informative."

A bell rang out in the meadow, and when she blinked, Vano disappeared.

SHE SPOTTED BENJAMIN VECCHIO AS HE WANDERED THROUGH the crowd, chatting and making conversation like he was some kind of club promoter. Everyone seemed happy to see him.

Except his mate.

The petite woman was sitting in a small group near the center of the festivities at Radu's table with René, the French vampire, on one side and Kezia on the other.

Kezia and Vecchio's mate were leaning together and talking in whispers. If anything, it appeared that they were telling secrets behind the American's back.

It wasn't like any mating Tatyana had seen. She was accustomed to Kato and Alexander, who were practically joined at the hip. Benjamin and his mate seemed to avoid each other.

What would Oleg be like as a mate?

Tatyana banished the thought from her mind. By his own admission, Oleg's dead mate had been a nightmare. The last thing he likely wanted to do was take on another one.

"What are we now?"

"Us. Just... us."

And that was likely all they ever could be. Or maybe they wouldn't even be that after she told him Vano had spotted him.

It was probably for the best.

As much as Tatyana desired Oleg, if they kept going the direction they seemed headed, he would take over her life. He was a king. A *knyaz*. She didn't hate him for it. She didn't even resent him anymore.

But she didn't want or need a king.

Oleg was who he was, and Tatyana had to learn how to exist in this world. She had to learn how to survive. She had to make alliances of her own.

She felt like a newborn colt, all legs and wobbly balance. She might run someday, but for the moment she was far more likely to fall down.

"This is nice."

Tatyana looked over and saw Vecchio walking toward her. He was gesturing at the gathering around the bonfire.

"Yes. It's quite a show for the little ones." It appeared that every Poshani child in the camp had gathered around the campfire and was excitedly pointing at the sky.

"Nice for grown-ups too."

Nice? Yes, but much work. The area around the fire had been mowed and raked. Buckets of water had been set out.

"One errant spark and this all goes up in flames," she murmured.

"Such an optimist."

"A realist." She never said it wasn't worth the work. But valuable things took work. Valuable people deserved it. The Poshani children deserved something delightful, and it was worth the work to give it to them.

Benjamin was looking at the stream by Kezia's beautiful old vardo. "Keeping an eye on things?"

"I'd be a fool not to," she said quietly. "Even water vampires can burn."

"True."

Vecchio was watching the camp with a gaze that whispered secrets. Tatyana narrowed her eyes and saw him take in the vardo, clock the Hazar hovering overhead. He noticed everything around him.

Watchful. Always watchful.

Oleg said he had been raised by an assassin, but what was he doing in the kamvasa now? What was *his* purpose?

"Radu asked me to keep an eye out for any errant fire, and I was willing. There are not many of my kind in the camp." Most of the Poshani vampires were wind vampires like Vecchio.

Did he think that qualified him to take one of the jewel goblets that Rumi and Desiree were talking about? Maybe Vecchio—as much of a newborn as she was—was also looking for a home.

Or his own kingdom to rule.

He smiled at her, still putting on his gregarious mask, though she could see the calculation behind it. "You're generous to help."

"I've become quite good at putting out fires. I used to work for Oleg."

Oleg the Terrible. Thinking about him already felt bittersweet.

Vecchio was still there, still watching her. "I see."

"I very much doubt that." She lifted some water from the creek and rolled the liquid in her palm. The focus broke her memory of Oleg, and she felt her body cooling down. "But I'm ready when I need to be."

He gave her his biggest grin. "Good vampire."

"Ugh." Did he know how garish his fangs were? He looked like he was getting ready to bite something. Tatyana tossed the water back in the creek. "Put your smile away. I'm not in the mood for your teeth."

His laughter seemed genuine, and the glance he cast toward the collection of vampires where his mate was sitting was as conflicted as Tatyana's own mind.

When he spoke again, she barely caught his words. "Vampire life is complicated."

"So it is."

What was going on in his mind?

Despite his looks and the vast power differential between them, she felt older than Vecchio. Or maybe she was just more jaded. Maybe his life had been a privileged, soft life of ease.

Probably. If he was the adopted son of a powerful immortal, it was easy to imagine him slipping easily through life, drifting from one amusement to another like the children of the rich she'd seen vacationing in Sevastopol when she was growing up.

She heard the sound of air moving overhead. "The Hazar are coming to watch. Radu will call them down."

The last thing that Radu wanted would be wind vampires in the air with fireworks going off. That sounded like a recipe for disaster.

Vecchio narrowed his eyes. "Seems like you've gotten to know the ins and outs of this place pretty well."

"I'm observant. Some of us don't come into immortal life with riches, connections, and extraordinary power." She watched him from the corner of her eye. "We have to watch for our opportunities."

Radu shouted at the Hazar, "Come closer. Put out your lights."

The Hazar started toward the ground, leaving the skies above the kamvasa unguarded.

Radu kept talking to the gathered audience, and Tatyana looked over her shoulder, expecting to see Vecchio standing behind her, but the wind vampire had disappeared.

Moments later, the sky above her exploded with the first firework.

Tatyana nearly jumped out of her skin.

Tatyana returned to her trailer a few hours before dawn to find Oleg already working on a new puzzle. He had cleared off the table and was spreading tiny pieces across the surface.

The moment she saw him, the erratic energy skittering through her system eased, but the wariness remained. "There's something very strange going on."

Oleg stood without another word and turned to her. "Tell me."

He was ready, and his fangs were already down. His body was a coiled spring, and Tatyana suddenly understood why warriors followed this man into battle.

"I am a king who is a weapon."

She had the unnerving realization that in that moment, she could point Oleg at anyone she wanted and he would destroy them.

Vano. He'd be happy to get rid of Vano.

Vecchio.

Even Radu or Kezia.

She didn't need that kind of power. She didn't want it.

Tatyana could wait to tell Oleg about Vano's threats. Because in the end, he hadn't really made any. Not anything overt.

"It's not like that." She walked to him, put her hands on his shoulders, and his muscles eased. "It's fine. I'm fine." She stood on her tiptoes and lifted her face to his. "It's not an immediate thing."

When Oleg kissed her, his amnis smoothed down her neck, her

back, and her shoulders, calming her without his saying a word. It was a full-body hug from his energy to hers.

Oleg cupped her cheek. "What is wrong?" He bent down and put his nose to her neck. "I smell a wind vampire. Strong."

Oh damn. She was going to have to tell him about Vano or he was going to overreact.

But she'd also seen another wind vampire that night.

"Vecchio," she blurted. "We were talking while I was watching for sparks from the fireworks earlier."

"Was he bothering you?"

"Not in any dangerous way. He... asks too many questions. It's probably nothing."

Oleg took Tatyana's hand and led her to the sofa. "Sit with me. I can sense the tension in the camp even though I'm hiding in this trailer," he growled. "It's not unexpected, particularly this close to a power transfer."

"Transfer?" She sat next to him, but she didn't reach for the puzzle. "So one of the terrin *is* going to give up a goblet?"

According to Rumi, when one terrin was ready to retire, that was what they did. They handed over the jewel goblet to their chosen successor, and the Poshani people either accepted that successor or voted for someone more popular. The people always had the final say.

Oleg had said nothing, and a frown dominated his features.

"Is it Radu?" Tatyana got the impression that Radu was the terrin Oleg liked the most. "Is he giving up his power?"

"I do not know," he said softly. "I tried to discover his intentions months ago, but I cannot say for certain. I know he has an idea that it might be time."

"It should be Vano," she blurted. "Not Radu."

Oleg narrowed his eyes. "Did he threaten you again? I am more than happy to kill him."

"That seems... excessive." Yes, she was definitely keeping that to herself right now. "Actually, he's been keeping his distance. Maybe I smell like you now."

"You probably do." He leaned over and sniffed her neck, smiling with satisfaction. "Yes, you do."

Perhaps she could warn him away without mentioning Vano. "Do you think anyone knows you're sneaking into the camp? I don't want you hurt. And I don't want to create problems for the Hazar."

"Radu has probably guessed." Oleg sat back and stretched one arm across the back of the sofa, playing with a piece of her hair. "But he also likely knows that I am only sneaking in to meet with my lover, so as long as you do not object to me, he will not say anything."

That wasn't what she was expecting. Perhaps Vano's threats had even fewer teeth than she'd imagined. "He doesn't care that you've broken the security of the kamvasa?"

"This deep in my territory, he cannot be surprised that I know they are here. We're only a hundred kilometers from my castle right now."

"Your castle," she whispered. "I nearly forgot about the castle."

"You will like it. Of course, you cannot live there because I am sure you will want your internet, and I have not allowed them to put internet into the castle." Oleg pursed his lips. "But if you prefer it, I will allow internet to be built there."

"You don't build..." She shook her head. She wasn't going to try to explain how broadband cables worked to a thousand-year-old vampire when that wasn't really the issue. "Oleg, just because you're... courting me doesn't mean that I'm going to start working for you again."

"Don't be ridiculous." He stood and started pacing. "It's the only place for you. In less than two months, the kamvasa will be finished for the season. You will not be welcome back in the Fire King's court."

She watched him pace, and she felt his amnis changing, his energy shifting from waves to spikes. Hard and biting.

"I will find a place," she said calmly. "I have a few avenues that I am investigating, though I would like to go visit my mother if—"

"The fact that you are even asking permission is an insult to me!" Oleg snapped.

Tatyana kept very still. "I'm not trying to insult you."

"Stop that." He pointed at her. "You cannot still be afraid of me. This stubborn independence is—"

"I am *not* one of your people." She stood and allowed her amnis to wake. She wasn't a scared newborn anymore. She might not have a fraction of his power, but taking his blood had given her new insight.

She had power too.

"You are *mine*," Oleg said deliberately. "Whether you admit it or not. Your blood knows the truth."

Tatyana could feel his energy surging in her blood. She wanted to go to him. She wanted to curl into his body, rub her body against his, and drink him in. Her body was primed for him. Her fangs were long. She could walk to him, take his blood, bathe in their shared amnis, and forget everything they were fighting about.

"This is the problem," she said quietly.

This had always been the problem.

He marched toward her and crossed his arms over his chest. "What are you talking about?"

He was so powerful, so potent, that he burned everything else away, and if she returned to his territory, submitted to his aegis, her soul would turn to ashes.

She would be nothing.

"Oleg," she whispered. "Please don't ruin this."

"I am not ruining anything." He lowered his voice. "You are the one running. Again you are running."

"Because I am not one of your people," she said again. "I'm not a minion to order around. I'm not your soldier. I am not your book-keeper. And if I—"

"You can take any role you would like. I would value your counsel on any—"

"If I started working for you again" —she could not let him run her over— "then all this?" She motioned between the two of them. "It changes. You *have* to realize that."

"Why?" He leaned down until their eyes were level. "Are you saying you like this?" He pointed to the door. "Hiding our connection? Sneaking in the shadows? I would be *proud* to have you stand at my side, Tatyana Vorona."

"I like being at peace."

He took a step back as if she'd struck him. "And I do not give you peace?"

"I want to be with you." She stepped toward him. "But who you are to the world and who you are to me?" She put her hand over her heart and shook her head. "They are not the same."

"This place is an escape for you." His jaw tightened. "And yet I cannot escape the world. Not even here. Not even with you."

"What are you talking about?"

Chapter 29

Oleg

He could lie. It would be so easy to lie to her.

But she was leaving him again. Running away like a frightened rabbit, and in his anger, Oleg didn't think. "You think you are the only reason I am here?"

Her chin lifted, and she stepped away from him. The amnis that had been roused and hungry for him stilled. It watched. It waited. He could feel her blood in his body chill.

"Of course not." Her voice was mechanical. "Because this year the Vashana Zata is happening. Power is changing hands, isn't it?" She pushed a finger into his chest. "And *nothing* that important happens in your territory without your having a say in it."

She grasped the connection immediately.

Of course she did. His future mate had a brilliant mind, but Oleg would not be dissuaded.

"Milaya—"

"Don't call me that." She shook her head. "Don't use sweet words when this is just another... maneuver. I'm such a fool!" She reached down and swept the tiny pieces of the puzzle off the table, scattering them to the ground in a sudden and unexpected burst of anger. "We never stopped playing chess, did we?"

Oleg stared at the scattered pieces of the game. He had sent Mika to the nearest town to find the elaborate wooden picture, and his boyar had come back with five choices. Oleg had picked the lavender field because he was hoping it would remind her of home.

Now the broken picture mocked him.

Foolish. The voice in his mind had the insidious whisper of his sire. *Foolish vampire.*

Perhaps he *was* foolish.

But was Oleg foolish to want her or foolish to have hidden the truth?

"You didn't come here to find me, did you?" Tatyana asked. "You came here because you know that something is happening with Vano, Radu, and Kezia. You know that something strange is happening with those new vampires who showed up."

"Thieves." He kept his voice soft and his eyes on the purple and green pieces on the floor. "Radu invited three thieves to the kamvasa. And I don't know why."

"The Frenchman. He's the other thief."

"Very good, volchitsa." Oleg walked to the desk, pulled out a chair, and dragged it across from the sofa. He snapped at it. "Sit."

"Fuck you," she spat out. "I am not your dog."

"No, you are my *headache*," he hissed. Oleg pointed to the chair with gritted teeth and fangs that wanted to punch through his jaw. "You want to know why I am here? Then sit."

She kept her eyes narrowed, and her energy was as cold as the Baltic Sea, but she sat.

Oleg sat on the sofa and leaned forward, his eyes level with Tatyana's. "Every Poshani terrin has their own responsibilities. Radu runs their hospitality and also takes the lead on running the kamvasa. Kezia is the diplomat. She travels and negotiates with other vampires as needed. And Vano—"

"Is the businessman." Her eyes didn't leave his. "I know this part."

"He's the one who pays for... well, most of this. He runs the books, and he runs most of the human businesses for the clan."

"Which is why he was questioning Rumi and the other cooks about the food budget."

Oleg waved a hand. "That's nonsense. They have plenty of money."

"Unless he's stealing," Tatyana said. "Like Zara was."

Oleg nodded. "That is a possibility. More damning, he is also going behind Radu's and Kezia's back and causing trouble in Russia with Ivan."

She frowned. It was the first break in her cold wall. "Ivan your brother?"

"Ivan is my brother, and he's also my governor for much of Russia. He's the most like our sire, and he's not a person I want anywhere near you."

"But if I come to work for you, I would have to deal with him."

"*If* you come to work for me?" Oleg's eyebrows went up. "So now it's a possibility?"

She blinked, opened her mouth, then closed it.

Aha. He smiled. "It *is* a possibility."

"N-no," she stammered. "It's a hypothetical that's not going to happen."

He brushed his hand at her imaginary problem. "Because of your... minion thing."

She reached over and snapped in his face. "Because of this bullshit."

Oleg smirked.

Tatyana narrowed her eyes. "Don't laugh about the snapping thing. Everyone hates it."

"I know. That's why I do it."

She rolled her eyes. "You are such an asshole."

"Too bad you like it so much when I fuck you," he muttered.

"Don't be crude."

Oleg barely kept from laughing. She might protest his crudeness, but her body reacted to it. She liked his roughness as much as his sweet words. He could smell her arousal in the trailer. It bloomed in the air like the scent of the roses.

He looked at the meeting of her thighs and licked his lips.

"Stop it." She shifted in her seat.

"Do you want me to?" His eyes ran over her body. "Truly?"

"Yes." Her hand was trembling. "Truly."

"Very well." Oleg had mercy on her. He pulled back his energy, but he couldn't fail to notice when her eyes dropped to the prominent erection in his pants.

Nevertheless, she kept her words focused. "So Vano and Ivan are making trouble?"

"Yes, which goes against everything the Poshani stand for. I am their host. To steal from me, ambush my people—even kill and wound them—"

"Vano killed some of your people?" Tatyana blinked. "Oleg, he—"

"Ivan hired Vano to hijack our trucks. Paid him to hijack our trucks, and some of Ivan's own people were killed in the process."

Her eyes went wide. "Your brother would kill even his *own* people?"

Oleg leaned back and folded his arms over his chest. "Our sire did it all the time, milaya. Ivan learned from Truvor, but this is not a practice that I have continued. If my people are loyal to me, I take care of them. The Poshani are the same, which is why we have historically been allies."

She pressed her lips together. Hard. "Radu and Kezia would be horrified by Vano doing things like that with Ivan."

Oleg nodded. "Exactly. When I officially arrive for the Vashana tomorrow night, I plan to expose Vano's and Ivan's scheming when I meet with Radu. If I am guessing correctly, Radu will decide to stay in power, and he and Kezia will force Vano out."

"And then what?"

"I will kill Vano" —Oleg shrugged— "if Radu and Kezia don't do it first. But not until he tells me everything he knows about Ivan's plans."

She kept her voice soft. "And what will you do with Ivan?"

"I haven't decided yet. Ivan has many who are loyal to him."

She cocked her head. "They may not be as loyal when they discover that he was paying Vano to kill some of their brothers."

"See?" He leaned forward and pinched her chin. "This is why I need you working for me. You see things quickly. You think politically, but you are not afraid of me."

She was like Mika.

No, she was better than Mika. Tatyana had a fatalistic streak that Mika didn't have. She didn't fear death, which made her utterly fearless when he needed to hear the truth.

You're going to fall in love with her. You're half in love already.

Oleg hated when Lazlo was right, but he couldn't deny it any longer.

"You think I came to this camp with ulterior motives?" Oleg said. "I cannot deny it. But you have things backward. I was looking for an excuse to hunt for you, Tatyana. Vano and Ivan only gave me the reason I needed."

Oleg left Tatyana's trailer an hour before dawn. He'd kissed her for so long he could still taste her, but he would not see her again until he was officially a guest of the kamvasa. It was better to be cautious at this point with so many of the Hazar gathered for the Vashana.

The puzzle pieces were still on the floor when he left.

"What is that face?" Mika asked Oleg when he reached their camp.

Ludmila was smoking her pipe by the fire. "He is in love with her, and she kicked him out. Can't you tell?"

Oksana's eyes went wide. "You're in love with Tatyana?" The water vampire nodded. "You know, I approve. She's a bit young but—"

"I do not need any of your opinions or your approval." He glared at Ludmila as he sat across from her. "Tenzin of Penglai is mated now. To a *man*."

Oksana burst into laughter, and Ludmila took her pipe out of her mouth. "Fuck you both."

He couldn't stop his smile, not even when Lazlo heard the commotion and came out of their cave. "Who is Tenzin?"

"That mean little thief who killed your friend Alfonso in Naples," Mika said.

"Hmm." Lazlo grunted. "He probably deserved it."

"Why are there three thieves in the kamvasa?" Oleg asked. "René, Tenzin, and the Vecchio boy. As far as I can tell, Radu invited three thieves to the kamvasa. Why would he do that?"

Ludmila shrugged. "Do we care?"

"Maybe we need to."

"Is there reason to think that their arrival may interfere with exposing Vano?" Mika asked.

"I do not know." Oleg crossed his arms over his chest and surveyed the four vampires surrounding him. "But I want all of you in my personal retinue when I arrive for the Vashana."

Lazlo winced. "Oleg—"

"Okay, fine." Lazlo would grumble so much about doing anything social Oleg might end up killing him, and then he'd have to replace a governor and not just a CFO. "Lazlo can guard the camp, and Ludmila, I want you in the trees, watching the Hazar." He pointed to Oksana and Mika. "The two of you are with me."

Oksana nodded. "Yes, Knyaz."

Mika was staring at the fire. "How are we going to prove to Radu and Kezia that Vano is betraying them?"

Ludmila took her pipe out again. "And are we sure they do not know about it?"

"I don't think so, but we can't be until we tell them," Oleg said. "We watch, we wait, and we see their reactions."

Ludmila nodded, but Mika still looked skeptical. "How are we going to prove it?"

"Polina sent the transaction details?" Oleg asked. "And a statement from her informant?"

Mika nodded.

"We have that, but mostly we need Juliya to get our hostage to turn on Vano." Oleg stretched out his legs and crossed his ankles. "And to convince him... Well, just leave that to me."

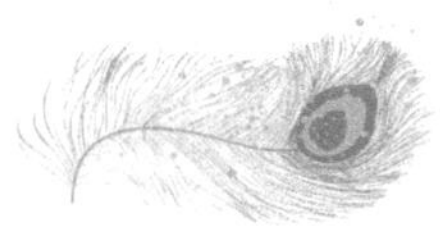

THE FOLLOWING NIGHT, MIKA CALLED ESEN—ONE OF THE WIND vampires in Oleg's druzhina—who met them at a prominent point near a small lake. Oleg took to the air with his soldier, who flew him through the dark clouds toward the citadel where Danior the vampire was locked in his dungeon.

Oleg didn't like flying, but Esen was part of Oleg's inner circle, and flying was the fastest way to get where he needed to be.

He landed on a high parapet that overlooked the river valley and turned to survey his territory before he walked inside the castle.

The rich, tree-covered folds of the Carpathian Mountains stretched behind him, and rolling hills in front of the castle dropped down to a river that cut through the valley. The village in the distance was lit by bright gold electric lights, and the wind swept through the trees, wafting the scents of pine, cedar, and moss to his nose.

The air was sharp and cold. A thread wrapped around Oleg's neck and crept down his spine.

"Knyaz?" His house manager arrived at the doorway.

"Get me a telephone, Omar. And a very long extension. I should like to call Polina."

Moments later, Oleg was sitting in the dungeon with Danior, the Poshani vampire who had killed his people and beat his driver nearly to death. The prisoner wore an ancient iron collar around his neck that was chained to the wall, keeping him on the ground.

Torture for a wind vampire.

Juliya's interrogations had not loosened Danior's tongue, and the wind vampire stared at Oleg with haughty eyes, daring him to kill him.

"I am not going to end you yet," Oleg muttered. "We're going to call my daughter first." He dialed the old rotary phone and listened to the device click as it turned. "There is no internet here." He glanced at Danior. "But I may have them build something. The vampire I am planning to take as my mate likes computers and internet things."

"Young," Danior muttered.

"I know, but what can I say? I am fond of a well-balanced battle-ax, so we are all biased toward the modern technology of our human years, are we not?"

The phone started ringing, and a few moments later, Polina was on the phone.

Oleg winked at Danior and put his finger to his lips to mime "quiet."

"Papa?"

"Lisichka, I know you spoke to someone at the gold exchange about Vano getting the money from Ivan, yes?"

"You owe me for how much I had to bribe him, but yes. Did you want—"

"I don't need the name." He glanced at Danior and put a finger to his lips again. "Can you tell me the dates of the gold transfers again?"

"Give me a moment."

There was a rustling sound on the other end of the line, and Oleg watched Danior, whose eyes were fixed on the phone with a most intense expression.

Danior was a Poshani vampire. He worked for Vano. If he was any kind of Poshani, he believed that whatever Vano had ordered him to do was in the service of his own people, not a Russian earth vampire who ran an organized crime network.

Torture wasn't working, so it was time for the truth.

"There was a payment on the fifth of August last year. Then another on the seventh of November." Polina listed off three more dates, and Danior's eyes never wavered from the phone.

Oleg asked, "And you're sure these transfers weren't going to Poshani accounts?"

"The payments I make to Vano for construction or other contracts all go through a holding company in Poland so the Poshani workers can collect their government pension credits. These appear to have come from Ivan's personal accounts going to Vano's personal accounts. Though I have some questions about other gold I'm seeing transferred into Vano's accounts when you have time to speak to Radu."

"Oh?"

"I can't say for certain," Polina continued, "but I believe Vano may be skimming money from the clan. I'd have to have a bookkeeper look for it, but there are regular and significant amounts flowing into his personal gold stores in the days after we record transactions with our company."

"I see." So Tatyana was correct again. Oleg glanced at Danior. "Tatyana said that Vano has been accusing the human cooks of over-feeding the children in the kamvasa, so he may be trying to cover his tracks."

The moment that Danior heard "overfeeding the children," his eyes went wide and Oleg felt his energy change. The air in the dungeon started to whip around the four stone walls.

"That's despicable." Polina added, "Let me know if you'd like me to fax this paperwork to you. You're at the citadel?"

"I am." Oleg angled himself toward Danior. "And yes, if you have records you can fax to me, do that. Omar will bring them to me."

"Of course."

"Have a good night." Oleg hung up before Polina could mention her daughter or mate. He stared at Danior, who was glaring at him.

"Your boss betrayed his people by asking you to do Ivan's dirty work," Oleg said quietly. "What is more, Ivan paid you to kill his own men. His own drivers and guards. People whose families depend on them and who had pledged loyalty to Ivan."

Danior remained silent, but Oleg could see his fangs were long, and the vampire swallowed visibly.

"Is it bitter?" Oleg whispered. "That taste on the back of your tongue when you learn that your own terrin is stealing so much that he would take food from the mouths of Poshani children to cover his deceit?"

Danior curled his lip and glared at Oleg. "What do you want?"

He spread his hands. "I am a reasonable man. All I want is the truth. Give me that, and I will hand you over to the terrin."

The hollow look in the vampire's eyes was enough to tell Oleg that he knew he would die no matter what.

"Your fate will be what the Kali demands," Oleg continued. "But the manner in which you face that fate is entirely up to you."

Chapter 30

Tatyana

Tatyana was shocked to find herself in an entirely new location when she opened her door that night. She hadn't realized they were moving that day; they had only been in the previous location for one night.

The Vashana Zata is almost here.

She felt the tension in the air, and as she stepped down into the long grass of the meadow where the wagons had been circled, she looked around, trying to understand what felt so different.

The camp setup felt... hasty. The usually meticulous preparations of the darigan were not evident. Grass hadn't been trimmed. Wagons were still in the process of setting up. It felt like the kamvasa had moved quickly, and she wasn't sure why.

Security breach?

She couldn't feel Oleg, and she wanted the assurance of his blood nearby. Anger tumbled with longing in her mind. She wanted him, but she didn't *want* to want him.

Her craving for the vampire was bordering on obsessive. Was this how he felt after taking her blood?

Tatyana had thought that his taking her blood was a greedy,

selfish move to control her, but now that she'd taken his, she realized that it was also a huge vulnerability.

I was looking for an excuse to hunt for you.

She was still being hunted, but was it truly personal—as Oleg claimed—or was he hunting her as an amusement while he had other motivations?

She wanted to believe what he said, that she was his true reason for being here. That he wanted her for herself, not as part of some scheme or power play.

And part of her did believe him, but was that the influence of his blood in her system?

Vano and Ivan only gave me the reason I needed.

Vano and Ivan. Tatyana didn't know the full implications of what they were scheming, but she knew that a Poshani terrin cutting deals with a regional governor under the nose of the other vampire authorities could not be good.

"Tatyana!"

She turned and saw Kezia walking toward her. "Good evening."

"An unexpected move." Kezia was smiling, but Tatyana saw tension around her eyes. "No doubt there was something unsatisfactory about the previous location. The darigan want everything perfect for Vashana."

Tatyana saw that Kezia was trying to convince herself. She remembered making excuses like that in university when she was the new student and the others in her dormitory had done something that left her out. It was an excuse to justify the anger and worry of being excluded from a decision.

"The darigan decide much for the kamvasa," Tatyana said.

Kezia nodded. "We trust them with our lives." She crossed her arms over her chest and watched the humans scuttling around the camp.

"How are they chosen?"

Kezia cocked her head. "You are very curious for a guest."

"I'm curious…" Tatyana started. "I'm curious about everything, I suppose. I'm new to this life."

Kezia smiled. "I forget that you are so young. It's rare for us to have a vampire in the kamvasa who is so new to this life. Most have not accumulated the wealth necessary to buy passage."

Tatyana shrugged. "Unless their sire dies and leaves them a fortune and they are left at loose ends."

"Is that what happened to you?"

"Are you asking where I got my money?"

Kezia's eyes brightened. "No, I am not. I don't believe women should have to explain themselves. Men usually don't."

"Exactly."

Kezia inclined her head toward her own trailer. "Would you care to join me for a drink?"

Why not? Perhaps Kezia could shed light on the strange tension that seemed to waft through the air like the scent of paprika and meadow grass.

"Thank you. I would enjoy that."

They walked across the meadow toward Kezia's trailer, a large wooden affair with a rounded top made of heavy cloth. There were windows on each side and one on the back.

As Tatyana looked closer, she realized they were false, only a decoration bordered by carved wooden shutters. The side panels were painted deep green with gold and red flowers detailed in intricate designs.

Tatyana paused to admire it as Kezia stepped onto the back porch.

"It's a vardo." She smiled. "I know my brothers prefer more modern conveniences like your trailer, but my houses in town are quite modern, so when I am in the kamvasa, I enjoy being sentimental."

"It's beautiful."

"And it's more secure than it looks." She waved Tatyana closer. "Come. We should share a drink. You're quite private, you know. A little hard to get to know."

Was she?

"I think I'm still more comfortable around humans," Tatyana said quietly as she ducked her head to enter the trailer.

"That's understandable," Kezia said. "Vampires are scheming liars who plan in centuries instead of years. You're quite right to distrust us."

It appeared bigger on the inside, and the top arched overhead, also painted with traditional Poshani designs.

"Your vardo is a work of art."

"Yes." Kezia looked up. "Many years ago, I had a human lover who painted all this." She waved a hand. "She was very gifted."

"You must have trusted her very much."

Something flickered in Kezia's eyes. "I've heard it said that to be trusted is a greater gift than being loved."

Tatyana tucked that away in the back of her mind as Kezia pointed her toward a velvet-upholstered sofa built into the side.

Her nose twitched. "What is that scent?"

Kezia glanced at her from the corner of her eye. "Peppermint schnapps. A bottle mysteriously fell from my bar."

"Mysteriously?"

Kezia poured two glasses of blood-wine and handed one to Tatyana before she sat across from her. "Quite mysteriously."

"You think someone broke into your trailer?" It wouldn't even occur to Tatyana. "Would someone do that to a terrin?"

"A Poshani would not," Kezia said. "But we have outsiders in the camp."

Benjamin Vecchio.

Tenzin.

Madina.

Not Darius.

"René," Tatyana murmured. "The Frenchman?"

It wasn't René who had been lingering around Kezia's trailer the night of the fireworks though. It had been Benjamin Vecchio.

Kezia narrowed her eyes and leaned forward. "Now why would you suspect René?" She lifted a hand. "I'm not saying you're wrong."

"I don't know." She did know; Oleg had confirmed that René DuPont was a thief. "Perhaps he reminds me of the young men in Sevastopol when I was a teenager. You could tell the ones who were only pretending to be rich to get money from people."

Kezia's fangs glittered in the gold light from her glass lamps. "You think René is a con artist?"

"Maybe not a con artist but an opportunist?"

She leaned back and smiled. "You are not wrong. My brother Radu asked that I invite him this year."

"Why?"

"That's an excellent question." Kezia tasted her blood-wine. "Both my brothers have been keeping secrets from me."

Tatyana sipped her wine. "You don't look angry."

"Why would I be? I have secrets of my own."

Tatyana offered another name even though her gut was saying she was wrong. "Benjamin Vecchio might be considered an opportunist by some."

"By me." Kezia sipped her wine. "But apparently he and his mate decided to leave us, and as I am not missing anything other than a broken bottle of schnapps, I doubt it was him or Tenzin. They are both very accomplished thieves."

Tatyana blinked. "What do you mean?"

"Ben and Tenzin are both very good at... we'll say *retrieving* lost things. It's their business these days."

"But you said they are gone?"

"Yes." Kezia's eyebrows went up. "Vano said they requested permission to leave. Quite extraordinary, but he made it sound like it was some kind of family emergency, and considering both their families—"

"They're *gone*?" That's what had felt off. There were two trailers missing from the kamvasa. That was the imbalance Tatyana sensed when she stepped outside.

"Things like this happen rarely, but they do happen." Kezia lifted one shoulder. "What can you do? They will not be welcomed back for a century at least. That is the penalty for breaking one's contract even in an emergency."

Well, that explained why the darigan had moved. If Vecchio and his mate had truly demanded to leave, the kamvasa could not remain in the same position for security reasons.

That meant that Oleg's presence was still undetected unless Vano had chosen to rat her out.

"And how are you finding the kamvasa this season, Tatyana Vorona?" Kezia lifted her glass of wine. "It seems you have made yourself very much at home."

She was tempted to tell Kezia what she'd witnessed between Vano and Rumi or that Vano had threatened her, grabbed her in the shadows, and tried to intimidate her.

Tell on me, and I'll tell on you.

"I love it here." Even with Vano's scheming, it was the absolute truth. "In all honesty, given the choice, I think I would never leave."

THE FOLLOWING NIGHT, TATYANA WALKED TOWARD THE cooking wagons, needing to reassure herself that Rumi, Desiree, and Katrina were still there. She hadn't seen them in a few nights, and now everything seemed uncertain.

The tension was even more distinct in the human areas of the kamvasa, though more humans had gathered and there was a general air of festivity.

Children ran through the camp, chasing each other while wearing flower crowns and fancy dresses as their mothers shouted at them to keep clean.

Dogs barked in happy chorus, and slow-blinking cats peered from the tops of trailers and covered wagons, watching from the darkness with gold eyes.

Small fires had been lit in each circle, and men and women gathered around them, chatting and smoking cigarettes and pipes. She drew a few curious glances, but the Poshani who knew her nodded and drew the curious stares away.

"Tatyana!"

She turned when she heard her name and saw Rumi waving for her. She walked over, and Rumi greeted her with an embrace.

Tatyana asked, "How are you?"

Rumi's eyes were bright. "Vampire drama, yes? This move disrupted all the original plans for the dinner because we were going to do a pit roast, but what can you do, right?" She shrugged. "The security of the guests come first."

"We don't deserve you."

Rumi smiled and reached for a bottle of beer. "You don't." She waved at Tatyana. "Walk with me."

They moved from Rumi's trailer through the circles of Poshani wagons and trailers, and Tatyana felt her tension start to drain away.

Rumi kept her voice low. "I understand that Oleg is arriving tomorrow night."

And the tension was back. "Oh?"

"I didn't want you to be shocked when he arrived," Rumi said. "I know that you have your issues with him."

"Thank you." She glanced at Rumi. "Do you truly think he would win a vote for terrin if one of them steps down?"

Rumi waved a hand. "No. I don't think he would even put his name forward, because he has a huge empire to run, doesn't he?

That would be like asking a prime minister to sit on a school council."

"He would be lucky to lead the Poshani," Tatyana snapped.

"Ha!" Rumi threw an arm around Tatyana's shoulders. "I love that you think so, but truly, he is a host to us and that is all. Most of our roaming areas overlap with his territory, and he has always been fair with us, which is not like his sire." She patted Tatyana's shoulder. "Still, I can tell that things are not easy between you."

"We're not..." How was she supposed to explain? "Anytime I was around Oleg, I always felt like he was keeping secrets from me, that he had an ulterior motive."

Rumi nodded. "That seems accurate for most vampires, don't you think?"

Her shoulders slumped. "How am I supposed to live with people like that for centuries? It's so much... bullshit, Rumi." Tatyana snapped, "I am surrounded by bullshit."

Rumi laughed. "So don't put up with it. Just be yourself and make the rest of them change if they want to be around you."

"I might have a very short life," Tatyana muttered.

"But it will be *your* life," Rumi said. "Yours and no one else's. That is all we can do, my friend. Human or vampire, we must live the life..." Rumi's eyes locked on something in the distance, and she curled her lip.

Tatyana knew before she even turned to look. "Vano."

"He's been lurking around the kitchen trailers all week." Rumi kept her voice to a murmur. "I don't trust him."

"How was he elected terrin when so many of the Poshani seem to dislike him?"

"He put on a good face for decades," Rumi said. "But now? Everyone is hoping he will give up the ruby goblet. He's greedy. There are rumors that the two vampires who left paid him off to let them out of their contract."

"It would have to be a lot, correct?"

Rumi nodded and started walking again. "Even for emergencies, there is a penalty because it disrupts everything about the planning. But we adjust."

"Did you report his attack on Katrina to Radu or Kezia?"

Rumi turned to her. "How did you know about that?"

"I saw it," Tatyana admitted. "I was coming to meet you, and I saw him threaten you."

Rumi's voice was fierce. "Did you say anything?"

"No, but Vano knows that I saw. He... he wasn't happy."

Rumi's hand tightened on her arm. "You must be careful, Tanya."

"I'm a guest here. Are you telling me I may not be safe?" She was curious what Rumi would think of Vano's threats, but she didn't want to put the woman at risk. "I thought the safety of the guests was the first priority of the kamvasa."

"The kamvasa doesn't last forever," Rumi whispered. "And you don't have an aegis. Vano could hurt you. He knows horrible people."

She lowered her voice. "What kind of horrible people?"

Rumi shook her head. "Just don't cross him, and forget what you saw."

The night after her meeting with Kezia, Tatyana heard a polite knock on her door. When she opened it, Oleg Sokolov, high lord of the Kievan Rus, was standing at her doorstep, wearing a formal grey suit with an intricately embroidered cape over his shoulders.

She stared at him, and he took her breath away. She felt the idiotic urge to swoon, so she quickly snapped, "So where is your crown?"

The corner of his mouth turned up. "I left it at the castle. It's quite heavy."

She kept her face pointed toward him, but her eyes darted around and she saw the humans and vampires watching them. "Is this a formal... something?"

"A formal greeting, of course." His voice was low and smooth. "After all, you are a vampire of my extended clan and a former employee, so it's only proper that I greet you on my arrival."

"Right." So this entire meeting was for show. "Give me a minute to grab a jacket."

Oleg nodded deeply. "Miss Vorona, I wait on you."

She was only wearing a simple dress and sandals, but she grabbed a silk jacket that Rumi had helped her buy, then fixed her hair before she returned to the door.

Oleg's eyes were warm as she walked down the steps of the trailer. "You look more Poshani than Russian now."

"Do I?" Good. That had been her intention. There weren't many blond-haired, blue-eyed Poshani, but she had tried to blend in. She switched to speaking in Poshani as they walked. "How was your journey, Lord Oleg?"

"Oh, I do like it when you call me lord." His voice was as seductive as ever. "I've missed our chats, Miss Vorona. You've picked up the language quite well."

"I'm not fluent yet." She nodded at a human server she recognized. "Where are we going?"

"We are taking a public walk around the camp to show the world that we're good friends now." Oleg nodded at Darius as they walked past him.

"You want them to think I'm working for you again?"

"Oh no." Oleg saw another vampire across the meadow and nodded at that one too. "You have made it very clear that you are not working for me again. That's not what this is about."

"What is this about then?"

"It is showing that we are friends," Oleg said. "Polite allies if nothing else. If there is going to be any conflict in the kamvasa, I want it known that Tatyana Vorona has my protection whether she is under my aegis or not."

She felt her heart move. "Oleg—"

"This is not a time to argue with me. Now— Forgive me." Oleg walked over to exchange polite words with Madina before he rejoined her. "Now is a time to project strength and unity between us. Do you understand?"

He was protecting her. Always protecting her. Maybe it was hard to recognize it because she had always been the one holding everything together, but no matter how she pushed him or how much she antagonized him, he was protecting her.

He was conniving, manipulative, and brutal.

Overbearing, bossy, and arrogant.

And Tatyana was falling in love with him.

What are we?

Us. Just us.

Oleg repeated the question. "Do you understand me, Tatyana?"

She kept her hands held behind her as they walked, resisting the ache in her blood. "I understand."

His amnis was in her veins, whispering to her and wrapping around her young and erratic energy. Oleg's energy was fire. It could burn her; it would hurt.

It could also keep her warm and safe and alive.

In the darkness that was her new eternity, Oleg's fire would never let her feel cold or alone. "I feel your blood in me," she murmured. "It's very hard to walk next to you and not react."

His steps didn't slow, but his voice got even softer. "Now you know how I feel, volchitsa." His voice was delicately scornful. "Do you think I want this? To walk beside you as if we are mere friends?"

Are you saying you like this? Hiding our connection? Sneaking in the shadows? I would be proud *to have you stand at my side.*

Tatyana's throat burned. "Oleg."

He smiled at someone across the meadow and raised a hand. "There will be more immortals showing up tonight. A few trusted dignitaries and friends who were invited to witness the ceremony. There will be a formal ceremony of greeting in a few—"

"I want to bite you again."

Oleg didn't speak for many minutes.

Tatyana felt the admission soft and lush in her mouth. "I want to bite you again."

"I heard you." His voice was a low growl.

"You have meetings tonight?"

They reached a stand of trees that cast a heavy shadow between two wagons, and before she could blink, Oleg had her in the shadows, pressing her body to his and claiming her mouth with his own.

Tatyana's blood leaped in her veins. She gripped the back of his neck and felt every molecule of her body reach for him. She wanted his fangs in her neck. She wanted to taste his blood on her tongue and feel his cock between her legs; she wanted to lose herself in the fire that was Oleg Sokolov.

He ripped his mouth from hers. "I will meet you before dawn."

"I'll be waiting." She needed him desperately, but if they were gone another moment, the others would notice.

He ran a shaking hand over her head to smooth her hair, then angled his shoulders toward the meadow again.

In seconds, they were walking as if nothing had happened.

Tatyana kept her hands behind her back again. This time they were trembling, and she gripped them hard to stop. "What do you want me to do?"

"Be safe, be smart, and be quiet," Oleg said. "I'm meeting formally with the terrin in an hour, then with Radu privately to tell him about Vano."

"There is tension among the humans. I noticed it when I was talking with Rumi earlier."

"I feel it."

A few minutes later, they had made a full circle and were back at her trailer.

Oleg nodded. "Miss Vorona."

She let her voice drop to a breathy whisper. "Lord Oleg."

The corner of his mouth turned up. "Save that for later. Right now give me a bit of your sharp tongue to bring down the mountain between my legs."

"That cape makes you look like you're going to a wizard convention." She loved the cape, but if he asked for insults, he would get them. "Shall I find a stick in the forest so you can pretend to have a wand?"

He crossed his arms over his chest. "I'm quite certain I have all the wood I need. That's not working, and I can't go to the terrin's tent with a cock hard as a tentpole."

"You like it when I'm rude to you." She sighed. "Fine. When Satoshi Nakamoto published his white paper in 2008 and the concept of cryptocurrency was first introduced to the world—"

"What are you talking about?" Oleg scowled.

"I was going to explain the history of Bitcoin to you."

"There." He nodded. "Well done. That completely killed my arousal."

"It always does."

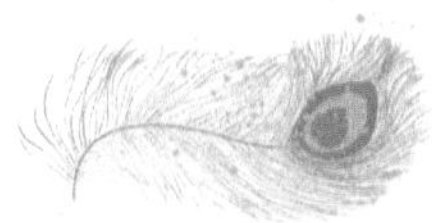

She was standing near the cooking wagons, sipping wine and trying to kill empty hours until Oleg was finished with his meetings, when she heard someone whisper her name.

"Tatyana."

She looked up at the last person she expected to see. "Benjamin Vecchio?" She looked around, but no one else seemed to have noticed the black-clad vampire wearing an odd cap and lurking in the shadows.

What the hell was going on?

"I am surprised to see you here," she said to the shadows, "where you *definitely should not be*."

He had left the kamvasa. He shouldn't even know where it was, but he was a wind vampire.

He kept his voice low. "Did Radu... make my excuses for me?"

His voice was wavering. Something was very wrong.

"He told us nothing." Tatyana shook her head. "Only that you and Tenzin had chosen to leave the caravan. Is everything well with your family?"

"Yeah. I don't know if Radu knows what's going on."

Oleg had implied the same thing, but Tatyana didn't want to mention Oleg to this stranger even if everything about his demeanor was setting off her protective instincts.

Vecchio turned his head, and when Tatyana followed his eyes, she saw Vano speaking with a group of the Hazar and darigan guards.

"Stay away from Vano," Vecchio said. "He's dangerous."

"You tell me things I already know. That man makes my skin crawl."

"Tomorrow night." He seemed to struggle with his words. "Anything you can't live without, keep it with you. If you need to run, be light."

Another vampire implying that something bad was going to happen at the Vashana. "What do you know?"

"Enough to know that something is coming and it could be violent."

"This is the kamvasa. Radu would never—"

"Radu would not." His voice was low and urgent. "Others might."

So something bad *was* going to happen at the Vashana. She had felt it. Oleg had implied it. Now this stranger was confirming it. Tatyana nodded.

"I like you," Vecchio said. "Take care."

The wind shifted, and she smelled him. His energy had changed, and his skin held the faint scent of cardamom and incense.

"You smell like her now," Tatyana said. Vecchio smelled like his mate. The combined scent was lovely in an entirely unexpected way. "Did you resolve your dispute?"

Would her scent change when she took Oleg's blood again? Would his? There was something intensely satisfying about the idea of leaving her mark on him at the cellular level.

Vecchio smiled. "You're very observant. You know that, right?"

She shrugged. "It usually gets me into trouble."

"Good luck." He tipped his hat and then casually walked to the edge of the forest.

In seconds, he had melted into the darkness.

When she turned back to the wagons, Vano was nowhere in sight.

Chapter 31

Oleg

I want to bite you again.

Oleg let her whisper linger in his head as Mika helped him dress for the meeting with Radu that was about to take place. He was wearing the same suit he'd worn when he took a walk with Tatyana, but the formal cape he donned to meet Radu was far more elaborate and—though she had joked about it—he did have a crown, though it was not a traditional piece of finery.

Mika lifted the heavy cape trimmed in ermine and draped it over Oleg's shoulders. "Remember, the first point of this meeting is to get a verbal pledge from Radu that he is still an ally and get assurances that he will *not* be surrendering a goblet."

"And you're still confident that Radu is ignorant about Vano's actions?"

"You'll have to make that judgment when you see him, but all the information that Polina, Juliya, and I can find says that Vano is in this alone with Ivan."

"And you have the statement from Danior?"

Mika held up a tablet encased in plastic. "I do."

Oleg walked to the bathroom, and the moment he looked through the door, he was back in Tatyana's trailer, fucking her against the wall of the shower as he barely held on to control.

"Whatever you're thinking about right now," Mika muttered, "stop."

"Tatyana is not going to come back to work for me."

"Are you seriously thinking about the woman right now?" Mika snapped. "We're talking about the security of the empire, and you—"

"I'm talking about a woman who is not only going to be very important to *my* future but also the future of our territory." Oleg turned and glared at his boyar. "Be very careful what you say right now."

Mika snapped his mouth shut; then, after a long moment of silence, he carefully said, "Then I suggest you focus on securing that territory, reinforcing the power of an ally, and rooting out the snake that has been living in the grass."

"Fine." Oleg walked into the bathroom, and Mika handed him an elaborately carved wooden box. He opened it and saw Truvor's crown sitting on a bed of red velvet.

Mika glanced at the old thing. "It's impossible to look at it and not see his helmet."

"I know; that's the point."

Oleg had hammered the circlet from the twisted remains of the iron helmet Truvor kept hanging on his fortress wall. The metal had been crusted with human blood, and the ridge of osprey feathers was broken and battered.

It was hideous, yet Truvor had kept that thing and all of his armor hanging on the wall of the castle where he'd brutalized his army and especially his offspring.

After Truvor and all his loyalists were dead, Oleg had marched into the fortress's massive throne room and burned everything his sire had touched. To this day, the seams between the stones were filled with black ash from his fire.

He'd ripped Truvor's helmet from the wall, and the parts that hadn't burned he'd fashioned with his bare hands into a crude crown that he'd shoved onto his forehead when it was still red-hot. The scar the crown left was so severe he'd worn it for a century.

Every brother who faced him. Every enemy he killed. The last thing they saw was the twisted remnants of Truvor's helmet burned into Oleg's forehead.

Eventually he'd hammered something decent-looking from it, then coated the circlet in gold and set a ruby in the center where the crown rested on his forehead, a reminder of the blood that had forged the immortal Kievan Rus and the blood that it took to hold it.

Oleg lifted the crown and put it on his head. It wasn't beautiful, and it was heavy.

The crown hadn't been made for beauty. It had always been meant to send a message.

"Radu is a friend," Mika reminded him. "Remember that. He's an ally, but he's going to resist you telling him what to do. The Poshani are fiercely independent."

"He's ready to move on," Oleg said. "He's been serving for centuries. I think he wants a break."

"And you're asking him to commit to another century," Mika said. "I know."

"We know." Oleg stared at his reflection in the mirror for a moment. What would she think of this bloody crown? Would she be willing to stand next to the man who wore it?

She'd taken him as a lover. Even confided in him. There was trust growing between them, and their blood was mingled. But would Tatyana Vorona—so new to immortal life—be willing to publicly stand with a vampire known to the immortal world as one of its most brutal leaders?

Oleg turned to leave the bathroom, and Mika shut the door behind him.

"Oleg Sokolov, Varangian of Gardariki and Knyaz of the Kievan Rus."

The Hazar at the door announced his presence in the terrin's tent, and Oleg strode forward with Mika following him and Oksana bringing up the rear.

Radu, Kezia, and Vano sat on low sofas on the far side of the highly decorated tent that had been set up the night before. The center pole of the tent was the size of a large cedar tree and carved with intricate decorations higher than Oleg's eye.

As he passed it, he noticed the personal crests of Radu's family, then Kezia's, then Vano's. The next terrin would carve their own crest into that pole and add their name to the list of immortals who had watched over the Poshani people.

Radu rose to greet him. "My friend."

Oleg stopped a few feet away and bowed slightly. "Radu le Basarab, Kezia le Almásy, Vano le Krizenov, you honor me with your invitation to this most sacred event."

"Welcome, Lord Oleg, and thank you for your attendance," Vano said. "It has been too long since we have been in our company."

"Thank you, Vano." Oleg looked over and winked at Kezia. "I see that you've convinced your clever sister to let you live another few years."

Radu and Kezia both chuckled.

"I try to be gracious," Kezia said. "Welcome, Lord Oleg."

Oleg sat down on a low couch across from them, and Mika stepped forward to present the gifts that he'd brought for them.

Bars of gold. Bottles of the finest vodka. Cattle horns to signify the beef they would be gifting to the kamvasa. And, finally, a whole sturgeon that the darigan brought in and laid on a low table in front of Oleg.

He made the first ceremonial cut into the belly of the fish, revealing the shining black roe the darigan would clean and process to produce a rich harvest of salted caviar for the Poshani to enjoy after the Vashana.

"Lord Oleg, you honor us with gifts," Radu said. "Please know that while you are here, the hospitality of the kamvasa is yours. No blade will touch your neck, no light will touch your skin, and no hunger will be left wanting. Our home is your home; our Hazar and our darigan will protect you with their own lives."

"Thank you, Radu." It wasn't proper to address Poshani terrin with any sort of title as they were considered servants of the clan. "I accept the hospitality of the kamvasa. While I reside with you, my axe belongs to you and I will defend your sovereignty with my blood and fire."

Formal greetings and oaths taken, most of the darigan retreated, leaving Oleg alone with the three terrin while Mika and Oksana sat at a distance.

"Truly," Kezia said, "it has been too long since you've visited, Oleg."

"Agreed." Vano reached for a goblet of blood-wine. "Far too long."

Oleg smiled. Did Vano know he'd been sneaking in to see Tatyana? He wouldn't be surprised. No doubt the scheming vampire had tucked that information away for his own use later.

"We'll finish this drink," Radu said, "then we should settle that question about the Bucharest property, don't you think?"

"Agreed." Oleg was eager to leave the terrin's tent, but he forced himself to finish his wine.

"Business talk on the eve of the Vashana, brother?" Kezia asked as she lifted a glass to her lips. "You are working hard."

"I never thought we'd be saying that about you." Vano laughed, but the humor had an edge.

Radu cut his gaze to the side, but Oleg kept his eyes firmly on

Radu and only smiled. "I'm sure we can settle our discussion quickly. I am looking forward to the ceremony tomorrow night."

Go on and joke. Oleg's tone was clear. *The adults in the room have important matters to discuss.*

"We're all ready for the Vashana." Kezia sat back, and her eyes narrowed when she looked at Vano. "It's been an interesting season. We should catch up later, Oleg."

"I'll make sure to reserve the time."

The four vampires exchanged pleasantries for another hour, sharing blood-wine, previously prepared caviar, and delicate bites of traditional Poshani delicacies as they chatted about the weather, the entertainment and plays the humans had performed, and other light diplomatic talk.

Soon enough, Oleg and Radu were leaving the terrin's tent and walking into the night, moving from the center of the caravan to Radu's personal trailer.

Mika handed him the tablet while Radu's secretary handed him a folder; then Mika, Oksana, and Radu's people were stationed at a distance while the two friends talked inside.

"It's a good thing I like you," Radu said. "And her."

"I have no idea what you're talking about."

All the trailers in the kamvasa were luxurious, but unlike the generic ambience of a five-star hotel in Oleg's and Tatyana's lodgings, Radu's trailer had the feeling of a very eclectic, very wealthy home.

There were stacks of books piled behind wire-framed cabinets. A conversation area with fresh flowers on a gold-painted table. Wooden cabinets lined the walls, and there were thick Persian rugs layered on the floor.

Radu sat on a leather sofa. "You're good, but you're not that good. You think I can't smell your smoke trail a mile away?"

"Again, I have no idea what you're referring to." Oleg smiled and removed the awkward crown. "I can take this off, can't I?"

"Of course you can." Radu grimaced. "It's hideous. Surely you can create something more beautiful of your own design. I've seen your work."

Radu was one of the few vampires who had seen the citadel and all of Oleg's extensive mosaic work there.

"You're kind, but you of all people understand the importance of tradition." Oleg sat across from Radu. "So you spotted me, did you?"

"The first visit, my guard detected the security breach, but it wasn't until I went to investigate personally that I knew it was you. I told them to watch and wait."

"She didn't report me."

"She didn't." He shrugged. "If it were anyone else—"

"You know I would never if it wasn't important."

The corner of Radu's mouth turned up. "She must be a true wizard with a spreadsheet, old friend."

Oleg allowed himself to smile. "She is mine. So I thank you for your consideration in this."

"If she'd complained to me, you'd already be dead, and I'd have a massive international incident on my hands. But I would have had to kill you."

Oleg smirked. "You would have tried."

"So we are fortunate that whatever kind of charm you have used on the woman has worked. What piece of art from your collection are you going to give me as an sincere apology for breaking the sanctity of the kamvasa? I was thinking the new Chagall you mentioned a few months ago. "

Oleg tried not to snarl. "The Chagall... would look beautiful in your office in Bucharest."

"And of course a contribution to the Poshani Children's Fund would be a thoughtful gesture of our mutual interest in the next generation."

Now Oleg had to smile. "I am always looking toward the future, my friend."

"Excellent." Radu tapped on the leather folio on the table. "What are we talking about that could not wait until after Vashana?"

Oleg kept his voice low. "Are you going to step down?"

"I believe I am." There was some kind of conflict in Radu's expression. "I may not have a choice, Oleg. There are... complications, and I don't know if telling you—"

"Are those complications the reason you invited three well-known thieves to the kamvasa this year?"

Radu cocked an eyebrow. "It's a long story."

"We may be old men," Oleg said, "but I plan to live forever. I have time."

"Someone stole the emerald goblet."

Oleg had expected trickery from Vano. He hadn't expected this. "The dishana?"

"Yes, it's been missing for quite some time. I've searched for it myself, hired the Vecchio boy, but now he has left the kamvasa." Radu shook his head. "I have failed my people. I must step down."

If the emerald goblet was missing, there was no way that Radu would have been scheming about anything with Ivan. He wouldn't have had the time.

Oleg considered the other two thieves residing in the caravan. "Tenzin? René DuPont?"

"They were both suspects." Radu smirked. "As were Darius, Madina, and Fynn. I invited all of them so that Vecchio could discover the truth, but he has failed me."

"You cannot step down," Oleg said. "I am truly sorry, my friend, but no matter what happens with the goblets, it is vital for your people that you do not step down from the terrin's seat."

Radu's eyes narrowed. "What are you talking about?"

Oleg pulled out the tablet and opened it, spinning it around to the video that Mika had already opened. "Danior Kosinski didn't die in those attacks on my trucks. We found him, and I think you're going to want to hear what he has to say."

Two hours before dawn, Oleg finally left Radu's trailer and walked to Tatyana's. He'd met with both Radu and Kezia, faced the heat of Kezia's anger, and gotten a better picture of what was happening with the terrin's seats.

He didn't know what would happen with Vano or the missing goblet, but for now Kezia and Oleg had managed to convince Radu that it was vital he stay in his position for another century and that Vano was double-crossing them.

Tatyana opened the door while he was still a few feet away and stepped back so Oleg could enter.

"It's so strange to have you walking up to my door with everyone watching." She looked around and waited for him to walk inside before she closed it. When she turned to him and saw him in the light, she blinked. "What is that?"

The corner of his mouth turned up. "What? I thought you liked my wizard robe?"

"No, that." She pointed to his head. "It looks... painful."

Oleg pried off the twisted circle of iron and gold. "It's my crown."

"It doesn't look like a crown."

He put it on the coffee table, then unclasped the heavy silver brooch that secured his cape. "Help me get this off."

"Oleg—"

"Unless you want me to fuck you while I'm wearing my ceremonial regalia," he muttered. "That can be arranged. In fact, I think I would enjoy you riding my cock while I was sitting on the throne in the citadel."

Tatyana froze, and her pretty pink lips fell open.

"Hmm." Oleg cocked his head. "I see that you're getting ideas now, but these trailer walls are thin, so we'd best save that one for later."

He gripped the ermine-trimmed cape with one hand and pulled the heavy garment from his shoulders, tossing it on the sofa before he walked to her. "I believe," he murmured, "that you wanted to bite me."

When he reached Tatyana, her arms went up automatically, resting on his shoulders. Oleg felt the sudden ease in his neck. He inhaled and the scent of her was salt air, honey, and some hothouse flower he couldn't put his finger on.

"I want you." He reached down and lifted her into his arms. "I have been rattling on for hours about business and politics, and I hate politics."

She pressed her face into his neck and inhaled deeply. "You may hate politics, but you're good at it."

"It makes me want to light everything on fire," he growled. "Or bash something with an axe."

"Does it?" She started playing with the fine hair at the back of his neck, and Oleg nearly fell to his knees.

She's nothing you want and everything you need.

Lazlo was wrong after all. Tatyana was everything he wanted *and* everything he needed. He loved her. The truth of his feelings settled in his bones and eased through his veins.

Every lover he'd had before her—even his disastrous mating with Luana—it had only been so that he could recognize Tatyana when she came into his life.

As he walked to the bed with her in his arms, Oleg relished the delicate weight of her body in his hands. Her legs wrapped around him. She clung to him, and the kisses she pressed to his neck felt delicate and shy.

He didn't want shy. He wanted the wolf.

Oleg pried her off and tossed her on the bed. "Do you have something for me?"

As expected, his haughty expression provoked her acid tongue.

"Do I have something for you?" She smirked. "I'm not the one who went hunting, Oleg Sokolov. Do you have something for *me*?"

He unbuttoned his jacket, watching her as she watched him. He tossed his outer garment to the side, then unbuttoned his shirt at the neck and wrists before he pulled it over his head.

The scent of her arousal filled the air, and by the time he unbuttoned his trousers, her heart was thumping as if she were still human.

He stepped out of his pants and kicked them to the side, standing before her naked and erect. He grasped his cock in his right hand and felt the heated flesh pulse in time with her heartbeat.

She was lying on the bed, her lips flushed and her body splayed out. He wanted to fuck her and sink his teeth into her neck, but he wanted to play with her first.

"How is your control, volchitsa?" He stared at her mouth. "I want to see your pretty lips wrapped around my cock."

She crawled forward on the bed, and Oleg nearly came just from seeing her on her knees. She looked up as she ran her lips along the length of his erection, and it was everything.

Tatyana opened her mouth, wrapped her lips around his cock, and took him deep in her mouth. Oleg reached out, grasping the long braid of her hair in his fist and moving her back and forth along his length.

She relaxed her throat and took him deeper.

Oleg nearly exploded. "Not this time." He gently pulled her off his cock.

"I wasn't finished."

"It's been too long since I've been in you." He dragged her to her knees on the bed, nearly ripping her clothes off.

"Wait." Her lips were shining and swollen red. "Let me."

She pulled the dress over her head, and his body trembled as she removed her undergarments. Then she was naked before him, a delicacy of soft skin, pink lips, and deliciously plump breasts.

He leaned down and pulled her up by the waist, capturing her breasts with his mouth, sucking her nipples into his mouth and scraping them to hard points with his dull front teeth.

"Oleg." Her head fell back, exposing her neck to him. Her arms were limp, and their mingled blood surged through her body.

His fangs ached to come out, but he waited. He could feel flames erupt on his shoulders, but before he could react, Tatyana reached up and pulled a gentle mist over his skin.

His entire body shuddered at her touch.

"Please." Her fingers dug into his shoulders. "I need—"

"Yes." He laid her down, parted her legs, and hesitated for a moment. He wanted his mouth on her sex, but he wanted the blood at her neck too.

Tatyana decided for him when she gripped his cock in one hand and pulled him closer, parting her legs and wrapping one leg around his waist as he thrust up and inside.

A feral growl ripped from his throat as he seated himself in her body. She hooked an arm around his neck and pulled him closer, squeezing her pussy around his cock and nearly sending him over the edge like a newborn vampire.

"I could live with your cock in me," she whispered.

The unexpected words slipping from her lips made his fangs grow long, and he arched into her body, harder, longer.

His fangs nicked her ear. "Too much?"

She shook her head, and Oleg licked the drop of blood from her ear.

The taste of her blood was a bright, soft kiss against his amnis, and his fire calmed from a raging blaze to a smolder.

For a second Oleg hesitated. She was too fine. Too clean and bright for his life. He was a fool for thinking she would ever want to be his.

The moment passed when he felt her shove his shoulder as she rolled him to the side, onto his back, and then she was arching over him, riding him in glorious, languid strokes, her long legs bracing her body over him as she took control of her pleasure.

Her braid had come loose, and her long blond hair fell over her shoulders. He gripped her thighs and slid his thumb to her clitoris, stroking the sensitive point as he felt her sex tighten around his cock.

The moment she started to climax, he sat up, slid his hand along her shoulder, her neck, angling her head to the side and lowering his fangs to her skin.

The bright, pure taste of her blood burst in his mouth as his fangs pierced her skin. She shuddered violently in pleasure as her amnis flowed into him, entering his blood, covering his body.

The fire danced from his hand to the small of her back where it teased the air over her skin, heating and licking along her body, provoking the rise of her own amnis that met his in a steaming kiss.

Oleg drank deep, sealing the small wounds in her neck with his tongue before he captured her mouth in another blood-tinged kiss.

Tatyana's body was electric, her skin alive with goose bumps as the hairs on her body burned away at Oleg's touch.

He leaned back, braced his arms behind him, and still she rode him. His erection was aching and ready.

He caught her eye and tilted his head to the side, exposing his neck.

Tatyana's fangs grew long. She licked her lips, then leaned forward, and Oleg fell back so that she was draped over him and her golden hair fell around them, curtaining them as they made love.

"Milaya," he whispered as he trailed his fingers from her temple across her cheek. "Take what you want." He cupped the back of her head, sliding his long fingers through her silken hair and pulling her mouth to his neck. "Take it."

He thrust his hips up, driving into her, and as she slid her fangs into his vein, the most delicious wave of pleasure crested over him; the release of elemental fire singed the silken sheets beneath him before Tatyana pulled the heat away from his body, wrapping her amnis around him even as she took his blood into her body.

They were one in that moment. She was his, and he was hers. The heady pleasure wrapped around him as Tatyana drank him in.

His body stilled as he continued to release, holding her tightly as she fed from him. His right hand rested gently on her head, and his left stroked her back, dancing along her skin as their energy spun together like threads in the wind.

By the time she finished drinking, Oleg was wrung out with pleasure and his entire body was at peace. She licked at his wounds and raised her head. Her eyes were cloudy and unfocused.

"Oleg?"

He tucked a long strand of hair behind her ear. "Tatyana Vorona."

"What is this?" She blinked. "I feel..."

"Connected," he murmured. "Our bond will be even stronger now. If we exchange blood like this again, it will be... quite binding."

It would be permanent. It would be a blood bond that would last for centuries. She would live in his blood, and he would live in hers.

Tatyana started to move away, but he held her still, their bodies still joined, their blood and amnis mingling, twisting together even as they lay spent.

"I want you as my mate," he said.

She froze. "What?"

"My mate," he repeated. "I want you as my blood mate. Not my employee. Not a minion like you said. Not ever. If you are my mate, you will be my greatest counselor, my most trusted friend. There will be no hierarchy between us because your will will be as my own."

Tatyana pulled away from him, and this time he let her go.

She crawled off his lap, though she stayed on the bed next to him, staring at the wall.

Oleg didn't press. He waited.

What he was asking was no small thing. It wasn't a passionate whim or an impetuous decision. What he was asking was no less than a bond that could be eternal and a role that would require her sacrifice.

"Oleg." She looked everywhere but at him. "I don't... I mean—"

"You must take time to think about this." He sat up and propped his back against the headboard. "You are new to our world, so let me put this in human terms."

Oleg took her hand in his and waited until her eyes met his.

He locked his gaze on wide blue eyes the color of the summer sky. He kept his voice and his hand soft even though everything in him wanted to grab, to conquer, to steal her away like the barbarian he was.

"Call me your husband, Tatyana Vorona. Grant me your love. Ask me for my protection and you will have it. You will be my mate. No one will touch you. I will care for you, your family will be my own, and you will want for nothing ever again."

Chapter 32

Tatyana

Her mind was *shattered*.

"I'll leave you now. Just think about what I asked."

Oleg kissed her forehead and returned to his trailer before dawn, leaving Tatyana staring at the wall.

He wasn't asking her to marry him, he was asking for her to be some kind of queen. A ruler. His *mate*.

Tatyana barely understood what that meant.

She'd jumped straight from falling in love with the scary, dangerous, and strangely honorable vampire lord to considering whether she was willing to tie her life to his for eternity.

Nothing really prepared a person for that.

Tatyana wanted her mother, but that wouldn't help either. Anna would sit her down, tell her that marrying a king was a horrible idea, that she'd never have a moment's peace. Wasn't there a nice clerk at the city office who didn't mind a wife who only came out at night?

No, her mother was not going to be any help at all.

What would Rumi say?

Oleg Sokolov's marriage proposal was not something that Tatyana could ask Rumi and Desiree for advice about. She had a feeling Oleg would end up wiping their memories quite thoroughly if she did something like that, and she didn't want her friends' brains altered without their consent.

Marriage?

Like... in a church? Could vampires go into churches?

They must have been able to because Oleg told her he was godfather to Elene's children, which would imply that he'd been at their baptisms, which would mean—

She was spiraling.

What he was asking was crazy. She wasn't old enough to get married, especially to a thousand-year-old vampire. She wasn't anyone's queen. She had no idea what it would be like to lead.

Did that mean she'd have to occasionally take up a battle-ax and go defeat his enemies like when Zara had attacked the house in Sochi?

Would she have to sit in on business meetings?

Were there diplomatic events?

What exactly did a vampire queen do?

If Tatyana hadn't been vampire, she would have been awake for hours. Luckily, the sun rose as inevitably as the turning of the clock and dragged her into a deep and dreamless sleep.

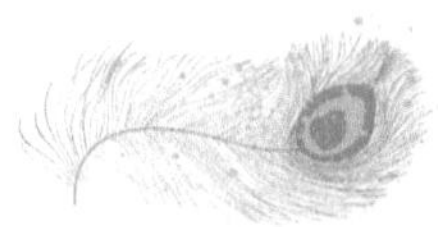

THE FOLLOWING NIGHT, TATYANA WAS STANDING IN THE meadow and watching the final preparations for the grand Vashana Zata with thoughts of Oleg still racing around her mind.

She didn't want to sit with the rest of the immortals who seemed to be in some kind of grandstand that faced the stage, so she lingered in an area just to the right of the main stage and waited for anyone who looked familiar.

Oleg was in the stands, wearing another immaculate suit and the cape he'd had on when they walked around the camp. He caught her eye from across the meadow but offered only a nod. She saw him speak to several immortals sitting nearby, but mostly he spoke to Mika, who was sitting to his left.

He left the seat on his right side empty.

Madina and Darius were sitting behind him. René DuPont was also there, along with the other vampire guests, most of whom were wearing traditional clothing of various sorts.

Between the flower garlands draped everywhere, the stage in the middle of the meadow, and the general aura of revelry, Tatyana felt like she'd accidentally walked onto a movie set.

"What's wrong with you?" Rumi walked up to her, waving a hand in front of her face. "You look like someone walked on your grave."

The vampire lord of the Kievan Rus asked me to marry him and be his queen.

"I had a strange night last night." It was all Tatyana could manage. "And tonight feels..."

"Even stranger?" Rumi grimaced. "The tension is high. Everyone is putting on a good front for the children because they're so excited, but Vano had another altercation with some of the darigan last night."

"Oh?"

"I don't even know what it was about this time, but he was accusing them of insubordination and implying that he was going to get revenge on their families." Rumi sighed. "It's such a mess. He needs to go, but then there's just going to be another power-hungry old man taking his place, so I don't even know what's best anymore."

Ben's warning about events turning violent popped into her mind, and she kicked herself for forgetting to bring some of her essentials and her gold.

Damn Oleg. He'd completely distracted her.

"What are you doing down here?" Rumi asked. "You need to be up with the guests."

Tatyana crossed her arms over her chest. "I wanted to sit with you and Desiree."

Rumi smiled. "I know you forget sometimes, but you do have fangs." She cocked her head to the side and looked at Tatyana. "There's something different about you tonight. Did something happen?"

I exchanged blood with a very powerful vampire, and I feel like I could throw a vardo across the lake.

Tatyana shook her head. "Not really."

"Is it Oleg?"

She blinked. "What? No!"

"Is he bothering you?"

You have no idea.

"No, it's not that. I just..." Tatyana sighed and stood up from where she leaned against the wagon. "I don't have any formal clothes. I didn't bring any and there aren't any to buy."

"You look perfect," Rumi said. "You look *Poshani*." She lifted a finger. "Wait a moment." She waved a woman over who had a rack of flower crowns. "Here." She grabbed a flower crown with ribbons woven through the branches and placed it on top of Tatyana's head. "There you go. You're as fancy as any of them now."

Tatyana wanted to hug her, but that would be awkward. She wanted to thank Rumi for accepting her. Thank her for the simple and profound gift of calling her a friend.

"I'll go with the other vampires," she said, "but find me later? I have a feeling that I'm going to miss the good parties if I stay with the old people."

Rumi laughed. "You're not wrong."

Tatyana made her way through the crowd, and as she approached the platform, she hesitated for a moment when she saw the finery of the vampires in the stands. But remembering Rumi's words, she lifted her chin and walked up the steps.

"Surati, welcome to the Vashana Zata." A Hazar guard stepped aside and allowed her up the steps into the dignitaries' section. "You are most welcome."

"Thank you."

"Tatyana!" René DuPont waved her over. "Come and sit with me unless you're royalty and I don't know about it."

Tatyana cast a quick peek at Oleg, who glanced at the seat next to him.

She froze, her eyes sweeping over the gathered group of vampires who were all staring at her. Oleg must have seen the panic in her eyes because he shook his head slightly and flicked his cape out so that the seat next to him was partially covered.

Okay, so no public statements if she wasn't sure yet.

"Thank you." Tatyana spoke to René, but she was looking at Oleg. "I'm not royalty, just a grateful guest." She sat and folded her hands in her lap.

"Poshaniya!" Kezia stood on the stage and shouted.

A roar from the crowd that sounded like they were ready for a show or a sporting event.

"Poshaniya!"

Another, louder roar.

Kezia was clearly running the program. "We gather tonight!"

She stepped to the front of the stage, and the crowd of Poshani roared and waved their hands in greeting.

René leaned over and spoke softly as the audience erupted. "I believe you're friends with Ben Vecchio, are you not?"

Wait, what? Why was René talking about Vecchio?

"We're... friendly."

"So you know that he and Tenzin did not leave willingly."

Tatyana's eyes went wide. "What?"

"Vano tried to dispose of them," René said. "Very unpleasant, but no harm done. I have been instructed to keep an eye on you if things become complicated."

"What do you mean, dispose?"

"I mean exactly what I say."

She glanced at Oleg. Did he know about this? Should she tell him?

She tore her eyes from Oleg. "Thank you for your concern, but I'm sure I'll be fine."

"If you're worried about the Russian, don't be." René chuckled a little bit. "He's as slow as all the old ones."

Oh, you are an idiot. "That's an interesting assumption."

Tatyana suddenly wished she'd been less shy about publicly claiming her relationship with Oleg.

The Frenchman nodded at the stage. He couldn't seem to keep his mouth shut. "Do you see them? All lined up, the humans who actually think they have a chance to become a terrin?"

"Do they?" Tatyana looked at the front of the crowd and saw a group of mostly middle-aged men and a few women sitting with what looked like cheering sections behind them. "I thought only vampires could become terrin."

"Yes, but they expect to be changed," René said. "That's what they want, the immortality. Only the most foolish want the power."

The power. Yes, only a fool would want the power.

"Brothers and sisters," Kezia shouted, "welcome to Vashana!"

Another ecstatic cheer from the crowd, and the vampires in the grandstand clapped politely.

"As all of you know, this is the Vashana Zata, a special night held only once every hundred years. Because of this occasion, we have invited a few trusted guests from the kamvasa." Kezia gestured to where Tatyana was sitting. "Our guests honor this trust and the privilege they have been granted."

There was murmuring in the crowd as all the humans in the audience turned.

Tatyana smiled and waved, but then she noticed that no one else was waving and dropped her hand.

René chuckled beside her. "You're a lamb, aren't you?"

"Oh?" She was tired of him already. She turned to René and gave him the most dead-eyed stare she could muster. "People usually call me a wolf."

Was it her imagination, or did Oleg clear his throat? Was he hiding laughter?

The corner of Tatyana's mouth turned up.

They had a private joke, and something about that felt warm and thrilling at the same time.

Kezia was still talking on the stage. "This night will decide the next hundred years of leadership."

René was still whispering to her. "A little bird chirped in my ear that you and Vano are not friends."

"Who told you that?" He was right, but Tatyana didn't want to share her business with a thief.

Kezia was still trying to talk, but someone shouted from the back of the crowd, and then others joined in. It took Tatyana a few moments to understand what they were saying.

Dishana. They were calling for the goblets.

This entire ceremony seemed wildly chaotic, and Tatyana just wanted to leave. The breeze had died down, and the humidity in the air was bordering on oppressive. But she couldn't leave; that would be horribly rude.

"Have you seen them before?" René asked softly. "The sacred goblets of the Poshani, each carved from a single jewel?"

Tatyana shook her head. "I haven't. Have you?"

He looked amused. "I may have caught a quick glimpse once."

The crowd continued to chant. "Dishana, dishana, dishana!"

Tatyana's eyes locked on Kezia, who appeared frozen.

Something was wrong. Something was very wrong.

Tatyana leaned forward. "What is happening?"

"Here we go," René whispered. "Pay attention, my little lamb."

Why did men seem obsessed with giving her animal nicknames?

Tatyana muttered, "I'm wide awake, my arrogant fox."

All René did was laugh as the crowd stood and continued chanting.

Dishana, dishana, dishana.

The vampires in the stands were all reacting to the mass of humans growing more and more excited. She could feel the elemental energy buzzing, and it was everything she could do to remain calm herself. Blood was flowing. She could smell the sweetness of it wafting from the assembled humans, and her fangs elongated in her mouth.

The Hazar took to the air, circling the camp in wide swoops.

What was going on?

Tatyana's eyes locked on the three terrin on stage. Vano was looking at Radu. Radu was staring straight ahead with his jaw locked. Kezia seemed to falter.

When Kezia spoke again, Tatyana could barely hear her. "Sadly, the trust of the kamvasa has been breached."

Madina hissed from her seat behind Oleg, and all the vampires around her froze. Nothing moved. No one spoke.

Oh God. Was it Oleg? Had they found out? Were they going to try to... What? Confront a millennia-old fire vampire publicly? Kezia couldn't be that foolish.

"Someone has used our hospitality against us." Kezia was looking directly at Oleg now. "The dishana, the goblets gifted to our first terrin, have been stolen."

Tatyana felt like she might vomit the blood she'd consumed at sunset. Oleg would never steal. Never. Tatyana turned to René. "You," she muttered. "You are exactly the type to—"

"No, my sister. Not stolen," a woman shouted from the edge of the crowd, and in that moment, a massive whirlwind of flower petals rose in the air, and Tatyana saw two figures flying within it.

The air turned electric as the vampires in the stands rose, a few of them shouting, another taking to the air, and still others bolting immediately from the meadow.

What. Was. Happening?

Whispers and names were thrown around the crowd.

"Tenzin!"

"It's Zasha. It's just like them to—"

"No, I saw the Vecchio lad. He's making a power grab."

Tatyana turned to Oleg, who was watching her. He lifted his palm slightly and met her eyes. There was no surprise. No panic, and Tatyana didn't even smell a hint of smoke.

Oleg was calm, so she tried to relax.

"Be safe, be smart, and be quiet."

She sat and watched as the blizzard of flowers went on and on. It whirled and tossed in the air like a wild storm, and the flower crown flew from her head, sucked into the vortex of flower petals that filled the sky over the meadow.

René sighed beside her. "They are such attention hogs."

"Who?"

The wind died down, and two vampires landed on the stage, flower petals falling around them like confetti.

If Vecchio and his mate wanted to make an entrance, they'd made a dramatic one.

The tall young vampire walked over and lifted a winking emerald-green goblet over his head. "They were not stolen, my friend. Protected."

Tatyana could barely see the goblet from a distance. It was small, only a little larger than his palm.

As if it were one of the scripted plays, Radu stepped forward and took the green cup from Vecchio's hand.

Then Vecchio turned to the grandstand and pointed at René. "Monsieur DuPont? If you would."

"My turn, chérie." René winked at her, then sauntered down the stairs and walked through the parting crowds to the stage. He strolled toward Kezia, kissed her knuckles, and when he stood, a bright yellow-gold crystal was in her hand.

Now Tenzin was the last one in the center of the stage, and in a blink, Tatyana saw a blood-red goblet held to her chest.

Tenzin was looking at Vano with a cold stare, and Tatyana realized there was someone who hated Vano way more than she did.

And that tiny, terrifying vampire looked like she was seconds away from murder.

When Tenzin spoke, her voice carried across the meadow. "Shall I tell them, Vano, how I came to have this goblet in my possession?"

Vano erupted. "Because you are a thief." He pointed at Tenzin. "Hazar!"

Tenzin and Vecchio rose into the air, and while the Hazar gathered at a distance, no one approached to challenge them. Vecchio held a sword in his right hand, and the way the formerly friendly American was watching the circling vampires, Tatyana had zero doubt that he would murder all of them if they touched his mate.

She heard the seat next to her creak, and when she looked, Mika was sitting next to her, his eyes fixed on the drama in front of the crowd.

"I swear," Mika said, "there is nothing that woman likes more than a hostile takeover."

"She's taking over?" Tatyana didn't like that. Who was Tenzin to the Poshani? They spoke about her like her old partner, the assassin. She was a ghost. A legend. She would be a horrible terrin.

Tenzin let her mate stare down the Hazar surrounding them as she addressed the audience. "Long have I honored the Poshani and admired their hospitality. But four days ago, the trailer where I was promised shelter was abandoned, left behind when the kamvasa moved on."

"What?" Tatyana frowned. "They *left* her?"

"I was not expecting that," Mika said.

Kezia rose to her feet, her goblet in her hand. "Vano told us you had asked to remain. He showed us a letter signed by you and Benjamin."

Tatyana couldn't look away. She watched Vano. The snake. He was already starting to slink away.

What have you done, you fool?

For the Poshani, the kamvasa was sacred, and a promise was

never to be broken. Everything in their culture centered on intricate laws of hospitality.

"It was not written by us," Vecchio said. "Your brother lied to you."

The Poshani crowd—who had been watching in utter silence—all started to speak at once.

"Let Vano speak!"

"He should explain himself."

"They are lying thieves!" an old man at the back of the crowd shouted. "They stole the dishana and are trying—"

"Let Vano explain himself!"

"Vano, tell us the truth!"

"Vano, speak!"

Tatyana caught the look on his face, and even though she knew he was an evil, manipulative asshole, she was still shocked by his expression. "He did it," she murmured. "He *left* her."

Tenzin turned away from Vano and spoke to the vampires in the grandstand. "Then, while I was in my day rest, Vano's allies burned my shelter with me inside."

Oh fuck.

The surge of amnis around her felt like a battle call.

Oleg rose to his feet. Madina rose. *Every* vampire in the stands rose, their eyes sweeping over the crowd that was quickly turning to chaos in front of them.

Fangs were bared, and more than one immortal seemed to reach for a weapon even though all of them had been surrendered to the Hazar before the ceremony.

But one vampire didn't need a weapon.

One vampire in the stands overlooking the crowd *was* a weapon.

Every eye on the platform turned to Oleg Sokolov.

The Hazar rose into the sky, circling the crowd and drawing their swords.

"No." Tatyana's heart began to beat and she rose. "Oh no."

"Tenzin is going to start a riot going on like this." Mika whispered, "Oleg, I have her."

Tatyana smelled the scent of burning cedar a second after Mika spoke. She saw Oleg glaring at Vano as if he would murder the vampire as entertainment for the crowd.

"He's going to kill Vano," she whispered.

"Who, Oleg?" Mika nodded. "Possibly. He would annihilate an entire clan if they threatened his mate."

"I'm not—" Tatyana's protests were cut off as the Poshani crowd erupted in angry shouts and pointed fingers. Some were fighting among each other, and many were fleeing from the meadow with children in tow, anticipating violence when the vampires turned against them.

Radu finally walked to the front of the stage and raised his hands. "Brothers and sisters!" He looked at the vampire guests. "There must be an explanation for this. Patience."

Oleg did not sit down, but the other vampires did.

"There *is* an explanation." Mika folded his hands in his lap and stared at the stage. "Vano is a snake."

Tatyana slowly took her seat, and she felt her entire body heat as Oleg's amnis stirred in her. She felt... pleased. She'd wanted Vano to be the terrin that retired, and it looked like that decision might be made for him.

She'd wanted him to pay for threatening her friends, for threatening her.

He'd betrayed his people, schemed with Oleg's brother, and killed innocent humans and vampires.

It looked like payment was coming, and that payment was going to be very, very public.

Radu turned to Vano. "Brother, tell me our former guest is mistaken. That there has been a misunderstanding."

If Tatyana hadn't already known Vano was guilty, she would have discerned it from the furious expression on his face.

She glanced at Oleg, but her lover was watching everything with a slight smirk and his arms crossed over his chest, clearly trying not to laugh.

"There is no mistake," Tenzin shouted. "The ashes left behind prove my tale. Vano attempted to kill a guest of the kamvasa and lied to the Hazar and the darigan about it."

No one said anything until a group of Poshani men shoved a man forward.

Tatyana recognized them. They were some of the humans who were tasked with moving the trailers during the day. Tatyana knew from her own experience with these men and women that the darigan were deadly serious about security.

"I am one of those whom Vano ordered to burn the caravan." The man pointed at Vano. "He told us the vampire inside had murdered a Poshani girl. That she was a murderer and the terrin had ordered her death for betraying our hospitality. He showed us a paper signed by all three. That is the only reason we followed his orders."

"What an idiot."

Tatyana turned and saw that it was Darius who had spoken.

Everyone in the stands turned to look at the old Persian in shock.

"Vano." Darius shook his head, then stilled again, appearing more like a statue than a man.

"I think that's the first time I've heard him speak in weeks," Tatyana whispered.

Mika said, "His sense of timing is impeccable."

They all turned around to see how Vano would respond to the accusations the human darigan leveled at him.

Kezia spoke plainly. "The terrin made no such order."

"I know of no murdered girl," Radu said.

Tenzin shouted again. "This is a mystery easily solved. Is anyone missing a daughter?"

Tatyana leaned toward Mika. "She really likes to make a scene, doesn't she?"

"This is like watching a soap opera." Mika kept his eyes on the stage. "But I am pleased. This is the best outcome for Oleg."

Ah yes. It was all about Oleg for Mika.

She leaned closer as the vampires argued on the stage. "I know about his dealings with Ivan, but did Oleg know of the stolen goblets?"

"I'm not sure this wasn't all a stunt to take Vano's goblet from him." Mika nodded at the stage. "You notice that the little thief still has it in her hands."

"She probably wants to keep it."

Mika let out a dry laugh. "But then she'd be Poshani terrin for a century. You think she wants that?"

Oh no. Tatyana's heart sank. She looked for Rumi and Desiree in the crowd. This was going to throw everything into chaos, wasn't it? Yes, they were getting rid of a cruel terrin who was probably stealing from them, but Tatyana knew from experience that the devil you knew was often better than the devil you didn't.

"She's lying!" Vano screamed out. "They are thieves! I would never—"

"Why would she lie?" Radu lifted his goblet. "Our goblets have been returned to us. Only yours is withheld. Would thieves do that?" Radu spoke to the Hazar. "Take him."

A fight erupted in the air, and once again, everyone in the stands rose, watching the violence.

Swords clashed, Poshani screamed and ran, and punches of wind battered the assembly.

There was chaos on the ground as many tried to flee, and even some of the vampires in the stands seemed to disappear, melting into the woods around the meadow.

Benjamin Vecchio was the one to capture Vano, and the two wind vampires moved so quickly that Tatyana almost felt ill trying to watch them.

The fight did not last long. A few moments later Vano fell to the stage with a hard thump, and the waiting Hazar overwhelmed him.

Vecchio landed next to his mate, and a few words passed between

Vecchio, Tenzin, and Radu, but Tatyana couldn't hear anything until Kezia stepped forward again.

"Tenzin, you possess the ruby goblet of the Poshani terrin! You are an old friend, known to the kamvasa." Kezia addressed the Poshani crowd. "Tenzin of Penglai, commander of the Altan Wind, daughter of the Kali, protector and bearer of the ruby dishana!"

"Huh," Mika said. "I didn't think she'd take it."

Tatyana looked at Oleg again, but she could read no expression from him, and the bond between their amnis was deadly quiet.

This wasn't over.

"He's hiding his feelings," Tatyana said. Why was he hiding his feelings?

"Oleg?" Mika shrugged. "He has no say in this. To interfere with the election of the terrin in any way would create distrust within the Poshani. If you interfere in the internal matters of an ally, are you truly an ally?"

Tatyana kept her eyes on Oleg, wondering what was going through his mind as he leaned farther forward, his harsh gaze intent on the stage.

The vampires on the stage seemed to be arguing in whispers as the Hazar led Vano kicking and screaming away, but a few moments later, Tenzin—the new Poshani terrin—stepped forward.

"Poshaniya," she said. "You are kind and hospitable. You honor your guests and your history, and I would travel with you for a century if I could. But I am not suited for the honor of serving on the terrin."

Mika muttered, "So they'll have an election after all. Well, that's not a bad—"

"But there is among the kamvasa guests a woman of honor and cunning!" Tenzin continued.

"Madina?" Tatyana whispered to Mika. "Is she handing the goblet to Madina?"

"No." Mika's expression went carefully blank. "I don't think she's talking about Madina."

"—a vampire who respects your traditions and has learned your language and your history."

Wait... what?

Tenzin turned and looked straight at her. "Tatyana Vorona."

Oh no.

Oh no no no no no no.

Hot fear flooded her chest.

Mika was whispering furiously. "You have to answer. Tatyana, you have to answer."

Tatyana stared at Tenzin, a tiny vampire who had—perhaps unknowingly or perhaps not—blown up her entire existence.

She'd wanted to remain with the Poshani. She could admit that now. She wanted to remain. But she was no one's leader. She was barely a vampire herself.

Mika hissed, "Stand up. You have to do *something*."

She stood and turned to Oleg, but he said nothing.

Tatyana's eyes went wide with a silent plea: *Tell me what to do!*

Oleg only gave her one infuriating raised eyebrow. *Your decision, little wolf.*

His silence was everything and nothing.

Oleg couldn't help her. He couldn't say anything. Any influence would be a sign of interference, and it would damage his alliance with the Poshani.

The crowd was quiet when Tatyana walked down the steps, her feet moving on a kind of autopilot.

She couldn't do this.

There was no way she could do this.

She saw the Hazar who had greeted her at the bottom of the stairs.

"Surati." He smiled and inclined his head. "Surati."

She made her way forward as the crowd parted, her mind racing about what she should say. What she should do.

Surely they would pick someone else.

They *had* to pick someone else.

Other Poshani took up the address as she walked.

"Surati," an older man said. "Surati!"

"My sister, you are called!"

This could not be happening.

She saw Rumi and Desiree at the end of the makeshift aisle the Poshani crowd had formed for her, and as she reached her friend, Desiree held up a hand and put another flower crown on her head.

The old women she had chopped onions with nodded and muttered their approval. "Good," one said quietly. "Yes, it's good."

"Please," Rumi whispered. "Tatyana, you have been called to this."

"This was meant to be," Desiree said from beside her. "Tanya, the Kali has spoken."

Rumi continued her hushed encouragement. "If you take it now, no one will question it."

Desiree whispered again, "It is the will of the Kali."

With one last parting look at Rumi, Tatyana mounted the steps, the whispered entreaties of the people who had welcomed her into their community ringing in her ears.

Kezia said something, but she didn't hear it.

Radu tried to speak, but it was as if he was mumbling through water.

Water.

She took a deep breath and called the mist in the air to steady her.

Yes.

She looked at Oleg, and the fierce devotion in his eyes nearly brought her to her knees.

A hundred years?

A century of service.

She looked at the hopeful faces spread out in front of her. Wide-eyed children and skeptical youths only a few years younger than she had been before everything in her life turned upside down. Mothers. Aunts. Uncles and grandfathers.

She wasn't qualified to lead any of them.

But she did remember what it felt like to be human.

"You have opened your arms to me." She choked back a sob that threatened to escape from her mouth. She could not cry. She would not. She would be strong for the people who had given her a place. A home.

The family that had welcomed her. Who had cared for her.

"You opened your arms to me," she said again. "But you must be the ones to choose."

The humans in the crowd kept their eyes on her.

She heard the word *surati* again.

Sister.

"If you want me as your terrin," Tatyana continued, "I *will* do my best. I will devote myself to this even though I am young and I am learning. I will make so many mistakes, but I promise you that I will do my best."

Someone in the crowd said again, "Surati."

"Rusa Surati," another said, and there was gentle laughter.

"*You* must choose me." Tatyana smiled. "Not anyone else. I will only accept the ruby dishana if it is the will of the Poshani people."

"Surati!" a young woman shouted. "You are our sister, Tatyana le Tala!"

She had no idea what all that meant, but she lifted her eyes to Oleg's.

His chin was lifted, and in his eyes, she saw both grief and pride.

Milaya. Her lover mouthed the endearment before his face settled into a stoic mask.

"Tatyana le Tala!" more of the Poshani shouted. They threw flowers on the stage. "Terrin of the Poshani! Terrin Surati, holder of the ruby goblet!"

Tatyana lifted her chin and touched the flower crown on her head as Tenzin, the fierce little thief who had put this knife to her neck walked over and held out a bright red goblet a little larger than a pomegranate.

"I believe this is yours."

Tatyana looked at Vecchio, her hands hanging at her sides. "This was you."

"Sometimes the wrong things happen to good people," Benjamin Vecchio said. "And sometimes the right things happen to the right people."

The goblet lingered in Tenzin's hand, taunting her with its beauty, and all she could think was: *Oleg couldn't have made it more beautiful than this.*

Tatyana turned to Kezia and Radu, the two vampires who would sit with her. Not as authorities but as equals. "I will never take this responsibility for granted. I will always look out for the most vulnerable."

The corner of Kezia's mouth turned up in a slight smile. "Then sister, take your goblet."

Tatyana took the ruby dishana from Tenzin's hand and lifted it to the cheers of the Poshani. She didn't look at Oleg. If she did, she might burst into tears.

She glanced at Vecchio from the corner of her eye as they cheered. "I am never going to forget this."

She wasn't sure if that was a threat or not.

She was pretty sure it was a threat.

Chapter 33

Oleg

Oleg strode toward Tatyana's trailer, but there was already a company of Hazar stationed outside.

He halted and addressed the one who seemed to be in charge. "Please tell Tatyana le Tala that Oleg Sokolov requests an audience."

The Hazar inclined his head. "Yes, Lord Oleg."

Things were moving very fast. The night was still young, and Vano was being tried within hours. The vampire would be dead by dawn, and Oleg needed information.

And he needed to see her.

Oleg didn't know what he was feeling, but there would be time to sort all of it out later. Right now he had a unique opportunity with the new terrin of the Poshani people, and he couldn't—

"Oleg?"

The moment she opened the door, he rushed inside.

"It's fine, it's fine!" She reassured the Hazar seconds before she slammed the door in their faces, and then she completely collapsed in his arms.

Oleg picked her up, carrying her to the sofa as she sobbed silent cries into his chest.

"They cannot hear me," she whispered.

"I know."

"I cannot let them hear me."

His little wolf didn't want to admit her fear to those who had chosen her.

"Shhhh. I have you." Oleg held her in a fierce embrace, kissing the crown of her head, pressing his lips to her golden hair. "I have you. You're fine."

She could not stop crying, her body heaving with silent sobs.

He whispered, "Tatyana le Tala."

Tatyana the Gold.

Someday she would appreciate the beautiful name they had given her, but as she wept in his arms, he felt her fear and her grief in the blood he carried within his own veins.

No one knew their connection, and they would have to be very, very cautious.

"Milaya," he whispered, "you did the right thing."

That only seemed to make her cry harder.

She was wrung out, and he tilted her face to his, hoping his kiss would give her strength. The kiss grew from a gentle reassurance to a desperate joining as she threw her arms around his neck and held him in an iron grip.

When their lips parted, she buried her face, wet with bloody tears, into his neck.

"What did I do?" she whispered. "Oleg, what have I done? I can't do this."

"Yes, you can."

"I can't. They picked the wrong—"

"They picked wisely." Oleg took a deep breath and let it out slowly. Then another. "Breathe with me."

After a few moments, her breathing matched his. She was so precious. And so very, very human still.

He kissed her forehead. "You were presented with an impossible situation, and you took the lead."

"You asked me to—"

"Now is not the time to talk about that." He pressed a quick kiss to her temple, refusing to think about the questions hanging between them. "Your fellow terrin are going to execute Vano tonight for betraying the clan, and I need your help."

She perceived the situation immediately. "You need to ask him about Ivan."

"Radu and I reached an agreement the other night, but in the heat of the evening's revelations, I don't want to take a chance that they will kill him before I can interrogate him."

She sat back and took another breath, steadying herself. Her lips were trembling, but he saw the steel enter her spine as she stood up and wiped her face. "We should go."

"Give yourself a moment," he whispered. "You have a moment. They will not judge him without your presence."

Her mouth settled into a line. "They're going to kill him."

"They might ask you to kill him yourself," Oleg said, "as you are the one taking his seat."

Her eyes went wide. "But he didn't hand it over. I didn't... I didn't *take* it. I didn't battle him for it."

"Exactly. The goblet was taken from him because he betrayed the clan. If you were the one to execute justice, it would cement your position."

"They chose me," she whispered, "but I never wanted this. Oleg, you have to know I never—"

"Vecchio was right." Oleg kept his voice low. "Often horrible things happen to the wrong people. This time something good happened to the right person. Take it, Tatyana."

The irony was not lost on him. She had been without a clan, without aegis of any kind, and now the woman he loved and wanted above all others was the leader of an ancient and powerful clan known for their fierce loyalty.

For the rest of her eternity, Tatyana Vorona—Tatyana le Tala—would be a valued and protected member of the Poshani clan. She would have the family she wanted. The clan she deserved. She would belong to a family as devoted to her as she was to them.

There was nothing that Oleg could offer greater than that.

"You can bring the Poshani into the new century," he continued. "Modernize their businesses, lift up those who have been overlooked, and provide guidance to a proud people that will last centuries. You are the leader that they need right now."

Her eyes cleared, and the lip that had been trembling steadied.

Purpose. His mate needed purpose to be happy.

"Yes." She nodded. "I can do that."

"And you won't do any of this alone." Oleg stood and held out his hand. "Come, milaya. Let us go meet your fellow terrin."

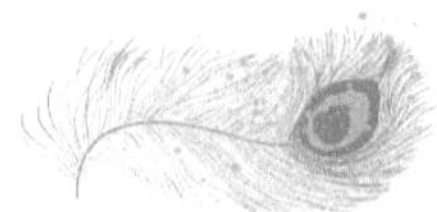

Oleg helped her dress in a dark frock and a cape that one of her human friends brought to her trailer. It was embroidered with a bright border of red and blue flowers. She washed her face, brushed her hair, and Oleg braided it in two long plaits that he wove together and pinned on her head.

"There. You look like a queen."

She looked over her shoulder. "How do you know how to braid?"

"You doubt my skills? My hair used to be longer than yours."

"I would have liked to see that." She took a steadying breath. "I'm ready."

He kissed her forehead. "Yes, you are."

As they left the trailer and walked to the terrin's tent, Oksana walked over to meet them, holding the gift that Oleg had quickly arranged.

"Terrin Tatyana." Oksana paused and inclined her head. "A gift from the Kievan Rus to the new leader of the Poshani."

It was a battle-ax in the Varangian style, forged with a single curved head and balanced for Tatyana's weight. Ludmila, being closer to Tatyana's size and weight, had picked it from the weapons she'd brought from the citadel, and Oksana had overseen the quick construction of the guard and belt by a Poshani craftsman.

If Tatyana was going to execute Vano, she would use Oleg's blade to do it.

Tatyana's face revealed nothing when she held out her hands to take the weapon. "Thank you, Oksana. It is a beautiful gift."

She handed the axe to the Hazar on her left, who looked at Oleg and gave him a nod of approval.

Oleg walked behind Tatyana, a little to her right, and watched as the frightened young woman who had wept in his arms put on the mental armor to face a century of leadership.

Mika came to walk beside him. "She will do well once she gets the feel for it."

"I know."

"You always did have a weakness for powerful women," Mika muttered. "There was that queen in Spain for a while. Several Scandinavian princesses. That clan leader from Bohemia in the twelfth century."

"Mika, shut up."

As she approached, the Hazar guards pulled back the entrance to the tent, and then everyone except Tatyana stopped and she walked forward.

She turned and met Oleg's eyes. "I will speak to my brother and sister first."

The Hazar seemed to approve of this, judging by their pleased expressions.

Oleg stood next to the Hazar holding Tatyana's weapon and asked, "Have you tracked down all of Vano's people yet?"

His expression revealed nothing. "We have."

"And?"

"Hazar take an oath to the clan, not the terrin." The vampire turned to Oleg. "If any of our number violate that oath, they are dealt with by their brothers and sisters."

Oleg had a feeling that any of the Hazar who had knowingly cooperated with Vano were going to face the same fate as their former terrin.

After some time, Radu poked his head from the tent and pointed at Oleg, snapping his fingers as he motioned for him to come.

Oleg paused just long enough to hear Mika let out a sigh. "Oh, that is the most satisfying—"

"Shut up," Oleg said. "If you do not want me to kill you."

Oksana snickered as Oleg walked forward, ducking his head underneath the entrance of the terrin's tent.

Vano was bound by heavy chains at the neck, the wrists, and the ankles, and those chains were locked around the central tent support that had been carved with the terrin's crests.

Oleg was already mentally designing Tatyana's crest, which she would carve into the beam before the next kamvasa.

Vano sat on the ground, staring at the far wall with a slight smile on his smug face. One of his ears was missing, and blood dripped down his neck.

Judging by the blood trail, Kezia had been the one to take the ear.

The wind vampire couldn't fly. He couldn't reach any weapons. And he could not escape the condemnation of his clan.

"The terrin of the Poshani have come to a unified agreement now that our sister has joined us," Kezia told Oleg. "Vano's execution will be public as a warning to any and all who think to betray their clan."

"A public execution?" Oleg nodded. "A wise choice for both your clan and your guests."

"Yes," Tatyana said. "A statement must be made that betrayal of the clan or the clan's guests is punishable by painful death."

Oleg locked eyes with her. "How will he die?"

"He will burn."

Oleg cocked his head. "Are you asking—"

"Vano will face the sun," Tatyana said, "chained to the ground until he burns to his death, and his ashes will remain visible until the kamvasa moves. Both humans and vampires must see that betrayal of the clan will not be tolerated."

Radu added, "He will not return to his element. His ashes will be ground into the dirt where animals can tread on his remains."

Oleg looked at his old friend. "It is a statement."

"It is." He held his hand out toward Vano. "You are welcome to question him about your brother if you would like. The Poshani value our alliance and trust that our relationship will remain strong in the future now that this cancer has been exposed."

"Thank you, old friend." How much did he want Radu and Kezia knowing about the weakness in his own empire? Oleg looked at Vano, and the man's haughty expression told him that an interrogation was expected.

Oleg pulled up a small stool and sat in front of Vano. "We did business for many years. How much of that money did you steal from the clan?"

Vano blinked. He'd been expecting questions about Ivan. "Enough."

"Oh, don't be foolish," Oleg said softly. "Is it ever enough?"

The prisoner said nothing.

"When you attacked my trucks, did you know they had vampire guards accompanying them?"

"Yes."

"So you knew that the Poshani you'd ordered to hijack those trucks would more than likely die."

The corner of Vano's mouth turned up. "Yes."

He heard Kezia and Radu reacting behind him, but he never let his eyes leave Vano. "What did you buy with the money Ivan paid you?"

Vano's smile was broad. "He didn't give me money."

"Ah, forgive me. What did you do with the gold?"

Vano pursed his lips. "Hmmm. I think I will let your lover find it. Do you think the Poshani will love her as much when they discover she's more loyal to you than them?"

Oleg chuckled. "If you think that Tatyana le Tala is more loyal to a man she allows in her bed than to the family she has chosen, you have no knowledge of her. Your ignorance is showing, Vano."

"Ivan has plans for you, old one."

"You think I'm old? Ivan's older—he's just not as powerful and he never was." Oleg winked. "Don't worry. I will discover Ivan's tricks without your help."

"So you don't want to know who else in your clan is plotting against you?" Vano's eyes were wide.

Oleg stretched out his legs. "Do you want to tell me?"

"Polina."

Oleg chuckled. "Is that so?"

"Pavel."

He nodded slowly. "Fascinating. Anyone else?"

"Rudov." Vano cocked his head. "Am I lying?"

"Oh yes," Oleg said. "And maybe no."

"She will never choose to return to you now," Vano said. "Your little bookkeeper belongs more to me than you now."

"Is that so?" The man had limited time on the earth—Oleg would let him talk nonsense.

"I will be ashes, but she will still belong more to me than to you because my blood" —Vano lunged forward, rattling his chains— "*my* blood still runs through this clan, and she is now its servant. How does that feel, Oleg Sokolov? To know that your blood will serve mine?"

"An interesting perspective." Oleg reached into his right boot, grabbed a dagger, and plunged it into Vano's leg, making sure to miss any vital arteries.

The man howled, and Oleg looked up at the three terrin.

"Sincere apologies," Oleg said. "My hand slipped."

Kezia linked her arm in Tatyana's and watched Vano raging with all the sympathy of a lion observing an antelope. "I hate when that happens."

"Moisture in the air," Radu muttered. "It's foggy tonight."

Tatyana was staring at Vano, and Oleg could see that what she'd heard disturbed her.

Oleg was not disturbed. "Vano." He pulled out the knife and cleaned it on the man's wool trouser leg. "As much as you would like me to kill you before you have to feel your skin peeling and burning at dawn, I am not going to interfere."

"You'll die." Vano laughed. "Your brothers will kill you soon. Your precious empire is cracking, old man. You were never strong enough to hold it."

Oleg put the dagger back into the sheath in his boot and stood. "Goodbye, Vano. I would say farewell, but that is not your future. You will fare very badly."

He turned, inclined his head to Radu, Kezia, and finally Tatyana. Then Oleg left Vano to his fate.

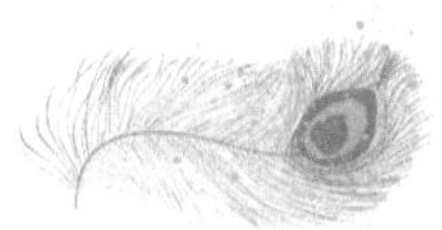

THEY SAT IN HER BED, PROPPED AGAINST THE HEADBOARD, Tatyana's head on his shoulder as he sketched in a notebook he'd found on the desk.

"There, see?" He flicked the pencil over the paper. "There must be a wolf in the center."

She laughed a little bit. "Why?"

"Because you are my little wolf." Oleg kissed her forehead. "And a wolf on your herald symbolizes bravery and loyalty, so it is perfect for you."

Tatyana grew very quiet, but Oleg allowed her to ruminate. There was not much he could do for her now other than design something worthy of the house and line she would build.

"I didn't want this," she whispered.

"I know." He kept sketching. Two axes behind the wolf. A dove with open wings at the top.

"What we were—"

"We still are." Oleg's pencil paused on the page. "Do you think that your position makes you any less attractive to me? I told you, milaya, I enjoy your fangs." He sketched the wolf's muzzle and added comically large fangs coming down from its jaw. "See?"

Tatyana laughed. "No, you can't do that."

"Why not?" He pretended to bite her hand when she reached for the paper. "Are you an artist? No. You must trust my genius."

"Your genius, is it?"

"Yes, obviously."

She snuggled closer into his side and tucked her arm around his waist. "You should replace the dove with a firebird."

He grunted. "Too dominant."

"Is it my crest?"

"Obviously yes."

"Then I want a firebird, not a dove."

He erased the dove and considered her request. A firebird would throw off the balance of the crest he was making for her. "Why?"

"Because I would not be a wolf without the firebird," she said softly.

Oleg set the notebook aside. "Tatyana—"

"What have I done?" She closed her eyes. "I don't know how to lead a huge clan like this. When I imagined being part of the Poshani, I thought I could work for them. Maybe update their accounting systems." She laughed a little; then her laugh turned into a cry, and she covered her mouth with her hand so no one heard her.

She would never let them hear her cry. Never let them know that she hadn't wanted this. The fact that she let Oleg see her tears was an honor he had never expected. One he wouldn't have thought he would even want.

But he would never take her trust for granted.

Tatyana's eyes filled with tears, and Oleg pulled her to his chest.

"Shhh." He stroked her hair, unpinning the braids and slowly loosening the plaits of golden hair. "Remember what I told you? Right after you'd been turned?"

"You told me a lot," she whispered. "Because you are very bossy and controlling."

"That's correct." He tilted her head back and kissed the blood-tinged tears from her cheeks. "And I told you that I would see you dance." He framed her face with his hands. "This is your dance. Your life will be long, milaya. *My* life will be long. Right now this is your dance."

She looked into his eyes, and Oleg had to fight the urge to throw her over his shoulder, battle the Hazar, race out of the kamvasa, and disappear into the wilderness with Tatyana Vorona on his arm.

He loved her, and she was not his anymore. She could not be. Perhaps she never would be.

She whispered, "You asked me a question."

Oleg shook his head. "We don't have talk about that."

"I want to talk about that."

"You're the terrin now, and your loyalty must be to your clan. Of all people, I understand this and I respect it." Oleg knew she would not say yes because she could not. And damn the shreds of his honor, because he loved her even more because of it. "I know what I envisioned for the future is not possible now, so please don't—"

"Yes."

Oleg froze. "What?"

"Yes, I will marry you, Oleg Sokolov. If you will still have me."

Chapter 34

Tatyana

Warsaw, Poland
Six months later

Tatyana closed the folder with printouts of the prospectus that the new chief financial officer of Sokolov Industries handed to her.

"I don't see any reason to think they will *not* agree," she said, "but of course, I will need to go over the details with my brother and sister."

The middle-aged man nodded. "Of course, Miss Vorona. I would also add that structuring this trade complex outside Lublin this way is likely to bring outside investment that will benefit both parties. Since it will be a multiuse space, there has already been an inquiry from Wallace Enterprises about a longer-term hospitality complex."

Wallace Enterprises becoming involved meant that Tatyana's plan to build a vampire free-trade zone in cooperation with Oleg would have legs. Wallace was known for strict standards of neutrality, which would lend weight to promises by Oleg, the Poshani, and the Polish vampire court based in Krakow.

She stood and shook Bernard Lazareva's hand before her guard Henrik saw the human out. Moments later, she was on-screen with Radu and Kezia.

"Did he agree to using Poshani labor contractors?" Kezia said. "I was on the phone with Polina about that last week."

"Yes." Tatyana held up a finger. "As long as at least half the management comes from Sokolov Industries."

Radu nodded. "That's standard for our contracts with them."

Rebuilding the Poshani businesses without Vano was a little like reconstructing dinosaur bones. There were so many pieces missing, at times Tatyana felt like she was creating as much as she was recovering.

Add in a lot of dust and debris, and she had her work cut out for her.

Luckily, the bones of the organization were solid and the people left after Kezia and Radu's purge of Vano loyalists were grateful to still be employed. Reconstructing things with the help of modern technology and improved logistics had turned the somewhat dire business enterprises of the clan around significantly in the past five months.

"What do you think of the new CFO?" Kezia asked. "As good as Elene?"

"No, but no one was ever going to be, especially with only three months experience," Tatyana said. "He's quick and he's the right age. Good experience in international shipping, and I think that was the priority for them."

In fact, she knew that had been the priority.

"It was a bit of flattery for him to negotiate personally for this contract," Radu said.

"Agreed," Tatyana said. "If Elene were still alive, one of her deputies would have been in this meeting."

Radu nodded. "Go ahead and approve it if you're satisfied," he said. "I trust you."

"I'll have the lawyers look over everything then?" She looked at Kezia, who was often a harder sell.

"Let me think about it for a couple of nights," Kezia said. "I want to read through it one more time. There are some political implications with putting it in Lublin."

"Fair enough," Tatyana said. "Sokolov can wait. I'll look over the numbers once more too. Shall we schedule something for Thursday night?"

"That sounds good to me. Radu?"

"I am free Thursday after two in the morning."

"Good." Tatyana quickly scheduled an online meeting. "You're getting a link now in your email."

Both of them groaned.

"No arguments," Tatyana said. "We agreed about this."

"I hate the email," Kezia said. "It's so impersonal."

"But much faster than human messenger." She waved at both of them. "My mother made dinner for me, so I'm done for the night."

"Say hello to her from me," Radu said. "And tell her I need more of those ginger cookies she sent me."

"Enjoy dinner. Good night." Kezia's screen went blank.

Tatyana waited for the connections to cut out before she closed her insulated laptop and waved at her assistant outside the conference room.

Britta popped her head in the room. "Finished?"

"Finally. Can you ask Henrik to call the car?"

"Of course."

Tatyana packed up her trusty old messenger bag, sliding her laptop inside as a memory slipped into her mind.

"I found the connection between ZOL Enterprises and SMO International, so I'm smarter than whoever tried to hide her company, don't you think?"

"I'm the one who tried to hide her company. So you think you're smarter than me?"

"Maybe I'm just better at sorting through paperwork."
"Don't back away now, volchitsa. I like your teeth."

She pulled out her phone and tapped a message.

> Thinking of you.

Seconds later, a reply.

> As you should be.

> What did you think of Bernard?

> He's good. Easy to work with.

> That means you're making more money than us in this deal. I knew we agreed on numbers too quickly.

Tatyana smiled as she walked down the stairs, feeling a stir in her blood as she reached the foggy night air of the Polish capital.

Her amnis sat up, woke up, and her immortal nature stretched its legs after a full night of working in the human office.

Her phone buzzed just as a late-model black Mercedes pulled up to the side street where Henrik was waiting.

"Good night, Miss Vorona." Henrik opened the door. "Say hello to your mother please."

"Thank you, Henrik. And hello to Magda from me."

"Thank you, Surati."

The affectionate nickname had stuck, and Tatyana didn't mind a bit.

When things got to be difficult or when she had a hard time reminding herself why she was living in freezing-cold Warsaw, it was good to remember who she was working for.

The Poshani were her family.

Her driver's name was Essa, and she drove like a complete

lunatic, but luckily there wasn't much traffic at three in the morning, and Tatyana was back at the Poshani compound in twenty minutes.

The Hazar stationed at her house opened the car door as soon as she pulled up, and the minute Tatyana stepped outside, she could smell the scent of stroganoff coming from the kitchen.

"I am telling you, there is fresh tomato," Rumi said.

"And I am telling you there is not," Anna barked back. "Not in *good* stroganoff. I don't know who taught you how to cook but—"

Rumi let loose with a flood of Poshani curses.

Tatyana froze and took a few minutes to brace herself on the wall before she went in.

Rumi had been promoted to her house manager, and most of the time that was fine.

Except when her mother was visiting.

Everyone loved Anna, but Rumi wasn't keen on an old Russian woman teaching her how to cook, and Anna was suspicious of everyone.

Her phone buzzed in her pocket.

> Are you home yet?

She typed back.

> Mama is cooking. She and Rumi are arguing.

> What is it tonight?

> Tomato in stroganoff.

> I have no opinion on this.

She braced herself for battle and walked into the kitchen on the ground floor of the sprawling house within the Poshani compound in a residential neighborhood east of the Vistula River.

"Hello! I am home." She set her messenger bag in the office that was just off the downstairs entryway, then walked back to the kitchen to see Rumi and Anna glaring at each other.

Rumi broke off eye contact and looked at Tatyana. "How was work?"

"Good. As expected. No surprises."

"That's excellent."

Anna barked, "Dinner is almost ready."

"Good," Tatyana snapped back. "Because if you don't feed me, I'm going to bite you."

"Eh." Anna waved a hand at her as Rumi held back a laugh.

Tatyana walked around and placed a kiss on her mother's cheek, then put an arm around her waist. "Thank you for cooking."

Anna grumbled. "These people hug each other constantly, and now it is rubbing off."

"I know, what will you do?" She sat at the counter, watched her mother cook, while Rumi opened a bottle of blood-wine and poured her a glass.

If anyone had told her a year ago that she'd be settled in Warsaw, running a business and coming home to her mother complaining at night, with friends who kept gardens, an extended family living in the rambling compound around her, and kids running through her house when they were in trouble with their parents...

She would have thought that person was delusional.

But six months made all the difference. It was nearly time for the kamvasa to start again, though she wouldn't be able to join it for the entire season like she had last time.

No, she was needed at the office to build the future of her people.

And though there was ever more rumbling on the borders near Oleg's territory, for the first time in Tatyana's immortal life, she didn't just feel safe.

She knew she was home.

Elizabeth Hunter

There were two hours left before dawn when the black Mercedes pulled up to a town house in the center of Warsaw. The streets were dead, so when she stepped outside, there was no one to greet her.

The car pulled away, and she walked around the corner to the wrought iron gate, used her key to open the lock, and slipped inside.

If she were a wind vampire, this would be so easy, but she was not.

She smiled as she passed the large fountain in the back garden.

Water could come in handy at times too.

He opened the door before she reached it, and his blood, which lived in her, surged the moment their eyes met.

He smiled. "Hello."

Tatyana's silent heart flipped in her chest. "I knew he wasn't going to bring your plane here without you."

"You know me too well." He held out his hand. "Come inside. I've been waiting for you."

Tatyana and Oleg's story will conclude in Obsidian Empire.
Coming Spring 2026

ElizabethHunter.com
ElizabethHunterShop.com

OBSIDIAN EMPIRE

Coming

2026

Discover the Elemental Universe!

Did you find yourself intrigued by the characters Ben and Tenzin in this book? Perhaps you want to learn more about Giovanni Vecchio or the internal workings of the Poshani.

The Elemental Universe is a series of interconnected smaller series set in the same expansive world as *The Firebird and the Wolf.* To find out more, please visit ElizabethHunter.com.

And if you're intrigued by Ben and Tenzin's story in particular, please check out the Elemental Legacy series in paperback, ebook, and audiobook at all major retailers and at ElizabethHunterShop.com.

About the Author

ELIZABETH HUNTER is an eleven-time *USA Today* and international best-selling author of romance, contemporary fantasy, and paranormal mystery. Based in Central California and Addis Ababa, she travels extensively to write fantasy fiction exploring world mythologies, history, and the universal bonds of love, friendship, and family. She has published over fifty works of fiction and sold over two million books worldwide. She is the author of the Elemental Mysteries series, the Irin Chronicles, and other works of fiction.

ElizabethHunter.com
ElizabethHunterShop.com

Also by Elizabeth Hunter

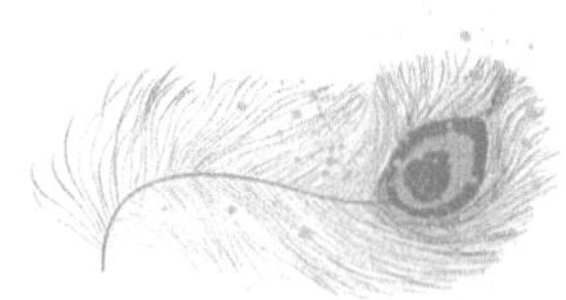

Valley of the Shadow

THE ELEMENTAL LEGACY

Shadows and Gold

Imitation and Alchemy

Omens and Artifacts

Midnight Labyrinth

Blood Apprentice

The Devil and the Dancer

Night's Reckoning

Dawn Caravan

The Bone Scroll

Pearl Sky

Tin God

THE ELEMENTAL COVENANT

Saint's Passage

Martyr's Promise

Paladin's Kiss

Bishop's Flight

Tin God

THE SHADOWLANDS

First Light

The Shadow Path

Broken Veil (Winter 2025)

THE IRIN CHRONICLES

The Scribe

The Singer

The Secret

The Staff and the Blade

The Silent

The Storm

The Seeker

<u>The Seba Segel Series</u>

The Thirteenth Month

Child of Ashes (Coming 2026)

<u>Cambio Springs</u>

Long Ride Home

Shifting Dreams

Five Mornings

Desert Bound

Waking Hearts

Stings and Arrows

Dust Born

<u>Vista de Lirio</u>

Double Vision

Mirror Obscure

Trouble Play

<u>Glimmer Lake</u>

Suddenly Psychic

Semi-Psychic Life

Psychic Dreams

Please visit ElizabethHunter.com or ElizabethHunterShop.com for more information about news and upcoming releases!